Whose Music?
A Sociology of Musical Languages

Whose Music?
A Sociology of Musical Languages

JOHN SHEPHERD
PHIL VIRDEN
GRAHAM VULLIAMY
TREVOR WISHART

Foreword by HOWARD S. BECKER

First published in 1977
by Latimer New Dimensions Limited
14 West Central Street, London WC1 1JH

SBN 901539 51 1 (hardback)
SBN 901539 62 7 (paperback)

Typeset by TNR Productions Ltd
and printed in Great Britain by
The Hollen Street Press Ltd

to
Bunny & Rosamond Vulliamy
Irene Wishart
and the memory of
Ted Shepherd

The publishers gratefully acknowledge the financial assistance of The Arts Council of Great Britain in the production of this book.

If it is art, it is not for all, and if it is for all, it is not art.

Arnold Schoenberg

The blues is the truth.

Lightnin' Hopkins

Something's happening, and you don't know what it is, do you Mr. Jones?

Bob Dylan

Contents

Acknowledgements

This book is a product of extended discussion and mutual criticisms on the part of the four authors. However we would like to thank the following people for contributions of ideas and criticism: John Cardale, Peter Coleman, Brian Davies, Annie Griffiths, John Hayes, Bryn Jones, Ed Lee, Ian Lewis, Richard Orton, Mike Peters, Jan Steele, Keith Swanwick, Stefan Szczelkun, Jackie Wishart, David Wood and Michael F. D. Young.

Also, John Shepherd would like to thank the Dean of the Institute of Advanced Studies, Manchester Polytechnic for allowing him time to prepare the final draft of his contributions; Graham Vulliamy, the Social Science Research Council for financial support towards the field work reported in Chapter Seven, the teachers and pupils at the school where this research was done, and the journal *Popular Music and Society* for permission to reproduce certain material used in Chapter Six; Trevor Wishart, *Interplay* and John Low for providing him with invaluable experience in the field of community arts, and the Arts Council for financial assistance.

Finally, we would like to thank Josie Dickson, Sue Hodges, Gillian Stirk and Brenda Wilson for typing the final manuscript and Linda Shepherd, Sue Hodges, Val Durkin and Jackie Wishart for bringing a certain degree of sanity to the whole project.

Foreword

To say that art or music is a social product, or that they are affected by social forces, or that they reflect the structure of a society — to use any of these common platitudinous formulae is simply to claim the domain of the arts for sociology in return for a promissory note for an analysis to be delivered, if all goes well, on some later occasion. Sociologists have left so many of these obligations unredeemed that artists and humanistic scholars have become justifiably wary of their pretensions. Add to this that sociologists like to theorise about these matters without acquiring a first-hand working acquaintance with the materials or characteristic social situations in which artists work and audiences absorb what they do (Trevor Wishart criticises the results of this in Adorno's writings in the last chapter of the present book), and you find still further reason for readers to avoid any further sociological treatment of the subject.

Shepherd, Virden, Vulliamy and Wishart have not left us another promissory note. They have paid in cash. They combine historical, musicological and sociological materials and styles of analysis in ways that really connect. Analyses of social class systems speak in translatable ways to analyses of musical forms. Not only that, both are connected to an understanding of the organisations through which art works get distributed to their ultimate audiences. And, further, we see how people learn, in school, what kinds of music are to be taken in what ways, what is "serious" and worthy of our attention, and what is "mere" popular music to be treated as cultural trash. Finally, and very importantly, we see that theorising about all these matters is an integral part of the process by which dominant class groups justify their domination, cultural and otherwise.

To have done all this is a sizable achievement, and I do not mean to undervalue it when I say that there is still more to be done. There is always more to be done. My vote for the next focus of concentration would be the more professionalised areas of contemporary music worlds, those interconnected networks of composers, performers, publishers, recording companies, critics, aficionados, producers of hardware and software — in short, all those people and organisations whose joint efforts, coordinated through a more-or-less shared system of conventions, produce the works which audiences hear and respond to, and which work in the society in the ways the authors analyse here. Some work along these lines, far from enough, has been done in the United States and France, though seldom with the ample musicological and sociological context displayed here.

The book is provocative. I often found myself disagreeing, or wondering whether an assertion was true, or thinking of what seemed to be contradictory cases. That speaks to the book's fundamental interest, for it is clearly (at least to me) more important to get people thinking along new lines than to achieve the final word on a subject (as though that could be done), and I don't see how anyone can finish this book without being forced to think a little differently, at least, than they had thought before.

Howard S. Becker
April 1977
Chicago, Illinois

Introduction

In relating musical 'languages' to wider social structures and media of communication, this book argues that any particular kind of music can only be understood in terms of the criteria of the group or society which makes and appreciates that music. This theme is in sharp contrast to established attitudes to music, which utilise an 'objectively' conceived aesthetic. These attitudes are revealed in the assumptions underlying most musicology and musical aesthetics including, perhaps paradoxically, the work of a number of cultural radicals, such as Lukacs and Adorno. On a more practical level, these prevalent attitudes to music manifest themselves both in music education policies and in the policies of arts and broadcasting administrators, who have the power to promote some kinds of music above others.

Whilst the contributors to this book share a common critical stance to their subject matter, the central theme of the book, that music is an aspect of a wider social reality, is approached from diverse perspectives — musical, aesthetic, sociological, and educational. The cooperation of a number of authors has thus overcome one of the limiting tendencies of most previous work in this area, in that musicians have traditionally been sceptical of sociological approaches to their 'art-form', whilst sociologists have tended to shy away from study of such an 'abstract' mode of communication. Thus practically all sociological studies of music have been concerned with the sociology of musical life (that is the conditions surrounding the production and 'consumption' of music), rather than with giving a sociological analysis of the music itself.

1

INTRODUCTION

The opening three chapters by John Shepherd are based on a consideration of what might be seen as the central methodological problem facing musicology. This problem may be indicated by asking in what way music can be said to have significance or meaning. It is the word 'meaning' which is problematic in this context, since music does not *obviously* have any relation to the world of objects and ideas. Basing his argument on lines of thought drawn from the sociology of knowledge and media philosophers (such as Marshall McLuhan), the author demonstrates that this central difficulty of the aesthetics of music may ultimately be attributed to the underlying epistemology of the modern Western world. In particular, he argues that the essentially a-social approaches adopted by Langer and Meyer towards this problem, whilst seemingly transcending it, are in fact ultimately compromised because they depend on categories of understanding drawn from that same epistemology. The second half of Chapter One seeks to illustrate — by considering prevalent modes of social organisation and intellectual activity — why institutionalised musicians and aestheticians find it difficult to recognise the inherently social nature of music.

Drawing on concepts basic to structural anthropology, and stressing the role of symbols, Chapter Two then puts forward a view of the social process which transcends the epistemological problems raised in Chapter One, thus leading to a valid social theory of music. Chapter Two concludes by relating the inherent difficulties of *writing* about *music* to many of the topics already indicated. Specifically, it is shown how concern with analysis on the one hand, and with philosophical, psychological and biographical considerations on the other, directly reflects the categories of understanding responsible for the central aesthetic difficulty.

Chapter Three seeks to substantiate the mainly aesthetic and sociological arguments of the first two chapters by analysing the 'deep structure' of three kinds of music — pre-literate, sacred Medieval and tonal — and then relating these deep structures to the social milieux of their creation. In this way it can be shown, both from a general theoretical viewpoint and from specific analysis of music, that the meaning of music is indeed inherently social.

Trevor Wishart, in Chapter Four, by considering the effect of writing on verbal communications, seeks to illuminate the impact of notation on the way music is both perceived and conceived of in the

2

West. Notation is seen as focussing musical perception on a specific and limited set of notatable parameters and their permutations. Despite its evident advantages it also has important drawbacks. Furthermore, in permitting the music which flows from it to be more easily controlled by a class of 'scribes', it has led to a devaluation of music as an alternative, and yet equally valid, mode of communication to the written word. It has also led to a rejection of coexisting oral-aural musical traditions. In addition, the dominance of notation has encouraged the conception of music as being essentially abstract, leading to a puritanical culture-specific notion of musical value. At the same time the equation of musical form with the visual forms of its notations has led to a sterile rational formalism in compositional practice which reflects the current ascendancy of rationalistic positivistic ideology. The invention of sound-recording has, however, shattered the hegemony of this dominant visual-rational viewpoint.

Against the theoretical approach developed in Part One, the majority of Part Two is taken up with a consideration of the relationships between social stratification and twentieth-century music. Chapter Five, by Phil Virden and Trevor Wishart argues that the stratification of music is an expression of general social class structures within modern industrial societies. Differences in musical production and appreciation are both symptomatic of, and reinforcements for, the class-structuring of what people find relevant and how they relate to their world. The authors first establish that a division of labour has systematic consequences for the ways people orientate their lives and hence how and why they communicate in general. This wide theory of the stratification of symbols, derived from the socio-linguistic work of Basil Bernstein, is then applied to music itself. It is suggested that musics can be analysed in relation to a continuum, the poles of which embody at one extreme high mediation, explicitness and lineal structure and at the other more immediacy, implicitness and circularity. The latter we might expect to find originating amongst dispossessed groups of people and therefore, in order to illustrate more fully this sociological approach, the second half of the chapter examines the blues as an ideal-typical example of such music.

It is argued that the blues has an underlying pentatonic structure. A distinction is drawn between 'the blues scale as used in jazz' and the authentic blues tradition. Various analyses proposed by

3

musicians trained in the 'classical' or jazz traditions are considered and rejected in favour of this alternative theory, which views the 'bending' of notes and chords as intrinsic to the musical language. The blues is elaborated 'intensionally' within a rigid cyclical structure and this is interpreted as supporting our ideas concerning the world sense articulated by such music.

Graham Vulliamy's chapters are related to current debates in the sociology of education and reflect a growing interest in applying a phenomenological sociology of knowledge perspective to education. Michael F. D. Young in his introduction to *Knowledge and Control* (1971) notes that unfortunately we have few studies of how 'contemporary definitions of culture have consequences for the organisation of knowledge in the school system'. Chapters Six and Seven attempt to do this for one particular area of the curriculum by focussing first on wider cultural definitions of music and then on definitions of music in the school system.

In Chapter Six the musical establishment's conception of 'serious' music is questioned by reference to its reaction to a new tradition of music during the course of this century — the Afro-American tradition, springing from the negro blues and now covering such diverse fields as jazz, rock music, soul and Tamla Motown and so on. By focussing particularly on jazz and rock music it is argued that the establishment's interpretation of these new styles of music is fundamentally misguided and serves to perpetuate false dichotomies between 'serious' and 'popular' music. This artificial distinction is then maintained by dominant groups by means of selective financial subsidies, particular types of mass media policy and in what counts as valid knowledge in the curricula of schools and universities. In the process, questionable assumptions concerning aesthetics, the production of 'art-works' and the 'seriousness' of artists are perpetuated, together with misleading interpretations of cultural forms other than those associated with high culture. The particular case of music exemplifies the problems associated with more general distinctions between so-called high culture, folk culture and mass (or popular) culture, which are often made by sociologists, educators and various guardians of high culture. The chapter ends with an alternative interpretation of these distinctions — an interpretation influenced by the work of the French sociologist, Pierre Bourdieu.

In Chapter Seven the focus is narrowed from definitions of music and culture in society to their definitions within the school system.

4

Recent theoretical debates in the sociology of education have centred around the phenomenological critique of much of the positivist empirical work in the traditional sociology of education. As a consequence, a plea has been made for more ethnographic studies of classroom interaction, which examine the social assumptions underlying teachers' definitions of knowledge and ability and their influence on the success and failure of pupils. A major section of the chapter is a report of such a participant observation study in a particularly interesting and unusual music department of a large mixed comprehensive school. Data from the case study suggest both the possibilities for and the constraints on changing traditional definitions of music teaching. In comparing this case study material both with other schools and with other possible definitions of music teaching, it is suggested that the various ways in which 'what counts as music' is defined are associated with differing criteria of success, differing relationships between teacher and taught, and different assumptions made by teachers concerning the relations between pupils' intelligence, family background and musical ability.

The argument to date in Part Two highlights the problem of the relationship of the committed artist to his audience in a highly stratified society. In the light of the previous discussion, Chapter Eight attempts a reassessment of the notion of radical or 'progressive' cultural action, seeking to avoid the group-centred, culture-specific assumptions which have been criticised earlier in this book. The views of two prominent left-wing critics (Adorno and Lukacs) are rejected on the grounds of their implicit elitism. It is then proposed that 'radicalness' be judged by practical results in changing the consciousness of specific groups, and not by the comparative intellectual analysis of the forms of works *in abstracto* with its implicit assumption of the universal validity of the cultural values assumed by the critic. Case studies of the work of Shelley and Cage are used to illustrate the real practical problems and difficulties facing any artist who attempts to put his radical conception into practice.

The major concerns of this book are central to practising musicians, musicologists and sociologists. However, one of the problems in writing a book of this type is the difficulty experienced by both sociologists and musicians in approaching each other's disciplines. This is particularly the case when one considers the complexity of musical vocabulary. We have therefore included an appendix on musical terminology which, we hope, will give the interested non-musician enough of an insight into the workings of different musical 'languages' to understand our main points of argument. For the interested musician, who may find the *sociological* perspective of this book somewhat unusual, we would suggest that the fresh insights that it gives into the processes of musical creation are well worth any difficulties he may encounter.

Needless to say, any book of this kind, which seeks to break new ground, more easily lays itself open to criticism. However, it is not our aim to be definitive, but rather to stimulate a re-examination of traditional assumptions about music and in the process to open up new avenues for both research and activity.

PART ONE

Chapter One

Media, Social Process and Music

JOHN SHEPHERD

The central assumption of this book is that any significance assigned to music must be ultimately and *necessarily* located in the commonly agreed meanings of the group or society in which the particular music is created. This assumption can neither be proved or disproved. However, it will be the principal purpose of this chapter to argue that prevalent, 'a-social', views of music are inherently problematic, and that these views form an integral aspect not only of industrial man's outlook on the world, but of the political structures within which he lives, and which he largely takes for granted. Chapter Two will then put forward a view of the social process which eliminates the problems referred to, and allows for a vital and acceptable social theory of music.

Implicit in the central assumption of this book is the view that the meaning of music is somehow located in its function as a social symbol. It is the word 'meaning' which creates the greatest problem in this context. For most people a symbol has meaning because it refers to something outside itself. Pictures have meaning because they refer to something in physical reality, and words have meaning because they refer to concepts and ideas. But to suggest that a piece of music has meaning because of extra-musical references is, at the least, highly contentious. The logical alternative has thus been to look for the meaning of music within the structure of individual pieces, an alternative whose strictest formulation, as Leonard B. Meyer indicates (1956, p.33), is to be found in the attitude of the absolutists:

The absolutists have contended that the meaning of music lies specifically, and some would assert exclusively, in the musical processes themselves. For them musical meaning is non-designative. But in what sense these processes are meaningful ... they have been unable to state with either clarity or precision .... This failure has led some critics to assert that musical meaning is a thing apart, different in some unexplained way from all other kinds of meaning. This is simply an evasion of the real issue.

The real issue can be stated in terms of the following comparison. Because their meaning is 'located outside them', words and pictures may be thought of as 'carrying' their meaning and 'giving' it to the recipient. The symbol, in other words, survives the divulgence of its message. If, on the other hand, musical meaning is acknowledged to lie within the musical process itself, then in 'giving away' that meaning, a piece seemingly compromises the very being or essence responsible for the meaning in the first place. As Susanne Langer (1960, p.236) has put it, the absolutists 'seem to feel that if musical structures should really be found to have significance, to relate to anything beyond themselves, those structures would forthwith cease to be musical'.

This difficulty results from confusing a symbol which has no referent in the world of objects and ideas with one which is informationally a closed system. Music certainly falls within the former but not, as the absolutists imply, the latter category. It is this distinction which facilitates the theories of Meyer and Langer. Broadly, both authors locate musical significance in 'psychological constants' (Meyer, 1973, p.14) or 'psychological laws of "rightness" ' (Langer, 1960, p.240). That is, since all music originates in the minds of individual people, and since all minds are assumed to possess similar psychological characteristics, it is taken that there will be a certain conformity of patterning or structure between all music and all minds. Consequently, all minds are presumed to be suitably predisposed for the superimposition of the particular structure that constitutes a piece, and there is no longer any need to have recourse to the notion of symbols which divest themselves of externally referential meanings. 'Information' is conveyed by another method.

On the surface, this might seem to be a suitable and adequate explanation of musical process. It is ultimately compromised, however, by resulting from exactly the same mode of thought responsible for the original difficulty. In order to understand this anomaly, it is necessary firstly to argue that the collective reality of any society is mutually constructed by its members, rather than being externally given, and secondly to indicate the role played by varying media in the construction of that reality.

The Social Construction of Reality [1]

An approach to the understanding of the social construction of reality may best be made through a consideration of the role played in that process by symbols. A symbol may be thought of as any occurrence in the world, whether or not produced by man, which carries a *generally* agreed meaning for the members of a particular group or society.

Societies can only arise and continue to exist through communication, that is, the creation and exchange of symbols [2]. Symbols are not self-contained phenomena. They are not God-given, but created by people to cope with the many varied situations in which they find themselves. The meanings of symbols and sets of symbols are originally derived from *specific* and *real* situations. But there is another side to the coin. Once a symbol or set of symbols have been created in response to a new situation these symbols, in retrospect, colour that situation. When people look back at a series of events they do so by means of and *through* the symbols created to define it. Furthermore, the new symbols may be used in other situations. Since the symbols are not specifically created for these other situations they bring to them meanings which although not necessarily irrelevant or wrong, are obviously coloured by previous usage. The reverse, of course, is equally true, for new situations modify the meanings of the already existing symbols used to denote such situations. In other words, situations and symbols have a mutually interdependent, but not determinant [3], relationship crucial to the constantly changing dynamics of the social process.

This relationship is most easily understood with regard to words, which constitute man's most important symbolic mode. Not only do the meanings which arise in social situations give rise to words and continually modify the meanings of pre-existing words, but words and complete symbolic languages bring pre-conceived meanings to bear on our everyday sense of the world. Indeed, any new situation and/or symbol is mediated to an extent by pre-existing adjacent meanings. The world we live in has meaning for us only because we symbolically mediate the events that take place in it with other people, and we do this primarily with words. Reality — often conceived as an objective fact which cannot be changed, but only misconstrued — is thus *constructed* by people through the mutual *agreement by words and other symbols* on experiences undergone by individual people:

> 'World-view' is an elusive term, but when we speak of some-one's world view in any sense, we do not mean simply the world impressing itself upon his passive receptors, sensory or intellectual. A person does not receive a world view, but rather takes or adopts one. A world view is not a datum, a *donné,* but something the individual himself, and the culture he shares partly constructs; it is the person's way of organising from within himself the data of actuality coming from without and within. (Ong, 1969, p.634).

For the purpose of clear understanding, a theoretical distinction may be drawn between environment and everyday reality: environment is the unqualified situation (reality as we might *imagine* it to be as objective fact) in which a person finds himself; everyday reality is the result of that person's interaction with the environment and the interaction of this subjectivity with other subjects. In practice, the distinction is invalid for two related reasons: firstly, no person finds himself without society and therefore pre-existing cultural support; and secondly, subjectivities and ensuing inter-subjectivities become legitimated or integrated into a world sense[4] through which the environment is mediated to people. Society is quintessentially symbolic. That is to say, world senses and the legitimating structures that integrate inter-subjectivities into a world sense — the meanings of society — are created and maintained in and through people's collective externalisations. Every perception made and every symbol externalised is done so as a contribution to and in the context of the symbolically mediated and, since new situations are constantly arising, dialectic field of meaning peculiar to any group or society.

Any culture-specific field of meaning is predicated upon assumptions which evolve as a result of the inter-subjective legitimations of perceptions, events and situations that articulate that field. These assumptions may be regarded as the paradigmatic framework or structure upon which all sensory or intellectual interaction is unconsciously grounded. The realisation of the existence of such assumptions does not negate the dialectic concept of society (one might conclude that it encouraged people to perceive the nature of all perceptions, thoughts and externalisations as mechanically determined). Assumptions serve, on the contrary, to mediate, process and in some cases repress socially efficacious information in one way rather than in any other. Society is not a one-level mono-linear cause and effect sequence, but a mosaic of simultaneously interacting and complementary fields of action and influence. It must be further emphasised that assumptions are implicitly agreed upon inter-subjectively, and as such are themselves, at times of great stress and rapid or fundamental change, subject to the dialectic processes of society.

The Oral-Visual Split

The principal line of argument in this chapter is that the assumptions underlying the world sense of industrial man are ultimately responsible for current difficulties in music aesthetics. The form the assumptions or world sense of a particular society takes would perhaps seem largely to depend on the way the symbols of that society depict, denote and categorise what might be *imagined* as a previously undifferentiated world. But as well as being influenced by the content-categories of symbols, the world sense or reality developed depends even more pervasively on the medium of mediation (for example, the spoken word, writing, typography or electronic communication) prevalent in any society. Once again, this assertion cannot be proved one way or another, and there is insufficient space to make out a supporting case for it. The following descriptions of pre-literate and industrial world senses do, however, seem to provide considerable substantiation.

Before proceeding to a description of the way in which writing and typography have engendered certain fundamental categories of analysis in the industrial world sense, it is necessary to briefly indicate why the comparison with what may be taken as a pre-literate world sense is made. Sociology is concerned with the study of human relatedness in society — in practice mostly modern industrial society. It is apparent that if a sociologist wishes to understand the relationships people enter into in an area of society in which he is interested then, to produce a description or explanation that is as *meaningful* as possible, he must attempt to lay bare the assumptions upon which the structure of the relation-

11

ships is grounded. If the sociologist does not attempt this, he may well fall prey to two related dangers. Firstly, if the society is other than his own, he may see the workings of the other society in terms of the unspoken assumptions prevalent in his own. This would serve to render his description or analysis useless. The avoidance of this danger not only involves the sociologist in the process of exposing the assumptions of the other society, but also in making clear the underlying implications of his own position, which are part and parcel of his own existence. Secondly, if the society under examination is his own, the sociologist, by explaining human relationships in terms of the unspoken assumptions common to himself and his society, achieves little else but a reinforcement of those assumptions and, consequently, of the *status quo*. The workings of his own society, in other words, remain a mystery towards which he has contributed, a process which hardly adds to the understanding of that society. Whether the society is his own or not, therefore, the sociologist must constantly question his own position. In this particular case, the questioning will be achieved by making the comparison with a vastly different world sense, that of pre-literate man.

Practically all communication in pre-literate societies takes place in face-to-face situations. And it is because sound thus takes on a great importance in pre-literate man's world[5] that, in order to understand the way this world is structured, it is necessary to understand the inherent qualities of sound *as a perceived phenomenon*. For sound has certain qualities not generally associated with the other phenomena that impinge on our senses. Sound is evanescent. It can only exist as it is going out of existence. It is never static and can only be considered sequential by the application of discontinuous analytic thought to its existence. A sight, on the other hand, can generally be more easily isolated in its ongoing effect and examined without destroying the inherent quality of the experience to anything like the same extent. The only way a sound can be so examined is by repeating it in its entirety if, indeed, the circumstances of its creation allow this.

Sound is thus more symptomatic of the flow of time than any other phenomena that impinge on our senses. Although all other phenomena occur within a stream of time, the fact that they may be generally isolated and examined at leisure demonstrates that, *as far as the influence on the arrangement of man's sensorium is concerned,* they are not so inexorably tied to that stream as sound is.

Sound evokes a sense of space very different from that evoked by other phenomena. A person can only look in one direction at a time, and can easily rid himself of an unpleasant sight by closing his eyes or turning away. Taste is very much a sense of acceptance and rejection, and the power to escape a tactile stimulus is obvious. Smell, although it has something of sound's all-encompassing quality, may still be avoided by holding one's nose or moving away. In all these cases avoidance involves the parameter of visual space. The sound of the world, on the other hand, impinges on our ears from all directions and all distances at once, and the ability to totally cut out or ignore sound is severely limited:

> Auditory space has no point of favoured focus. It's a sphere without fixed boundaries, space made by the thing itself, not space containing the thing. It is not pictorial space, boxed in, but dynamic, always in flux, creating its own dimensions moment by moment. It has no fixed boundaries; it is indifferent to background. The eye focuses, pinpoints, abstracts, locating each object in physical space, against a background; the ear however, favours sound from any direction. We hear equally well from right or left, front or back, above or below. If we lie down, it makes no difference, whereas in visual space the entire spectacle is altered. We can shut out the visual field by simply closing our eyes, but we are always triggered to respond to sound. (Carpenter and McLuhan, 1970, p.67).

Sound is symptomatic of energy. Something has to be going on for sound to be generated, and with sound that is not electronically conveyed (if we treat the loudspeaker as a translation device), the source usually occurs within a geographical range that means it can have an immediate effect upon the listener. Total staticity and the generation of sound is very rare. An example of this aspect of sound is given by Ong (1967, p.112) when he points out that 'a primitive hunter can see, feel, smell and taste an elephant when the animal is quite dead'. When, however, 'he hears an elephant trumpeting or merely shuffling its feet, he had better watch out. Something is going on. Force is operating'.

Sound is therefore dynamic. It requires a more immediate response, and does not allow so much time or the space necessary for initial avoidance, subsequent, cooler exposure, and considered rationalisation.

Pre-literate man thus sees himself as being at the centre of a sound universe, which is dynamic and bounding with energy. Furthermore, since the paradigm of sound for people is the human voice, he imputes power and influence to the physical phenomena that surround his existence as he would impute it to the human voice. This orientation of pre-literate man to his world is noted by Mary Douglas (1970, pp.103-104):

> In all the cosmologies mentioned so far, the lot of individual humans is thought to be affected by power inhering in themselves or in other humans. The cosmos is turned in, as it were, on man. Its transforming energy is threaded on to the lives of individuals so that nothing happens in the way of storms, sickness, blights or droughts except in virtue of these personal links. So the universe is man-centred in the sense that it must be interpreted by reference to humans.

The world of pre-literate man is a revelationary and relatively unpredictable world over which he exercises *comparatively* little conceptual control. This lack of control over environment is reflected in, and partly caused by, a lack of control over knowledge, which again relates back to pre-literate man's orality. There is thus much impetus for the creation of a firm and comparatively unyielding legitimating structure:

> Man knows what he can recall — all else is so ephemeral as to be negligible. In an oral culture this means he knows what is cast in fixed thematic formulatory patterns. Anything else will seem unreal, nonknowledge, reprehensible and dangerous. This is the noetic foundation for the traditionalism stemming from oral cultures. What is non-traditional . . . is dangerous because it is slippery and unmanageable. Oral-aural man does not like the non-traditional because, beyond his limited means of control, it advertises the tenuousness of his hold on rationality. (Ong, 1969, p.640).

The hermetic and revelationary world of oral-aural man, with its tight grip on the supporting mythological structures, militates against the easy acceptance of change in pre-literate societies. Freshly perceived phenomena tend to be contained by and mediated through the rock certainty of orally accretive legitimations. This does not mean that the legitimating structures in pre-literate societies do not change in a manner that would prove historically contradictory, but merely that pre-literate man, because of his orality, is unlikely to realise the contradictory nature of successive legitimations, a fact illustrated by Goody and Watt (1963, p.309):

14

Early British administrators among the Tiv of Nigeria were aware of the great importance attached to ... genealogies which were continually discussed in court cases where the rights and duties of one man towards another were in dispute. Consequently they took the trouble to write down the long list of names and preserve them for posterity, so that future administrators might refer to them in giving judgment. Forty years later, when the Bohannans carried out anthropological field work in the area, their successors were still using the same genealogies.... However, these written pedigrees now gave rise to many disagreements, the Tiv maintained that they were incorrect, while the officials regarded them as statements of fact, a record of what had actually happened, and could not agree that the unlettered indigines could be better informed about the past than their literate predecessors. What neither party recognised was that in any society of this kind changes take place which require a constant readjustment in the genealogies if they are to continue to carry out their functions as mnemonics of social relationships.

Neither does the orality of pre-literate man's noetic foundation mean that relatively sudden breaks in the legitimating structures that are quick enough to impinge on his consciousness do not occur. But unless the break was occasioned by a literate society, it would seem more than likely that the new world sense would quickly assume the features already described. Change in pre-literate societies, then, tends to be continual and gradual rather than infrequent and radical, and something of which pre-literate man is not obviously conscious.

Pre-literate man's attitude and relationship to change is symptomatic of his sense of time. Just as he exists in a man-centred world where events in space are threaded onto the lives of himself and significant others, so events in the past and potential occurrences in the future are mediated by him in terms of the present. This is evidenced by Goody and Watt's story concerning the Tiv of Nigeria. In this sense pre-literate man lives within time. And against the background of industrial man's spatialised and objective concept of time, with its sense of the pastness of the past, and the futurity of the future, it is not being merely redundant to say that, for pre-literate man, all past and potential events are irrevocably tied to the present.

Living within time and therefore having little consciousness of time as we conceive it, pre-literate man may not be said to have any abstract temporal sense. Time unfolds and is revealed to him through specific events which recur and which are of great importance for the ordering of his existence[6]. Such events, as Edmund Leach has pointed out[7], are most likely to be seasonal changes of some sort. It must be emphasised, however, that these recurring events are *not* used as a means of dividing up abstract continuous time into a mechanical succession of separate segments or instants[8]. As A. I. Hallowell put it (1937, p.660) in discussing the time concept of the Saulteaux Indians, 'the "moon" is not a division of continuous time, it *is* a recurrent event'.

Experiencing time in a concrete and cyclical fashion, therefore, pre-literate man does not conceive of time as regressing or progressing into the vanishing points of past or future infinity. Although pre-literate man undoubtedly has a sense of the past, it is seldom lineal and quickly melts into the contemporary simultaneity of mythology:

> On the whole, then, events that are believed to have taken place 'long ago' are not systematically correlated with each other in any well-defined temporal schemata. There are discrete happenings, often unconnected and sometimes contradictory. Yet the past and present are part of a whole because they are bound together by the persistence and contemporary reality of mythological characters not even grown old. (Hallowell, 1937, p.668).

Corroboration for this feature of pre-literate time is to be found in Dorothy Lee's (1970) description of Trobriand time concepts.

All these aspects of pre-literate time are, of course, closely inter-related, and are best summarised by Edmund Leach (1954, p.114):

> Primitive time can be regarded as a recurring cycle. Certain events repeat themselves in definite sequence. This sequence is a continuity without beginning or end, and thus without any clear distinction between past and present. The most important time-sequences are seasonal activities and the passage of human life. Both these cycles are conceived as of the same kind. For such thinking there is no chronology, and time is not measurable.

For pre-literate man, then, time is a revelationary circumjacence of concretely recurring events, which is constantly in flux, and over which, in Western terms, he exercises relatively little control.

This 'lack of control' is also evidenced in pre-literate man's concept of space. His ordering of space results from the particular and immediate configuration of objects and not from a preconceived abstract framework. With Western man space is an empty hopper made up of horizontal and vertical dimensions into which objects are placed with direct relevance to the visual relationship that an observer has with these objects. This is reflected in art during and after the Renaissance. In this art, 'everything is dominated by the eye of the beholder'. There is 'a space conception that is graphically depicted by the perspective projection of long level vistas upon a plane surface' (Giedion, 1970, p.74). And within this unified and centrally-oriented perspective there is a *lineal* ordering of objects which presupposes and reinforces sequentially segmented time. Pre-literate art completely denies any such abstraction however:

> It is this manner of seeing things without any 'relation to myself' that distinguishes primeval art from all later art. It is not disorder but a different order that is being followed — an order to which we, in our sophistication, have lost the key. (Giedion, 1970, p.78).

Not surprisingly, perhaps, a vital characteristic of this different order is a total lack of emphasis on a vertical-horizontal framework or background:

> The distinguishing mark of the space conception of primeval art is the complete independence and freedom of its vision, which has never again been attained in later periods. In our sense there is no above and no below, no clear distinction of separate-ness from an intermingling, and also, certainly, no rules of proportional size . . .
> Primeval art never places objects in an immediate surround-ing. Primeval art has no background.... This is inherent in the prehistoric conception of space: all linear directions have equal right and likewise all surfaces, whether they be regular or irregular. They can be tilted at any angle with the horizontal throughout the entire 360 degree range. To the eye of primeval man, animals that to us appear to be standing on their heads, do not appear inverted to him because they exist, as it were, in space free from the forces of gravity. Primeval art has no back-ground. (Giedion, 1970, pp.85-87).

With its concrete situation in specific objects, its lack of concern with fixed boundaries and backgrounds, its easy acceptance of intermingling and consequent lack of concern with separateness, pre-literate space is essentially auditory in nature[9]. And just as the visual bias of industrial man links his temporal and spatial

17

orientations, so are those of pre-literate man linked through his oral-aural bias. This is most easily demonstrated with regard to the lack of concern for spatial separateness:

> All is within the continual present, the perpetual flow of today, yesterday and tomorrow .... Whenever possible previous lines are not destroyed, but the lines of both earlier and later works intermingle till they sometimes — but only to our eyes — appear inextricable. It was recognised quite early that this superimposition was not due to idle chance but to a deliberate reluctance to destroy the past. (Giedion, 1970, pp.85-86).

The juxtaposition of past and imminent events in the ongoing present, in other words, requires a spatial sense that transcends the mutual separation of all objects in visual space. As industrial man has tended to spatialise time, it could equally well be said that pre-literate man temporalises space.

From whichever angle it is approached, therefore, the world of pre-literate man displays an instancy and immediacy which industrial man, given his rational control over the events of the world, finds it difficult to empathise with. It is dynamic, in a constant state of flux, and at all times pregnant with happenings. It is a world whose encroaching massivity is constantly requiring response.

$$* \quad * \quad * \quad * \quad *$$

Literate man possesses the ability of storing the information of his socially constructed reality, which then attains a permanency and safety not before possible. Within this innovation lies the potential for preserving inviolate discrepancies between succeeding legitimations, and so for the emergence of an historically based dialectic and the concomitant growth of a comparatively based rather than myth-ologically mediated critical method. The keeping of records there-fore makes possible a sense of the pastness of the past, of historical perspective, and so lays the foundation for the separation of history from myth.

As well as encouraging an historical and analytic perspective, literacy also emphasised the visual at the expense of the auditory. And whereas sound underlines *the dynamic immediacy of the environment,* visual stimuli underline *the distancing and separateness of events and objects both from each other and individual people.* As sound underlines immediacy in time, so vision underlines distancing

18

in space. Further, since literacy facilitates the safe and permanent storage of information *apart from people's consciousness,* it also induces a psychic spatiality. This psychic spatiality is, as we shall see, closely inter-related with the physical distancing just indicated.

Literacy may be broadly divided into two categories: ideogrammatic and phonetic. Whereas phonetic literacy encodes the sounds people make in speaking, ideograms directly encode the objects and concepts about which people speak. Ideograms therefore require a knowledge/acceptance of the ideas they ideally represent, because, in terms of the already existing set of ideograms, there is no way in which the ideas may be critically discussed. This aspect of ideogrammatic literacy has considerable political consequences, as a later section of this chapter will make clear[10]. The point at issue here, however, is that the world sense of an ideogrammatic culture cannot be transcended, because the ideograms are only capable of encoding that world sense, and not what people say in it, or about it. And since orally mediated knowledge is, as we have seen, slippery and evasive, its power to avoid assimilation of important aspects of ideas encoded ideogrammatically (which are more manageable, permanent, and therefore influential) is very limited. The power of literacy to radically alter orally mediated knowledge is so all-embracing and massive compared with the ability of oral people to influence literately encoded knowledge that, when a literate and oral society come into contact, the thought patterns of the former always tend to be superimposed on those of the latter. Any meaningful or consequential questioning of ideogrammatic intellection is thus severely circumscribed.

When the sounds of words are encoded in written words, however, oral questioning of visually encoded ideas may itself be encoded visually *in terms of already existing symbols.* Criticism which was originally oral may more easily influence knowledge which was literately encoded at the time the original criticism was made. In this way sound and sight provide mutual yardsticks of comparison and criticism. Not only may the written word be questioned in terms of the spoken word, therefore, but the efficacy of the spoken word becomes such that questioning it in terms of the written word is deemed to be a continuing necessity. As well as questioning what people meant in contradistinction to what they 'actually' wrote, then, one may also question what people meant in contradistinction to what they 'actually' said. The word is no longer restricted to

19

face-to-face communication, and the idea may be prised out of its pictorial prison.

In thus facilitating a divorce between meaning and symbol, phonetic literacy creates an epistemological dichotomy, that between content and form, which has been extremely pervasive in the thinking of modern Western man, and which is clearly of the greatest importance to any discussion of music aesthetics. Of more importance to the present line of thought, however, is the manner in which the divorce between meaning and symbol encourages a comparative and analytic, rather than mythological dialectic, and so aids the growth of historical dialecticism implicit in any literate society. One concomitant of this growing historical/analytic approach is the ability a *phonetically* literate person may develop to put a *great deal* of temporal/spatial distance between himself and the phenomena or knowledge he is examining. Initially, of course, this ability derives from the permanent storage of information in a place entirely removed from human consciousness. Gradually, however, the possibility of critically examining the spoken word in a manner similar to the written word *leads to the distancing principle being applied to face-to-face communication.* The distinction between meaning and symbol, content and form, and the distancing involved have become so pervasive in industrial man's cognitive and intellectual orientation, that it is extremely difficult for him to understand the immediate power words possess for pre-literate man. Indeed, without a conscious realisation of how this distinction and distancing arose, any meaningful insight into the role played by language in pre-literate societies is almost impossible.

Because the spoken word in pre-literate societies cannot be divorced from its everyday use in face-to-face communication, and *because of the indissoluble links that exist in those societies between man, the universe and sound,* words come to have an immediacy and power unknown in industrial society. And *because of the imposing massivity of pre-literate man's world,* there is no way in which this immediacy and power can be diluted or questioned. Words and referents are inextricably intertwined, a phenomenon illustrated by J. C. Carothers (1959, p.309) through reference to his non-literate son:

> Some years ago my little son said: 'Is there a word "pirates", Daddy?' When I replied in the affirmative, he asked 'Are there pirates?' I said, 'No, not now, there used to be'. He asked, 'Is

there a word "pirates" *now?*' When I said, 'Yes', he replied, 'Then there must be pirates now'. This conversation, which might have come straight from Parmenides' doctrine of twenty-four centuries earlier, is a reminder that, for a child, a thing exists by virtue of its name; that the spoken or even imagined word must connote something in the outer world[11].

As J. W. Carey has put it (1967, p.10), words in pre-literate societies 'become icons, they do not represent things, they are themselves things'. They are instrumental in *all* their aspects, and certainly efficacious over and above any hard information that we, industrial men, might distill from them. There is no attempt on the part of pre-literate man to separate meaning from symbol, content from form, and then to relegate symbol or form to a position of neutral insignificance. As *sound* the word is dynamic and pregnant with consequence.

$$* \quad * \quad * \quad * \quad *$$

In view of this comparison of the different kinds of significance assigned to words in pre-literate and industrial societies it may be concluded that, firstly, the distinction between content and form that we take so much for granted is in fact specific to phonetically literate societies and that, secondly, the conundrum the absolutists find themselves in is inextricably linked to that distinction. That is, if the form of music is its content, how can it have any content (or significance) at all?[12]

What is not so clear is that there is a second distinction, *inter*dependent with that just indicated, on which the theories of Langer and Meyer are predicated. Because this second distinction *is* interdependent with the first, the significance assigned to music by Langer and Meyer is largely spurious, and the positions they adopt are not very far removed from that of the absolutists. This distinction, its interdependency, and the consequences that interdependency have for the theories of Langer and Meyer will now be described.

The distancing inherent in the meaning/symbol dichotomy of phonetic literacy greatly reinforces the emphasis on visual space that results with any form of literacy. This reinforcement has important consequences for man's relationship to himself, to others, and to the physical environment. The inter-subjective designation of self no longer exclusively requires the presence of the 'significant other', since socially efficacious information may be received in writing. If one thinks of consciousness, which is socially mediated through communication with others, as communication with self, then it follows that the reception of written information, which originates with others, but whose perusal (silent or oral) is essentially communication with self, induces a shift of emphasis to self. Literate man can put others at a distance and in so doing becomes self-conscious to a degree not possible with pre-literate man.

In the same way that literate man may put others at a distance he may also put the environment at a distance. The analytic method inherent in phonetic literacy serves to reduce pre-literate man's lack of conceptual control over his man-centred universe[13]. Not only does literacy enable comparisons through time of environmental events, but, in enabling man to be increasingly conscious and analytic of self and others, also permits the energy and events of the environment to be unravelled from the lives of people. In other words, as phonetically literate man distinguished symbol from meaning, so he began to draw a line between himself (the words *he* uttered) and the external world, (the *things* to which the words referred). *A vital distinction between the physical and the mental thus grew up,* in marked contrast to oral societies, where the difference between physical and mental, non-human and human, 'outer' and 'inner' is of relatively little significance.

The spatiality and distancing of literacy provides the essential link between increased self-consciousness and 'objectivity'. Through the provision of a surrogate other, literate man possesses the capability of becoming conscious of his consciousness, and of his position in the universe — of partially stepping outside himself and, in a move formalised by Copernicus, of vacating his central, orally-enveloped position in the cosmos. This, as we have seen, is simply an impossibility for pre-literate man: 'for early man, the world was something he only participated in, not an object to be manipulated in his consciousness'. (Ong 1969, p.635).

This objectivity is closely linked with industrial man's sense of time. The historical perspective (distancing) possible with literacy leads to a straight-line or linearly sequential sense of time:

> In our culture, the line is so basic that we take it for granted, as given in reality. We see it in visible nature, between material points, and we see it between metaphorical points such as days or acts. It underlies not only our thinking, but also our aesthetic

apprehension of the given; it is basic to the emotional climax, which has so much value for us, and, in fact to the meaning of life itself. In our thinking about personality and character, we have assumed the line as axiomatic. (Lee, 1970, p.142).

Furthermore, through his ability to record events and through his sense of the pastness of the past, literate man can halt the events of time in their ongoing flow and so, in effect, halt time. Coupled with the development of his analytic ability, therefore, literate man also developed a tendency to examine time, as it were, from the outside, a tendency which reached full fruition with the Renaissance:

> With the end of the Renaissance the feeling of spontaneous inter-communication in all individual activity within the cosmic *becoming* has also disappeared. Human thought no longer feels itself a part of things. It distinguishes itself from them in order to reflect upon them, and is thus no longer upheld by their own power of enduring. From the motion of bodies which inexplicably and incessantly modified it, human thought feels itself to be disengaged by the very act of thinking, for in this act it places itself outside the motion which is its object. (Poulet, 1956, p.13).

Literate man therefore exists outside time in the same way as he can partially exist apart from himself and his society, and in the same way as his self-consciousness and objectivity allow him to unravel the events of the environment from a human-like volition. But in becoming conscious of his consciousness literate man also becomes as conscious of his own temporal flow from which he cannot *totally* escape, as he does of the events of the environment which he can now fix in a sequential linear order. There thus rises up in Western thought a distinction between time concepts as relating to the physical world and to the mental:

> When Hermann Weyl claims that the objective world *is* and does not become, he has to admit that at least our 'blindfolded consciousness' *creeps* along the world line of its own body into the area of the universe called 'future', or when it is said that we meet the pre-existing future events *on our way to the future,* we concede that even if the future is completed, our way to the future is still going on .... Thus arises an absurd dualism of the timeless physical world and temporal consciousness, that is, a dualism of two altogether disparate realms whose correlation becomes completely unintelligible. (Capek, 1961, p.165).

This 'absurd dualism' clearly underpins the human/non-human, mental/physical, inner/outer, subjective/objective epistemological split already noted.

* * * * *

It is now possible to understand why neither Meyer nor Langer transcend the limitations of their own intellectual tradition. For by restricting musical significance to the inner, emotional and subjective side of this split, they have in reality failed to transcend the first, *interdependent* form-and-content dichotomy. By restricting music to the inner and mental worlds, in other words, they are in fact still denying music any *substantial* significance beyond its 'mere existence' as form. Indeed, a *purely* psychological significance can only be assigned to music — and the difficulty of the absolutists' position thereby overcome — by unjustifiably *denying the interdependency of the two dichotomies.*

This criticism implies that the significance attached to music by these two authors is largely spurious. Symptomatically, Langer claims music to express *'the Unspeakable'* (1960, p.235)[14], and goes on to assign such significance a low rational priority:

> Music is a limited idiom, like an artificial language, only even less successful; *for music at its highest, though clearly a symbolic form, is an unconsummated symbol.* Articulation is its life, but not assertion; expressiveness, not expression. The actual function of meaning, which calls for permanent contents, is not fulfilled; . . . (1960, p.240).

Because she assigns such a low rational priority to musical significance, Langer's stance seems to come perilously close to that of the absolutists. Meyer, on the other hand, allows for a much more explicit significance through his emphasis on rigorous analysis. Yet it is again symptomatic that this analysis, by Meyer's own admission, ultimately fails as a method of elucidating that significance. He tells us that ethetic relationships — which constitute the 'kinesthetic sensing of the ethos and character of a musical event' (1973, p.242) — 'are unquestionably important . . . but . . . hard to analyse with rigor and precision' (1973, pp.245-246), that 'there is an absence of an adequate theory of ethetic change and transformation' (1973, p.246), and finally, that 'the rigorous analysis of ethetic relationships is beyond my knowledge and skill' (1973, p.267).

At this stage in the argument, the reader may think that Meyer's difficulties can be traced to the fact that music does indeed encode that which is genuinely 'unspeakable' or unutterable. It might be thought, for example, that because music refers outside itself to psychological constants, the inner-outer distinction has been truly transcended. But as a symbol may only have meaning in relation to something outside itself, so a thought or feeling might only exist because it too relates to something in the outside world. More specifically, there exists an equivalence between the inner-outer distinction as it applies to both symbols and consciousness: a symbol may only refer outside itself to something because a thought (itself having the same external referent) gave that symbol its meaning; conversely, a thought may only exist because it possesses an external referent implanted by a symbol (itself having the same external referent). This point will become clearer in the light of arguments presented in Chapter Two.

Now although there is little doubt that people possess deep-seated desires which are genetically programmed, there is equally little doubt that a high proportion of the way we relate to the world results (as already argued) from symbolic interaction with other people. As far as each of us is concerned, these other people exist 'out there' in 'objective reality'. If, therefore, it is maintained that there is no need to transcend the inner-outer distinction as it applies to the mind (because all psychological constants or psychological laws of rightness are genetically programmed, thereby making reference to the outside world unnecessary), then that is something the aesthetician or music theorist needs to argue in some detail. Symptomatically neither Langer nor Meyer undertake this argument.

Meyer does, however, paradoxically indicate the possible solution to his difficulties by concluding that it is impossible to distinguish between psychological constants and the conventions of a particular musical language:

> In theory it is possible to distinguish between archetypal patterns and schemata. The former would be those patterns which arise as the result of physiological constants presumed innate in human behaviour. The latter would be those norms which were the result of learning. But the distinction breaks down in practice. For most traditionally established norms have some basis in innate constants, and on the other hand, patterns derived from innate constants become part of tradition. (1973, p.214).

If this is the case, why does Meyer not seek the basis of ethetic relationships in these different and identifiable norms? To pose a parallel question, if Langer can reach the conclusion that *what music . . . actually reflects is only the morphology of feeling'* (1960, p.238) why does she not further enquire into the origins of that morphology? Why does she implicitly doubt, with Meyer, 'that the explanation of musical practice needs to be pushed back this far' (Meyer, 1973, p.8), and thereby effectively ignore the entire sociological tradition?[15]

✳ ✳ ✳ ✳ ✳

One reason for this 'psychological' barrier may be located in the one aspect of industrial man's world sense which has primarily resulted from the advent of movable type printing.

Literate man's ability to view time as a lineal sequence of discrete instants[16] gradually fed back upon his understanding of language until all language, whether spoken or written, was conceived in terms of the sequential and segmented nature of the *written* word. One discrete word, in other words, was thought of as following another in set order to give a specific meaning. Pre-literate man, by contrast, did not think in terms of the discrete homogeneous word, but rather in terms of utterances relevant to the face-to-face situation in which meaning was to be conveyed:

> Man without writing thinks in terms of sound groups and not in words, and the two do not necessarily coincide. When asked what a word is, he will reply that he does not know, or he will give a sound group which may vary in length from what we call a word to an entire line of poetry, or even an entire song. The word for 'word' means an 'utterance'. When a singer is pressed to say what a line is, he whose chief claim to fame is that he traffics in lines of poetry, will be entirely baffled by the question; . . . (Lord, 1964, p.25).[17]

It was the concepts of linear segmented sequentiality and arrested time that made possible the invention of movable type printing; the visuality of handwriting acted back upon itself and created the potential for mentally arresting and splitting up the action of scribing. Furthermore, the difference inherent in phonetic literacy between word and meaning, form and content, enabled man to conceive of the blank page as a container into which could be poured meaning in the shape of interchangeable bits of type, linearly and sequentially arranged. Finally, consciousness of linearly segmented processes itself facilitated the invention of the actual process of movable type printing, which involves a number of different steps, sequentially arranged.[18]

It was undoubtedly the invention of movable type printing which both facilitated and actively encouraged the formulation of Western man's epistemology in its most extreme and crystalline form. Although manuscript literacy permitted the rise of all the visual concepts so far mentioned, it could not allow for the rise of uniformity (homogeneity) and repeatability to the extent possible in post-Renaissance society. Manuscripts of the same 'article' or 'book' were copied at different times by different people with different handwriting. Quite clearly, a copy made by one person would, in all probability, *look* quite different to a copy made by another, and there was no guarantee that the wording of one copy would be identical with the next[19]. Furthermore, the number of copies that could be made by this method was obviously limited. Movable type printing, on the other hand, made possible the production of hundreds of copies all of which were identical.

This development of uniform outlook may be said to have two aspects, one physical, the other mental. Firstly, the extreme visuality and segmentation encouraged by printing, together with the regularity and repeatability of the printed page, instigated the concept of a unified pictorial space. The encroaching immediacy and tangibility of pre-literate man's environment, his disunified, multidimensional but 'uniquely structured spaces and times' (McLuhan, 1962, p.178) were eventually syncretised into the depth of a single three dimensional space. The visual stress of printing thus gave a focal point to the distancing and spatiality of phonetic literacy.

But this development of a single physical point of view has an intellectual analogue, as Goldschmidt indicates (1943, p.113):

> It cannot be doubted that for many medieval writers the exact point at which they ceased to be 'scribes' and became 'authors' is not at all clear .... We are guilty of an anachronism if we imagine that the medieval student regarded the contents of the books he read as the expression of another man's personality and opinion. He looked upon them as part of that great and total body of knowledge, the *scientia de omnia scibili*, which had once been the property of the ancient sages.

The organic wholeness of knowledge is split into *segmented* and *individual* points of view, a development that Marshall McLuhan links to the advent of silent reading[20] (1962, p.125): 'The reader of print . . . stands in an utterly different relation to the writer from the reader of manuscript. Print gradually made reading aloud pointless and accelerated the act of reading till the reader could feel "in the hands of" his author.' But it was not only the reader who reacted to this desire for uniformity of feeling:

> Individual writers throughout the sixteenth century varied tone sentence by sentence, even phrase by phrase, with all the oral freedom and flexibility of pre-print days. Not until the seventeenth century did it become apparent that print called for a stylistic revolution. The speeding eye of the new reader favoured not shifting tones but steadily maintained tone, page by page, throughout the volume. . . . By the eighteenth century the reader could depend on a writer controlling the purr of his sentences and giving him a swift smooth ride. Prose became urbane, macadamised. The plunging, rearing horses of sixteenth-century journalese were more like a rodeo. (McLuhan, 1970, p.129).

Instead of partaking of the dialectically ongoing *scientia de omnia scibili* therefore, typographic man internalised a segmented, permanent, finished and individually propagated piece of knowledge[21].

In the same way that historical dialecticism inculcated a lineal sense of the past, so the predictable repeatability of the printed page reinforced the lineality of the future. This reinforced sense of lineal futurity found its clearest expression in the concept of applied knowledge: 'The Medieval Book of Nature was for *contemplatio* like the Bible. The Renaissance Book of Nature was for *applicatio* and use like movable type'. (McLuhan, 1962, p.185). The analytic method inherent in phonetic literacy and historical dialecticism coupled with the concept of repeatability gave typographical man the idea of projecting the analytically examined causes and effects of past events into the future. Science as we have understood it since the Renaissance grew out of this one level (the *single* point of view), lineal, mono-causal epistemology. And the acid test of the accuracy of scientific prediction lies in the *visual* observance of repeatability, an approach unknown before the Renaissance. As McLuhan (1962, p.184) points out in referring to the work of Nef (1958, p.27):

> Observation and experiment were not new. What was new was insistence on tangible, repeatable visible proof. Nef writes . . . 'Such insistance on tangible proof hardly goes back beyond the

times of William Gilbert of Colchester, who was born in 1544. In his *De Magnete,* published in 1600, Gilbert wrote that there was no description or explanation in the book that he had not verified "with his own eyes".' But before printing had had a century and more to build up the assumptions of uniformity, continuity and repeatability, such an impulse as Gilbert felt or such a proof as he offers would have attracted little interest.

Indeed, nowhere is the epistemology of modern industrial man so clearly evidenced as in the Newtonian/Laplacian view of the universe. As words are locked into the homogeneous printed page, so the universe is viewed as homogeneous empty space peopled by discrete and ultimately immutable units of matter. The indestructability of matter is itself a concept analagous to the idea of permanence engendered by the keeping of written records, and the juxtaposition and motion of matter in space may be predicted by invoking laws derived from the past observation of matter in space. Future events may thus be *determined* and ultimately *controlled,* and the increased control of knowledge resulting from the distancing and objectivity of phonetic literacy may be said to have reached its highest pitch.

The Newtonian/Laplacian view of the universe, in being induced by an epistemology generated by phonetic literacy and typography, in turn reinforced that epistemology to the extent that modern Western man *failed to differentiate between what was legitimately predictable and controllable in terms of Newtonian mechanics and what lay outside the field of those laws.* The crucial step in formulating this all-inclusive cosmology is the unfounded assumption that all reality consists in the material. This assumption derives from conceiving matter, which is *not* maintained by people, in the image of eternal unchanging type which *is* maintained as such by people. In this way matter was assigned a spurious eternity and immutability which encouraged people to think of it as somehow basic or fundamental to the operations of the universe. As a result the concept of matter tended to obscure all else: 'For psychological reasons[22], the concept of matter sometimes obscured the concept of void or both concepts obscured that of motion; and nearly always the concepts of space, matter and motion tended to obscure that of time'. (Capek, 1961, p.135). It was this assumption that all reality was ultimately grounded in the material that both facilitated and encouraged the hegemony of scientific thought in modern Western culture:

29

> Science is, of course, the unquestioned source of authoritative knowledge in the modern world. Scientific myths enjoy the claim of being factually true even if they are in no way demonstrable, even if they must be taken on faith, even if they attempt to answer what are, after all, unanswerable questions. Scientific myths have the great advantage in this self-conscious society of not appearing as myths at all but as truths, verified or capable of being verified by the inscrutable methods of the scientist. (Carey, 1967, p.38).

This hegemony was in many ways inevitable, because not to support it would have necessarily resulted in a questioning of the single unified pictorial space upon which Newtonian physics is predicated, a questioning hardly likely to be undertaken in view of the enormous practical 'benefits' derived therefrom. In this way the seduction became complete, and typographical man assumed that the behaviour of all phenomena could ultimately be explained and predicted in mechanical terms. As Helmholtz put it, 'To understand a phenomenon means nothing else than to reduce it to the Newtonian laws'. (Quoted, Hanson, 1965, p.91).

A similar, if paradoxical[23], process occurred with the more metaphysical aspects of industrial man's world sense. As people gradually filtered out experiences which did not conform to the order of matter in space, so they began to filter out the inflectionally coded information of spoken discourse:

> Inflectional complexity, in written form, is not only burdensome for the ear; it is also in conflict with the spatial order that the scanning eye finds natural. To the eye, inflections are not part of the simultaneous order of linguistic variations, which they are for the ear. The reader's eye not only prefers one sound, one tone, in isolation; it prefers one meaning at a time. Simultaneities like puns and ambiguities — the life of spoken discourse — became, in writing, affronts to taste, floutings of efficacy. (McLuhan, 1970, p.125).

Because of this inherently paradoxical parallel with industrial man's approach to the material world, it is important to make perfectly clear the relationship between the Newtonian/Laplacian view of the universe and the more general 'material-factual' mode of thought intimated by McLuhan. For, *from the point of view of the analysis of industrial ideology,* the Newtonian/Laplacian world view is no more than a particularly lucid expression of that ideology. The ideology also finds expression in the analysis of other spheres of activity which, on the face of it, have little to do with classical

30

physics. But so seductive is the Newtonian/Laplacian world view, and so strong is scientific mythology that some people, such as Helmholtz, believe that, at least in theory, every phenomenon can be reduced to its constituent material parts and satisfactorily explained through classical physical theories. All that such people will usually admit is that in many cases this procedure is prohibitively complex and detailed. This constitutes the strictest formulation of the industrial world sense. A further, less strict, formulation remains possible without however resurrecting those aspects of experience filtered out through the approach under discussion. That is, that although all phenomena may theoretically be reducible to their constituent material parts, a completely adequate explanation of these phenomena according to material-factual modes of thought does not require this. This latter position is the one that has been *unconsciously* adopted by many people in European civilisations since the Renaissance. For them everything is rationally explicable when *reduced* to the appropriate analytic constituents. Anything which cannot be so reduced and which therefore cannot be made *visually explicit,* immediately becomes non-knowledge:

> The inflectional suggests, rather than expresses or spells out, relations. Technology is explicitness. Writing was a huge technological advance in this respect. It expressed, it made explicit, many relations that were implicit, suggested in inflectional language structures. And what writing couldn't make explicit quickly got lost. Far more than writing, printing was a technological means of explicitness and explanation. But those auditory inflections and relations which could not be made visually explicit by print were soon lost to the language . . . (McLuhan, 1970, p.132).

This is not to say that the power of this mode of thought has not varied considerably over the last five hundred years[24]. At no time, however, was it as pervasive as during the Enlightenment:

> Seeing the beautiful demonstrations of Descartes and Newton as they explained the heavens with their co-ordinates, the great classical minds sought to rival this perfection and simplicity on earth. Philosophers used the geometric method to arrive at moral and religious truth; social scientists reduced government to mechanics; the tragic muse imitated the tight deductive gate of Euclid; and I am not merely playing with words when I say that poetry itself adopted one common meter as if scientific accuracy depended on it. In all the imponderables of life, conduct, and art, the test was no longer the flexible, 'Is it good,

31

true or beautiful for such and such a purpose?' but 'Is it correct?' (Barzun, 1943, p.40).

The paradox indicated at the beginning of the previous paragraph occurs because the epistemological dichotomy of industrial man is capable of acting back on itself at more than one level. In other words, the tendency described in the previous two paragraphs for industrial man to suppress the inner, mental, subjective and emotional side of the dichotomy and emphasise the outer, physical, objective and intellectual, operates in *both* the physical *and* metaphysical (oral) aspects of his world sense. This paradox thus points up the central ambiguity of the world sense, an ambiguity already indicated in respect of industrial man's temporal sense[25]. For although industrial man tends to think that all phenomena are susceptible to material-factual modes of thought, he cannot, if pressed, deny the temporal flow of his own consciousness. Unfortunately, because world senses are processual phenomena to be lived in rather than examined, industrial man is seldom pressed. His consequent inability to differentiate between what is genuinely material-factual in the universe and what isn't has thus led to an unfounded assumption of *total* objectivity. He has, in other words, *unconsciously* slid into the position of thinking himself to be *totally* outside time and ultimately *totally* capable of knowing about everything, including himself (a proposition which is inherently schizophrenic). Industrial man *tends* to see existence projected before him on one long, flat vista[26].

* * * * *

In view of this exposition of the industrial world sense, it is useful to briefly indicate why Marshall McLuhan's theories have met with such a tentative and negative response in many quarters. It will be remembered that one of the corollaries of the meaning/symbol split was a concentration on what somebody 'actually' meant, in contradistinction to what they may have spoken or written. The result of this process is a desire to fix the hard information from the uncertain flux of the original utterance. In this sense content may be thought of as the significant *matter* which may be poured into the empty *form* provided by the spoken, written or printed word. As McLuhan has so succinctly put it (1962, p.252): 'The effects of the phonetic alphabet in translating the audile-tactile world into the visual world was both in physics and literature to create the fallacy of "content".' Since content has been equated with the side of the epistemological dichotomy traditionally assigned the higher reality, it is not surprising that, for typographical man, media, the forms into which meaningful content is poured, are inconsequential, neutral and certainly not, in themselves, constitutive of knowledge.

As already suggested, this 'view' of media is fallacious. Media influence the balance of the very sensory processes that people use to filter the information coming to them from the environment. In the words of the crowning McLuhanism: 'The medium *is* the message' [Italics mine].

* * * * *

One reason for the 'psychological' barrier which prevents Langer and Meyer from adopting a sociological stance towards the question of significance in music may now be briefly given. Because a higher rational priority is traditionally assigned to the material than the metaphysical, there has been a tendency to think of the 'materials' of society, the people and the environment on which they depend, as somehow more important to the social process than the symbols those people emit. The symbolic superstructure is taken to depend for its significance on the organisation of people and goods that constitutes the kinship/political/economic infrastructure. This view once again depends on a multi-level interpretation or transformation of the epistemological dichotomy described above. In the first place, as we have seen, the *matter* or content of a message is given a higher rational priority than the medium of its conveyance. But precisely because the matter of a message is divorced from the *materiality* of its inconsequential conveyancing medium (*all* symbolic transfer involves *some* articulation of the material universe), it appears as thoroughly metaphysical in comparison with the materiality of people and the goods they manufacture. Symbolic utterances thus come to be given a lower rational priority than people and goods, and to be seen to depend for their significance on the social infrastructure. Were the materiality of symbolic transfer not discounted in this fashion, such division of the social process (itself interdependent with the epistemological dichotomy of industrial man) would be impossible. This understanding of the social process is, of course[27], entirely consistent with the view that a symbol has

33

meaning because it refers to something outside itself, in this instance some process in the infrastructure. This being the case, the significance of music cannot be socially situated because such situation would again invoke the notion of extra-musical concepts:

> Yet the explanations furnished by reference to political, social and cultural history tell only part of the story. For stylistic changes and developments are continually taking place which appear to be largely independent of such extramusical events. Although an important interaction takes place between the political, social and intellectual forces at work in a given epoch, on the one hand, and stylistic developments, on the other, there is also a strong tendency for a style to develop in its own way. If this is the case, then the causes of these changes must be looked for in the nature of aesthetic experience, since for composer and listener style is simply the vehicle for such an experience (Meyer, 1956, p.65).

Once again, the music theorist is caught on the horns of Western man's epistemological dichotomy.

Media and Social-Intellectual Structures

The reason given above for the lack of a sociological approach to the question of musical significance is not the only one. Before going on to put forward a theory for musical significance which transcends the epistemological dichotomy of industrial man, therefore, it is necessary to briefly discuss two other *interdependent* reasons. These two reasons form aspects of the social-intellectual structure prevalent in industrial society, a structure which, in being predicated on the industrial world sense, is again *interdependent* with that world sense.

This section thus seeks to situate the social-intellectual structure of modern industrial man both historically and across the boundaries of the class stratifications which are symptomatic of it. The historical perspective serves to emphasise the necessarily culture-specific nature of any structuring, while the concern with anti-classical movements within the structure serves to demonstrate that, despite shifts in power between social classes, and despite an increasing degree of democracy, the overall structure remains essentially the same. Anti-classical movements, in other words, *tend to be articulated in terms of classical structures*.

Social-intellectual structures are primarily the result of the inter-subjective legitimations of political-economic power groups *dialecti-*

cally mediated through the influence exerted by media on man's sensory and cognitive faculties. The process of legitimation — whether achieved by all the members of a society turning their attention to the process at one time, or by specific members appointed by society who do little else — involves encompassing the entirety or a part of everyday reality, and putting its imposing massivity, within which everyday tasks are carried out, at a distance. The automatic acceptability of everyday reality is potentially suspended, and the legitimators voluntarily place themselves in a position where they are more exposed to the impact and implications of fresh phenomena and events. The recession from everyday reality that is inherent to legitimation thus results in an intensification of individual awareness, the degree to which this awareness may progress being determined ultimately by the means of communication and media available to a society.

So, for reasons already discussed[28], increased awareness in a pre-literate society cannot help but be re-integrated or sublimated into the collective ego during the ritual that symbolises legitimation. The potential for divergent opinions which impinge closely on the assumptional framework of these societies is low, as the political-economic power group is, to a large extent, constituted by the entire society.

Ideogrammatic literacy, however, encourages the formation of a distinct group of legitimators who align themselves with the ruling elite in a society. Ideogrammatic languages usually entail a vast number of signs (some 50,000 in Chinese, of which 3,000 are necessary for a reasonable degree of literacy[29]) which can thus only be learnt and manipulated by a small group of specialists, a phenomenon which in itself brings about an emergent division of labour. Because of the vast potential contained in any form of literacy for the improvement of the administrative and commercial activities of a society, these specialists were of great importance to rulers. There thus existed a natural propensity for the scribe and the ruler to act together in common purpose. As a result of this propensity, and the fact that ideograms do not code sounds[30], the only information coded is that relevant to the ruling elite; to become literate is to unavoidably acquire both the outlook and the ideas of the ruling class, ideas which are of little use or relevance to the ruled oral classes. Goody and Watt have noted the emergence of these characteristics in ancient Oriental civilisations (1963, p.314):

35

... it is a striking fact that ... in Egypt and Mesopotamia, as in China, a literate elite of religious, administrative and commercial experts emerged and maintained itself as a centralised governing bureaucracy.... Their various social and intellectual achievements were, of course, enormous, but as regards the participation of the society as a whole in the written culture, a wide gap existed between the esoteric literate culture and the exoteric oral one, a gap which the literate were interested in maintaining. Among the Sumerians and Akkadians, writing was the pursuit of scribes and preserved as a 'mystery', a 'secret treasure'.

Unlike the various forms of hieroglyphic literacy, phonetic literacy is relatively easy to learn, the number of symbols involved usually varying between twenty and forty. Also, as it is possible for phonetic literacy to encode the spoken language of the *entire* society, it does not inherently militate against the interests of any particular group in that society. Phonetic literacy could thus be viewed as a potential democratising influence on a previously autocratic regime. Whether or not this influence held sway in any particular society depended on other factors which there is insufficient space to discuss here[31].

There can be little doubt, however, that phonetic literacy also aided the incipient division of labour facilitated by ideogrammatic literacy (that is, a basic split between mental and physical tasks). As the concepts of spatialism, segmentation, sequentiality and control developed from the influence of phonetic literacy, so the literate elite were more and more exposed to the conceptual parameters within which it was possible to conceive the idea of fragmenting the individual processes of a physical task, and assigning them to different persons. Once this stage had been reached, it was then possible to conceive of tasks which could not be completed by one man, or by a very few men working according to the principles of a relatively unsophisticated division of labour, but which, for reasons of time or skill, would necessarily require the efforts of several men working in succession. This principle, as will be shortly indicated, can then be applied to the whole existence of a society, so that its different activities can be achieved with the maximum of skill and efficiency. Consequently, not only is the role of the legitimator entrenched by the division of labour, but the division itself, facilitated by the legitimator's intellectual orientation, allows for the growth of class and enables the ruling classes to utilise the services of the legitimator in preserving the *status quo*. As instigator and as part of the division of labour, the legitimator tends to have a vested interest in its preservation. Until at least the end of the eighteenth century, therefore, a literate elite governed the 'civilised' world in autocratic fashion.

Typography is as equally a double-edged weapon for encouraging democracy as phonetic literacy. On the one hand, the typographical process, in which individual bits of type can be changed around to form the desired page, engendered the projection of organised mechanisation and regimentation right throughout society. As uniform printing gave rise to the mechanistic view of space and matter, so it gave rise to the idea of using men like the mechanically interacting parts of a machine. Man has become, in the industrial process, the inter-changeable atomistic parts of a mono-causal lineal process, and, as the interchangeable cog in the nation's machinery, he became necessarily homogeneous. The division of labour reached a new peak in efficiency.

The homogeneity of industrial society was achieved through the destruction of the 'mutuality' of feudal society. No longer did a person play a universally understood and specific role in his local society. Through increasing urbanisation he became a depersonalised source of labour to be slotted into a huge centralised scheme. McLuhan describes the transformation in the following way (1962, p.162): 'The feudal system was based on oral culture, and a self-contained system of centres without margins . . . This structure was translated by visual, quantitative means into great centre-margin systems of a nationalist mercantile kind . . .' As the simultaneously divergent viewpoints[32] and time-spaces[33] of medieval man were snapped into three-dimensional focus, so the disparate functioning of feudal units were unified into a single national point of view. But as society changed from one of centres without margins to one of a centre with margins, so did man. Formerly a 'centre' whose activities were mediated by the oral immediacy of other 'centres', industrial man floats comparatively rootless in a constantly changing social milieu. No longer is the rationale of social existence to be located in an immediate self-contained society, but in a remote centre — that of nationalism:

> . . . the development of writing and print ultimately fostered the breakup of feudal societies and the rise of individualism. Writing and print created the isolated thinker, the man with the book, and downgraded the network of personal loyalties which

37

oral cultures favour as matrices of communication and as principles of social unity. (Ong, 1967, p.54).

Industrial man, in other words, must provide his own margins, a process increasingly enabled through the advent of literacy, that surrogate other. The alienation of homogeneous atomistic individuality essentially constitutes the agony of post-Renaissance objective self-consciousness.

Besides being encouraged by the uniformity of function induced through the homogeneity and repeatability of print, the growth of nationalism was also aided by the improved control at a distance made possible by the easier production and propagation of knowledge. Clearly, this control yet again helped to entrench a high division of labour. Moreover, since the market potential for printed books was greater than could be satisfied by a clerical elite reading in Latin, an increasing number of books were published in the vernacular. Ethnic groups thus became more conscious of their own national identity because they could, in a very literal sense, see themselves.

But, as suggested earlier, typography may also act as a force for democracy. This possibility — and hence the double-edged nature of both phonetic literacy and typography — ultimately exists because of the central ambiguity inherent in the industrial world sense. The nationalism just described, for example, both contains and is predicated upon the suppressed distinction of physical and mental time indicated above. For while homogeneous individuality is a necessary adjunct of nationalism, in that men with self-contained margins are required to act interdependently for the centrally dictated aims of the nation, those same men, increasingly more literate and critical, came to be more conscious of the self and its relationship to others, and so gained an increased possibility for formulating and voicing anti-classical opinions: 'individualism, whether in the passive atomistic sense of drilled uniformed soldiery or in the active aggressive sense of private initiative and self-expression, alike assumes a prior technology of homogeneous citizens.' (McLuhan, 1962, p.209). The growth of self-expressive individuality fostered and was in turn reinforced by the emergence of the concept of authorship in post-Renaissance Europe, a concept, as noted, that is uncommon in the Middle Ages.

The possibility inherent in phonetic literacy for an analytic approach towards the discrepant bodies of knowledge that may be stored in a society thus approached something like full fruition during the Renaissance, and the phenomenon of cultural lag consequently becomes of importance in examining the *entire* body of knowledge in modern society. The vast dissemination of books and knowledge that has resulted from printing has encouraged divergent opinions simply because the actual body of knowledge a person may be exposed to could well be, and probably is, different in every case. No one man can now know everything. As Goody and Watt have pointed out (1963, p.324): 'the content of the cultural tradition grows continually, and in so far as it affects any particular individual he becomes a palimpsest composed of layers of beliefs and attitudes belonging to different stages in historical time'. In literate societies, therefore, where the legitimator, as assignor of values, constitutes the class of person most intimately exposed to discrepancies and contradictions, there exists the potential for the legitimator's high degree of self-consciousness to be at variance with his role as maintainer of the established social symbology. Which direction he takes will largely depend on whether he has a vested interest in a *status quo* or is indifferent or hostile to it. Those legitimators who choose to erect new symbolic structures act as catalysts and initiators in the process of change or 'progress', a process which figures prominently in the consciousness of modern Western man.

The role played by printing in creating the intellectual fervour of the Renaissance need not be recounted. However, it was not until the late eighteenth century that anti-classical movements took on a strong *class* orientation. Raymond Williams (1961, p.50) tells us that 'from the third and fourth decades of the eighteenth century there had been growing up a large new middle-class reading public, the rise in which corresponds very closely with the rise to power and influence of the same class'. Because of this increased market, the author no longer needed to work for a patron but could make his money in the open market-place. As Dr Johnson indicates (writing in 1750), a change of subject matter results:

> The task of our present writers is very different; it requires, together with that learning which is to be gained from books, that experience which can never be attained by solitary diligence, but must arise from general converse and accurate observation of the living world. Their performances have, as Horace expresses it, *plus oneris quantum veniae minus*, little indulgence, and therefore much difficulty. They are engaged in portraits of which everyone knows the original, and can detect

any deviation from exactness of resemblance. Other writings are safe, except from the malice of learning, but these are in danger from every common reader . . . (Quoted, McLuhan, 1962, pp.273-274).

The result was that, in reading material produced for them and about them, the middle classes began to gain a consciousness of their political position and of its desirability. This consciousness gradually spread to the working classes during the nineteenth century[34].

Increasing class consciousness was aided by other developments, such as the mechanisation of transport systems and the close proximity of the working classes in the emerging urban areas, both of which can be related to the growth of industrial nationalism. Consciousness led to and went hand in hand with a demand for increased education, until the foundations were laid for an ongoing critical, political and economic dialectic. The legitimator in society, instead of exclusively aligning himself with a ruling elite who have a vested interest in class stratification, may now be found as the representative of practically any class or group.

Phonetic literacy and typography have thus been heavily instrumental in generating a class dialectic, but *within* the framework of political and economic nationalism. From the situation where individual feudal units *were* very much the people that constituted them, industrial society has moved to a situation where the nation state has become a big hopper in which occupants can be placed and shifted in a highly mobile fashion. Nationalism is founded upon the fallacy of form and content; it is not of the people because it contains them. It is permanent while people are mortal. And as the nation is not constituted of specific individuals it has appeared as a pre-existing and generally unquestioned fact of life: 'Because the national state does not belong to the citizens of any particular generation, it must not be revolutionised' (McLuhan, 1962, p.221).

Class dialogue has thus been overwhelmingly concerned in practice, if not in theory, with who shall wield the centralised power of nationalism and to what effect. Only very recently have there been signs of a general awareness of the inherent paradoxes of industrial man's social and intellectual organisation, and a general realisation that perhaps only a fundamental restructuring of that organisation will remove some of its major problems[35]. In a parallel fashion anti-classical legitimating *structures* have generally been conceived within the intellectual, political and economic frameworks outlined in this chapter[36], and so grounded very much on the noetic structures induced through phonetic literacy and typography. Literate legitimators, in other words, in self-reflexively receding from the immediacy of everyday reality, have had great difficulty in recognising the consequences of their own literacy.

The intellectual analogue of this social structure is easy to identify. Due to the high division of labour, hierarchical class structure and centralism of nationalism, the legitimator, in all spheres of society, remains very much in the position of producing and defining knowledge for other people[37]. At the national level academics and artists have generally been associated with those who govern, as this statement by Adam Smith strongly suggests:

> In opulent and commercial societies to think or to reason comes to be, like any other employment, a particular business, which is carried on by a very few people, who furnish the public with all the thought and reason possessed by the vast multitudes that labour. (Quoted, Williams, 1961, p.52).

For the central dissemination of knowledge to remain unchallenged, it is necessary that knowledge is arbitrarily conceived. This arbitrariness is closely inter-related with the notions of objectivity, and form and content — form and content because the *matter* of a message is removed from the social location of its communication, and objectivity because reality is thought of as given rather than socially constructed. The supremacy of this independent and objective knowledge over that resulting from social mediation was symbolically asserted through Plato's expulsion of the poets:

> Plato's banishment of the poets and his doctrine of ideas are two sides of the same coin. In banishing the poets from his *Republic*, Plato was telling his compatriots that it was foolish to imagine that the intellectual needs of life in Greek society could still be met by memorising Homer. Rather than deal in this verbalisation, so much of a piece with the non-verbal life-world, one needed to ask more truly abstract questions. (Ong, 1967, pp.33-34).

Thought and action, mind and body, self and physical environment were separated to such a degree that a considerable amount of importance was able to be given to the 'cerebrally derived' at the expense of the socially experienced:

> In classic Hegelian thesis-antithesis fashion Plato's ideas, the 'really real' *were polarised at the maximum distance from*

the old oral-aural human life-world. Spoken words are events engaged in time and indeed in the present. Plato's ideas were the polar opposite: *not events at all but motionless 'objective' existence, impersonal and out of time.* (Ong, 1967, p.34).

Meaning is thus isolated from its social context and comes to be grounded in a scheme of *absolutes:*

> In oral culture words — and especially words like 'God', 'Justice', 'Soul', 'Good', — may hardly be conceived of as separate entities, divorced both from the rest of the sentence and its social context. But once given the physical reality of writing, they take on a life of their own; and much Greek thought was concerned with attempting to explain their meanings satisfactorily, and to relate these meanings to some ultimate principle of rational order in the universe, to the *logos.* (Goody and Watt, 1963, p.330).

Quite clearly, any assertion that the reality or knowledge of a society is *socially constructed*[38] not only brings into question the notion of absolute objective knowledge, but also implicitly *questions the right of one group of people to define that knowledge for everyone else.* Ultimately, the entire centralised structure of nationalism comes under scrutiny.

Music and the Structure of Industrial Society

At the beginning of the previous section it was stated that there were two inter-related reasons why Langer and Meyer could not assign a social significance to music. It was also suggested that these reasons formed integral aspects of the social-intellectual structure prevalent in industrial society. It is now possible to briefly argue and illustrate the reasons.

Firstly, if the significance of music is taken to be socially located, then it must be understood to form an aspect of the socially constructed reality of the group or society responsible for producing the music in question. In other words the music can only legitimately be understood in terms of the categories of analysis which themselves form an aspect of the reality of that particular group or society. The tendency of the musician or aesthetician in industrial society to approach *all* music in terms of certain *arbitrarily* defined categories thus comes seriously into question.

Secondly this questioning would in turn question the propensity of institutionalised musicians[39] to impose centrally a certain kind of 'musical knowledge' on the rest of society. In particular, it would question the propensity of those musicians to decide what 'counts as music' and, furthermore, to decide what counts as 'good' music for the remainder of society[40]. Such centralised decisions of course necessitate arbitrary categories of analysis and understanding.

Examples of such arbitrary categories are not difficult to find. The notion that musical significance is ultimately located in 'psychological constants' or 'psychological laws of "rightness" ' is itself arbitrarily derived. But perhaps the best example is provided by Victor Zuckerkandl (1956, pp.222-223), when he asserts that musical significance is located in *laws* which may only be discovered by the composer in *objective reality:*

> It is not that the mind of the creative artist expresses itself in tones, words, colours, and forms as its medium; on the contrary, *tone, word, colour, form express themselves through the medium of the creative mind.* The finer that medium the better tone, word, colour, form can express themselves. The greater the genius, the less it speaks *itself,* the more it lends its voice to the tones, the words, the colours, the forms. In this sense, then, music *does* write itself — neither more nor less, by the way, than physics does. The law of falling bodies is no invention of the genius of Galileo. The work of the genius consists in bringing the mind, through years of practice, so into harmony with things, that things can express their laws through him[41].

The above passage from Zuckerkandl well illustrates the way in which arbitrarily derived categories of understanding are not surprisingly grounded in the world sense of industrial man. This phenomenon finds explicit musical expression in the work of Meyer, when he attempts to extrapolate a universally applicable theory of music from albeit insightful analyses of tonality[42]. Again not surprisingly, pre-literate music does not fair very well:

> The differentia between art music and primitive music lies in speed of tendency gratification. The primitive seeks almost immediate gratification for his tendencies whether these be biological or musical. Nor can he tolerate uncertainty. And it is because distant departures from the certainty and repose of the tonic note and lengthy delays in gratification are insufferable to him that the tonal repertory of the primitive is limited, not because he cannot think of the other tones. It is not his mentality that is limited, it is his maturity. (Meyer, 1967, p.32).

This statement of Meyer's represents a classic case of ethnocentricism. He refuses to consider that pre-literate man's world sense is so greatly different from industrial man's that criteria derived from tonality *are simply inappropriate* to pre-literate music[43]. The search for objective standards of value must be maintained:

> At this point some of our social scientist friends, whose blood pressure has been steadily mounting, will throw up their hands in relativistic horror and cry: 'You can't do this! You can't compare baked alaska with roast beef. Each work is good of its kind and there's an end of it'. Now granted both that we can enjoy a particular work for a variety of reasons and also that the enjoyment of one kind of music does not preclude the enjoyment of others . . . this does not mean that they are equally good. Nor does it mean that all modes of musical enjoyment are equally valuable. In fact, when you come right down to it, the statement that 'each is good of its kind', is an evasion of the problem, not a solution of it. And so we are driven to ask: are all kinds equally good. (Meyer, 1967, pp.34-35).

It should now be abundantly clear why Meyer and other music aestheticians cannot possibly locate musical significance as an aspect of socially constructed reality. For not only does such location raise the all-pervasive problem of form and content[44], but it also ultimately brings under scrutiny the entire centralised social-intellectual structure of industrial society. No music aesthetician is likely to begin such a scrutiny even *implicitly,* for as an institutional-ised academic he has an *unconscious* vested interest in that structure. In other words, if a musician or aesthetician questions not only what he says about music, but, in so doing, his right to speak exclusively to and on behalf of other people, he *potentially* puts himself in the unenviable position of questioning the legitimacy of his own socially designated role. The workings of the musical process tend to be conceived as absolute, permanent and ultimately discoverable beyond the vagaries of human thought and perception because such an approach aids mystification and so role-security. To ignore the social nature of music is thus to articulate the social-intellectual structure of industrial society.

The tendencies described in the previous paragraph do not arise from any *conscious* political motive. There can be no question of an 'autocratic conspiracy'. They result rather from the *unconsciously-seated* inability of musicians and aestheticians to follow through the logical implications arising from the *related aesthetic and political* problems surrounding the 'meaning' of music. And given the particular characteristics of the industrial world sense and the inter-related social-intellectual structure of industrial society, there can be little doubt that these problems have been extremely intransigent. Because of its inherent nature, music, perhaps more than any other phenomenon to impinge on our sensory and cognitive faculties, has highlighted the assumptions and deficiencies both of our social organisation, and of our traditional outlook on the world.

In this respect, one final point can be made. At the beginning of the chapter it was stated that the question of meaning in the representational arts is not necessarily problematic. Meaning in these arts can be 'adequately' located in content. Consequently, analysis in social terms becomes easier and, moreover, of little danger to the traditional social-intellectual structure, because it is carried out in terms of the categories mutually interdependent with that structure (that is, the categories of form and content). What is said within a structure is of little consequence to the structure unless it actively questions the assumptions upon which the structure is grounded. *It is precisely the very great difficulty of coming to grips with the meaning of music in terms of form and content that has paradoxically made arbitrary and central definition with regard to music extremely easy.*

To put it another way, there can be two possible responses to the difficulty of the 'meaning' of music. One is to avoid the difficulty. In this case, because traditional ways of looking at the world are totally unsuited for an adequate understanding of music, it becomes extremely difficult to use the categories of that world sense to question any central and arbitrary theories[45]. The other response is to confront the difficulty, and construct a sense of the world which allows for an adequate understanding of the musical process. This is the purpose of the following chapter.

NOTES

1.   The discussion in this section owes much to the work of Berger and Luckmann (1971), and Cicourel (1973).

2.   This proposition is argued by Duncan (1968, pp 44-46).

3.   The necessity for this indeterminacy or creativity is argued below in Chapter Two.

4.   The term 'world sense' is used in preference to the term 'world view', since 'world view' betrays the strong visual orientation of modern industrial man and so encourages the same culture-specific concepts that Chapter Two attempts to transcend. 'World sense', on the other hand, continually underlines a social construction of knowledge which is mediated by the effect of all media on the balance of the senses. The distinction will become clear during the course of the chapter.

5.   The reader may have difficulty in gaining an insight to this importance. It may help, therefore, to draw a comparison with typographical civilisations where the printed word tends to take on an authority and importance that is not always warranted. In a different way, messages conveyed in and through sound have an equal kind of authority and importance for pre-literate man.

6.   cf. Hallowell (1937, p 669).

7.   cf. Leach (1954, pp 115-120).

8.   The contrast between industrial man's spatialised concept of time, and pre-literate man's intuitive processual understanding is reinforced through the structure of their respective languages. cf. Whorf (1971, pp 142-143).

9.   cf. p 13 above.

10.   cf. *Media and Social-Intellectual Structures*, p 34 below.

11.   Further substantiation of this 'sense' of the word for non-literates is given by Riesman (1970, pp 109-110).

12.   cf. pp 7-8 above.

13.   cf. Ong (1967, p 45).

14.   Langer is here referring to a statement by Wagner in *Opera and Drama* that 'orchestral language expresses just what is unspeakable in verbal language, and what, viewed from our rationalistic standpoint, may therefore be called simply *the Unspeakable*'.

15.   For a more detailed application of this line of thought to Meyer's most recent (1973) publication, see Shepherd (1976, pp 42-43).

16.   This view results both from industrial man's ability to 'halt' time in its continual flow and from the importance the line plays in his mode of thought.

17.   The transition indicated in this paragraph was, of course, extremely slow, and one which went through many stages. One such stage is represented by the way in which 'words' were frequently 'joined up' in the writing of antiquity. Oral flow, in other words, still permeated some chirographic literacy. cf. Goody and Watt (1963, p 319) and Kenyon (1937, p 35).

18.   cf. Ong (1967, p 48).

19.   cf. Chaytor (1970, p 123). This difference in look meant that recognition of a particular 'article' or 'book' was as much aural as visual, a fact which again underlines the gradual nature of the shift from oral-aural to visual culture (cf. *n*.17 above). Further evidence of this gradual change is provided by the comparative difficulty that medieval and ancient civilisations experienced in reading (cf. Chaytor, 1970, p 117 and p 122) and by the way in which reading aloud persisted as the norm until well into the Renaissance (cf. Ong 1967, p 21, p 55 and p 58).

20.   cf. *n*.19 above, especially Ong (1967. p 58).

21.   This move towards uniformity and the single point of view is reflected in the standardisation of spelling and of the meaning of words. In this latter regard McLuhan (1970, p 129) comments that 'even nowadays a medieval dictionary would be impossible, since individual writers assumed that they were free to define and develop any given term as their thought proceeded'.

22.   Capek (1961, p 135) makes a direct connection between these psychological reasons (which correspond very closely to the arrangement of industrial man's sensorium) and the repression of certain aspects of experience he is indicating: 'In the classical model physical reality was constituted by four fundamental entities: space, time, matter and motion. All other concepts, including that of energy and momentum, were derived ones; similarly, attempts to reduce the number of basic entities to fewer than four were not successful . . . . Tactile sensations disclosed the reality of matter, visual sensations the reality of space. Since visual and kinesthetic sensations disclosed the reality of motion, motion, too, was a sensory datum. But to what sensory datum did the reality of time correspond? It can neither be touched nor seen; it manifests itself most conspicuously in the auditory sensations which since the time of the ancient atomists have been excluded from physical reality; or in the emotional introspective qualities which by definition do not belong to the physical world. It is true that in the sensory perception of motion we concretely experience succession and that the concept of motion presupposes the concept of time; but it is psychologically understandable that this logical order was forgotten and, as motion in the form of spatial displacement was more accessible to perception and imagination, it was made the very basis of the concept of time in the relational theory'.

23.   This paradox is explained in the subsequent paragraph.

24.   Generally speaking, it may be thought of as gradually increasing until the Enlightenment, and then decreasing until the beginning of the

present century, when changes of a rather different nature began to take place. Although pervasive, the mode of thought never went unchallenged, even at its height. One can think, for example, of the eighteenth-century satire of the book, or Blake's opposition to Newtonian thought.

25.   cf. p 23 above.

26.   It is in fact possible to derive two contrasting epistemologies from the industrial world sense. For convenience these epistemologies may be labelled the 'universal' and the 'dichotomous'. The dichotomous asserts that any particular phenomenon may be understood *either* in terms of the physical, outer, objective world, *or* in terms of the inner, mental, subjective world. This is the epistemology that, for obvious reasons, musicians implicitly support. The universal, in repressing this latter side of the dichotomous, accepts that *all* phenomena are explicable in terms of the physical, outer, objective world. This rigorous formulation of the industrial world sense is only possible in the light of the knowledge of how that world sense came into being. For people who do not question the assumptions upon which their sense of the world is founded and who consequently live largely *unconsciously* within the industrial world sense, the categories of understanding derived therefrom do not appear nearly so clearly formulated. Rather, there is an uneasy and nebulous vacillation 'around' and 'between' the two epistemologies that passes for one homogeneous epistemology appropriate to the common understanding of the world. This uncertainty is, of course, further aggravated by the way in which the categories of understanding may act back on one another at different levels. Precise analyses of the way in which the categories interact in any situation thus tend to be lengthy and tedious. The purpose in this chapter has been to convey a general impression of the principal features of the industrial world sense.

27.   That is, because it is interdependent with the epistemological dichotomy of 'form' and 'content'.

28.   cf. pp 13-18 above. More specifically (cf. Carothers, 1959, p 308), pre-literate man is relatively unable to partially step outside himself, and be reflexive or 'intellectual' where his own reactions to events are concerned. The facility for discussing a problem internally with 'self' is severely restricted, and so the problem is acted out externally with others. Ong (1967, pp 132-133) relates an incident which supports this analysis: 'The riots in the Republic of the Congo at the achievement of independence a few years ago perhaps provided more recent evidence of oral-aural anxiety syndromes. I recall in particular the press report of a Congolese officer whose comment when he was asked about the riots was quite simply, "What did you expect?" That is to say, "Don't armies everywhere riot this way from time to time when the pressure builds up?" '

29.   cf. Goody and Watt (1963, p 313).

30.   cf. p 19 above. The ossifying influence of hieroglyphic literacy is referred to by Goody and Watt (1963, p 313): 'Any system of writing which makes the sign stand directly for the object must be extremely complex. It

can extend its vocabulary by generalisation or association of ideas, that is, by making the sign stand either for a more general class of objects, or for other referents connected with the original picture by an association of meanings which may be related to another either in a continuous or discontinuous manner. Either process of semantic extension is to some extent arbitrary or esoteric, and as a result the interpretation of these signs is neither easy nor explicit'. Again (p 315): 'the conservative and antiquarian bias of hieroglyphic societies can perhaps be best appreciated by contrasting it with fully phonetic writing; for phonetic writing, by imitating human discourse, is in fact symbolising not the objects of the social and natural order, but the very process of human interaction in speech: the verb is as easy to express as the noun; and the written vocabulary can be easily and unambiguously expanded. Phonetic systems are therefore adapted to expressing every nuance of *individual* thought, to recording *personal* reactions as well as items of major importance'. [Italics mine].

31.   The different degree to which phonetic literacy aided or hindered the growth of democracy in Ancient Greek and Roman civilisations, for example, is discussed by Fisher (1936, p 44) Goody and Watt (1963, p 318 and p 322), Kitto (1951, p 66), McLuhan (1962, p 61), and Ong (1967, p 34).

32.   Marshall McLuhan, for example (1962, p 136) has pointed out that: 'it was disturbing to scholars to discover in recent years that Chaucer's personal pronoun or his "poetic self" as narrator was not a consistent *persona*. The "I" of medieval narrative did not provide a point of view so much as immediacy of effect. In the same way grammatical tenses and syntax were managed by medieval writers, not with an idea to sequence in time or space, but to indicate importance of stress'.

33.   Georges Poulet (1956, p 7) tells us that: 'For the man of the Middle Ages . . . there was not one duration only. There were *durations*, ranked one above another, and not only in the universality of the exterior world but within himself, in his own nature, in his own human existence'. Further, medieval man's concept of matter has clear implications for his concept of space (since space is ultimately articulated or 'marked out' by matter): 'To change was to pass from potentiality to actuality. But this transition had nothing about it necessarily temporal. By virtue of the Christian doctrine of omnipotence, it could have a temporal quality only if there were some cause which did not allow the immediate transformation by divine action of the potentiality into the act. And this cause which required that *time be involved in the change* was a certain defect of matter. . . .From this point of view, matter was nothing other than a resistance which, manifesting itself in the substance of a thing, hindered that thing from assuming instantly the fullness of being which its form would confer upon it; a resistance which introduced distance and tardiness, multiplicity and delay, where everything, it seemed, should have happened simultaneously and at once'. (Poulet, 1956, pp 4-5). This high degree of interdependency between matter and *different* 'times' or durations necessarily involves a diversity of *different* 'spaces' or extensions.

34.   This growing consciousness is evidenced in the change of meaning with words such as 'class' and 'democracy'. cf. Williams (1961, pp 14-15).

35.   This awareness has become possible because the media of our communication are again in the process of altering the arrangement of our sensorium and the orientation of our noetic foundations. Electrical forms of communication are restoring the immediacy and simultaneity of our awareness of world events. cf. McLuhan (1964).

36.   Marx is probably the first thinker to have broken from these frameworks and dispensed with the fallacy that knowledge is somehow absolute, permanent and ultimately 'discoverable'. In 'turning Hegel on his head', he and Engels provided a theory of historical and economic processes that saw these processes as manifestations of human contructs acting back upon themselves. And there is little doubt that media philosophers, in extending such an approach to the very language that mediates our existence, have vastly expanded the scope of the critical sociological tradition that began with Marx.

37.   Dissension among and between members and groups in nation states is not evidence of conflicting and different social-intellectual structures, because the dissension generally arises from the essential structural paradox of nationalism and so pervasively articulates that very structure. Legitimators still centrally define knowledge for their group, even if that knowledge conflicts with the knowledge of other groups, whether at the same or a lower or higher level in the overall hierarchic structure.

38.   cf. *The Social Construction of Reality*, pp 9-11 above.

39.   By 'institutionalised musicians' is meant those musicians who belong to institutions (such as conservatories, university music departments, orchestras and so on) dedicated to the 'serious' tradition of European music.

40.   This question of the social control of 'what counts as music' is considered in detail by Graham Vulliamy. cf. Chapters Six and Seven below.

41.   The outlooks of Langer and Meyer are not, of course, far removed from this view of Zuckerkandl's. Although Langer and Meyer allow the human mind a greater role in the compositional process, they still think of musical significance in terms of 'internal' (cf. Zuckerkandl, 1956, p 68) 'objective' 'laws', whether or not they are ultimately discoverable.

42.   This trend is particularly noticeable in Meyer (1956) and Meyer (1973). With regard to this latter book cf. Shepherd (1976). It is assumed here that tonality encodes and creatively articulates the industrial world sense (cf. Chapter Three below).

43.   Meyer's attitude (cf. Meyer, 1967, p 32 — also Meyer, 1956 and Meyer, 1973) is that all music should conform to a straight line sequence aimed at an emotional climax or culmination. Lee (1970, p 142) has already indicated (cf. also above pp 22-23) that this outlook on life is *specific* to modern Western man. Since music encodes and creatively articulates the structure of life and meaning for all men (cf. below Chapter Three), it is hardly surprising that, viewed through the criteria appropriate to tonality,

pre-literate music appears somehow inferior. For it is tonality, and *only* tonality, that encodes Western man's spatialised notion of time.

44.   cf. pp 33-34 above.

45.   The situation is aggravated of course by the fact that the 'central' and 'arbitrary' theories are themselves grounded in the categories of the industrial world sense. If they are questioned in terms of these same categories, they will *necessarily* be confirmed, cf. pp 11-12 above, the brief discussion of sociological method.

Chapter Two

The 'Meaning' of Music

JOHN SHEPHERD

Symbologies

It was argued in Chapter One that the positive feedback operating in post-Renaissance societies between visual stress and written language has been responsible for repressing important facets of life and experience to the collective unconscious. As a consequence of this process 'educated' industrial man has tended to relate to the world solely in material and reified terms — terms which he has not unnaturally equated with the rational objectivity of typography. This outlook has acted back on language so that in all its forms — even the spoken form responsible for the vastly different world sense of pre-literate man — it is ultimately conceived in terms of, and measured against the norm of rational objectivity. The 'oral' and 'emotional' both in life and language has at best been relegated to a position of secondary importance.

It was also argued in Chapter One that society can only arise and continue to exist through symbols externalised by members of society, and that although words constitute the most obvious and important symbolic mode, they do not constitute an exclusive symbology. The emphasis placed by industrial man on rational, verbal objectivity, however, has led him to relegate in significance the realisations of any symbolic mode which implicitly challenge his world sense. The unspoken — or more appositely, unwritten — assumption is that everything that is real can be expressed in objective, rational language and its extensions[1], and that reality as embodied in the rational word is somehow higher than, or ontologically prior to any other evidence of reality accruing from other sources. But although language constitutes the most important symbolic mode from the point of view of maintaining the technically highly developed civilisations of industrial man, it does not follow that the reality comprehended through language is more real than that articulated by other modes, nor, concomitantly, does it follow that language is potentially an exclusive mode in the sense of all other non-verbally coded experience being reducible to verbal terms.

Whilst it remains true that the different symbolic modes *emphasise* different aspects of reality by reason of their different media, it must not be thought that language and other symbolic modes additively contribute their different realities to the total field of meaning in a society. For the sake of discussion, it is convenient to think of the meanings of society as displaying two different aspects: those of *relata* and *relationships*. These terms are explained by Hugh Dalziel Duncan (1968, p.46):

> It has long been realised that any mode of social analysis will produce at least two types of entity: first, analytical elements called 'social facts' which can be observed easily enough, and second, the entities (not so easily observed) that arise in a system because analysis was made in the particular way in which it was made. In more specific terminology the easily observed elements are called relata, while the elements 'underlying' the system are called relationships of those relata.

Structures in society are revealed to people through the relata (other people and symbols) that they perceive, but the structures would not exist as such unless the relata were maintained in certain relationships that people cannot *directly* perceive but can only sense in consciousness through the individual constructions made possible by the transfer of symbols. The symbolic mode of language as conceived by industrial man has emphasised the relata of society at the expense of the relationships because the relata of society display a materiality consanguinous with the objects of the material universe — objects, however, which are not *necessarily* maintained in structural relationships. It was this emphasis that induced industrial man to apply a materialist and reductionist philosophy to human existence, an application which still finds expression in the positivistic social sciences. Yet it can be understood from the present discussion that language does not simply signify objects and reified concepts, as its rational written form might lead us to think. Rather, objects and reified concepts are the word-embodied materials or relata by and through which cultural constructs are articulated. Further, it is of crucial importance for an understanding of how music functions to realise that it has a tendency to emphasise relationships at the expense of relata, since its own relata are non-material and non-referential. Different symbolic modes, therefore, are quite capable of encoding similar structures but may, because of their method of encoding, stress different aspects of these structures.

As it affects individual consciousnesses the transfer of symbols in society presents two aspects. Firstly, as already indicated, there are the constructions instigated by the reception of socially efficacious symbols. Secondly, there are those constructions which result in socially efficacious utterances and externalisations. It is essential for a full comprehension of the concepts put forward in this chapter to emphasise that the dialectic process of consciousness indicated here cannot function without an element of creativity. By creativity is meant, in any specific situation, the formulation of a structure in consciousness which is both facilitated and, to a greater or lesser extent, pre-conditioned by the structures of previous symbolic transfer, but whose *precise* configuration could not have been predicted at the deterministic level of materiality appropriate to symbols themselves[2]. Such creativity may be efficacious at any level of generality, whether that of a comparatively inconsequential situation in everyday life, or that of the largely unconscious articulation of a group or society's assumptional framework[3]. It is the process of creativity at this greater level that is of most relevance for this chapter.

The possibility for creativity as described here is indicated by Lévi-Strauss (1968, p.79):

> ... between culture and language there cannot be *no* relations at all, and there cannot be 100 per cent correlation either. Both situations are impossible to conceive. If there were no relations at all that would lead us to assume that the human mind is a kind of jumble — that there is no connection at all between what the mind is doing on one level, and what the mind is doing on another level. But, on the other hand, if the correlation were 100 per cent, then certainly we should know about it, and we should not be here to discuss whether it exists or not.

The latter part of Lévi Strauss's argument may be extended, for if the correlation between culture and symbol were 100 per cent, then society would be reduced to the determinism and prediction of the industrial world sense. The extreme rigidity of such a society would make dialecticism a logical impossibility, and it is very difficult to see how society could either come into existence or survive under such circumstances. The creative element of individual minds is thus as necessary a pre-condition of structural changes in society as the flexibility of human behaviour in the face of environmental changes (social or physical) is for the survival of human individuals as biological organisms.

$$* \quad * \quad * \quad * \quad *$$

The position adopted, then, is that all symbolic modes are permeated by all-pervasive social symbolic constructs which are dialectically and therefore creatively articulated by and through specific consciousnesses and symbols. As a consequence of this position, it is impossible to conceive of society or culture as somehow basic or fundamental to the symbols of that society. For the inclination to regard the kinship/political/economic sphere of society as the sphere in which rests all primary causation for symbolic activity implicitly denies the efficacy of all symbols as potential instigators and pre-conditioners for subsequent utterances and externalisations. Futher, the concept under discussion reifies society, for what is society if not the *totality* of mutually efficacious and dialectically related *individual* consciousnesses *and* symbols? In this context it is again useful to emphasise that society can only arise and continue to exist by and through the symbols externalised by members of that society. Finally, it is not difficult to realise that both the primary causation and reification are themselves symptomatic of the reductionist, deterministic and materialist industrial world sense which it was necessary to elucidate in order to arrive at the position here adopted.

The fallacies of this concept of primary causation may be parenthetically illustrated by reference to the attitude of politicians towards music during the development of early Soviet Russia. For some years after the October Revolution, politicians were generally of the view that art would be influenced by political-economic events and that, consequently, there was not or should not be any need for political interference. Trotsky, for example, did not believe it was possible for a truly Soviet culture to emerge until the period of the dictatorship of the proletariat had ended, and Soviet society had become truly classless:

The cultural reconstruction which will begin when the need of the iron clutch of a dictatorship . . . will have disappeared will *not* have a class character. This seems to lead to the conclusion that there is no proletarian culture and that there will never be any, and in fact there is no reason to regret this. (Quoted in Krebs, 1970, p.34).

If the true Soviet culture is to emerge naturally from the synthesis of all classes, then state interference would merely be detrimental to this development: 'Art must make its own way, and by its own means. The Marxian methods are not the same as the artistic. The Party leads the proletariat but not the historical processes of history.' (Quoted in Krebs, 1970, p.35). Lunacharsky, who was the first Commissar of Education and Enlightenment, formulated an analysis of the relationship between the socio-economic situation of a class and the underlying nature of its artistic production which supported a liberal view of the arts. We are told that '. . . the logic of his aesthetic categories showed the logic, if not the letter of Marxism, and since Marxist logic was inevitable, then a liberal view encouraging a dialectic development should be adopted.' (Krebs, 1970, p.38). As Commissar, Lunarcharsky did everything possible to encourage any serious artistic enterprise. It may be concluded then that at least until 1927:

The Marxist-Leninist view on culture and art . . . was that they formed a part of the superstructure of whatever historical mode prevailed. The implication . . . was that the superstructure changed automatically with the change of the material basis of society. Although this concept was later shattered by Stalin it meant now that the State's sole leverage on the arts was through manipulation of the social mode. (Krebs, 1970, p.46).

It is essential for an understanding of subsequent events in Russian musical life to realise that this apparently liberal attitude towards the arts was accompanied by a strain of conservatism. In other words, although artists were given a free hand, artistic production was expected to develop within certain guidelines. Although Lenin, for example, acknowledged that 'every artist takes it as his right to create freely, according to his ideal, whether it is good or not', he clearly felt that there were limits which should not be transgressed: 'But of course we are Communists. We must not drop our hands into our laps and allow the chaos to ferment as it chooses. We must try consciously to guide this development and mould and determine the results'. (Klara Zetkin, quoted in Schwarz,

57

1972, p.19). In the same vein Trotsky felt it necessary 'to destroy any tendency in art . . . which threatens the revolution . . . or [which] arouses the internal force of revolution . . . proletariat, peasantry and intelligentsia to a hostile opposition to one another'. (Krebs, 1970, p.35). We are also told that 'Lunarcharsky fought one manifestation throughout his years: the perversion and destruction of the classical tradition'. (Krebs, 1970, p.38).

By the late 1920s and early 1930s it became clear to those in power that music was not progressing within the basically tonal and classical guide-lines required. The liberal line of thinking was thus abandoned and the more conservative strain was drawn on to ensure that the 'culturally safe' classical tradition was not threatened. In 1927, when Stalin had succeeded Lenin, the progressive Association of Contemporary Musicians was absorbed by the more reactionary Russian Association of Proletarian Musicians. In 1936 this organisation was replaced by the Union of Soviet Composers, an official organ of the Ministry of Culture. And in 1936, following the first All-Union Congress of Soviet Writers of 1934, came the criticism of Shostakovitch's *Lady Macbeth of Mtsenk*. Finally, in 1946 came the crushing general criticism of the country's leading composers[4].

The point for the present line of argument is the discovery on the part of the Russian authorities that the dialectic processes of society do not involve a slavish imitation of the material basis of society by a symbolic superstructure, but rather the potentially creative formulation of symbols through which, in any social realm, heretical structures may be articulated. Although the political-economic realm had come under determinant control in Soviet Russia it was hardly surprising that the creative element inevitable in the dialectic processes of society should still find an outlet in the unrestricted arts.

The initially paradoxical attitude of the Russian authorities towards music is symptomatic of an interesting contradiction within Marxist thought, that is, the contradiction between a dialectic, and a 'scientific' or deterministic and materialist approach to the social process. This contradiction situates the Russian-Marxist movement firmly in its nineteenth century context. It was the essential condition of Romanticism that it attempted to transcend the capitalistic and industrial world sense in terms of the categories produced by that very same world sense. Similarly, the October Revolution sought to replace the old capitalistic order with a new egalitarian one, but the attempt was compromised throughout by recourse to methods of rational determinant control. It therefore became a Revolution which, as it were, involved relata rather than relationships and structure, one system of centralised control, that of the Tsars, being replaced by another.

It is in terms of this attempt by the Russian system to halt any creative dialectic in the social process and replace it with rational control that Lenin's attitude to the arts, his combining of 'revolution in the social sphere with reaction in the spiritual' (Berdraev, quoted in Krebs, 1970, p.31) becomes clear. For, as is argued below, traditionally tonal classical music both encodes and articulates the structure of a centralised political-economic system, and so was entirely appropriate to the 'new' order of things in Russia. Given this affinity, it was hardly likely that music articulating other competing structures would be tolerated. This goes a large part of the way to explaining why the morbid frustration of Tchaikovsky and the neurotic eroticism of Scriabin were tolerated, while the clearer, more vigorous language of Prokofiev has often been castigated.

It may be argued, therefore, that the concept of dialectic materialism as applied in Russia provides an implicit contradiction in terms, for to *strictly* interpret Marx's statement that 'it is not the consciousness of men that determines their existence but, on the contrary, their social existence determines their consciousness' is to emphasise one aspect of the social process at the expense of the other. Moreover, it is to imply a unidirectional and sequentially determinant process where, as this section has attempted to illustrate, none can be unquestionably established. Political-economic and kinship structures are most probably no less symbolic or epiphenomenal than those of language, music or art, and any implicit categorisation of the social process into physical and spiritual, or objective and subjective realms, in being predicated upon the restricted world sense of industrial man, is of little use for understanding the essentially symbolic and dialectic nature of society.

The position adopted above may now be expanded. Insomuch as evidence of the existence of society or culture is revealed to us *only* through the symbols we perceive[5], culture and society can only be regarded as being immanent 'in' the potentially creative articulations of specific symbols, no matter to which realm of social activity they pertain. Furthermore, since these articulations originate from and are only efficacious 'within' individual minds, society must also be regarded as being immanent 'in' individual consciousnesses. Society, in other words, as a process of order-in-change, is immanent 'in' and 'through' the dialectic interaction of people and symbols.

The 'Meaning' of Music

It is the theme of this chapter that the meanings of society are encoded and creatively articulated by music to an extent that denies the assumptional assignation of a higher rational priority to both verbally encoded meanings and to the political-economic infrastructure of society. Music has meaning only insomuch as the inner-outer, mental-physical dichotomy of verbally referential meaning is transcended by the immanence 'in' music of what we may conceive of as an *abstracted* social structure, and by the articulation of social meaning in individual pieces of music. In this respect music stands in the same relationship to society as does consciousness: society is creatively 'in' each piece of music and articulated by it.

As we have seen in Chapter One, any meaning that may be assigned to music does not and cannot result or depend on the existence of physically external referents. In this sense music is its own meaning. But this does not imply, as Susanne Langer would have it, that music is an 'unconsummated symbol', for the presence of permanent contents that Langer requires for the fulfillment of the actual function of meaning in a symbol must surely be rooted in the inner-outer, form and content dichotomy of the verbal-physical world. Consequently, restricting musical meaning to the 'inner life' as Langer does, and thereby denying an 'outer', transcendent or social meaning, again seems to be a product of traditional industrial epistemology as witnessed in the inner-outer opposition. Music is not an informationally closed mode of symbolism relevant only to 'emotive, vital, sentient experiences', or 'inherent psychological laws of "rightness",' but an open mode that, through its essentially structural nature is singularly suited to reveal the dynamic structuring of social life, a structuring of which the 'material' forms only one aspect. Music is consummatory because of the social meaning immanent in the individual consciousnesses and pieces of music of a society and, conversely, because social meaning can only arise and continue to exist through symbolic communication originating in consciousness — communication of which music forms a part.

It would be wrong, of course, to imply that Langer's and Meyer's psychological view of music goes *absolutely* no way towards transcending the form and content dichotomy. In maintaining that there is a *structural* conformity between music and mind they have arrived at a position not totally dissimilar to the one put forward here. The crucial difference, however, is that they have implicitly assumed mind to be a delimited entity in all its aspects. But as the following statement by Gregory Bateson indicates (1973, p.436), it is entirely possible to arrive at a concept of mind consistent with the views expressed in this chapter:

> The individual mind is immanent but not only in the body. It is immanent also in pathways and messages outside the body; and there is a larger Mind of which the individual mind is only a sub-system. The larger Mind is . . . immanent in the total inter-connected social system . . .

The superimposition of the structure that constitutes a particular piece of music onto a suitably predisposed mind is indeed essential to all musical communication. But equally essential is the social interaction responsible for the particular structural disposition of that mind.

Again, it would be unfair to Susanne Langer to imply that her notion of music as an 'unconsummated symbol' is totally without insight. As her support for Wagner's understanding of music suggests[7], Langer tends to categorise experiences-in-consciousness into the 'unspeakable' and the 'speakable'. The former, *implicit*, category consists of those experiences which can only be sensed in consciousness and not specifically referred to; the latter, *explicit*, category of those objects and concepts which may be definitively indicated. Music is to be equated with the implicit category, writing with the explicit[8]. Now while it remains true that music may emphasise the implicit and writing the explicit, it does not follow that music cannot encode the explicit, nor that writing cannot encode the implicit. As previously argued, different symbolic modes are capable of encoding similar structures, but may, because of their method of encoding, stress different aspects of these structures (in this regard, the explicit may *simplistically* be equated with relata, and the implicit with the relationships 'underlying' those relata). A discussion of explicitness and implicitness as possible paradigms for social and musical elucidation is inappropriate here[9]. However, the following further relationship between media and world senses may be indicated. On the one hand, there are those media which communicate implicitly and those which communicate explicitly; on the other there are those world senses (such as the 'pre-literate') which tend towards the implicit and those (such as that of industrial man) which tend towards the explicit[10]. Music is quite capable of implicitly coding an explicit world sense, a process evidenced throughout the entire tradition of tonality. Langer's concept of the implicit and the explicit[11] thus has substance. But her tendency *rigidly* to equate music with implicitness, and writing with explicitness, her consequent implied denial of the social process immanent 'in' music, and her subsequent failure to assign any *real* significance to music, once again points to the inadequacy of the view that music is an 'unconsummated symbol'.

Writing about Music — 1

The attempt to establish in academic language that reality as embodied in the non-verbal and 'non-rational' mode of music is equal and coextensive with that embodied in language is, of course, inherently contradictory. If life and experience as encoded by music has equal reality with that encoded by words, why bother to verbalise about music? Is one not in fact denying the very theme being discussed and illustrated? Ideally, one might leave music to speak for itself were it not for the very fact that music, for reasons indicated in Chapter One, is often regarded as an elusive, epiphenomenal and somehow unreal occurrence, which can only be brought into the fold of reality through verbalisation. The self-evidence of musical reality is therefore insufficient for establishing that very reality. The only recourse available is to attack the epiphenomenalist on his own verbal territory, firstly by showing how his own kind of verbal approach to music is grounded in the physical-mental, form-and-content epistemology of industrial society, and, secondly by attempting to demonstrate that music does code social-intellectual structures.

These two processes are inextricably linked since the approach to musical meaning adopted here — itself a piece of writing — implicitly asserts the inadequacy of the traditional approach to writing about music. Also this traditional approach in itself, and regardless of what it may concretely say about specific pieces of music, belies a certain epistemological approach that makes implicit assertions about the nature of music inconsistent with those arising from a 'structural' approach. What one says about music cannot be legitimately differentiated from the approach one takes in saying it, since both activities are but different aspects of the initial process of reflecting on music. As well as putting forward a different view of music and how it may function (that is, a view of music as we might *imagine* it to be, 'out there' and 'beyond us' as 'objective fact'), it is necessary to constantly take into consideration how and why one is *constructing* that particular view. A view of music in itself cannot be isolated from the formulation of the view as part of the social construction of knowledge and reality, because such isolationism subscribes to the fallacy of form and content, whilst at the same time ignoring the efficacy of form[12]. Any discussion of music therefore involves, of necessity, a consideration of the method of discussion.

The separation of the objective from the subjective that is typical of highly literate society has resulted in two basically different approaches to writing about music. The first is the descriptive or analytic, which seeks to explain precisely what happens in the music. Realising perhaps that written language, with its overtones of determinacy and objectivity cannot adequately or usefully relate the subjective experience that music is, analytic writers seek to explain, or at least bring into high relief, the music as objective fact. The second approach recognises the emotional, psychological and subjective in music and seeks to underline the experience for the listener by means of words. The words in such a situation are usually separated to a degree from their hard rational bias, and the result is predominantly what Mellers has termed a 'prose-fiction'. Both approaches have obvious drawbacks. The first fails to go beyond the physical patterns of sound as perceived and notated, and so implicitly supports the notion that all reality is ultimately reducible to and explicable in terms of materiality. For reasons already put forward, it is therefore absolutely meaningless in itself and adds little or nothing to the aesthetic experience. The second — if well done, which is seldom the case, because it would require the services of a very talented poet — may succeed in paralleling the aesthetic experience and so help to elucidate it a little, but at the expense of totally ignoring the musical fact. Moreover, written language, by its very form, does not have such pliable parameters as music. As a result, the 'prose-fiction' used to describe one piece of music can become dangerously similar to the prose-fiction used to describe another, often very different piece[13]

The inadequacy of both approaches can be traced to their predication on the physical/formal (analytic) — mental/content (prose-fiction) dichotomy[14], a dichotomy whose continued existence is concomitant with the maintenance of industrial man's world sense. There is consequently a reluctance among some musicologists to try to relate the two approaches meaningfully, for the successful achievement of any such relating would ultimately lead to the articulation of a competing world sense. Robert Lyle, for example (1948, p.158), cannot accept that the findings of analysis might be related to more philosophical considerations:

> The scope of music has been, and doubtless always will be much debated. The problem arises as soon as musical criticism ventures to discuss the philosophical implications of a musical style or idiom. It must be faced, for analysis itself can only clarify; it cannot explain, nor can it relate its particular and highly specialised findings to the wider context of man's preoccupation with truth and beauty.

For Lyle, the creative impulse or generative kernel of a piece of music must either reside within the piece of music or outside it. Meaning cannot transcend. If extra-musical ideas provide the impetus for a piece, then analysis can be of no avail in understanding it:

> Much music, especially 'romantic' music can be understood only in relation to extra-musical ideas. This will seem obvious enough when we remember that the neglect of a purely musical logic does not by any means prevent a work of music being consistent, convincing and appealing. Only in such a case the consistency must derive from an initially non-musical source. To this *division*, criticism must constantly adjust itself, for the formal completeness of say 'Sea-Drift' [Delius] can only be *subjectively* felt, it cannot be *objectively* demonstrated in purely musical terms. [Italics mine]. (Lyle, 1948, p.158).

A method of writing about music that combines both approaches does serve to eradicate some of the inadequacies mentioned, but it, unfortunately, still fails to realise that music forms an integral part of the social process. With this method, the 'objective' and 'subjective' in music are still often regarded at base as being two separate entities, rather than merely different aspects of the same phenomenon, and the effect achieved is often that of a mechanical mixture, rather than that of the elucidation of the organic social whole that a piece of music is. The a-social view of music discussed in Chapter One and the specific approaches to writing about music mentioned here are thus facets of the same social-intellectual structure as manifest in the realm of musical thought and articulation. In the modern Western world music still tends to be regarded as being beyond the pale of even the symbolic superstructure of crude Marxism, let alone being regarded as an active constituent of the social process. Western music critics tend to deny the possibility of the Soviet position with regard to musicology — that is, that musical form and 'language' have ideological significance. The denial results not because Soviet musicology fails to transcend the categories of form and content (such transcendence being the purpose of these three first chapters), but precisely because, in mechanically equating musical form with the content of social dogma, it starts out on the road to the achievement of that very transcendence.

The traditional approach to writing about music does little but support a musically encoded ideology (that is, the coding through tonal classical music of the industrial world sense) through its own ideological implications (that is, the oppositional epistemological categories and centralised authoritarian structures symptomatic of that world sense), a process that is both ultimately tautological and of questionable critical value. The writer is tied to one viewpoint, the implication being that this viewpoint is sufficiently universal and objective for musical judgement to be authoritatively disseminated.

Two examples of such writing may be noted, examples which, because both writers are concerned with the social implications of musical style, are more disturbing than they might otherwise be. The first example is taken from the writings of Theodor W. Adorno, a man, who despite his radical pose, betrays the authoritarianism implicit in many elitist European academic systems. Adorno's musical outlook is rooted very much in the highly conscious and rational aesthetic of Schoenberg and, as a result, he finds it very difficult to tolerate Stravinsky's music which, at least in its early phase, creates effects *comparable* to those of pre-literate musics:

> Authenticity is gained surreptitiously through the denial of the subjective pole. The collective standpoint is suddenly seized as though by attack; this results in the renunciation of comfortable conformity with individualistic society. But at the very point where this is achieved, a secondary and, to be sure,

highly uncomfortable conformity results: the conformity of a blind and integral society — a society, as it were, of eunuchs and headless men. The individual stimulus activated by such art, permits the survival only of self-negation and the destruction of individuation; this indeed was the secret goal of the humour of *Petrouchka* . . . but now this obscure drive becomes a shattering fanfare. (1973, p.159)[15].

The second example is taken from the writings of an eminent Soviet musicologist, Israel V. Nestyev. It should immediately be pointed out that his approach lacks any of Adorno's arrogance, and that his discussion of music generally seems interesting, informative and perceptive. Nevertheless, the party line is maintained and judgement delivered. Summing up Prokofiev's achievements as a composer, Nestyev says:

> In his affirmation of human virtue and his exposure of negative forces, Prokofiev was not always equipped with clear ideological aims. He never gave enduring expression to the heroism and pathos of the people's life in the period of the victory of socialism. He was more successful in depicting the past . . . than in portraying revolutionary struggle and socialist creation. (1961, p.458).

The principle reason for this attitude towards Prokofiev's music has already been indicated.

It would be self-contradictory to imply that the approach to writing about music adopted here does not also make implicit ideological assertions. It does, but there are two differences. Firstly, the position adopted acknowledges that the writer, as a social animal, is his own prisoner, a phenomenon implicitly denied by those who espouse the traditional approach. Second, the realisation of necessary social involvement in what is written, instead of putting blinkers on an observer and diminishing the usefulness and validity of his observations, adds considerably to his insight. The writer may cast off from his safe haven of authoritarian objectivity and realise that no one viewpoint, no one musical language is sacrosanct. Only by uncovering his own material and absolutist assumptional framework, therefore, can industrial man step beyond the aesthetic implications of his own music, and so simultaneously realise the equal worth of other musical languages and the social significance of all music.

NOTES

1.   The best example of such an extension is provided by mathematics.

2.   Although symbols comprised of sound implicitly question the concepts of materiality and determinism (cf. pp 12-18 above), sound itself obeys physical laws.

3.   cf. pp 10-11 above.

4.   An excellent account of this incident is given in Werth (1949).

5.   It may be thought that other people may be perceived independently of any symbols they emit. But since no person can be arbitrarily isolated from his social milieu (with which he is constantly interacting), it may be asserted that the mere existence of the 'other' is incipiently symbolic. People and the symbols they emit cannot, in other words, be legitimately separated in this arbitrary fashion.

6.   cf. Langer (1960, p 240).

7.   cf. Chapter One, *n.* 14.

8.   Once again, this division is a clear expression of the epistemological dichotomy of industrial man.

9.   This discussion has been undertaken elsewhere by the author. cf. Shepherd (1975b).

10.   The pre-literate world sense may be said to be implicit because it is a sense which is very much 'lived within'. The industrial world sense, on the other hand, is one in which all experience tends to be set out or understood in a totally 'objective' and 'rational' fashion.

11.   cf. Langer (1960, p 245).

12.   cf. pp 32-34 above and pp 41-42. It is precisely because the materiality of symbolic communication is ignored that ideas may be isolated from the context of their creation.

13.   Not all books on music display such a marked dichotomy as has been described here. Moreover, there are some books which tend very strongly in the direction of transcending the strict form and content categories. In spite of this, however, it does seem fair comment that a great number of books and articles implicitly take this dichotomy, in one form or another, as the assumed methodological starting point for their enquiry and presentation. The number of books written along the lines of 'the man and his music' provides some testimony for this assertion, as do the number of books which seek to pass judgement on a work or body of music without making explicit reference (through musical examples or other devices) to the actual music itself. Again, more evidence is provided by the great number of purely analytic articles published each year. This is not to imply, however, that such material is of little value. The reverse is often patently the case. The argument is that by re-arranging the methodological basis for

musicological enquiry it will be possible to gain greater insight into the music under examination, whilst retaining a more truly phenomenological sense of the music as *music*.

14.   This formulation of the dichotomy as applied to the traditional approach to music may appear confusing as, in the Newtonian cosmology the physical or material is regarded as the content of a homogeneous, three-dimensional, spatial form. It should be remembered, however, that the Newtonian/Laplacian view of the universe only constitutes one example of the articulation of the industrial world sense (cf. pp 30-31 above). The fundamental epistemological dichotomy engendered by phonetic literacy finds expression in many ways which, on the surface, may appear contradictory or paradoxical. (cf. p 32 above).

15.   A fuller discussion of Adorno's attitude to twentieth-century music is to be found in Shepherd (1975a).

Chapter Three

The Musical Coding of Ideologies
JOHN SHEPHERD

Introduction

The purpose of this chapter is to indicate the way in which analysis can, *within certain limitations,* elucidate the social meaning inherent in music. The limitations, of course, result from the fact that analysis is an overwhelmingly explicit procedure, that music is an implicit form of communication, and that some world senses tend towards the implicit. But as it is impossible for any musical language to be *completely* explained through analysis (since all musical communication must to some degree or other be implicit), so it seems extremely unlikely that any world sense exists which is so completely implicit in its nature that some, at least superficial, analysis of its music would be totally impossible. Nevertheless, it is extremely important that the limitations are observed, for stepping over them necessarily involves the imposition on certain musical languages of categories of analysis totally inappropriate to the ones encoded in those languages. That is, explicit categories of analysis would be imposed on implicit musical languages and, as the following discussion of plainchant and tonality so vividly illustrates, any development from an even partially implicit to an explicit language necessarily involves fundamental changes in the syntax of that language. Mary Douglas has indicated the dangers of explicit analysis for ethnology in general:

> The anthropologist who draws out the whole scheme of the cosmos ... does the primitive culture great violence if he seems to present the cosmology as a systematic philosophy subscribed

to consciously by individuals. We can study our own cosmology — in a specialised department of astronomy. But primitive cosmologies cannot rightly be pinned out for display like exotic lepidoptera, without distortion to the nature of a primitive culture. (1970, pp.110-111).

It is precisely for this reason that the structural method adopted in the previous chapter to illustrate the way in which music can be thought of as having an inherently social meaning remains no more than an illustration. For although it transcends the form-content, mental-physical dichotomy of Western man, and thereby allows for a consideration of the implicit[1], structural analysis remains a largely visual and explicit procedure. Its use in relation to any highly implicit languages — and most pre-literate music must be counted as such — would thus be highly distortive. Further, any attempt to use it as a universally applicable method of 'musical' or 'social' elucidation would again invoke the notion of an objective aesthetic.

The approach[2] indicated in this chapter can be applied at any level of generality, whether that of one work within a composer's total output, the style of a composer as it articulates meaning within his social milieu, or a musical language as it embodies the social-intellectual structure of an entire society. It is best, however, to demonstrate the method at the greatest level of generality, because, until the articulation of a social-intellectual structure through the musical realm of knowledge has been consciously realised, any examination of a composer's piece or style is likely to be compromised through ignorance of its articulation at that greater level[3]. The descriptions and discussions which follow therefore explore the musical articulation of social-intellectual structures and frameworks in different societies, and so give an idea of the culture-specific nature of such articulations. The intention is not to give a definitive or conclusive exposé of the musical articulation of meaning in any society or group of societies, nor is it to present an historical survey, although there is some discussion of the factors affecting the development of tonality from plainchant. Rather it is, using a restricted amount of material, to argue the validity and legitimacy of a particular sense (view) of music, and of a way of elucidating the social meaning inherent in music in a practical and specific fashion.

One final comment is necessary by way of introduction. It was argued in both the preceding chapters[4] that there cannot be a determinant relationship between symbol and social meaning. That is why all symbolic exchange is potentially creative. It follows from this relationship that factors other than social meaning may influence the precise configuration a symbol assumes. Two of the most important factors are biological characteristics of the human organism and the inherent qualities of the material through which a symbol manifests itself[5]. Since biological characteristics are species-specific they can be assumed to be constant or neutral as far as the overwhelmingly social meaning of any particular music is concerned[6]. But since the harmonic series has clearly been highly influential in the formation of both plainchant and tonality, technical explanations for these languages will be taken as far as reasonably possible in the ensuing discussion. The impossibility of purely technical explanations will, however, point up the ultimate necessity of a social understanding.

Pre-literate Musics: Some General Observations

Any attempt to generalise about pre-literate musics is fraught with difficulties. Not only are there a great variety of pre-literate cultures whose individual musics can display a vast number of 'contradictory' characteristics, but the implicit nature of these cultures would seem to militate against a high degree of explicit analysis[7]. Initially, therefore, some tentative suggestions will be made about the relationship of music and society in pre-literate cultures. Only then will two *possible* ideas be mooted about the way in which the internal 'structure' of pre-literate musics might be said to encode and articulate what has previously been described as a pre-literate world sense.

In view of pre-literate man's relationship to the universe, it seems more than likely he experienced music as an all-enveloping happening. It was the medium of sound, it may be remembered, which was largely responsible for the creation of a world sense through which pre-literate man encountered the universe as revelationary and relatively unpredictable. Unlike literate and typographical man, who fearlessly regards the universe as something to be controlled and manipulated, pre-literate man holds tight to a relatively unyielding legitimating structure, and tends to view anything which does not fall inside the confines or patterning of that structure as reprehensible and potentially dangerous. Non-knowledge in pre-literate societies, that which is disorder to the carefully maintained order, has two opposing but inter-related aspects:

> Granted that disorder spoils pattern, it also provides the materials of pattern. Order implies restriction; from all possible materials a limited selection has been made and from all possible relations a limited set has been used. So disorder by implication is unlimited, no pattern has been realised in it, but its potential for patterning is indefinite. This is why, though we seek to create order, we do not simply condemn disorder. We recognise that it is destructive to existing patterns; also that it has potentiality. It symbolises both danger and power. (Douglas, 1970, p.114).

There is a striking parallel between this ambivalent attitude towards disorder and the attitude that exists in some pre-literate societies towards musicians. In more than one society[8] musicians hold a lower status:

> [but] in such cases there is a definite question as to whether the attitude towards musicians is not ambivalent and whether musicians may not in fact occupy a special situation in which behaviour not tolerated in others is considered acceptable, or is at least tolerated for them. (Merriam, 1964, p.134).

Thus, although the behaviour of musicians is often regarded as reprehensible, and although they are frequently the recipients of derisory jokes, there can be little doubt that musicians are nevertheless essential to the social process. In Basongye society, for example:

> the reaction to the facetious suggestion that these ne'er-do-wells should be banished was one of extreme seriousness and even real horror. Life in a village without musicians is not to be considered, and people spoke of leaving the village were no musicians present. This reaction cannot be taken lightly, for the bonds of kinship and economics which tie an individual to his village are extremely difficult to break. (Merriam, 1964, p.136).

In some societies musicians might well provide a form of mediation between order and disorder, between that which is safe and normal, and that which is dangerous and powerful[9].

This mediation would seem to be reflected in one of the compositional processes to be found in pre-literate societies. By this process, an individual receives a song from the supernatural[10]. In Flathead Indian society, for example:

> While it is recognised that some songs are individually

composed by human beings, and that some other songs are borrowed from neighbouring peoples, all true and proper songs, particularly in the past, owe their origin to a variety of contacts experienced by humans with beings, which, though a part of this world, are superhuman and the source of both individual and tribal powers and skills. (Merriam, 1967, p.3).

Moreover, 'the Flathead believe that in former times all songs derived from such experiences and that none were made up by individuals or borrowed from other tribes' (Merriam, 1967, p.3). One example of an experience can be given:

There was a man who was out hunting. He was sneaking up on the game by sitting at a spot on the game trail when he heard somebody singing. He thought 'There must be people around'. So he stood there and waited to see who was coming. Pretty soon a spike bull elk came out from the bush and told him, 'This is your song. If you really need this song, sing it'. It was a love song. So he didn't kill the spike, and never killed an elk again. (Merriam, 1967, p.7).

Mediation with powerful and dangerous disorder is further suggested by two aspects of this compositional process. Firstly, whether the occurrence is accidental, as above, or purposefully sought, as in the case of plains or plateau vision quests, the recipient leaves his village. This might be interpreted as a symbolic departure from 'conceptual surroundings' that are normal and safe. Secondly, the power of the supernatural is invested in the recipient:

Songs which derive from the supernatural lead to two types of power for the individual who receives them. In one case this is shamanistic power, while in the other, power is scattered and of such a nature that the individual remains simply a person with special capabilities for doing or effecting special things. Thus while a person may have special powers in love, gambling, hunting, war, or other social situations, the shaman has a concentration of songs which centre primarily about curing, although he may have obtained other skills through song as well. (Merriam, 1967, pp.3-4).

Whether or not these aspects carry the significance ascribed them may be debatable, but there seems little doubt that the revelationary and unpredictable nature of this compositional process directly reflects pre-literate man's revelationary and unpredictable world.

In those societies where musicians do not hold an ambivalent position and where composition is not revelationary, it is still the case that music is assigned much greater social relevance and power than it is in the Western world. In other words, pre-literate man possesses neither the objectivity nor the high division of labour[11] necessary to divorce music from the immediacy of its social context. Merriam (1964, p.262) makes this contrast:

> ... we can and do isolate music as a thing in itself and look at and analyse it as an object quite apart from its context. For example, we can turn on the radio, hear a piece of music being performed, and listen to it without having to know who the composer is, what period he represents, or what the function, if any, of the music is. We can take music out of any other context and treat it objectively or subjectively as something which exists for itself. We do this not only in the listening process, but in our analysis of music; the student of music form looks at it as an objective entity which can be divorced both from himself and from its context.

By comparison, 'neither the Basongye nor the Flatheads do this. For the Basongye, to the contrary, every song depends heavily upon its cultural context and is conceptualised in this relationship'. (Merriam, 1964, p.262). Again, Venda music is clearly of great social relevance:

> Venda music is overtly political in that it is performed in a variety of political contexts and often for specific purposes. It is also political in the sense that it may involve people in a powerful shared experience and thereby make them more aware of themselves and of their responsibilities toward each other. (Blacking, 1973, p.28).

One aspect of the social relevance of pre-literate music may be described in more detail. Much important knowledge in pre-literate cultures is commonly stored in tales or songs[12] whose repetition is based on commonplaces, that is, set verbal formulae and themes[13]. These formulae and themes often feature complex but strongly similar rhythmic patterns which are part and parcel of the method by which a reciter remembers the essential unvarying segments of the tale. It seems likely that song as we understand it came about as the result of the vocal inflexions peculiar to each commonplace. The singing of an epic tale, or songs which are part of a tale, could thus be regarded as a stylisation of the everyday speech[14] upon which the creation and maintenance of vital information rests. Since the retention and repetition of the knowledge is essential for the survival of the society in question, the tale takes on a highly affirmative moral value[15], and the melodic shapes it generates become *generally* symbolic of the emotional security felt at reinforcement of the legitimating structure.

Walter J. Ong underlines the inseparable intertwining of epic tales and music with the everyday life and concerns of pre-literate men. Talking about the lack of a fundamental differentiation between the objective and subjective in pre-literate cultures, he goes on to say that:

> by the same token, in one way or another, everything was caught up in the polemic of the human life struggle. The action of the heroic figures generated in an oral economy of narration would naturally at root consist of a battle between forces of good and evil. When so much of the lore of a culture was retained through narrative tales or songs about great heroes, even what would be otherwise completely neutral material thus acquired a moral flavour by association with the polemic or *agonia* of the hero and his adversaries. The entire world thus tended to be polarised in terms of 'good guys' and 'bad guys' . . . (1969, p.641).

Besides straightforward reinforcement of the *status quo,* music in pre-literate societies can also provide a means whereby a person *collectively* and *externally* copes with his problems. Titiev (1949, p.2) describes this process with respect to the Mapuche of Chile. Unaccompanied songs are improvised at social gatherings by men or women:

> who take advantage of the occasions to 'blow off steam', or to call general attention to some matter of personal concern to the singer. Songs of this kind are called 'assembly songs', and their moods may vary from naive and joyful to slanderous, bitter or ironic. (Quoted, Merriam, 1964, p.203)[16].

Through this process the integrity of society is maintained. It is interesting to speculate that this is another fashion in which music mediates between the order of the *status quo* and potential disorder. This disorder may derive from the desire of the singer to alter the *status quo,* or from his wish to point out some misdemeanour or abuse of power on the part of someone else.

Since pre-literate man possesses neither the objectivity nor the high division of labour necessary to divorce music from the immediacy of its social context, it would seem highly unlikely that he would be able to distance himself to any appreciable extent from the musical experience. Two inter-related aspects of pre-literate man's attitude towards music would seem to substantiate this claim.

75

JOHN SHEPHERD

Firstly, it appears probable that music is 'composed' or 'manipulated' in a far less determinant and 'conscious' manner than is the case in industrial society. The revelationary process of composition already described partially backs up this assertion, but it would also seem to be true in situations where songs are made-up. It is Merriam who once again draws the distinction between Western and pre-literate culture:

> The second factor which, in conjunction with the others, contributes to the total Western concept of the aesthetic is the *manipulation of form for its own sake*. This is a strong part of Western music culture where change is a value, and it seems logical that where music is treated as an abstract thing in itself the manipulation of form for its own sake might be regarded as a criterion of the presence or absence of abstractability (1964, p.263).

However, in Basongye and Flathead cultures, 'there is no apparent verbalised concept of such things as intervals, polyphony, melodic lines, melodic range, tonics, and so forth . . .' (Merriam, 1964, p.263). Consequently:

> If there is relatively little recognition of formal elements of music, it seems doubtful that music form can be consciously manipulated, for manipulation implies a juggling of the elements of music structure in order to arrive at a fresh form[17]. (Merriam, 1964, pp.263-264).

Secondly, because music cannot be 'viewed' or manipulated as an abstract entity, there is little question, as Merriam has already implied, of Western-like aesthetic considerations being applied to it:

> The concept of music as 'beautiful' seems to be generally undeveloped in primitive cultures. Informants speak of songs as being 'good'. No doubt the prevailing functionality of music is responsible for this designation, for beauty is an end in itself, while 'good' implies usefulness for a specific purpose: a song may be good for curing, good for dancing etc. In some tribes informants also describe songs as 'powerful', probably because the songs have some sort of supernatural function (Nettl, 1956, p.20).

The fact that pre-literate man feels it necessary to mediate his relationship with a revelationary and unpredictable universe through music, that he does not possess the objectivity or high division of labour necessary to divorce music from its social context, and that he is not sufficiently distanced from his music to develop

76

'conscious' modes of composition or a Western-like aesthetic — all these characteristics of his attitude to music speak of a world sense which is essentially lived 'within'. So too do some claims made about the 'internal structure' of pre-literate musics.

A high proportion of pre-literate music is monophonic. That which is not would seem to demonstrate from its nature that pre-literate man has not really escaped the confines of the monophonic line. He is unable, in other words, to place himself to any extent outside his music. Firstly, 'the tone systems of polyphonic material in a given style do not often coincide with the tone systems of the individual parts; this discrepancy is strong evidence against the beginnings of polyphony from a feeling of latent harmony'. (Nettl, 1956, p.79). Because harmony *as we typically understand it* depends largely upon the distancing from phenomena possible in phonetically literate society[18], it would have been extremely difficult for the specific pitch relationships and more general intervallic structures of pre-literate melodic lines to be externalised in the relationships obtaining between those lines, or, conversely, for the relationships obtaining between those lines to be internalised in the individual lines themselves. It is hardly surprising, therefore, that Nettl claims that 'there are no known rules of consonance or dissonance operating in primitive music comparable to the strict European ones'. (1956, p.87). As a concept involving the explicit statement of tonal relationships, *tonal* harmony would most likely have been alien to pre-literate cultures, because it involves a relationship to the sound experience, and so to phenomena in general, that pre-literate man simply did not possess.

The arguments presented in the previous paragraph are certainly consistent with the theory put forward in Chapter One[19]. However, it seems that there are some pre-literate cultures where the inherent qualities of melodic lines are *externalised* in harmony. Blacking, for example, tells us that in some Venda melodies:

> The companion tones in a pentatonic scale differ because of the spacing of the intervals, but the basically social principle that a tone must have a companion tone still applies, and it may be expressed explicitly in the 'harmonies' improvised by other singers. (1973, p.85).

If evidence such as this does weaken the arguments just put forward — and further, more detailed analysis would be necessary to establish that it did — then the difficulty could probably be traced to an invalid equation of melody with implicitness, and harmony with explicitness. This is by no means the case. Many harmonic devices used by Debussy and Delius are undoubtedly implicit in their operations, and it appears more than likely that melodies such as *Summer Is Icumen In* are explicit. Although evidence such as that presented by Blacking would therefore require refinement of the arguments put forward in the previous paragraph, such refinement is not necessary in the context of the remainder of this chapter[20].

It is also possible that pre-literate man's world sense is revealed by the 'temporal' as well as the 'spatial' aspects of his music. Since pre-literate man lived within time, the difference between the subjective and mechanical temporal span which is symptomatic of industrial man's world sense — together with the tendency to repress the subjective and emphasise the mechanical — was a difference that did not impinge on pre-literate man's consciousness. *In the spatialised terms of industrial man,* pre-literate man could not have been conscious of time. The rhythms of pre-literate musics, which are either corporeal or spiritual[21], articulate this time-sense:

> As the term suggests, corporeal rhythm comes from bodily movements, from physical gestures in time, associated with work or play. It thus tends to be accentual; the regularity of the stresses measures off Time without necessarily having any relationship to melody .... The effect of this Time-measuring thus tends to be incantatory and hypnotic. In becoming habituated to Time's beat we cease to be conscious of it, and this unconsciousness of our earth and time-bound condition is precisely the magic effect that primitive man sought through his music.... The other kind of rhythm, which we have called spiritual, arrives at a similar effect by the opposite means. Whereas corporeal rhythm is accentual, spiritual rhythm is numerical, having the minimal relationship to bodily movement. It thus tends to be subtle and complex in its organisation; to suggest, indeed, a self-generative spontaneity that counteracts any sense of periodicity or beat . . . . In effect it is liberative and therefore ecstasy-inducing[22]. (Mellers, 1968, p.3).

Both the externally emotive nature of the incantory and hypnotic corporeal rhythm, and of the liberative, ecstasy-inducing spiritual rhythm is indicative of pre-literate man's propensity to mediate his life and consciousness externally and collectively[23].

The Case for the Underlying Pentatonic Structure of Plainchant

Although the advent of literacy substantially altered man's orienta-

78

tion towards himself and the world, the strong residue of orality effectively prevented the development of any 'consciously' or rationally organised harmony or metre until the late Middle Ages. The phonetic literacy of Ancient Greece, for example, provided the conceptual framework within which Pythagoras could evolve the mathematical basis of Western melody and harmony, and within which it was thus possible to step outside the all-encompassing confines of the melodic line (or, in some cases, of implicit harmony). Yet the orality which largely underlay the society would not allow further musical exploitation of the discoveries made by Pythagoras; the 'passionate religious mystical matriarchy . . . remained at war with, and was too powerful to be absorbed by its new, empirical, rationalistic patriarchy' (Mellers, 1968, p.8). This dualism was most probably reflected in the music, as Peter Crossley-Holland points out. 'Practising Greek musicians', we are told, although 'by no means unaware of the role of the mind in defining their materials, naturally placed more emphasis on the evidence of their ears than on the mathematics of the specialist theorists'. (1960, p.100).

Again, in early medieval society, although a certain degree of objectivity and 'reason' were used to maintain a theocratic world, the orality which was still strong and very much at the basis of the theocracy prevented any development of organised harmony. Man still thought of himself as being at the centre of the universe, and even the learned stock of knowledge was still reinforced orally. A student in a university, for example, 'proved his ability in logic, physics or natural philosophy, ethics, metaphysics, law or medicine, as well as in theology, by disputation and possibly a final oral examination in a disputation like form. There were no written papers, written exercises or written examinations at all. Writing was used a great deal, but in connection with oral expression' (Ong, 1967, p.59).

It would be impossible to begin a discussion of any Western musical language [24] without mentioning at least the bare essentials of the Pythagorian discoveries, since it is the *social organisation* of the natural phenomena brought to man's notice through these discoveries that results in those languages. The discoveries may be summarised as follows [25]: when a note is sounded, certain harmonics are given off above the fundamental, in vibration ratios of 2 to 1, 3 to 2, 4 to 3, 5 to 4 and so on. These ratios constitute the octave, the fifth, the fourth and the major third, and are just the beginning of a whole series of gradually diminishing intervals that constitute the harmonic series, (see Example 3.1).

Example 3.1 The Harmonic Series

(N.B. The notated pitches are only approximate.)

As social constructions utilising this series[26], the underlying structures of the Western musical languages possess the common element of being variously grounded upon the intervals of the octave, fifth and fourth. The keynote in tonality, for example, is dependent on the primacy of the octave, and is also harmonically defined by its relationship to the dominant (at the fifth) and subdominant (at the fourth) of that key. Again, the fundamental interval of the music of Ancient Greece — at least in its theoretical aspect — was the fourth of the tetrachord, two of these tetrachords being put together — 'either disjunctly with a note to join them, or conjunctly with a tone to complete their downward series' (Crossley-Holland, 1960 p. 102) — to form the octave scale or *harmonia*. But there also exists another structure, that of pentatonicism[27], which is based on the intervals of the fifth and the fourth, and which, it can be argued, is the structure underlying a great deal of medieval music.

* * * * *

It is a principal theme of the remainder of this chapter on the musical coding of ideologies that both the pentatonically generated modality of plainchant (and of some popular medieval songs) and the subsequently developed language of tonality are mutually exclusive systems derived from the harmonic series; further, that medieval society retained pentatonicism for reasons of ideological implications, and that post-Renaissance society developed tonality as an integral facet of its own new ideology.

The first step in this argument is to put forward the case for the underlying pentatonic structure of plainchant. Before doing this however, the indigenous nature of the octave, fifth and fourth, both to the music of the Western world in general, and to medieval music in particular, may be more fully illustrated by reference to early organum (that is, parallel singing at the interval of a fifth or the interval of a fourth), and to the reasons that can be put forward for its development. Indeed, starting with the simple element of a monodic line, and assuming that the properties of the harmonic series influenced the manner in which people of different voice ranges sang with each other, it is not difficult to speculate on how parallel singing at the octave, fifth and fourth originated. Not only are the octave, the fifth and the fourth the intervals (audible as harmonics) which occur first in the harmonic series[28], but the fifth and the fourth provide convenient 'half-way' points between the two notes of the octave (which again, we may assume is the most natural interval for parallel singing) for those whose voice-range does not easily fall within either of the two lines of the octave. Gustave Reese is substantially in agreement with this analysis:

> Another explanation [for the 'origins' of parallel organum] is offered by the natural ranges of the four main classes of human voices, which, roughly speaking, lie at pitch levels a fifth away from one another, in consecutive order from bass to soprano. The congregations that sang responses at services did not consist of trained singers, but sang with the ranges they found comfortable. Machabey, on the basis of this, writes: 'The division of men's voices into two parallel lines, and of the high-pitched (women's and boys') voices into two other lines paralleling the first, must have followed as a matter of course, without the executants noticing it'. In 1908 in France, he heard an untrained congregation singing in organum without, apparently, intending to. The men and women each broke into two groups singing a fourth or a fifth from one another, according to the texture of the melody. (1940, p.250).

It should be noted in this context that the interval which is midway between the two notes of the octave (that is, the interval comprised by the defining note of this octave and the sixth note of the semi-tone scale — see Appendix) is the augmented fourth of our tempered scale. This is the only interval that is not even approximated between two adjacent notes of the harmonic series. Moreover, if it is conceived in terms of two non-adjacent notes, the vibration ratio is never the same (5:7, 7:10, 12:17 etc). In comparison to the fifth and the fourth, therefore, which maintain exactly the same ratios throughout the harmonic series, the unstable augmented fourth seems less of a natural choice as an interval for parallel singing.

The interval of the fourth is, of course, one removed from that of the fifth in the harmonic series, and it could be argued, in the case of parallel organum, that the fourth arises as the inversion of the fifth. Dom Anslem Hughes gives this impression in discussing the organum of the *Musica Enchiriadis* (see Example 2):

> From the *Musica Enchiriadis* we learn about four types of organum: (1) in parallel fifths, with the plainchant melody on the top line; (2) in the same, with the higher voice, or *vox principalis* doubled at the octave below and the lower voice, or *vox organalis* doubled at the octave above, thus resulting in a four part effect . . .; (3) taking either the higher or the lower pair of these four voices and running on in parallel fourths . . .; (4) a variant of this last method. (1955, p.278).

Example 3.2: A Section of the *Musica Enchiriadis*

By inversion, therefore, the occurrence of the perfect fifth also underlines the existence of the perfect fourth, even if the fourth cannot be said to arise in the first place by reason of its position in the harmonic series. But even then, it does not seem legitimate to conceive of a perfect fourth on the fundamental, since no such fourth occurs either in the harmonic series or by inversion of the fifth. However, it could equally well be argued that, once the fourth was established as an equal partner of the fifth, it would not be a very great development for the fourth to become established in its own right as an interval directly relating to the fundamental. Moreover, notwithstanding this theoretical 'difficulty', there still remains much evidence that the fourth, for whatever reason, was as much a natural modification of the original melodic line as the fifth.

Given the indigenous nature of the fifth and fourth to Western music, it is not difficult to see how the pentatonic scale could have come into existence[29]. If one takes the fifth and fourth on the original fundamental, and treats them in turn as fundamentals with their own fifths and fourths, then one arrives at a structure of five

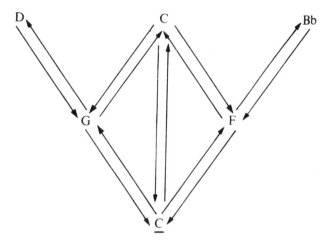

Figure 1

notes (see Fig. 1). It might seem to the reader that this is a somewhat cursory explanation for the origins of the pentatonic structure in early medieval society. Surely there are many more detailed causes and influences that may be brought to light and put before him? There are two related answers to this possible criticism. Firstly, there can be no ultimate and complete explanation for the occurrence of any social symbol. In the final analysis all that can be said is that *this* pentatonic structure, as specifically articulated in the plainchant repertory, was *creatively* evolved[30] in early medieval southern Europe as part of the ongoing construction of social reality. Given this construction of reality, however, *other* structures with similar features and articulating similar meaning might well have come into being. Secondly, even it it were possible to adduce detailed causes for the creation of this structure — a research project, which, given the almost total lack of written records, would be difficult in the extreme — then such causes would never furnish a complete explanation, and, moreover, would be *symptoms* of continuing structural change, rather than causes in the strict meaning of that word.

One of two further questions might also arise in the reader's mind regarding the structure in Fig. 1. The first is that, having accepted the indigenous nature of the octave, fifth and fourth to Western music, why is it that the progression of fifths and fourths shown in Fig. 1 stops at the second level? Why does it go as far as that and no further? The second question is this: once having generated a fifth and a fourth from the original fundamental (the underlined C of Fig. 1), why is it that another fourth and fifth are generated above the G and F rather than other subsequent intervals of the harmonic series? After all, this alternative suggestion does not negate the primacy of the fifth and the fourth, and would allow for the introduction of other intervals (audible as harmonics) into the underlying structure. There are not, and never can be, intra-musical answers to these questions, for the organisation of musical structures is ultimately a dialectic correlate of the social reality that is symbolically mediated by and through the music of a particular society. *The answers will only emerge, therefore, as an attempt is made to demonstrate the way in which pentatonicism and tonality have respectively mediated the medieval and industrial world senses.*

There are fundamentally three pieces of evidence [31] which support the hypothesis that Gregorian chant in particular, and medieval music in general, have an underlying pentatonic structure. Firstly, as Reese has noted, many chants [32] are purely pentatonic: 'Whether or not virtually the entire ancient repertoire was based on a pentatonic groundwork . . . , the fact remains that a considerable number of Gregorian melodies are clearly pentatonic'. (1940, pp.159-160). Furthermore, it is interesting to note that medieval German songs also display a pentatonic character [33], a feature which, according to Sir Jack Westrup, has 'obvious associations with Gregorian chant' (1955, p.259). But even where a Gregorian chant does not display pure pentatonic formulae throughout, there is often convincing evidence from opening phrases and subsequent motives that the pentatonic structure plays a generative role in that chant:

> Furthermore, many Gregorian compositions betray their pentatonic origin through characteristic opening phrases of a

84

purely pentatonic nature (usually sung by the cantor alone). These produce an impression of being 'principal themes' and are sometimes subsequently developed on a six or seven-tone basis. One finds a still greater abundance of the so-called 'trichordal' motives — the nuclei of pentatonic formations. These are composed of three notes within the interval of a perfect fourth and contain no semitones. Thus C-D-F, D-F-G, G-A-C, A-C-D, as well as their various permutations and transpositions, used either consecutively or intermittently are trichordal motives. (Yasser, 1937, p.181).

The most obvious objection which can be raised against the hypothesis of pentatonically structured medieval music is that very frequently more than the five notes of the pentatonic scale are in evidence. It seems more than likely, however, that the remaining two notes of the natural gamut which may appear in a chant do so in the role of passing notes:

> Still another important piece of evidence should be taken into account in determining the true scalar basis of medieval music. We refer to the *quilisma*, the symbol for which is today generally believed to have indicated the sounding, within a minor third, of a very light and transient ornamental note. (Yasser, 1937, p.182).

As Yasser indicates[34], a striking precedent for this procedure is to be found in the Chinese *pien*-tone. Moreover, there is a considerable amount of statistical evidence in support of the theory:

> Out of nearly 1600 Gregorian items which at present constitute the principal musical material of the Catholic liturgy, only a little more than 700 contain no quilismas at all. The number of those which do contain quilismas, impressive as it is (amounting to almost 900), must have been greater at the time when, as is supposed, the use of the quilisma was universal for all melodies that employed more than five notes within an octave.
> The total number of quilismas found in the 900 compositions referred to is 3100, of which 81.5 *per cent* are placed within minor thirds, 17 *per cent* within major thirds, and 1.5 *per cent* within perfect fourths. (Yasser, 1937, p.344).

It may also be pointed out that the passing note theory does much to explain B flat as the sole example of notated 'chromaticism' in early medieval music — that is, it can be heard as one of the two possible passing notes between A and C: 'The *pien*-tone theory, when its implications are fully worked out, shows that B flat is not merely a faintly undesirable substitute for B natural, as the theorists too often imply, but its peer; and the melodies themselves, with their frequent use of B flat, bear this out'. (Reese, 1940, pp.160-161). Finally, if the original objection is still maintained by asserting that the passing notes are bound to immediately destroy any feeling for pentatonicism, and are likely to create an incipient feeling for tonality, it may be pointed out that the existence of chromatic passing notes in tonal music does not immediately imply the destruction of tonality and the creation of atonality. It is not necessary, in order to demonstrate the existence of a particular musical structure, that only the notes of that structure be present in the music itself. What is necessary is to indicate that the structure, as articulated by and through the music, determines both the relative importance and function of the notes as used, as well as the more general characteristics of the archetypal melodic (and harmonic) formulae.

This second line of argument for the generative function of pentatonicism in plainchant has been greatly substantiated by Jacques Chailley in two recent articles. Chailley's position is that the traditional eight modes of plainchant are in fact extensions of pentatonicism:

> Qu'est-ce qu'un mode grégorien? Dans l'optique de l'étude ci-dessus, nous pouvons répondre, en simplifiant au maximum: c'est un modèle formulaire provenant de l'amplification ornamentale d'un schéma melodique reliant une tonique à une corde de récitation ou teneur (dite plus tard dominante), sur une échelle pentatonique fixe comblée ad libitum par des dégrès faibles plus ou moins mobiles[35]. (1970, p.85).

These modes, it may be argued, cannot be regarded as tonal formations in quite the same way as tonality can. For whereas tonality is a musical language universally evident in European cultured music between approximately 1600 and 1880, many individual chants are either modally ambiguous, or do not convincingly fit into any mode at all. Moreover, without denying that much plainchant does fit into modal analysis, and may therefore be said to articulate different concepts of time-space within that more generally articulated by the generative pentatonic structure, it seems very likely that the theoretic concept of the eight modes originally had as much to do with theological numeric symbolism as it did with rationalising strictly musical evidence[36]. The theory of tonality, on the other hand, was completely derived from the music of the tonal period and is consequently universally applicable to that music.

Chailley takes as his point of departure two 'facts' which, in his opinion, have been largely ignored by traditional theory: the pentatonic nature of very old melody[37] ('le caractère pentatonique de la melodie la plus ancienne'), and the historical importance of chanting the psalms, and so of the reciting note or tenor used in that chanting ('l'importance historique de la psalmodie et par conséquent de la corde de récitation ou teneur'). The importance of the tenor lay in the tendency of most chants to move around it before descending to the final ('Les usages universels de la cantillation nous enseignent que la tendance la plus courante de celle-ci conduit d'une part à des broderies autour de la teneur, d'autre part à une chute melodique finale au grave de celle-ci, . . .'). These legacies, argues Chailley, were highly influential in the development of both the Gregorian chant and the eight modes, these latter evolving from the interaction of four factors:

1. The range defined by the tenor and the final (the final gradually replaced the tenor in importance and traditionally became the somewhat unsatisfactory method of assigning a mode to a chant). This range could be a minor or major third, a perfect fourth, a perfect fifth (these perfect consonances being the most 'fertile' generators of modes) and, exceptionally, a minor sixth.

2. The shape of the melodic kernel whose range has been fixed by the tenor and final. If one takes a strict pentatonic scale (and Chailley is very precise in his definition: 'l'échelle de base étant celle du pentatonique anhémitonique divisant facultativement ses trihemitons incomposés par des *piens* faibles et souvent mobiles dont la hauteur . . . se seraient vu fixée par l'attraction'[38]), then, by starting in turn on each of the five notes it is possible to arrive at different internal shapes for the intervals of the fourth and fifth (this explains their 'fertility'). i.e: (In the following scheme 'T' indicates a whole tone and '3' a minor third.)

Perfect fourth:

C	D	F	G	A	C	=	T	3	T	T	3	}	Shape 'I'
G	A	C	D	F	G	=	T	3	T	3	T		
D	F	G	A	C	D	=	3	T	T	3	T	}	Shape 'II'
A	C	D	F	G	A	=	3	T	3	T	T		

The remaining 'scale' does not give an initial interval of a fourth.

Perfect fifth:

F G A C D F = T T 3 T 3   Shape 'I'
C D F G A C = T 3 T T 3 ⎫
G A C D F G = T 3 T 3 T ⎬ Shape 'II'
D F G A C D = 3 T T 3 T   Shape 'III'

The remaining 'scale' does not give an initial interval of a fifth.

3. The fixing by attraction of the weak notes to be found in the two intervals of a minor third created by a pentatonic scale.

4. The manner in which the range of the melodic kernel was extended to give the *ambitus* (range) of a chant. This determined whether a mode was authentic or plagal.

Unfortunately, there is insufficient space in this chapter to reproduce all of Chailley's very detailed arguments. Nevertheless, it may be pointed out that Chailley's analysis has the advantage over the traditional classification of being able to account for modally ambiguous chants and chants which do not fit properly into the modal scheme.

Finally, it would seem that the importance of the fourth and the fifth to both the pentatonic structure itself and that structure's generation of chants and modes finds expression in the method of analysis used by medieval theorists in regard to the modes. All eight modes (in the symmetrical systematisation of Hermannus Contractus) were viewed as being founded on these two intervals:

> The system of the octave-species . . . soon yielded ground in the analytical writings, being replaced in large part by consideration of what might be called the *modal nucleus* consisting of the notes immediately above the final, and of the various species of pentachords and tetrachords. The admissible pentachords were TSTT, STTT, TTTS and TTST; the admissible tetrachords were TST, STT and TTS; the diminished fifth and augmented fourth were inadmissible species. (Reese, 1940, p.156).

This classification is closely linked with the designation of the octave, fifth and fourth as the only admissible consonances in medieval music, at least until the thirteenth century:

> The classified species of the Middle Ages are bounded solely by medieval consonances — the fourth, fifth and octave. To obtain a full complement of early medieval consonances one need add to these only the unison and such octave-compounds as the twelfth. The compass of the authentic modes is often extended downwards by one degree . . . but these modes,

nevertheless, continued to be classified according to the species, not of their ninths, but, like the others, of their octaves .... The sixths also, dissonances in the early Middle Ages, are among the intervals that never bound classified species: the hexachord, though used for purposes of classification, was not applied to the distinguishing of species. It could not have been, in its Guidonian form, since its TTSTT structure never varied. (Reese, 1940, pp.156-157).

The exclusive use of the octave, fifth and fourth as consonances in early medieval music and as the distinguishing features of modal species provides striking parallels to the exclusive role of the fifth and fourth in generating a pentatonic structure. Moreover, given the exclusive use of these intervals as consonances and distinguishing features, it would be surprising to find that any other interval or intervals were fundamental to the structure of Gregorian chant. Indeed, if the melodic formulae of the chant do in fact articulate the fifth and the fourth as basic structural elements, then it is but a small step to the externalisation of these implicit elements as analytic tools.

The Articulation of an Ideal Feudal Structure through Pentatonicism

Unlike those of tonality, the fundamentals of pentatonicism are interlocking and mutually dependent; they do not point outside themselves. It is both impossible and invalid to hear only one note of the structure as the one to which all others irrevocably and necessarily tend. Assuming that passing notes are not important structural elements in pentatonicism, six relationships only are possible for a pentatonic melody. The notes referred to are those of Fig. 1. Example 3.1 may also be consulted:

1. Any note can be heard as its own fundamental.
2. All the notes (except B flat) can be heard as the third harmonic relating to a second (perfect fifth).
3. All the notes (except D) can be heard as the fourth harmonic relating to a third (perfect fourth).
4. D can be heard as the fifth harmonic relating to a fourth (major third).
5. F and B flat can be heard as a sixth harmonic relating to a fifth (minor third).

6. C, D and G can be heard as an eighth harmonic relating to a seventh (whole tone).

Which of these relationships will be heard for any particular note will depend entirely upon its position in any particular melody, with the preceding note (ignoring passing notes) most probably being the most important factor. One can, of course, make a similar assertion for tonality. Any note of the major or minor scale may perform a number of different functions, all of which depend upon specific context. But whereas the function of tonal notes depends upon a definite hierarchy in which certain relationships may be heard as more important or fundamental than others — thus giving rise to the oppositions of concord and discord, and the distancing of modulation — the relationships of pentatonicism have no hierarchy. Any one relationship is as important or fundamental as any other; it exists to a very large extent by and for itself, having no hierarchical function outside itself.

Yet, although no one note of a pentatonic melody can become a basic fundamental to which all others must at some time resolve, many pentatonic and modal melodies give the feeling that one note is more important than the others. This feeling is created simply by stressing one note (such as the tenor of a chant) more than the others, and this sense of importance, as Rudolph Reti has pointed out[39], is of a 'melodic' rather than a 'harmonic' nature[40]. Reti also demonstrates that a melody which possesses 'melodic' rather than 'harmonic' centrality can be brought to rest on the important note at any point in its duration. To attempt the same with a melody of harmonic tonality would be to 'destroy the innermost sense of the whole line'.[41] (Reti, 1958, p.16).

As was briefly noted in Chapter One feudal society was of a highly decentralised and localised type. The collapse of the Roman Empire, itself strongly centralised, created a situation favourable for the emergence of small social units whose population, at least in theory, were mutually dependent upon one another:

> To seek a protector, or to find satisfaction in being one — these things are common to all ages. But we seldom find them giving rise to new legal institutions save in civilisations where the rest of the social framework is giving way. Such was the case in Gaul after the collapse of the Roman Empire.
> Consider, for example, the society of the Merovingian period. Neither the State nor the family any longer provided adequate protection. The village community was barely strong enough

to maintain order within its own boundaries; the urban community scarcely existed. Everywhere the weak man felt the need to be sheltered by someone more powerful. The powerful man, in his turn, could not maintain his prestige or his fortune or even ensure his own safety except by securing for himself, by persuasion or coercion, the support of subordinates bound to his service. On the one hand, there was the urgent quest for a protector; on the other, there were usurpations of authority, often by violent means. And as notions of weakness and strength are always relative, in many cases the same man occupied a dual role — as a dependent of a more powerful man and a protector of humbler ones. Thus there began to be built up a vast system of personal relationships whose intersecting threads ran from one level of the social structure to another. (Bloch, 1961, pp.147-148).

The creation of a social system which 'involved a far-reaching restriction of social intercourse, a circulation of money too sluggish to admit of a salaried officialdom, and a mentality attached to things tangible and local', (Bloch, 1961, p.443), naturally favoured the oral and face-to-face mediation of social relationships. Both medieval society and medieval man became 'centres without margins'[42]:

Imagine two men face to face; one wishing to serve, the other willing or anxious to be served. The former puts his hands together and places them, thus joined, between the hands of the other man — a plain symbol of submission the significance of which was sometimes further emphasised by a kneeling posture. At the same time, the person proffering his hands utters a few words — a very short declaration — by which he acknowledges himself to be the 'man' of the person facing him. Then chief and subordinate kiss each other on the mouth, symbolising accord and friendship.Such were the gestures . . . which served to cement one of the strongest social bonds known in the feudal era. (Bloch, 1961, pp.145-146).

In this fashion one became the 'man of another man' rather than an anonymous cog of a strongly centralised bureaucracy.

In commenting upon the cross-fertilisation of medieval sacred and secular music, Professor Mellers has drawn a striking analogy between music and society:

Not only had the religious art-music of the Middle Ages and the popular folk music many qualities, technical and spiritual, in common; there was a continual interaction between them which is of crucial importance from both a sociological and a musical point of view. There have been many learned arguments as to which came first, which influenced which, that seem to me irrelevant. If the feudal order meant anything (and one knows it nearly always failed to live up to its pretensions) it was an order in which cleric and peasant mutually succoured each other, one providing for the needs of the body, the other for the needs of the soul. They were complementary parts of a social organism, allied in their very differences, and their respective musical manifestations likewise complement one another. (1946, p.26).

It is possible to go much further than this, however, for the pentatonic structure underlying much medieval music in itself serves to articulate the *ideal* feudal structure. The fundamentals of pentatonicism are complementary and mutually dependent on one another. They are also centres without margins in the sense that the relationships they form are made *directly* with other fundamentals, something that is simply not the case with tonality. Indeed, insomuch as one note of the pentatonic structure may be stressed more than the others, Bloch's statement that feudal society was 'unequal . . . rather than . . . hierarchical' (1961, p.443) is one that could equally well be applied to the structure of pentatonicism as found in medieval music.

The structural articulations of medieval music are not restricted to the 'spatial' sphere alone, however. Both the spiritual rhythm of plainchant[43] and the corporeal rhythm of folk-song[44] conveyed a revelationary sense of becoming rather than an incarnate sense of being[45]. Time was a product of becoming:

> To change was to pass from potentiality to actuality. But this transition had nothing about it necessarily temporal. By virtue of the Christian doctrine of omnipotence it could have a temporal quality only if there were some cause which did not allow the immediate transformation by divine action of the potentiality into the act. And this cause which required that time be involved in the change was a certain defect of matter. From this point of view, matter was nothing other than a resistance which, manifesting itself in the substance of a thing, hindered that thing from assuming instantly the fullness of being which its form would confer upon it, a resistance which introduced distance and tardiness, multiplicity and delay, where everything, it seemed, should have happened simultaneously and at once. (Poulet, 1956, pp.4-5).

The instaneity of oneness with God stands in stark opposition to the spatialised temporality of industrial man. Both negate the subjective flow: oneness with God implies a complete losing of the self, a solipsistic consciousness, whereas the conceptual control of spatialised time indicates a consciousness of consciousness, together with a sense of history, progress and all the other categories of understanding symptomatic of the industrial world sense[46]. In negating the instaneity of oneness with God, however, the temporal flow of consciousness reveals time without making it incarnate as objective fact. The conceptual control medieval man has over the universe, therefore, remains slippery: 'these men, subjected both externally and internally to so many ungovernable forces, lived in a world in which the passage of time escaped their grasp all the more because they were so ill-equipped to measure it.' (Bloch, 1961, p.73). But, as Bloch indicates, the lack of measurement (and measurement is so vital to the time of industrial man) 'was but one of the symptoms . . . of a vast indifference to time,' (1961, p.74) and so of the fact that medieval man still largely existed *within* time.

The revelationary nature of becoming is therefore closely related to medieval man's lack of self-contained margins. Medieval man feels much more intimately involved with and affected by events than does industrial man. Both the mutual dependency of the pentatonic fundamentals of medieval music and that music's spiritual and corporeal rhythms articulate this revelationary immediacy. It is hardly surprising, therefore, that from the standpoint of industrial society, the music of medieval man seems to negate the individuality which is a dialectic correlate of that society's world sense[47]. Mellers, for example, is of the opinion that the singer of plainchant 'is not interested in the "expression" of the individual' but in 'the medium through which the voice of God manifests itself'. (1946, pp.24-25). Again, in noting certain similarities between plainsong and some secular songs, the same author infers a link between musical structure and the structuring of medieval society and consciousness:

> The rhythms are extremely flexible, flowing naturally from the spoken inflection . . . there is a tendency towards fluid pentatonic vocal figurations analagous to the plainsong tropes; there is an habitual avoidance of leading notes and implied full closes, the same insistence on conjunct motion and the absolute and perfect consonances. The impression still tends, that is, to the merging of the personality in something outside itself; for all the local details of the songs, the effect is not that of the incarnation of a 'personality', but of a creative act which is independent of any particular person, made manifest through the human voice. (1946, p.25).

The Development of Tonality: A Structural Approach

Accepting the notions of implicitness and explicitness, and the assertion that all musics articulate social-intellectual structures, the difference between the *monody* of plainchant and the initial *harmony* which develops into tonality might not appear as great or as fundamental as one might think. For the parallel fifths and fourths of organum make explicit in this first form of Western harmony the fifths and fourths of the underlying and implicit pentatonic structure of much early medieval music. Such externalisation only represents a transient stage between the pure monody of pentatonicism and the fully-developed harmony of tonality, however, for pentatonicism, in thus becoming harmonically explicit, began to destroy its own implicit qualities. As we have seen, the only inequality existing between the fundamentals of pentatonicism resulted from the stressing of one note through repetition — a stressing which did *not* serve to break up the mutual dependency (and therefore the ambiguity of relationship) existing between the fundamentals. The creation of the *vox principalis* and the derived *vox organalis,* however, destroys this mutual dependency by creating a hierarchy. The *vox organalis* only exists insomuch as it is a function of and refers back to the previously self-sufficient *vox principalis.* Although the *vox organalis* taken on its own (as in the *Musica Enchiriadis* — see Example 3.2) could well be a self-sufficient line of plainsong, the way in which it is conceived and heard by medieval man negates such a possibility. It is now possible to extend Figure 1 to include these externalisations (see Fig. 2).

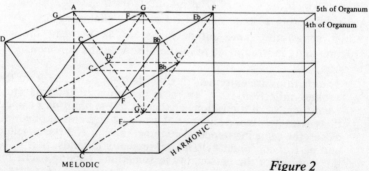

Figure 2

Furthermore, organum may give notes which were previously *quilismas* a different hierarchical function, thus weakening their

previous role as passing notes. In Example 3.3, for example, a note
which is a passing note within the mode is now heard as a function of
a fundamental. The process is more obvious in Example 3.4, where a
piece of disjunct motion utilises the note in a fashion that denies any
possibility of its being heard as a passing note. Notes which were
previously *quilismas* and, as such, were unessential, here become
essential parts of the structure of organum [48]. This is demonstrated
in Figure 3.

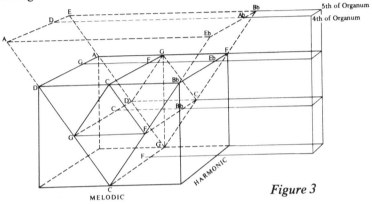

Figure 3

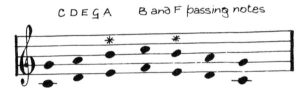

Example 3.3

Example 3.4

The role of organum in negating the very structure it is
externalising can be further explained by considering the increasing
importance of *musica ficta* to the emerging polyphony of the late

Middle Ages. It has already been noted that the augmented fourth or diminished fifth, as approximated from the harmonic series, is a very unstable interval that falls roughly halfway both in an octave and between the intervals of the fourth and the fifth. Medieval theorists have labelled it *diabolus in musica,* therefore, not only because of its instability, but because any musical reference to it would tend to deny the natural function of fourths and fifths in halving the octave, *and so ultimately deny the underlying structure of pentatonicism.* As a corollary of this denial, there would exist a negation of the feudal structure of medieval society. It is furthermore worth noting, however, that the augmented fourth is the only interval that does not naturally result from the pentatonic structure and its passing notes. Fifths, fourths, major and minor thirds and whole tones can all be derived from the pure pentatonic structure, and the semitones occur as a result of *quilismas.* Augmented fourths can only occur in a pentatonic melody by a leap to or from a passing note, a procedure which negates the very function of a passing note. The fact that augmented fourths are not found in Gregorian chant not only supports the pentatonic theory, therefore, but again shows, from a practical standpoint, how the admission of augmented fourths would undermine a pentatonic structure by giving passing notes an emphasis they do not possess.

The parallelism of organum is therefore constrained to avoid the augmented fourths that would inevitably result (see Example 3.5) by resorting to *musica ficta.*

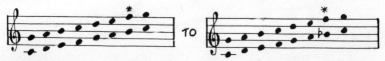

Example 3.5

Notes which were not previously part of the natural gamut of a mode thus become an essential part of the structure of organum originating in that mode. In Fig. 3, for example, three natural gamuts may be derived from the pentatonic structure (C D F G B♭):

$$
\begin{array}{ccccccc}
\text{C} & \text{D} & \text{E} & \text{F} & \text{G} & \text{A} & \text{B♭} \\
\text{C} & \text{D} & \text{E♭} & \text{F} & \text{G} & \text{A} & \text{B♭} \\
\text{C} & \text{D} & \text{E♭} & \text{F} & \text{G} & \text{A♭} & \text{B♭} \\
\end{array}
$$

$$
\text{*} \qquad \text{C} \quad \text{D} \quad \text{E} \quad \text{F} \quad \text{G} \quad \text{A♭} \quad \text{B♭} \qquad \text{*}
$$

The starred shape is inadmissible, since it does not conform to a natural gamut. From the three admissible gamuts, two different gamuts with one *musica ficta*[49] note may be derived:

$$\text{C} \quad \text{D} \quad \text{E}\flat_* \quad \text{F} \quad \text{G} \quad \text{A/A}\flat^* \quad \text{B}\flat$$
$$\text{C} \quad \text{D} \quad \text{E/E}\flat \quad \text{F} \quad \text{G} \quad \text{A} \quad \text{B}\flat$$

Figure 3 may thus be modified (see Fig. 4).

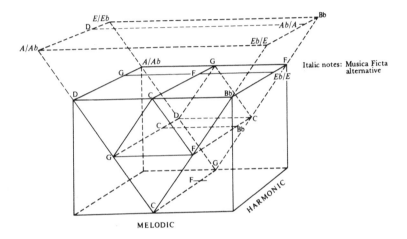

Italic notes: Musica Ficta alternative

Figure 4

This process, even more than that of making passing notes an essential part of the structure of organum, again serves to seriously weaken the pentatonic structure being externalised.

Organum, however, does not simply externalise the fifths and fourths of the pentatonic structure but also, in free organum, the seconds and major and minor thirds. Since major and minor thirds do not follow each other in free organum, they will be given as alternatives in Figure 5. For the reasons already discussed with reference to parallel organum, this procedure again negates the implicit qualities of the structure being externalised. A strong potential may therefore be said to exist in both parallel and free organum for the articulation of an explicit 'three-dimensional' structure at the expense of the already existing implicit 'two-dimensional' structure.

97

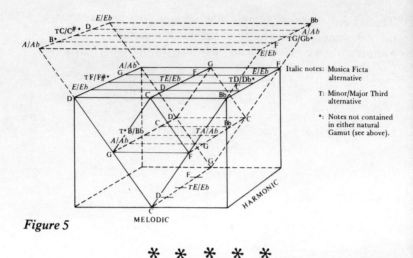

Figure 5

＊ ＊ ＊ ＊ ＊

Before proceeding any further with this brief analysis, however, it is necessary to examine a little more closely the pre-conditions necessary for the development of tonality together with some of the developmental features related to those pre-conditions. First of all, it is clear that the possibility of externally stating or reproducing elements of music which before were only implicit results from the development of phonetic literacy and its concomitant concepts as outlined in Chapter One. But, in contrast, it is by no means clear that the inception or creation of polyphony was coincidental with this 'conscious'[50] externalisation. Although Spiess is of the opinion that 'there is no scientific evidence extant to prove beyond question that there was a rudimentary polyphonic practice before the organum of the ninth century' (1957, p.15), such practice is a possibility that can hardly be ruled out[51]. The evidence relayed about by Reese to the effect that an untrained congregation may sing 'organum' with apparently intending to would alone seem to suggest that an 'unintended polyphony' was not uncommon in the early Middle Ages.

It might well be the case, therefore, that the process of writing down harmony was partially engendered by the pre-existence of polyphonic forms which, however, were not originally 'conscious' externalisations of the implicit plainchant melodies. It must not only be remembered that without the growing distancing and objectivity of phonetic literacy men might never have been able to recede far enough from the music to notice the implicitly structured and accidental or natural forms of polyphony (parallelism, heterophony and imitation), but, that without those very forms, literacy might have been used for much longer than was actually the case in encoding monophonic lines, whether implicit or explicit. Indeed, it is a distinct theoretical possibility that the development of an explicit musical structure might never have been harmonically mediated. There exists, in other words, a dialectic relationship between literacy and growing harmonic explicitness in which it is impossible to identify individual cause and effect. In the opinion of Denis Stevens, then, both the perpetuation and development of polyphony are linked with the importance of the book to the Carolingian Renaissance:

> The art of writing, of calligraphy, became wedded indissolubly to the art of music. Thus the polyphony of earlier times and distant nations, however well organised into parallel melodies, tunes-upon-drones, or thematic imitation, lacked the means to perpetuate itself unequivocally. It was the task of Western nations to transform sounds into symbols. (1960, p.211).

It is crucial for an adequate understanding of developing tonality that it is *not* viewed solely and simply as the result of the harmonic externalisation of a structure formerly implicit in the melodic lines of another culture. Tonality is not *just* a three-dimensional version of pentatonicism. It must not only be remembered that the phonetically literate concepts (described in Chapter One) which instigated and facilitated the creation of tonality in themselves changed the very structure of society and consciousness, but that evolving tonality itself represented a creative articulation and encoding of that change. The growth of a musical structure where harmony represents an *initial* externalisation of the structure as implicit in melody is therefore part and parcel of a fundamental change in the overall social-intellectual structure. Thus, although it is true that harmony may be regarded as the initial medium for growing explicitness, tonality as it finally evolved displayed a total explicitness which transcends any melodic or harmonic parameters[52]. From this point of view it is incorrect to hear the harmony of developed tonality *simply* as an externalisation of a structure formerly implicit in melody, or the melody of developed harmony as simply containing structural or harmonic implications that exist *only* because of the harmony. Any such line of thought ultimately depends upon the assumptional equation of melody with implicitness and harmony with explicitness. The validity of this equation was, of course, brought into question earlier in the chapter[53].

As a corollary of this discussion, it should be re-emphasised that music does not possess its own internal laws. Tonality was not generated simply from within previous musical forms, but was constructed and created as part of a continually developing social process. Even if music's dialectic relationship with wider social process is accepted, however, it could still be thought that the internal and self-sufficient musical laws which caused tonality paralleled wider social causation. But, as previously argued, social process knows no strict or prime causation. And, since creativity is an integral part of the social process, there can be no ultimate and complete explanation for the particular form that a symbol takes. Harmonic externalisation cannot therefore be regarded as a link in a causal chain which inexorably leads to the full development of tonality. Rather, it was a symptom of creative and transcendent social change. As already suggested, harmony might well *not* have been an absolute necessity for the development of an explicit musical language.

* * * * *

Two further developments were required before the evolving tonality as set out in Fig. 5 could achieve full fruition. Firstly, the third was accepted as a consonance and replaced the fourth as an important structural element. Apart from the fact that the major and minor thirds are, respectively, the next intervals to be generated in the harmonic series after the perfect fourth (see Example 3.1), the *pre-conditions* favouring the increasing importance of the third may best be elucidated by briefly considering the interplay between practice and theory in the Middle Ages. In an extremely interesting article Richard L. Crocker raises the question of why medieval theorists, given the legacy of the Greek Greater Perfect System, should bother with the construction of smaller theoretical units:

> What could be the purpose of articulating the scale into smaller units such as the tetrachord — as Hucbald did and as most other theorists did after him? Why, when early theorists had a complete scale — the Greater Perfect System — did they go through all this business with scale segments? (1972, p.28).

100

The probable answer, Crocker states,

> is ... that the Frankish musician started with the singing of the chant and worked his way toward theoretical constructions such as the scale, rather than the other way round. He was singer, teacher, theorist, in that order. *Cantus*, not *musica disciplina*, was his starting point; his curriculum was that of the monastic school of the 7th and 8th centuries, not the liberal arts curriculum of an earlier — or a later — time. The Greater Perfect System itself was not a basic assumption but rather a theoretical abstraction, relatively remote from practical experience. (1972, p.29).

'In terms of that experience', Crocker continues, 'there was a clear need for a scalar module of manageable size, such as a fourth or fifth'. (1972, p.29). In this context it must be made perfectly clear, as Crocker does, that the octave did not provide a suitable scalar module:

> Nor was an octave module itself very appropriate; we are so accustomed to thinking of the octave as the basic scalar module that we do not immediately recognise the circumstances under which it is inappropriate. From the Frankish point of view, the octave seemed too large a module .... in considering any extended scalar construction, we have to remember that there was no handy mechanical embodiment — no keyboard — for a standard reference .... Any tonal structure referred to must be sung and held in the ear. Hence the obvious advantage of using repertory pieces of chant to illustrate, or rather to embody, tonal constructions .... This is a specific demonstration of the central importance of chant repertory in the development of medieval theory. (1972, p.29).

It appears that the fifth might well have been the most important interval in this interplay between practice and theory. Not only is it the first interval to be generated by the harmonic series after the octave (see Example 3.1) — and therefore the largest consonance to be of any great practical use to the medieval musician[54] — but, in being the interval of duplication between the disjunct tetrachords around which hexachords were constructed, it was arguably an extremely pervasive common element in medieval theory. Crocker intimates as much in his discussion of the *Musica Enchiriadis* scale:

> Instead of octave duplication, the scale embodies consistent duplication at the fifth, comparable — but more consistent — to Guido's affinity at the fifth. As Handschin observed, Hermann's instructions, 'Take any tetrachord ... add a tone at either end ...' apply exactly to the constituent tetrachord of

101

the *Musica Enchiriadis* scale, the tones added at either end corresponding to the tones of disjunction between successive tetrachords. (1972, p.30).

Bearing in mind the overall importance of the fifth, it becomes clear that the preservation of the fourth as a consonance in any developed polyphony having more than two parts would almost inevitably, through inversion at the fifth, produce the unacceptable dissonance of the major second. If medieval theorists could not accept the third as a consonance, there seems little reason why they should have accepted the second. As intervals which occur next in the harmonic series after the fourth, and which come midway between the second and the fourth, the major and minor third could be regarded, therefore, as 'compromises'.

A preference for thirds rather than fourths in the harmonic dimension of Fig. 5 creates a situation highly favourable for the emergence of all the triads of the unified major-minor system. But before this could be achieved, it was necessary for one of the notes in each alternative situation indicated in Fig. 5 to be eliminated in such a way that the resulting structure only utilised the seven notes of the major scale. This development is indicated in Fig. 6 The scale chosen in Fig. 6 is F major. It should be pointed out, however, that

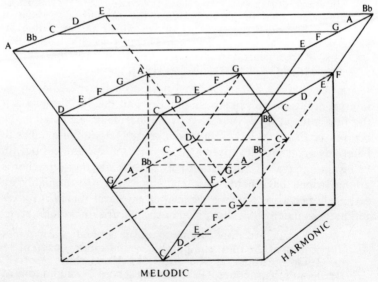

Figure 6

102

two other scales, B flat major and E flat major, would have been equally possible[55], and that the particular development shown in Fig. 6 is thus only indicative of a wider and more significant change. For the possibility of deriving three scales from the same structure is symptomatic of the relationship obtaining between the keys of those scales, and so of the homogeneity and repeatability[56] characteristic of the entire major-minor system. One major or minor triad of a particular key has relationships with other major or minor triads that may be precisely duplicated by those other triads if there is an appropriate key change. To put it in practical terms, a piece of tonal music involving modulation may be played in any one of twelve keys.

The homogeneity and repeatability of such inter-relationships are not characteristic of the modal system. In this system each mode has a unique structure which is largely unrelated to the other modal shapes. When the modes were first classified according to their finals, for example, there was no attempt to relate the finals on a common scale: 'It is essential . . . to notice . . . that the placement of the several finals on a common scale — so basic a step that we take it for granted — is actually distinct from the classification itself, which presumably came first as a separate step'. (Crocker, 1972, p.30). As Crocker points out, it is difficult for us, with our background of tonality, to imagine such a state of affairs:

> it . . . may require an effort to imagine the situation as it first presented itself to the chant singer: he would have perceived several autonomous groups of chants, each group with its own perceived set of tones and semi-tones, but he would not necessarily have been aware of any common scalar denominator that would relate the groups to each other. Indeed, there may have been no such demoninator. (1972, p.31).

Although there probably was no common scalar denominator which actually *related* the different groups of chant, it has, of course, been strongly argued that there existed, in the form of the pentatonic structure, a common *generative* denominator. In this distinction lies the difference between explicit musical structuring, where the relationships between relata are made perfectly clear in the music itself, and a more implicit structuring, where the music does not obviously display its own underlying structure.

A crucial stage in the development of tonality is therefore achieved when a scalar shape *itself* provides the module for relating the different shapes[57]. A parallel development took place in medieval

103

theory when the finals of different modes were placed on a common scale adapted and devised for that very purpose. This process does much to explain the importance of the tetrachord[58] to the scale of the *Musica Enchiriadis*[59] and other medieval theoretical schemes. But it was a process whose implications were only understood with some difficulty, and this difficulty gives a vital insight into the fundamental difference between the modal and tonal systems:

> The underlying moment in this process was . . . to understand the extended pitch realm of the scale (i.e. the Greater Perfect System as adopted by medieval theorists) in terms of the relationship among the finals — that is, the relationships among any one final and the pitches above and below it and then the relationships among the finals *when they themselves were taken to be the pitches above and below each other*. This step led outside of and beyond any one final; to put it another way, the ultimate purpose of the tetrachord of the finals was not so much to understand a particular final in terms of a scalar construction as to understand a scalar construction in terms of the network of finals. For it was the scale, not the finals, that needed understanding. (Crocker, 1972, p.33).

The difference between the development as it affected tonality and as it affected medieval theory is that whereas any medieval common scalar denominator was simply a theoretical concept having no *direct* musical expression, the tonal denominator was of *identical* shape with the scales being related. As such it had direct and explicit musical expression.

It has already been noted that, in order for the major scale[60] shape to emerge from any of the modal shapes, it was necessary for the alternative notes of plainchant[61] or organum to be eliminated according to a particular pattern. (cf. Figs. 5 and 6). It is now apparent that this pattern occurs as a dialectic correlate of the growing explicitness of evolving tonality, an explicitness which requires that the different modal shapes be syncretised into one homogeneous structure with a single unambiguous focal point[62].

The line of development so far argued in this section (see also Figs. 1-6) is echoed by Reese in his discussion of the Notre Dame School. Pentatonic melody and 'tonal' harmony balance each other:

> The upper voices, in weaving about the tones of the triad often supplemented them by the second and sixth, thus producing a strong pentatonic effect. But the forecefulness with which the triad makes itself felt, also, and in addition, the increasing

appearance of the third shows that the pentatonic and diatonic systems are poised in the balance. (1940, p.303).

The third, an interval originally regarded as needing resolution, gradually became a consonance in its own right, and superseded the fourth in its importance as a structural element:

> The feeling that thirds need resolution to perfect consonances is illustrated by Anonymus XIII . . . who states . . . that the major third should be followed by a fifth, and the minor third by a unison. . . . Practical music in the 13th Century, however, gave greater liberty to the third in particular. . . . While octaves and fifths predominate in the course of the pieces, the increasing recognition accorded to the third foreshadows the eventual downfall of a harmonic system based on unisons, octaves and fifths, and (originally) fourths — a system, that is, betokening a pentatonic feeling for melody . . . — and the approach of a harmonic system based on the triad. (Reese, 1940, p.295).

Tonality's Encoding of the Industrial World Sense

With the full development of tonality, the interlocking fundamentals of pentatonicism become separated. In Fig. 6, for example, it is perfectly clear whether C is heard as a fifth of F, as its own fundamental, as a third of A or a fourth of G, and, more importantly, at what level in the structure those relationships obtain. For tonality creates a hierarchy of fundamentals, all of which, through the various levels of the hierarchy, finally and ultimately relate back to one note.

In this fashion the architectonicism of the tonal structure articulates the world sense of industrial man, for it is a structure having one central viewpoint (that of the key-note) that is the focus of a single, unified sound-sense involving a high degree of distancing. It is, in other words, a centre-oriented structure with margins. But it is a further vital facet of tonal architectonicism that each note becomes a centre with margins. The more important structural notes relate to each other only insomuch as their precise function is defined by the less important notes belonging to higher architectonic levels, and these less important notes only relate to each other insomuch as *their* position is defined by their relationships to the more important structural notes.

The 'spatial' aspect of tonality is not, however, the only one to articulate the social-intellectual structure of industrial man. As the simultaneously divergent viewpoints and time-spaces of medieval man were snapped into a single three-dimensional focus whose necessary adjunct was a spatialised time, so the syncretisation of the different modal shapes into the unified structure of explicit tonality necessitated a precise vertical mensuration which could not help but articulate a spatialised time. The correct vertical co-ordination of the notes of the different melodic lines in tonality leads, as it were, to the possibility of making a 'spatial three-dimensional' cut along the 'time' axis of any tonal piece of music. The typification of such a cut is the bar-line. It is, moreover, a dialectic correlate of the spatialised time articulated by tonality that industrial man, in becoming increasingly objective and self-conscious, is able to stand back and objectify the passage of time. The revelationary nature of time as articulated by spiritual and corporeal rhythms is thus negated by a unified rhythmic structure which gains its effect from the pull of rhythmic patterns against pulse as contained in the strict metre essential to the three-dimensional cut already mentioned. By bringing the corporeal pulse of music into such *continual* high relief — and thereby altering and negating its original 'timeless' and hypnotic characteristics — the rhythmic structure of tonality helps to maintain industrial man's intense and constant awareness both of the passage of time, and of his own consciousness.

The vital change in man's orientation towards himself and the environment that occurred during the Renaissance created the fiction, if not the fact, of progress. The classical and cyclical idea of historical degeneration and recovery:

> . . . lost its hold on the imaginations of men as a result of profound changes in the outward conditions of life which occurred in Western Europe from the fourteenth to the nineteenth century. Among these changes were the rise of ordered secular governments, the growth of towns and industry, the geographical discoveries and the extension of commerce which brought Western Europe into direct contact with alien customs and ideas, and above all the rise of an educated middle class whose interests were hampered by a form of society in which both the power and the doctrines of the Christian Church supported the autocracy of kings and the privileges of a landed aristocracy. It was in this time of revolt against ecclesiastical and secular authority that the Christian doctrine of salvation gradually transformed into the modern idea of progress. (Becker, 1969, p.12).

The central point upon which the entire social-intellectual structure of industrial man is focused and from which the majority of power and influence in the structure is derived provides a defined goal towards which all other elements in the structure tend. It was argued in Chapter One, for example, that the phonetic literacy and typography responsible for the growth of the industrial social-intellectual structure was also heavily instrumental in generating a class dialogue that took place *within* the framework of political and economic nationalism, and was overwhelmingly concerned with who should wield the centralised power of nationalism. Progress, then, is concerned with impulsive movement towards the centres provided by the structure and its various sub-structures. But the concept is also a product of the temporal aspect of industrial society. The intense awareness of the passage of time that is concomitant with industrial man's increased control of the environment leads him to conceive of manipulating and 'improving' the environment (social as well as physical) in specific stages which can be achieved within certain segments of spatialised time relevant to his life span. For in being intensely aware of the passage of time and so of his own finite existence, industrial man tends to bring an urgency to his activities which medieval man, living more within a revelationary time, would probably find hard to understand. As we have seen, the syncronisation of events according to the clock which is so prevalent in industrial society would not have taken place in medieval society.

The concept of progress through spatialised time towards culmination at a focal point finds expression in tonality through the spatial and temporal aspects already mentioned. But perhaps the vital characteristic of tonality is its sense of *magnetic pull* towards the key-note, and it is this sense which provides the quintessential articulation of the concept of progress. Whereas the intrinsic nature of the relationships between the interlocking fundamentals of medieval music is partially responsible for its tendency towards temporal simultaneity, the sense of magnetic pull in tonality is achieved by utilising the hierarchy of fundamentals in such a way that the fundamental of each chord — as used in relation to the other notes of that chord — plays an explicit and *retrospectively*[63] pre-determined part in the passage towards a final and irrevocable statement. Tonal music is, above all, the music of explicitly sequential cause and effect — a cause and effect, that is, which depends, in the fashion of materialism, upon the reduction of a phenomenon undergoing explanation into 'indivisible' and discrete, but contiguous constituents that are then viewed as affecting one

107

another in a mono-causal and linear manner. The analysis of tonal music, for example, often concerns itself with 'showing' how the final satisfying effect of stating the tonic chord is 'due' to previously created harmonic tension. It is probably no accident, in this respect, that completed and satisfying harmonic passages are frequently referred to as 'harmonic progressions'.

The sense of direction and resolution produced in tonal music is symbolised almost totally by one chord — the dominant seventh. The importance of this chord can be accounted for in two stages. Firstly, it remains true that the three most important notes in the structure of tonality, and the ones which ultimateiy define the feeling for any particular key-note, are the key-note, the fourth and the fifth. If movement between these fundamentals and the triads which are built upon them occurs, notes I and V of the major scale are going to occur more often and so strike the ear as most important (See Example 3.6). This phenomenon coincides with the fact that the perfect fifth is, apart from the octave, the most basic and therefore the strongest interval in the harmonic series. As the two most important notes, and as an expression of an acoustical fact, these two notes, and, in consequence, the chords built upon them, are going to be heard as the most important factors in the establishing of a particular key.

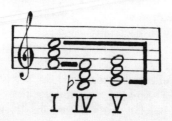

Example 3.6

Secondly, the next harmonic to produce a new note after the fifth harmonic is the seventh harmonic. This seventh harmonic produces the interval of a minor seventh above the fundamental, and so the chord of the dominant seventh. If this harmonic is added to the basic triads of the three fundamentals (I, IV and V), it becomes apparent that the one based on V is the only one to be included within the notes of the major scale derived from Fig. 6 (see Example 3.7). The

108

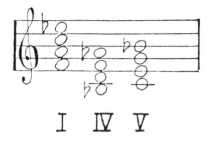

Example 3.7

importance of the V — I movement just described is therefore reinforced by the legitimacy of this seventh chord, which contains the unstable tritone (formed by the fifth and seventh harmonics). If the seventh chord on the dominant is sounded, and the first degree of the scale is sounded, then the unstable tritone is going to be attracted to the harmonics produced by this latter note (e.g. in F:B♭ — A, and E — F. The fifth degree of the dominant in this movement is strictly speaking redundant)[64].

As well as reinforcing the V — I movement central for the establishing of a particular key, the dominant seventh further emphasises the magnetic pull of tonality by being extremely important for the modulation without which any sense of progression in an extended piece would be lacking. The role played in modulation by the dominant seventh is related to the characteristics of the higher partials in harmonic series[65]— partials which, until the development of tonality, were not relevant as structural elements. Taking C as the fundamental and key-note, B flat and F sharp are stronger than B natural and F natural[66]. Thus when modulation is imminent, the introduction of these notes will not strike the ear as too unnatural. This is particularly true of the B flat, the seventh harmonic, which is audible to the ear.

It becomes apparent that the introduction of the B flat is the most natural manner of modulating. B flat is a relatively strong note in the harmonic series; it can be immediately inserted on top of the tonic chord to form a new dominant seventh; and it is slightly flat, thereby increasing its propensity to resolve to A. F sharp, on the other hand, is higher in the harmonic series than the B flat, and so relatively weaker. It is also flat[67], being almost half-way between F natural and F sharp, thereby weakening its tendency to move upwards to G.

Finally, although its relative importance over F in the harmonic series allows it to be fairly easily introduced at a point when the overall feeling of tonality is C, it cannot be directly introduced with C as the fundamental. A new dominant chord, based on D as the secondary fundamental, has to be introduced[68]. In this fashion the use of the dominant seventh emerges as the quintessential method of tonal modulation, a state of affairs which is underlined by the immediate ease of modulating flatwards.

The inherent instability of the augmented fourth, as underlined by the properties of the harmonic series, is in practice at the heart of a great deal of tonal movement and progression. Put another way, the tonal key system can be seen as the result of a conflict between man's attempt to organise rationally (through the tempered scale) the properties of the harmonic series, and the properties themselves. This conflict again serves to illustrate that no music can be regarded as a closed system having internally sufficient laws. Both pentatonicism and tonality are grounded in the relationships of the harmonic series, but both structures are extended and directed in different ways as dialectic correlates of the ongoing social-intellectual structure of the time.

It now becomes possible to understand why the original pentatonic structure (see Fig. 1) was limited to three levels of notes and two generative intervals[69]. In view of the creation of the structure represented in Fig. 6, it is apparent that the addition — in the structure as represented in Fig. 1 — of thirds to the original fourth and fifth (F and G), in probably encouraging a similar process with the fundamental (C), would have produced a structure involving a higher degree of distancing than was appropriate to the world sense of early medieval society. Furthermore, the addition of another level of fundamentals would have produced seven notes of relatively equal standing. In this situation the augmented fourth and semitone might well have been given more prominence than was the case[70]. Extension of the structure along the lines suggested, therefore, would have produced a totally different structure having more in common with tonality than pentatonicism. The medieval world sense which pentatonicism at the same time mirrored and articulated would have

110

been negated. Extension of the structure, in other words, could only occur as part of the continually developing social construction of knowledge and reality.

Some Comparative Remarks on Form

Finally, in discussing the musical encoding and articulation of social meaning, some comparative remarks may be made concerning 'form' in pre-literate musics and tonality. The differences in the formal aspects of the two classes of music reflect the difference between oral man's and typographical man's orientation with regard to time and memory, and are therefore respectively indicative of implicitly and explicitly structured music. In pre-literate music any 'unifying factors' of form are 'intrinsic' (Nettl, 1956, p.76) rather than extrinsic and externally imposed. Firstly, the most common melodic factor is that of the repetition and variation of short motifs. Secondly, we are told that 'most primitive polyphonic music employs identical or similar materials in each part'. (Nettl, 1956, p.80). Formal effect, therefore, seems to depend upon the immediately adjacent existence in the memory of the listener of material closely related to that which he is actually hearing. In this sense, the music is in a constant state of re-creation within time.

Form in Western music, however, depends very much upon comparison and long-term memory in order that the relevance of its constituent parts may take full effect. The rationally and visually[71] derived devices of polyphony (such as inversion, augmentation and diminution) lose much relevance if the listener does not consciously relate them to the initially stated subject. Furthermore, the whole principle of sonata form depends upon the relationship of one section to its antecedent. Development is meaningless without exposition, and recapitulation is meaningless without development. And if the recapitulation differs from the exposition, then the recapitulation cannot be said to have realised its full effect without comparison to the exposition in the light of the development. In other words theme or themes are discussed or externally manipulated, and discussion involves the separation of entities from their natural occurrence in time. In order to understand tonal music, industrial man must stand outside of time and music.

Writing about Music — 2

The attempt to indicate the social structuring that is inherent in particular musical languages and groups of languages has led to an approach to writing about music that transcends the categories of form and content. For, by means of comparing musical analysis with the world sense of the relevant societies it has been unnecessary to translate the musical experience into strictly verbal and substantive meanings. Since music is its own meaning there is, of course, no *need* to write about it. But it would be flying in the face of reality to ignore the fact that, because man's most useful and prevalent symbology is language, he will continue to legitimate the vast majority of his experiences, including music, through language. The academic who writes about music is merely indulging in an extension of this process[72]. Writing about music, then, is a legitimate activity insomuch as the 'meaning' of music is elucidated by reference to the social and mental structuring which is 'external' to the music, but which the music nevertheless transcendentally articulates from 'within' itself. In this chapter, therefore, the attempt has been to use words as indicators or probes of an articulated meaning that essentially lies 'beyond' not only the words used, but 'beyond' their referential significance. The intention has been to bring to life the relationships revealed to us through the material relata (and, derivatively, the relata of reified concepts) ultimately necessary for referential language, rather than to distort the musical experience into the reified confines of referential objects and concepts.

The limitations and implications of such an intention must be made fully explicit, however. Insofar as it remains necessary, at the present time, to verbalise about music, a structural approach would seem the most appropriate. But since the communication of this approach is as much rooted in the written word as more conventional approaches to writing about music, it should be realised that it *cannot* reproduce music's 'emotion' or immediate power. It would appear, then, that the *sole* contribution words can make to the musical experience lies in the realms of legitimation and criticism, a criticism, moreover that must ultimately be grounded in the individual's social situation.

As conceived in these chapters, therefore, writing about music is a maieutic process. It seeks to elucidate articulated meaning hitherto vague in the listener's consciousness, and so to heighten the awareness of self in relation to society. Society, as argued in the previous chapter, can only be regarded as being immanent 'in' the specific articulations of symbols, and, since these symbols originate from and are only socially efficacious 'within' individual minds, as being immanent 'in' individual consciousnesses. Given the culture-specific articulations and encodings of different musics, writing about music can never be an exercise in objective aesthetics. No one person or group of people is in a position to centrally define what good music is, what it should mean, and what the sophisticated and informed person should listen to. There never can be a simple one-way transfer of verbally pre-packaged artistic or cultural content. Writing about music is quite literally an extension[73] of the musical experience, and inasmuch as literacy aids recession from everyday reality, and so the process of being self-reflexive, writing about music becomes an extended exercise in looking at self and society through the medium of music. It is a means by which each person, writer or reader, can critically examine the structuring of his social and mental existence. What we like and what we do cannot be artificially divorced from the everyday life that constitutes such structuring, and no two structurings, either social or mental, and despite whatever underlying similarities may exist, can ever be identical.

It should now be more than apparent that the traditional ways of 'looking at' and writing about music discussed before deny the critically self-reflexive process that such writing could be, firstly by discussing a centralised and hierarchical music in centralised and authoritative terms, and secondly by developing a tendency to view other musics ethnocentrically. By not examining the assumptions of his own position the musicologist can only appreciate his own point of view, his own deep-seated preferences and phobias. In this respect he is in the identical position to the sociologist who, in examining a society, whether his own or another, does not examine the implicit assumptions of his own social position.

There is, however, a limit to the degree that one can uncover one's own assumptions. Not only is the conceptual level involved in self-reflexively receding from everyday reality circumscribed by the media available to aid such a process, but, within the conceptual parameters so circumscribed, there is a practical limit to the number of times one can examine one's own position. For every time one set of assumptions is uncovered, another is created as part of the meta-situation necessary for the initial examination. It is necessary, in other words, to have an assumptional framework in order to examine an assumptional framework. But continued pre-occupation with this infinitely regressive process precludes any real participation in the everyday world, and is liable to have one labelled as 'insane' by the people of one's own society[74]. As an antidote to central authoritarian objectivity, unremitting self-examination generates its own kind of useless isolationism. For although the observer continually interacts with what he is observing[75], there comes a point when he must leave behind the infinite adjustments of his own position and contribute to his own society.

Detachment-in-involvement thus seems to be the only realistic position to be adopted by any thinking (i.e. self-reflexive) person. One makes a contribution, not from the proverbial ivory tower of academia, but because one believes it to be relevant to one's situation and society. Again, it must be emphasised that activities carried out in recession from everyday reality (such as the academic) cannot be totally divorced from everyday reality. But this approach must constantly acknowledge its *necessary* limitations. Since the social-intellectual structure of any society is constantly changing, and since what any person says is — in some measure — part of the articulation of that structure, that person must accept that anything he says, on whatever time-scale, is necessarily ephemeral. The very act of *constructively* saying anything automatically makes the writer or thinker — to a certain extent — a prisoner of his own position.

NOTES

1.   That is, it allows for the existential equality of relationships with relata.

2.   It is in fact possible to have a 'universal approach' to understanding music, although not a 'universal *method* of elucidation'. cf. Shepherd (1975b).

3.   The reverse, of course, is also true, since the evidence of any musical language can only be established through the examination of individual pieces. However, until a piece has been examined in the context of other 'culturally adjacent' pieces, and in the light of the culture's particular world sense, it is doubtful whether its significance could be 'accurately' elucidated. Blacking seems to agree with this evaluation when he says that since musical patterns 'are always acquired through and in the context of social relationships and their associated emotions, the decisive style-forming factor in any attempt to express feeling in music must be its social content. If we want to find the basic organising principles that affect the shapes of patterns of music, we must look beyond the cultural conventions of any century or society to the social situation in which they applied and to which they refer'. (1973, p 73). Further, 'if you treat . . . melodies as things in themselves, as "sonic objects", which is the kind of approach I am objecting to, you can work out several different analyses. This procedure is very common in analyses of European music and may be one of the reasons why music journals are so full of contradictory explanations of the same music'. (Blacking, 1973, p 93). The dangers of extrapolating from the particular to the general has been pointed out in Shepherd's (1976) criticism of Meyer's (1973) theories.

4.   cf. p 9 and pp 55-56 above.

5.   That is, characteristics and qualities as we might *imagine* them to be, 'out there', in objective reality.

6.   This is not necessarily the case. It is entirely possible that the characteristics of different world senses might well emphasise or conversely distort elements of musical expression derived from biological constants. However, precisely because they are constants, it would be extremely difficult, if not impossible, to separate the elements of musical expression originating in them from those culture-specific elements which are socially mediated (cf. Meyer, 1973, p 214). Further it seems highly doubtful whether elements of musical expression originating in biological constants could have any meaning 'outside' those elements originating in the symbolic exchange essential to the maintenance of any society (cf. the arguments concerning Langer's and Meyer's theories, pp 24-26 above).

7.   An example of explicit 'musical' analysis relating to 'social' phenomena is, however, to be found in Blacking's work on the Venda (cf. Blacking, 1973, pp 79-88).

8.   cf. Merriam (1964), p 134 ff.

9.　　A very interesting parallel is provided here by attitudes towards jazz musicians in the United States during the 1920's (cf. Merriam, 1964, p 241 ff.). The jazz musician was regarded as undesirably deviant, but he was not tolerated, nor seen as essential to society, precisely because typographical man has such a 'rational control' on his world. Becker's (1963) work on jazz musicians is a classic study of deviance and attitudes towards it.

10.　　cf. Merriam (1964), p 167 ff.

11.　　cf. pp 34-42 above.

12.　　cf. Merriam (1964), pp 280-281.

13.　　cf. Lord (1964), Part I.

14.　　This might well be the origin of the 'elevated speech' to be found in many songs. (cf. Merriam, 1964, p 188 ff.).

15.　　cf. Merriam (1964) pp 204-206. The importance of music as a moral reinforcer is also underlined by the great emphasis placed on accuracy of rendition. cf. Merriam (1964) pp 115-116. Again, abuse of the power invested in a particular song can have grave consequences for the miscreant. These consequences may include death (cf. Merriam, 1967, pp 12-13).

16.　　cf. also Merriam (1964), pp 221-222.

17.　　Conscious manipulation of musical material becomes a lot easier, of course, when those materials can be notated in a permanent fashion.

18.　　cf. p 105 below.

19.　　cf. pp 12-18 above.

20.　　This is because plainchant is implicit *and* melodic, and tonality highly explicit *and* harmonic. Thus, although implicitness and melody, and explicitness and harmony cannot be strictly equated, the fact that plainchant and tonality *parallel* this equation will provide the reader with a relatively easy way of approaching the intuitive parameters of implicitness and explicitness as categories of musical/social elucidation. As it affects the development of tonality from plainchant, this topic is again discussed later in the text of this chapter (cf. pp 98-100 below).

The refinement indicated in the text has been carried out elsewhere (Shepherd 1975b). It could also be mentioned, in the light of the evidence presented by Blacking, that the Venda had been in contact with white men and their music for some considerable time before fieldwork was actually carried out. Although the Venda have as far as possible striven to maintain their identity, it is possible that some aspects of Western thought may have nevertheless surreptitiously permeated their symbolic output. cf. in this respect Worsley (1970) and Fanon (1970).

21.　　It is perhaps instructive to give two present day examples of music which may be taken to have corporeal or spiritual rhythms. A clear example of corporeal pulse is provided by the many different types of rock and pop music which have their roots in various dance forms. The reader must not think, however, that all rock and pop music displays a corporeal pulse. An example of spiritual rhythm is more difficult to find, but the singing of psalms in the Church of England can probably be said to display 'spiritual' qualities. Although the music for the psalm is notated in strict tonal fashion, the singing depends to a considerable extent upon additive and numeric characteristics resulting from the specific number and distribution of syllables within any particular verse. The chanting by the priest in the responses also displays 'spiritual' qualities.

22.   It should be pointed out that Mellers is speaking here with a certain amount of historical hindsight. It is strictly speaking incorrect to say that 'this unconsciousness of our earth and time-bound condition is precisely the magic effect that the primitive *sought* through his music' [Italics mine], because pre-literate man was already in the condition which, according to Mellers, he was 'seeking' through his music. It is extremely unlikely that pre-literate man has ever been aware of '*our* earth and time-bound condition' [Italics mine].

23.   cf. p 48 above, *n*. 28. Berger and Luckmann have also noted the external and collective approach of pre-literate man to life. For heuristic purposes they describe a society in which institutionalisation is total: '*all* problems are common, *all* solutions to these problems are socially objectivated, and *all* social actions are institutionalised. The institutional order embraces the totality of social life which resembles the continuous performance of a complex, highly stylised liturgy. There is no role-specific distribution of knowledge, or nearly none, since all roles are performed within situations of equal relevance to all the actors'. Although no such society exists, the authors point out that 'primitive societies approximate the type to a much higher degree than civilised ones'. (Berger and Luckmann, 1971, pp 97-98).

24.   There are certain forms of twentieth-century music, of course, to which this statement would not apply.

25.   For a fuller explanation, see the Appendix.

26.   The question arises as to how conscious these rationalisations are. The entire question of consciousness *vis-à-vis* music in any society is very difficult, and cannot be discussed here in any detail. However, some general comments may be briefly made. Firstly, 'explicit' cultures would seem to have a greater degree of consciousness regarding some aspects of the world (including, for example, the harmonic series) than 'implicit' cultures. This degree of consciousness may be musically encoded. But, secondly, the musical encoding itself may be a largely unconscious process. This seems to be the case with both plainchant and tonality. In each case theoretical rationalisation takes place after the language has become established, and in the case of plainchant, it is clear that the generative pentatonic structure is never made explicit. The fact of *ex post facto* theoretical rationalisation would seem to suggest that the 'rationalisation' of the harmonic series that initially takes place 'in' the music itself is largely unconscious. Thus, although Western man has been conscious of the harmonic series, its influence has still been an unconscious one as far as the formulation of musical languages is concerned. It is only during the twentieth century that a music's 'deep structure' has consciously preceded its composition.

27.   It is, in fact, quite possible that Ancient Greek music had an underlying pentatonic structure. Not only do the tetrachord and *harmonia* demonstrate a predilection for units of the fourth, octave, and subsequently, fifths, but the principal intervals of the diatonic genus (a whole tone) and of the enharmonic genus (a major third) are intervals that circumscribe units of conjunct motion within the scale (e.g., GAB DE). Moreover, the minor third of the chromatic genus is the interval derived from moving conjunctly between such groupings. This argument, however, must remain largely speculative.

28.   cf. Reese (1940), p 250 and Hughes (1955), p 275.

29.   There is some argument that a high proportion of pre-literate musics are based on the pentatonic scale. In this respect Reese (1940 pp 256-257) has noted that 'all the primitive music based on a definite tonality system displays as its most important structure-determining interval either the fourth or the fifth. Since the pentatonic scale, which we may indicate by the symbols CDFGac... is fundamental in all such music, the interval C-F... governs the melodic structure in some cultures (generally the more primitive) and the interval F-c... is predominant in others'. Yasser (1932, p 335) has also expressed the opinion that 'modern musical science . . . accepts . . . the historic universality of the pentatonic scale may be found in the past or present musical practise of almost every country'. It is, in fact, extremely doubtful whether any of the structural elements mentioned can be regarded as universals. Yasser, particularly, is on very doubtful ground. The Balinese Pelog scale, for example, is not very close to the pentatonic. Neither is much Venda music (cf. Blacking 1973). Yasser's theory smacks of an 'evolutionary' approach to music history.

30.   cf. pp 55-56 above.

31.   There is the possibility of a fourth piece of evidence in that parallel organum adopts the intervals of the fifth and the fourth, and these can be regarded as externalisations of the implicit melodic structure of plainchant. In that one has to assume the structure for this to become evidence, the argument might be regarded as somewhat circular, a criticism which could also be applied to the rationalisation of the modes in species of fifths and fourths. It has to be realised of course, that the processes under examination are dialectic and do not easily lend themselves to sequential analysis. Even in sequential terms, however, both 'externalisation' arguments take on more significance in the light of the first two pieces of evidence given in the text.

32.   According to Joseph Yasser (1937, p 344), some 700 out of the 1600 'which at present constitute the principal musical material of the Catholic liturgy'.

33.   cf. Reese (1940), p 233.

34.   cf. Yasser (1937) pp 182-183.

35.   'What is a gregorian mode? In the light of the following article we are able to reply with the utmost conciseness: it is a formulary pattern originating from the ornamentation of a melodic shape which links a tonic note with a recitation note or tenor (latterly called the dominant) in a fixed

118

pentatonic scale. This pentatonic scale is freely completed with weak notes which are more of less mobile'.

36.   cf. Werner (1948, pp 211-255). Two of the conclusions drawn by Werner are particularly interesting. The first (p 254) is that 'the principle of the octoechos originated *not in musical but in cosmological and calendaric speculations*. While the principle of eight modes is common to the entire Near East and, through Christianity, conquered Europe, its concrete musical implementations vary greatly according to the indigenous traditions of western folk-lore in the respective orbits'. Secondly, (p 255) Werner concludes that 'while the existing ecclesiastical modes must be considered *post factum* constructions of the theorists, the conception of an eightfold modality was an *a priori* postulate of a religio-mythical nature to which theorists had to adjust the various systems of modes'.

37.   It is far from clear exactly what Chailley means by this reference to very old melody. The work of P. Delalande and Y. Hameline is mentioned, but without a sufficient reference being given to enable it to be traced. From the context it is possible that Chailley is referring to the chant of the Near East, but it has so far proved impossible to determine whether this melody is pentatonic or not. In this situation one can only reiterate the reservations stated in note 29.

38.   'the basic scale being that of a pentatonic scale without any semitones in which the unfilled minor thirds are optionally divided by weak and often moveable *piens* whose exact placement within the minor third would seem to be fixed by attraction [to more important notes]'.

39.   Reti in fact uses the phrases 'melodic tonality' and 'harmonic tonality'. The word tonality was omitted in this context because it seemed confusing. 'Tonality' in this chapter refers exclusively to the musical language prevalent in Europe between approximately 1600 and 1900.

40.   Again, one must question Reti's use of the words 'melodic' and 'harmonic'. The classification Reti is attempting extends much beyond that which is simply melodic and that which is harmonic. The sense of importance of the key-note in a tonal melody *without harmony* is not in the slightest bit 'melodic' (according to Reti's categorisation) and there are some harmonies, such as are to be found in impressionistic music and the blues which work in a decidedly 'melodic' fashion (again according to Reti's categorisation). The specific reservations about the use of words such as 'melodic' and 'harmonic' have been made elsewhere (cf. pp 77-78 above, and *n.* 20). For the purpose at hand, however, Reti's classification is sufficient.

41.   This method is not the only one by which one note may be given more prominence than another in pentatonically based melody, and it is not to be suggested that it is the one which necessarily gives rise to the inequality of fundamentals as experienced in plainchant. Two other methods may be mentioned. The first is provided by the curvilinear shape of a melody which seems to create (possibly by the desire of the voice to relax the tension created by moving up and away from the first note) the propensity for the melody to return to its starting point. The second, which is related, involves

the use of reverse curvilinear shapes together with normal curvilinear shapes so that the melody pivots about a median note.

42. cf. p 37 above.

43. There is insufficient space here to describe the often vitriolic disputes which have surrounded the question of plainchant rhythm. For a survey of the dispute see John Rayburn (1964). For the purposes of this chapter it is adequate to note that all the three main schools of thought agree that plainchant rhythm was 'free', and that only an insignificant minority of scholars consider that it was strictly metred in the manner of tonality. No-one has ever suggested that plainchant had a rhythm founded on bodily movement.

44. As with pentatonicism (see note 29), spiritual and corporeal rhythm are elements that medieval music has in common with some pre-literate musics. Again, thorough comparative studies would be needed to establish that the rhythms of medieval music betray a conceptual framework essentially different from those of pre-literate musics. It is interesting to note, however, that medieval man's sense of time does involve a marked degree of distancing and historicity which one would expect to hear articulated in the rhythms of his music. cf. Georges Poulet (1956, pp 4-5).

45. These two phrases (a 'revelationary sense of becoming' and an 'incarnate sense of being') refer respectively to relationships with the world typical of orally mediated and typographically mediated societies.

46. cf. Chapter One above.

47. cf. Chapter One above.

48. Since the *quilismas* can thus become essential both in a harmonic *and* melodic sense, the melodic part of the diagram is extended up another layer. The relationship between the *quilismas* in a harmonic and melodic sense is thus indicated. See Fig. 3.

49. The examples and figures use a different set of notes, which serves to emphasise that the discussion is still centred around shapes rather than around notes having a precisely notated perfect pitch. The original pentatonic shape in the examples is therefore CDEGA, whereas in the figures it is B♭ CDFG.

50. The use of the word 'conscious' in this context has already been briefly discussed (cf. *n.* 26 above). Its use here is meant to indicate that a certain growth in consciousness is being encoded, and not that the process of encoding itself is explicitly carried out or 'conscious'.

51. As we have seen (cf. p 77 above), the Venda have a developed harmony, and, moreover, a harmony for which Blacking claims a degree of explicitness (cf. Blacking, 1973, p 85). What is true of the Venda in this respect is probably also true of some other pre-literate tribes (cf. Nettl, 1956, pp 77-89). Spiess is clearly aware of the existence of pre-literate polyphony, because he refers (1957, p 11) to Schneider's theory that polyphony as we now understand it evolved from such pre-literate polyphony. Spiess does make one comment on Schneider's theory which is

very important because it once again points up the possibility of white influence (cf. *n.* 20 above). Although admitting that Schneider's theory is 'logical' he says that 'there is perhaps room for speculation as regards the alleged "purity" of the aboriginal tribes from which stem the musical examples of Schneider's hypothetical first stage . . . it does seem that during the one thousand years that polyphony has definitely been known to be in existence . . . some influence, however indirect, may have reached such aboriginal nations and tribes . . .'

52.   It must be remembered that the harmony of developed tonality is just one aspect of a 'pre-existing' whole. With evolving tonality, therefore, growing explicitness is as much 'in' the melodic line as it is 'in' the harmony. Although in the case of evolving tonality, there would be no explicitness without harmony, the quality of explicitness is not restricted to the harmony alone. What is essentially a useful approach to understanding growing explicitness must not be allowed to distort the actual nature of such explicitness.

53.   cf. p 78 above.

54.   Although the octave was admitted as a consonance by medieval theorists, and although it is important in its relationship to the fifth and fourth, it was not itself an important structural interval in medieval music. Crocker indicates this when he says that 'when early theorists spoke of the octave, it was often in terms of its identity of resonance — "as when men and boys sing the same note".' (Crocker, 1972, p 29).

55.   This may be illustrated as follows:

B♭ C D E F G A B♭ — F major
B♭ C D E♭ F G A B♭ — B♭ major
B♭ C D E♭ F G A♭ B♭ — E♭ major

56.   Homogeneity and repeatability are key characteristics of the industrial world sense. cf. pp 27-29 above.

57.   The shapes are 'different', of course, only in that they have strictly notated perfect pitch. The actual shape is identical in all cases as regards modulation, but not as regards the triads built on each note of the scalar module. cf. *n.* 60 below.

58.   The tetrachord is important because there are four finals, each of which is appropriate to two (one authentic, one plagal) of the eight modes. The number of four is thus linked to the 'origins' of the eight modes as discussed by Werner (cf. *n.* 36 above). But it is also possible here to indicate a link between Werner's argument and the influence of the Greek Greater Perfect System on the formulation of the modes. For as Crocker indicates, although the classification of the modes is distinct from the placement of the finals of the modes on a common scale, 'it is not entirely distinct from the *number* of finals identified, for this number will depend to some degree upon the type of common scale selected'. (1972, p 30). This link again underlines the usefulness of Chailley's scheme in demonstrating how the eight modes could have evolved in a purely musical sense, whilst at the same

time not precluding the generation of plainchant which does not easily fit into any mode.

59.   Crocker (1972, p 33) points out that the scale of the *Musica Enchiriadis* 'was the most extreme exponent' of the development here being described. It is also interesting to note that the emergence of organum and theory (which can be regarded as an externalisation of implicit structure in the same way as organum — see above pp 88-89, and *n.* 31) occurred at about the same time and in the same area (10th- and 11th-century France) as the beginning of the breakdown of classic feudalism. This again provides evidence for the argument that music both encodes and creatively articulates socially constructed reality.

60.   The minor scale may be said to emerge as a result of the homogeneous nature of tonal structure. If every note of the major scale (the scalar shape which provides the module for relating the 'different' shapes) generated a major triad or scale within the key of that scalar shape, then the structure would immediately lose its characteristics of homogeneity and repeatability. This may easily be observed by reference to Fig. 6.

61.   As regards the shape of a strictly classified mode there are no alternative notes. Even if this was universally true in practice (which seems unlikely), then, according to Chailley's theory, there must have been alternative notes before the modes finally 'solidified' into their predominant shapes. The argument here is that as organum developed, these alternative notes again came into play, and became symptomatic of the weakening modal shapes. It is interesting to speculate that *musica ficta* had less to do with notated accidentals as it did with notes which were 'foreign' to the shape or natural gamut of a mode. Alternative notes would have provided instances of such foreign notes.

62.   The essential reification of this syncretisation is the scale of equal temperament as embodied in the keyboard.

63.   It is important to realise that such 'completeness' can only be realised when the work is viewed as a whole. While the piece is being composed and while it is being heard (at least for the first time), there are, at any one point, many alternative directions that the piece can take, although the number of such alternatives decreases as the piece progresses. Only when a piece is completed, therefore, can its 'inner logic' become apparent. One is not dealing with reversible time, therefore, even though reversible time is the logical and ultimate conclusion of the spatialised time articulated by tonal music, and is also a necessary correlate of the deterministic and reductionist world sense. Any reader who is further interested in the contradictions inherent in this description should refer to Capek (1961), especially pp 121-133, where the problem of reversible time is fully discussed.

64.   In a German sixth, for example, which functions in much the same way as a dominant seventh — except that a different type of resolution is produced by positing a different fundamental — the fifth can be changed to produce a French sixth, or omitted altogether, to form an Italian sixth.

65.   The following argument owes much to Deryck Cooke's analysis of the relationship of the harmonic series to tonal syntax (Cooke, 1959, pp 41-45). However, it should be pointed out that the conclusions drawn in these pages are only relevant once the separation of fundamentals has occurred. The crucial role played by fundamentals in the development of tonality is not mentioned by Cooke, his argument resting almost exclusively on the nature of the higher partials. Indeed, his argument is essentially a melodic one, which seems strange when the explicitness of tonality involves a highly developed harmony. It must be re-emphasised, therefore, that neither harmony nor melody in tonality can be legitimately separated from each other or regarded as logically prior to one another. Melody and harmony in tonality are but different aspects of one underlying structure that both encodes and articulates the industrial world sense.

66.   This is so because both notes occur earlier in the harmonic series than their counterparts and so are more likely to be audible to the ear.

67.   It must be emphasised that the B flat and F sharp only sound out of tune as a result of man's adaptation of the natural intervals found in the harmonic series to form the tempered scale.

68.   It is interesting to note, however, that both C and F sharp figure in a dominant seventh based on D.

69.   See the questions posed above on p 84.

70.   The augmented fourth was, of course, given no prominence at all. It is also relevant to note that the semitone in many circumstances was actively avoided. In discussing antiphonal psalmody, for example, Reese (1940, p 176), tells us that: 'The point of division between the two parts of the verse is known as the *caesura*. In settings of long texts the tenor of the first half of the verse may be interrupted by a downward inflexion called the *flexa*, which is also a type of cadence. If the tenor is sub-tonal (that is, if the scale degree immediately below it is a whole tone away) the inflexion descends a whole tone; if it is sub-semitonal . . . the inflexion descends a minor third'. Reese takes this to be 'an additional bit of evidence for the pentatonic nature of at least some of the Chant'.

71.   The processes of turning something upside down, or of elongating or compressing it are essentially 'spatial' rather than 'temporal', and therefore lend themselves more easily to visual rather than aural comprehension. The difficulty of actually hearing and identifying such devices as developed and used by the serialists is commonly accepted.

72.   The stance adopted here throws some light on the position of those people who maintain that analysis and writing about music can never be a legitimate or useful process. This position is based on the opinion that analysis and writing about music can never replace the musical experience, which is perfectly true. However, it does not follow from this opinion that analysis or writing about music is useless, because, although these activities cannot replace the musical experience, they can be an extremely useful aid to critical thought, as this chapter has sought to demonstrate. What people who hold to the above position are in fact doing is denying a critical and

123

self-reflexive approach to music. It is thus difficult to see how anyone in this position could be conscious of music's potentially creative role with regard to social and intellectual structuring. Strictly speaking, these people can only relate to music as a purely sensuous social ornament.

This last conclusion is only true in a strict sense, however, because there are very few people who do not externalise their responses to pieces of music. The person who maintains that analysis and writing about music are not useful processes is therefore really contesting the degree to which he should be critical and self-reflexive. There is no difference in kind between the initial verbalised reaction to a piece of music, and a detailed and considered exposé of that response which in effect elucidates many of the implications behind it. But, in elucidating all the implications behind his initial response, a person is much more likely to question its adequacy, rather than solely passing judgement on the music, which is frequently what initial responses are exclusively concerned with.

73.   An extension, that is, in the McLuhanesque sense.

74.   This is true of societies where reality is not recognised for the relative construct that it 'really' is. There is no 'ultimate' reality, merely different realities constructed by different societies. Where reality is considered as an absolute, another's differing reality appears as dangerous unreality, classifiable as 'insanity'. R. D. Laing indicates this process, at the same time illustrating the genuinely relative nature of differing realities through a demonstration of the relativity of insanity: 'When inside and outside have been flipped so that inside-outside for A is outside-inside for B and both think "absolutely", then we have spiralled into the most extreme inter-experiential disjunction in our culture — psychiatrists, sane: patients, psychotic. The psychiatrist in this case has no doubt about the diagnosis. The patient is psychotic and without insight. The patient thinks the psychiatrist is psychotic and without insight. The patient is psychotic and without insight *because* he thinks that psychiatrists are dangerous lunatics who ought to be locked up for their own safety, and if other people are too much under the spell of the thought-police to see that, he is going to do something about it'. (1971, p 43). If one thinks in terms of sanity and insanity, then it is just as valid to think of someone who has greatly indulged in the process of infinite regress as a sane person looking in on an insane world as the other way round.

75.   This statement is a necessary adjunct (in the social sphere) of the sociological stance adopted throughout these chapters. It is readily acknowledged, however, that the material sphere of activity in the universe is not appreciably affected by human observation, notwithstanding the dialectic interaction between object and observer.

124

Chapter Four

Musical Writing, Musical Speaking
TREVOR WISHART

Since very ancient times human thought and communication has been inextricably bound up with the use of the written word, so much so that it becomes almost impossible for us to disentagle ourselves, for a moment, from the web of written wisdom and consider the problems of meaning and communication, *in vitro,* so to speak. Ever since the Ancient Egyptians developed pictures into a viable form of hieroglyphic notation, our world has been dominated by a class of scribes, capable of mastering and hence capable, or deemed capable, of controlling what was to be written down and stored in the historical record. Although this function was often delimited or occasionally usurped by illiterate or semi-literate political supremos, such tyrants have usually succumbed to the literate scribehood's cultural web, as evidenced by the 'barbarian' invasions of the Roman and Chinese Empires, and to some extent by the Moslem conquests of Persia and Byzantium which generated a novel cultural epoch by throwing together the culturally divergent scribehoods of these two long-established cultures, under the unifying banner of Islam.

In the long era of scribery, all men regarding themselves as 'cultured' or 'civilised', as opposed to illiterate peasants and craftsmen, have lived within the confines of an enormous library whose volumes have laid down what was socially acceptable, and in effect *possible,* to know and to mean. Whilst those lying on the margins of 'civilisations' retained some sub-cultural independence (variously labelled as 'ignorance', 'backwardness', 'superstition', 'folk-lore' or 'folk-culture'), they equally had no access to the pages of history, and hence whatever the significance of their cultural world, it was devalued by default. The vast growth in literacy in the last century, with its numerous undoubted social advantages, has, however, further increased the dominance of our conception and perception of the world through that which can be written down.

So here we are in the library, and I would like to convey to you what I mean. If, for a moment, we could put all these volumes of words on one side, if we could face each other across this table and engage in the immediate dialectic of facial and bodily gestures which accompany face-to-face speech communication, perhaps you could appreciate that what I intend to mean is not necessarily reducible to the apparent meanings of the words I employ during this interchange; perhaps you could reach through my words to my meanings.

Unfortunately, however, you are not physically present as the other half of this discourse and hence I must ask you to bear with my necessarily impressionistic style as I attempt to convey, through the medium of the written word, the very limitations of that medium.

Writing, originally a clever mnemonic device for recording the verbal part of important speech-communications between real individuals soon grew to such a degree as to dominate, to become normative upon, what might properly be said. Divorced from the immediate reality of face-to-face communication it became objectified, generalised, and above all, permitted the new class of scribes (whether priests, bureaucrats or academics) to define and control what might 'objectively' be meant. Weber's conception of the advance of Western civilisation spearheaded by a specialist rational bureaucracy is the natural outgrowth of this simple development.

For Plato, the Idea of the object, which took on a new historical permanence in its notation in the written word, came to have more 'reality' than the object-as-experienced. This radically new stance reflects a permanent tendency of scribe-dominated cultures towards the reification of ideas, and the undervaluing of immediate non-verbal experience, which has special relevance to the history of music. Even for the average literate individual it might at first sight appear that what we can think is commensurate with what we can say, and hence to appear verbally confused or elliptical is easily interpreted as a failure of clear thought . . . rather than as a difficulty of verbal formulation of a perfectly clear non-verbal idea . . . (e.g. the idea of a good break in improvised musical performance is clearly understood by anyone who can play in the idiom, but has never been adequately reduced to a verbal description).

We would like therefore to propose that words never 'mean' anything at all. Only people 'mean', and words merely contribute towards *signifying* people's meanings. For the scribe, meaning appears to result as the product of a combinatorial process; broadly speaking, various words with more or less clearly defined reference or function are strung in a linear combination to form sentences, paragraphs etc., which have a resultant clearly specified meaning. For the individual speaker, however, meaning is a synthetic activity. He means. Not merely the combination of words but a choice from an infinitude of possible inflexions, tones of voice and accent for their delivery together with possibilities of movement, gesture and even song, enter into the synthesis of a speech-act which attempts to convey what he means, and in this way a speech-act may uniquely convey quantities of information about the state of mind of the speaker, his relationship to what is said and so on, which would be entirely lost if merely the words used were transcribed, but is certainly not lost on the person spoken to. Here it is abundantly clear that not meaning, but signification resides in the words, and the mode and context of use of these significations all contribute towards the speaker's meaning.

Now, immediately, we become aware of how thoroughly enmeshed we have become in our climbing-frame of notation. For all that remains of what we, or anyone else ever meant, once committed to parchment or print is these marks on the paper. Here in the library we *see* love, tragedy, joy, despair lying silently on the shelves, the entire history of the word. Open the pages, and Plato's 'Ideas' might appear to flutter into the air, like butterflies emerging from their pupae, or Hegel's invisible 'Spirit of History' might reveal itself to you on its great metaphysical march into the future, as a new edition of the history books appears to change the face of mankind. After all, it's safe and secure in the depths of the library, where the scribe knows what he reads, and so long as he remains the judge of what is to be admitted to his library shelves, what can impel him to venture outside for alternative verification?

Occasionally a gifted scholar does appear to question the very basis of a writing-dominated world-view. Lao-Tse, the Chinese philosopher, resorted to extreme verbal ellipsis in a late attempt to notate his philosophical stance. At the other extreme, a young scholar named Karl Marx, whose principle committment lay outside the scholarly profession, but who felt impelled to justify his world-view before the international scribehood, committed to paper the astonishing theory that the world is shaped by human *activity*, whilst talking, writing and the resulting development of ideas, constitute only one particular type of human activity, and this of secondary importance to materially productive, economic, activity. What had usually been regarded as *history-as-such* was, in his view, merely one particular reified result of human activity, the enscribed verbalisations of certain mortals with certain preconceptions, economic interests and systems of relevance.

Marx's great scholarly erudition won for his radical works a more or less permanent place on the library shelves, but in so doing it delivered his work into the hands of the continuing scribehood, who would promulgate his writings, but not very often their significance. The up-and-coming would-be radical scholar would learn about 'praxis' as a concept in 'Marxist epistemology', his understanding of alienation and class consciousness would be judged by its verbal competence.

At the other extreme, we have *music!* Ever since the world library opened there have been problems in this department. Somehow it seemed that music could mean something to people, judging by their reactions, but this something rarely seemed reducible to any definite verbal equivalent. Music as an alternative mode of communication, however, has always threatened the hegemony of writing and the resultant dominance of the scribehood's world-view. Therefore, from the earliest times, attempts have been made to lay down what could and could not be accepted as 'correct' musical practice. Both Plato and Confucius recognised the threat posed by uncontrolled musical experience to the 'moral fibre' of the rationalistic scribe-state, and advised the exclusive adoption of forms of music which seemed to them to be orderly in some kind of verbally explicable way. As, for the moment, there was no way of capturing music in the same way as speech, no notation procedure, it seemed safest to adhere absolutely to previous musical practice, while often ensuring that the music itself was subservient to an approved text. The codification and standardisation of church chant by Pope Gregory in post-Roman Europe may be seen as but one example of a tendency which is exemplified by the Chinese Emperor's great concern for the 'correct' tuning of the imperial pitch-pipes at the beginning of his reign, the execution of performers who made mistakes during ceremonial performances in the Aztec world and in many other cultures, and so on. With the appearance of musical notation, new factors came into play, which will be further discussed below. However, a rapid glance at the syllabi of most Western Universities will reveal the tremendous emphasis placed upon the study of composers who adopted a clearly, rationally codifiable (verbalisable) musical praxis, in particular the work of Palestrina (the champion of the Council of Trent), J. S. Bach, and in the case of the more 'go-ahead' departments of music, Schoenberg and his '12-tone technique'.

Even so, music continued to convey its alternative messages and holy men (like St. Augustine) were obliged to admonish themselves before God for being seduced by the 'mere sensuous quality' of musical sounds. This feeling that attention to aspects of sound beyond those which are capable of description, and hence prescription in, writing (and later in musical notation) is lascivious or morally harmful, is a recurring theme of scribe-dominated societies.

Returning now to the problem of distinguishing meaning from signification, we must begin by saying that if you are an absolutely committed verbalist, then there is no hope of your being convinced by anything we might write here. For the 'linguistic philosopher' all problems are reducible to problems of signification within language, and such a philosopher will merely deny the validity of our problem. Howevever, if you are capable of imagining that talking to your lover is not merely an exchange of syntactically-related arbitrary signs and bodily-gestures, that in fact there can be a dialectical communion between two people (at least), mediated and articulated through word and gesture, but not constituted by them, then read on!

But surely, you might say, if this communion exists, it can be named?

This is perfectly true. However, the point remains that its *articulation* is not the articulation of signs, and we must not assume that we can notate its articulation by attaching signs to different parts of it and articulating these signs.

To be more specific, let us first of all note that changes in our state ('bio-emotional state'? But let's not be deceived by the labels) are continuous and holistic, whereas verbal notations are discrete and combinatorial. We can never completely reduce the continuous to the discrete, or, to put it in another way, the processual to the combinatorial . . . this is also perhaps why our vocabulary for referring to internal states is so vague and ill-defined; where does one draw the lines of categorical distinction between the so-called 'emotions', 'moods', or 'responses' when there are, in fact, no such boundaries, but only a continuously varying something. Significant as this point may be (it is hinted at in Susanne Langer's *Philosophy in a New Key*), it is not, however, the central issue. For, ultimately, the important distinction lies between the experience, the state, as a state of ourselves, and the mere notations of it, the arbitrary-labels assigned to bits of the ongoing process . . . between the most immediate reality of me, now, and the reality of socially-interdefinable name-plates and syntactic laws. We may reach some agreement on how to use these name-plates, but that does not touch the heart of the matter. This problem is with us as soon as we begin to speak. But it is writing, with the consequent reification of ideas in written reportage, and the scribal control of world-view that forces the problem to the centre of civilisation. Very soon we are beginning to deny the existence of any sub-label reality at all, and the 'emotions' a convenient verbal fiction, become as mysterious as Platonic Ideals.

What the aural-tradition musician (at least those not entirely constrained by priest-scribe dominance) takes on faith is that music *does* touch the heart of the matter. With language, the actual medium used is of no special significance; it may be spoken (sound), written (visual), touched (braille), and so forth. In a certain sense, the message transcends the immediate concrete experience of the medium which carries it. Music, however, cannot be divorced from the medium of sound[1], and enters into our experience as part of an immediate concrete reality; it impinges on us and in so doing it *affects* our state. Furthermore, as Susanne Langer remarks in *Feeling and Form*, in its articulation of the time-continuum of concrete experience, it corresponds directly with the continuum of our experiencing, the continuous flux of our response-state.

Hence our pre-notation musician takes on faith that the way his musical articulating of sound impinges upon his own state is in many ways similar to the way it impinges upon the state of others. He seeks no verbal confirmation (except indirectly), understanding that there can be none. We might say that there is no divorce between the syntax of musical activity and the syntax of musical experience. Whatever is played is directly monitored, via the ears, by the player's immediate response to it . . . there is an immediate dialectic of musical action and experience.

By this immediate dialectic, music reaches directly to us, in a way which language can never do, communicating powerful messages which are not refutable within the socially-approved categorical systems of any scribe-culture. It is music's *intrinsic* irrefutability, its going behind the back of language, which has caused it to be viewed with so much suspicion and disdain by guardians of socially-approved order.

It is this immediate dialectic, however, which will be broken asunder by the advent of musical notation, causing a fundamental reorientation of musical conception and perception in the West, and rendering music susceptible to new verbal definitions and hence subjecting it to increasing interference from the verballigentsia.

Undoubtedly, musical notation, like 'speech-notation', originated first as a mnemonic device for already well-established musical practice but, like writing, it quickly grew to dominate that musical practice. Just as the original form of writing, the *ideogram*, did not attempt to convey the sound of words (as with alphabetic writing) but the ideas which were expressed through the word-sounds and hence demanded a familiarity with, and an adherence to, the sphere of those ideas, so the *neume* did not attempt to mark out what we now have come to regard as individual pitches and units of rhythm, but only shapes and contours of melodic lines customary in current practice, and hence also requiring a complete familiarity with current melodic practice, and an adherence to it, before becoming usable[2]. In this way, these first notation procedures tended to stabilise, if not to atrophy, the pre-existing ideological and musical praxes.

A more significant breakthrough occurs with the emergence of analytic notation systems. Here the verbal or musical praxis is analysed into constituent elements which are notated, and the notation combined to form the meaningful or characteristic units of verbal or musical praxis. In terms of language, the earliest example is afforded by the syllabary, as in Hebrew, where constituent (but meaningless) syllables are assigned separate written signs, and these strung together to form the combined sounds of meaningful words and utterances. However, the most significant form of analytic notation for language was the alphabet, probably invented in the Middle East but taken up by the Greeks as the foundation of the first literate *critical* culture. The alphabet takes the principle of the

131

syllabary one stage further, notating the (idealised) sound-constituents of the syllables themselves[3], and in so doing achieving such a considerable economy of means (twenty-six letters in the Roman alphabet, as compared to tens of thousands of Chinese ideograms) that universal literacy became a practical possibility for the first time.

The ideogram-writer had attempted to write down what was meant by the speaker in terms of the ideograms which were notations of conventionalised and traditional ideas; by the intrinsic nature of this system, novel ideas were extremely unlikely to be recorded, even if they did arise in speech-discourse. With the alphabet, however, the notation of the constituent *sounds* of language made possible the recording of what was actually *said,* and hence made possible the recording of conflicting statements and the emergence of a critical tradition (see Goody & Watt, 1963). Whilst this freed language from the domination of the tradition-bound ideas of a tiny elite of priest-scribes, it vastly expanded the spread and domination of writing as a vehicle for mediating and explaining human experience, and hence led to the devaluation by default of all non-verbal modes of action and communication . . . the ultimate triumph of a newly expanded secular scribehood.

The effect of analytic notation on music, in the context of a writing-dominated world was much more fundamental. This analytic notation for music, arising only in Western Europe, developed considerably later than alphabetic writings. The fundamental thesis of this system is that music is ultimately reducible to a small finite number of elementary constituents out of which all sounds possibly required in musical praxis can be notated by combining these constituents. It must be noted from the outset that this finitistic thesis is a requirement of notation rather than fundamentally necessary to conceivable musics. For a notation procedure to be of any use, it must use only a manageable (small) number of constituents which are then permuted; notation of the continuum is intrisically impractical. This is the same problem we have met in the problem of verbal categorisation of the internal experiential state.

The two features of sounds used in tenth-century musical practice which appeared most accessible to analytic notation were pitch-level and rhythm. Timbre was not tackled in this way (timbre, up till the twentieth century being limited by the available instrument technology); the continuum of possible dynamic levels has never been remotely accurately categorised, despite attempts to give it a notational rationale in some integral serial composition; while dynamic balance (remaining largely a matter of unspoken convention) and acoustics (usually the accident of performance location) have only come under accurate control with the advent of electronic sound-recording techniques.

However, even pitch and rhythm could only be captured in a very particular way, determined by the exigencies of analytic notation itself. Thus, whereas aural rhythm takes place against the silent backdrop of somatic rhythm, enabling the aural musician to indulge in the most intricate articulations of time, notated rhythm is limited by the problems of notational economy. We can divide time infinitely, and in performance can judge directly the effectiveness of the most subtle placements of sounds . . . but analytic notation is a finitistic procedure, we must be able to count the divisions in order to write them down (but not necessarily in order to judge aurally what is effective). Hence, analytically notated music is bound within the limitations of summative rhythms.

Similarly, discrete fixed pitches are idealisations of acoustic reality. In practice there are only sounds in their infinite variety of possible frequency, frequency-spectrum, timbre, dynamic envelope, phase and change and combination of all these. It might well be argued that we never hear the same sound twice. Consider the irreducible infinitude of tones of voice. But the infinite is not practicably notatable. What we must have is a finite set of pitch-levels, which we can permute and combine. The refinement of instrument technology attempts to impose this discrete permutational rationality upon the very production of sounds, and our ears learn to approximate our acoustic experience to the discrete steps of our imposed logic.

In the West, this rationalisation process is taken to its extreme. Thus from the infinitude of possible pitch levels which could give rise to numerous subtly different musical scales (such as the scales of the ragas of Indian music and probably those of Western medieval pre-notation chant, though this we will never know) a small set of twelve clearly specified pitch-levels is gradually selected partly through the tendency, intrinsic in the notation system (and its realisation in the technology of instrument design, especially keyboard instruments), towards a rational simplicity, a notational economy. The 'well-tempered' scale arrives, permitting a considerable opening up of the field of harmonic inter-relations among a limited set of fixed pitches, as Bach [4], and composers through Wagner and Schoenberg were to demonstrate.

In its constant search for new modes of expression, the Western classical music tradition was, however, constrained by its very concentration upon relationships of a limited set of thus notatable 'pitches', to extend the notatable field of harmonic relationships to the limit. The final step into a 12-tone, and thence 'integral', serial technique, rather than being a 'liberation' from this restricted-set tonality, must be seen in historical perspective as the final total capitulation to the finitistic permutational dictates of a rationalised analytic notation system, and the gateway to much sterile rational formalism (this concept is used here in a precise sense, to be discussed more fully below).

At the same time more subtle uses of pitch, such as sliding inflections, which can vary over an infinitude of possible speed, interval of sliding and curvature of the slide (there is in fact no real verbal equivalent, let alone musical notation, for the latter) were not amenable to this finitistic approach. It is interesting to note that the first units of music notated by the neume were not 'pitches' but melodic shapes, which strongly suggests that these shapes were more unified entities than the pitch combinations used later to notate them would imply. If we realise that frequency is variable over a continuum of values we can begin to see how inflections of normal scale pitches may have served to bind together these groups as single melodic 'gestalts'. Notice also how we are obliged to talk about inflections 'of pitch', already giving a greater reality to those units from the continuum of frequency which we have chosen to notate, and name as 'piches', as opposed to the equally real movement across micro-intervals between these selected few, which have been relegated to the status of 'inflections'. [5]

Hence, in a similar way to analytic writing, analytic musical notation notates what are conceived of as the idealised constituents of melodic and rhythmic practice, discrete pitches and units of rhythm, and hence what is notated can be freed from the necessities of established musical praxes. We can capture or generate in our notation new musical procedures and hence music is enabled to grow and develop in a way similar to critical thought in relation to language. In this way, we may, but *need not* discover new modes of musical experience. However, this begs the central question of what defines a musical experience, and this very concept has been fundamentally twisted by the impact of musical notation itself, gradually forcing music to kow-tow to the verbally definable.

These facts have only appeared to the view of some classically-trained musicians at this stage, when they have experienced working with electronic sound-recording media, which permit us to capture the sound-gestalt *in toto*, without the intermediate stage of a written-notation. In the intervening centuries the notational procedures which began as the servants of musical praxis have come, just as in the case of written language, to dominate our very perception and conception of music. After all, isn't music composed of notes, rather than sounds?

It is often noted in classroom experiments on notation that when left to their own devices, children often hit upon the idea of using lines and dots to represent pitch-levels, and summative units to represent rhythm, when attempting to notate music, from which it is concluded that this is perhaps the most natural way to write down music. But the process is of course circular, the large loop being closed by the long history of the dominance of our particular notation system which has become the norm for our musical praxis. Analytic notation has become a kind of grand-historical filter, selecting some elements of sound, those which it notates, as of musical significance and others, those which it can notate only inadequately or not at all, as of only secondary importance for our perception of sound *as music*. Thus the child perceives in the music that which the notation, and its realisation in the technology of instrument design demands. He attempts to notate what he hears, and not surprisingly the loop is closed.

Furthermore, what can be thus notated becomes what can be unequivocally talked about in a verbal-rational framework. And this point is of crucial importance, for what takes place is not merely a focussing of our *perception* upon the notatable and the consequent feedback upon our musical praxis, but a reorientation of our *conception* of music. Whereas previously verbal discourse had little of permanence to grasp onto in music except the very continuity and unity of established practice, which it could reinforce and stabilise by verbal decree, now musical process appeared to reveal itself concretely in the form of musical scores. The fleeting succession of musical experiences in time appeared to be captured in a continually present spatial representation which could be studied at any time, at any speed, and in any order. Just as the immediate dialectic of speech had been fundamentally subverted and devalued by the permanent monologues of the written word, so an intuitive and unverbalisable knowledge of music as an immediate dialectic of musical action and the fleeting and inscrutable musical experience was to be fundamentally challenged by the permanence and scrutability of the score. Permanently available and amenable to rationalistic verbal explication, the score rapidly usurps the sound experience of music as the focus of verbal attention and becomes the key-stone of an eminently verbalisable *conception* of what 'music' is.

Let us first consider the effects of the filtering or focussing effect of analytic notation upon our *perception* of music.

The most obvious consequence of the discovery of analytic notation is the emergence of the 'composer' who is able to challenge and expand existing musical praxis through creating notations of novel musical activities, his original scores. This development parallels remarkably the emergence of a critical philosophical tradition based on alphabetic literacy from the priest-scribe dominated world of ideogramic culture, although other social factors are clearly of importance in both cases. The novel split which gradually emerges between composer and performer, between the score and its 'interpretation' is the concrete realisation in musical praxis of the perceptual focussing upon notatable 'parameters'.

'Interpretation', still a semi-intuitive discipline, remains of great importance in the education of the musical performer who, however, remains somewhat outside the sphere of intellectual respectability. For the music scholar, however, raised in primarily verbally-based institutions, especially the new European 'University', the focus of attention is upon that musical syntax which can be discovered *in the score*. At the same time, the composer, whose musical tools are the notations at his diposal, will clearly tend to develop a musical syntax based on the organisation of these notatables. (He may concern himself with the 'interpretation' of his music, i.e. the determination of non-notatable aspects of the sound he intended, but the score will outlive the composer, and notatable syntax the unnotatable. Hence the scholarly study of any music which is not contemporary inevitably focusses primarily upon the notatable syntax).

Hence, whilst ever the musical scholar concerns himself with notation-composed works there will be a congruence of attention upon analytically notatable syntax, as scholar and composer have the same vested interest in notatability. The concatenation of scribal-domination, compositional necessity and the *limitations* of analytic notation, however, elevate the organisation of a certain limited range of musical variables to the status of 'music' as such and leads to an inevitable clash of values when the 'straight' musician comes into contact with music from an alien tradition.

Of course, not all musical praxis falls within the sphere of domination of the scribal elite. For those social groups (comprising most people at any one time in our history to date) who exist on the margins of the culture as mere economic functionaries of 'civilisation' (peasants, labourers, small-scale craftsmen and traders), music-making goes on regardless. But these groups have no access to, let alone control, of the society's symbolic records and hence their musical praxis merely goes unmentioned, and has never posed any threat to the scribe-dominated view.

On the other hand, where musicians schooled in the Western notation-tradition have taken a strong interest in folk musics for nationalist (Bartok, Janacek) or socialist (many Russian composers) reasons, the results have often been disastrous. Though well-intentioned, and sometimes (though not often) accompanied by painstaking research into the true pitch-practice etc. of the aural tradition (as in the case of Bartok), the very nature of the exercise (of transferring the full sound world of an aural praxis into the essentially restricted parameters of our culture-bound notation tradition) has often resulted in a trivialisation of folk art. One has only to compare a choral arrangement of a folk melody by one of the more workaday members of the Russian Composer's Union with an in-the-flesh performance of the original music to *hear* how much has been lost for the sake of 'harmonising' this music. Perhaps intuitively realising the dichotomy involved, Bartok was one of the few 'straight' composers to find some sort of compromise solution to this problem, compensating for the loss of pitch/rhythmic detail by the use of complex harmonic underlay. (Compare, also, the similar approach adopted by Messiaen in his 'transcriptions' of bird calls).

The twentieth-century discovery of the techniques of direct sound-recording, however, has enabled musical praxes which are not mediated via notation (at least not in the same overwhelming way) to be captured and distributed in their entirety and has hence shattered the hegemony of the notationalist view of music.

137

In the traditions of jazz and rock musics, the filtering mechanism of a notation procedure has been by-passed and elements such as subtle pitch-inflexion (especially deriving from the blues), complex rhythmic nuance, timbre control and inflexion, and subtle control of dynamic balance, acoustics and acoustic balance (made possible in the modern electronic recording studio) have returned to the foreground of musical concern for those people involved in these essentially aurally-based musical praxes.

What happens when the average 'straight' musician comes into contact with this music? Not surprisingly, we find his attention focussed upon relationships of 'pure' pitches, and rhythm insofar as it appears reducible to summative (i.e. notatable) procedures. The pitch inflexion deriving from the blues is sometimes even viewed as an inability to sing *in tune* i.e. on the 'pure' pitches laid down by our notation system. The subtlety of rhythmic nuance is summed up summarily as 'syncopation' which involves 'placing the accents off the beat'; but just how far off in each case, the notation-bound musician cannot conceive of nor, perhaps, perceive, as it is usually not measurable in simple summative-rhythmic terms. But just how far off in each case is the essential difference between an effective and ineffective *musical* experience in the genre in question.

Furthermore, the good mixing engineer achieves, by ear, the finest gradations of dynamic and acoustic balance, which are absolutely essential features of a good rock record (and of good electronic and tape musics). Yet how many musicians who have not worked in the medium are aware of this subtle art, and how many more might give it a second thought if it were brought to their attention? For the notation musician, pitch, rhythm, combinatorial timbre (the combination of instruments of traditionally-fixed timbre) and gross differentiation of dynamic level are the primary elements of 'music'; anything else is merely a kind of colouring-in of these ideal (notatable) elements, a distinction akin to that between Descartes' primary and secondary qualities. To such a view, a mere mixing engineer would hardly be worthy of serious consideration.

In the extreme case, the combination of pitch, rhythm and timbre inflexion in jazz and rock music is seen as lascivious, sexually suggestive and ultimately a threat to social order. As we can now see, this is more than a mere rejection of that which falls outside the clearly definable limits of a long-established notation (perception and conception) procedure with its verbal explicability and hence its

138

social-controllability. In a narrow sense this attitude is correct, for musical experience, even where apparently constrained by clearly explicable notation-based procedures, is ultimately irreducible to verbalisations and hence beyond any direct social control.

This dangerous state of affairs is apparent to many 'straight' music scholars and commentators, and dire moral warnings may be issued on the subject. For example, Leonard B. Meyer, in his essay 'On Value and Greatness in Music' warns against being affected by the 'mere sensuous' impact of the sound-experience itself, and goes on to praise the moral superiority of attentiveness, in both producing and listening to music, to what he sees as the musical structures, i.e. the relations perceivable by ear between elements of the music-as-notation. His view, of course, is not without reason within the framework of Western notated music, as here 'music' is conceived of (see below) as what is in the score, and the composer is confined to structuring those aspects of sound which he can portray in the notation he uses to compose with. Hence the music as heard will tend to rely strongly upon notatable structures. However, sounds still carry considerably more information, even in an ideal performance of notated music, than the notation ever could. This may be unfortunate from Meyer's point of view, but the untutored (non-filtering) listener can hardly be blamed for enjoying to the full his direct and unprejudiced musical experience. (Meyer would of course deny that this was a true 'musical' experience, but more of this later.) Furthermore, the two perceptual modes are not entirely incompatible.

Let us for a moment consider the direct response to music of the untutored, but sensitive, listener and his possible verbal explication of his experience, as compared to the Meyerian 'musician'. Most of the sounds they will ever hear are complex gestalts, even the individual 'notes' of specific instruments[6]. However, the gestalts they will hear in Western orchestral music, leaving 'interpretation' aside, are the results of combining (attempted realisations of) notatable ideal-pitches, note-values and timbres (in fact, in sound, these are merely less complex gestalts themselves). It is perfectly possible for the well trained (acutely filtering) 'musician', listening to the rich time-changing sound-gestalt of (say) the second movement of Debussy's *La Mer*, to select out the intricate inter-transformations of fragmentary motifs from which the notation of the sound-gestalt is constructed. He may listen analytically. But what of the untutored listener who says that in a somewhat vague way it reminds him of the sea? The 'musician' might respond that this response is superficial, his mind wandering . . . he was making an arbitrary association prompted by the title of the piece, or the picture on the record sleeve.

However, if we take his attempted verbalisation as a serious attempt to convey something about his, non-analytic, experience of the piece, what can we make of it? The answer is quite straightforward, though intellectually heretical. The time-changing sound-gestalt, as *sound*, has connected in that unverbalisable way we have labelled 'musical experience', articulating his 'state' in a way which is also ultimately unverbalisable . . . but in the only way he can, i.e. by citing a different experience which produced a similar articulation of his state, his experience of the sea (perhaps connecting via a similar sense of flow, breaking flow, non-precise repetition, etc.), or of the symbolic ramifications of his mental image of the sea, he is responding analogically (or poetically) to the musical experience *as such*. We might even suggest that his response was more honest in its very inarticulateness! Unfortunately, for him, however, verbal articulateness is normally regarded as the only passport to truth . . . even in music.

This is not to say that appreciation of musical syntax which can be traced back to the notation is, in itself, wrong, or necessarily unmusical in our original sense of the term . . . but that it constitutes only one factor *contributing* to our *musical* experience, and should not be given absolute priority merely because it is most capable of entering into rational-analytic discourse, as opposed to poetic-analogical discourse. The former remains immensely more valued in Western culture. (Why, otherwise, would we be writing this book!)[7]

$$* \quad * \quad * \quad * \quad *$$

Having considered the effects of analytic-notation upon our perception of music, we must now turn our attention to its impact upon our very *conception* of music and musical experience. We have already put forward the view that in an aural tradition which is relatively free from scribal coercion, the success of a musical act is judged by the player in the immediate experiential dialectic of musical action and musical experience. He will also make the assumption that his own musical response is at least similar to that of his listeners, and this assumption is confirmed in his playing with other musicians, or in the non-verbal or poetic-analogical responses of his listeners. Direct rational-analytical verbal confirmation is intrinsically impossible (what would be the point of music if it were possible?)

The first and most obvious impact of analytic notation is to transfer the musical structure out of the uni-directional continuum of experiential (Bergsonian) time (in which the musical dialectic takes place) into the spatialised perfectly reversible (Newtonian) time of the printed page[8]. In sound, the musical experience begins at the beginning and must be taken in the (irreversible) order and at the rate at which it comes to the listener. Furthermore, our experience of what arrives later is modified by our (perhaps inaccurate) memories of what has passed and, in this sense, there can never be a clear cut 'recapitulation'; everything is modified by the context of what went before. In the score, however, the whole span of the music appears to exist in a timeless, spatialised, present. We may peruse its content at any rate and in any order. In this way we may be able to perceive relationships, e.g. of recapitulation, which, however, after repeated and thorough aural experience of the music as sound we may never be able to hear. Can we thus treat such a recapitulation as an element of *musical* structure? This, of course, begs the central question of what constitutes *music,* what we experience in the sounds, or what we might theoretically appreciate of the score *through* the sounds, if our aural selectivity were more finely developed.

The best example of the split between a view of music based in unidirectional experiential time, and one based on the spatial reversibility of time as represented in the score is found in the concept of the 'retrograde' as found in serial music, and also in some medieval and Renaissance polyphony. Here the notational view is that by reversing the order of a group of notatable pitches such as:

(PRIME)

major 7th

we arrive at a pitch-set which is merely a derived form of the original:

(RETROGRADE)

major 7th

In the immediately present and spatially reversible time of the printed page the relationship of the two sets may be abundantly visually clear, but in the uni-directional and memory-dependent time of musical experience, a considerable aural retentivity and the performance of a rapid feat of mental inversion is necessary to grasp this relationship, i.e. in real time, unless the listener is forewarned that this sort of mental operation may be demanded of him, he will never become aware of such a relationship as, reading always from right to left as he *must do* in his experience, there is *no recapitulation . . .* no relationship between the sets.

Alternatively, on reaching the 'retrograde's' characteristic final leap of a major 7th, he may connect this with the similar but reverse leap of a 7th which begins the 'prime' version; he would then require a remarkably agile mind to perform a rapid mental comparison of his last ten interval experiences *in reverse order,* with the succeeding ten intervals he can remember from his experience of the prime.

In the case where the pitch set has a basically simple gestalt structure, for example:

(A)

which is basically the rising semi-chromatic scale-gestalt *x,* followed by the leaping gestalt *y,* he might retain these two shapes sufficiently to recognise a retrograde. But whether at a fairly brisk musical pace he would be capable of differentiating a true retrograde, B, from a very similar gestalt form (such as C) is highly doubtful.

142

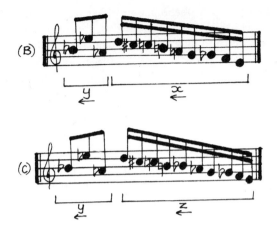

(It might be added that Schoenberg's constant use of the recapitulation of the pitch-shape of the prime using the inverted or retrograde set form but with the same intervallic direction as the original occurence of the prime, suggests that he was not unaware of this spatial-experiential dichotomy.)

When we consider even more extended use of retrograde or cancrizans form, such as the perfect arch-form of 'Der Mondfleck' from Schoenberg's *Pierrot Lunaire* where the entire movement runs in reverse order of pitches and durations from the centre point (except for the voice and piano, the latter having an elaborate fugato at the same time!), we must declare that experiential structure has been sacrificed to notational 'conceptual art'. (The idea of the cancrizans form derives from an idea in the text, where Pierrot sees his own back.) The retrograde of a 'duration series' as used in so-called 'integral serial' composition, is even more experientially problematic.

The second fundamental effect of the introduction of analytic notation and a praxis and scholarship which centres upon it is the emergence of a Platonic conception of music. Thus, just as the permanence and reproducibility of the written word 'table' appeared to Plato to project something more permanent and more 'real' than the many experienced tables of a concrete reality, so to the Western musical scholar, the musical notation appears to project something more permanent and more 'real' than the direct, but fleeting experiences of the sound of a musical performance. Music may

TREVOR WISHART

hence be regarded as a phenomenon which transcends immediate sense-experience. With the accompanying dominance of *composed* music, 'music' and its 'interpretation' can hence be distinguished from one another, and notatable syntax, discussable in a verbal space divorced from direct sense-experience, elevated to the position of Musical Syntax itself. This conception is exceptionally convenient as the fleeting moment of the total sense-experience could not be captured for direct verbal dissection in the musical mortuary, whereas the spatial, visual and non-time dependent score was ideally suited to abstract speculation.

Speculation about music *in abstracto* did not, of course, begin with analytic notation. The pythagoreans attempted to reduce the temporal experience of musical harmony to certain spatial-visual observations concerning the lengths of vibrating strings and hence began the long tradition of thought, especially prevalent in the Middle Ages and the twentieth century, which confuses musical experience with physico-geometric verbalisable laws and with abstract mathematical relations, coming to regard music itself as a form of abstract speculation. One can only wonder why such a concern with abstract form does not find fulfillment in pure mathematics, where symmetric or developmental forms may be enjoyed to the full, *in abstracto,* by a thorough study of group theory or catastrophe theory. By comparison, most musical form viewed *in abstracto,* is scarcely worthy of consideration. But the realisation of notated relations *in sound, in time* creates the experience of music, which has no such equivalent in any type of mathematical deduction (though it may be comparable to the excitement one may feel in perceiving mathematical elegance!) It is only the scribal desire to explain and control which forces the verbalisable to the forefront of their conception of music.

It was analytic notation, however, which formed the basis for closing the loop between musical perception *in abstracto* and musical conception *in abstracto,* between scholar-analyst and composer-synthesist, and which could make the Idealist conception of music appear inviolable from inside the notation tradition.

Hence, notation banishes the direct, unique, sound-experience from the realm considered as 'music' and reverses our appreciation of a sound-event. We are no longer to respond to the quality and articulation of the sound-gestalt in itself. Rather, we are only to respond to it as an attempted realisation of a conglomerate of Ideal (i.e.

144

non-existent) sound events approximated by proper attention to the notes, the counting, and the 'correct' instrumental timbre production. A musical performance is transformed from a unique trans-linguistic communion, where success or failure is directly internally verifiable for each listener, to a particular approximation to a notated Ideal form where success is validated by reference to this external form and hence taken out of the hands of performers and listeners alike and delegated to the scribehood's musical branch. Music comes under direct scribal jurisdiction.

Furthermore, there is an increasing concern to eliminate the unspecifiable effects of 'interpretation', which can be seen in the history of recent compositional practice as the interpretable 'simplicity' of Schubert's *Die Schöne Mullerein* gradually gives way to the technical complexity and specificity we find in Boulez's *Le Marteau sans Maitre* for example.

Where concrete musical relationships (at least originally based on their experiential successfulness) are represented by their notations in the score, and study and conception focuses upon this structure, divorced from the experiential (erotic) immediacy of the sound itself, these relationships, as *rediscovered* in the score, may be mistaken for *conventional* relationships, i.e. what, to direct musical experience may appear as *necessary* relationships, in that it is only through that particular musical structure that a successful communication of the kind intended can take place[9], can come to appear in the score as merely *arbitrary* permutations of 'notes' and 'time-values'. On the timeless flat surface of the score the visual-spatial relationships of the notes (used to represent real time) may be changed at will to produce arbitrarily arrived at visual-spatial structures, all having equal validity in visual space, but not necessarily so in experiential time.

Once, however, we demand that music be heard *in terms of* the score, then it is no longer experiential success which justifies notational visual-spatial arrangements, but notational arrangements become their own justification. Hence, 'musical form' may become freed from any restriction of direct experiential successfulness, in our original terms.

This leads ultimately to a rational formalism in music. The composer establishes certain visual relationships between entities in his notation, the musical scholar is trained to listen for these relationships, he hears them and a successful 'musical' communication is declared to have taken place.

The composer may even go to a great deal of trouble to determine exactly what it is possible to hear, in this rationalist sense. This is the basis of the aesthetic of a serial composer such as Milton Babbitt. However, the question of what differentiates one structure from another, what could impel us to listen to one piece rather than another seems unanswerable, except in the tautologous sense that the structures are *de facto* different, or in the ultimately absurd reductionist view that more, and more complex, relationships makes for 'better' music[10].

This beautifully closed rationalist view of music is the ultimate in scribal sophistication, it is complete and completely unassailable in its own terms. Music is hence completely socially definable and musical success may almost be measured with a slide rule. How much more tidy and convenient such a norm-adherent view of music than one bringing in the messy business of inter-personal, yet unverbalisable, (even erotic!) dialectics. The rationalist view of music fits ideally into a technocratic age with its linguistic and positivist ideologies . . . what we cannot talk about we cannot know, only that which we can talk about is real . . . so much for music!

Thus, ultimately, the score becomes its own rationale. It is what it is, and there is nothing more to say about it. The composer cannot be in error. (Of course, not all composers, even today, accept this absurd view! There are often other criteria involved in composition even where composers refuse, in a strictly positivist way, to talk about them.)

In contrast, an aural tradition, such as most jazz or rock, relying on the immediate dialectic between musical action and the musical experience *in toto* has no need and little room for these conventional fictions. (The long-established Indian scribal elite have, of course, attempted to make the necessary incisions in the Indian musical tradition for them to grasp and hold it.) The contrast between the autocratic centralism of the orchestra made possible through the normative authority of the score, and the democratic solidarity of the jazz group made possible by the immediate dialectic of a shared musical praxis and experience is not without wider significance.

It is only the advent of mechanical and electronic sound-recording techniques which has permitted equally thorough alternative, but non-filtering, traditions of musical study to take root. Here we can capture the unique musical experience *in toto* and study it time and time again, but in a real experiential time, not in the fictional spatialised time of the score.

Via these techniques also we have rediscovered the incredibly inaccurate fiction of the score, which attempts to notate the infinitely divisible temporal continuum of musical time in the finitistic code of analytic notation. When, for example, we play our tone row on the piano (example A), record it and play it backwards, not only is the pitch succession reversed, as in the notated retrograde (see example B), but the entire dynamic and timbral envelope of the piano sounds (see D), such that the resulting sound (see E), is barely recognisable as timbrally related to the original and is utterly different from the notated retrograde (B) as played on the piano.

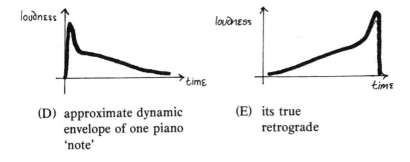

(D) approximate dynamic   (E) its true
     envelope of one piano   retrograde
     'note'

It is this direct experience of the continuum of musical time among other things, which has shattered the notation-bound preconceptions of many 'straight' musicians coming into contact with electronic studio work, and which still tends to divide off tape-music from mainstream 'straight' music as rarely worthy of serious musical scholarship. For this reason also, electronic musicians, still feeling that they must kow-tow to the verbal elite, have somewhat defensively tended to surround themselves with extensive technical tracts on 'generating procedures', 'hardware' and other matters acceptable, if not to the musical, then to the scientific branch of the scribehood, rather than risk their intellectual respectability by just doing the music and abandoning inadequate verbal rationalisations. (There is a sound practical politics behind this however: electronic equipment is expensive, and the scribehood holds the key to the purse.)

The tape-recorder in fact allows us to delay, recheck and refine the direct musical dialectic of an aural-tradition, performance-bound art. In the modern recording studio, with its multi-tracking facilities, we can lay down one track at a time, performing each line over and over again until it is judged, *aurally,* to be precisely what we desire, until the direct musical experience resulting from the musical action is thoroughly and precisely refined through direct unmediated reference to that, now repeatable, experience. Similarly, the tape-composer can work directly with the whole gamut of sound materials (electronic, notated-performed, improvised-performed, natural and so on) checking and rechecking his frequency, temporal-succession, dynamic balance and acoustic design against his direct and repeatable experience of the results. We can compose directly in experiential time.

In sharp contrast it is still possible, and common, in electronic music, usually pursued in scribal institutions such as universities (though not in pop music, where real musical dialectics holds the key to the purse!) to adopt the rationalist approach and produce utterly explicable, but un-musical experiences. In fact, the original response of the 'musician's' truncated conception of music to the advent of electronic sound generation techniques was to see the sine-wave as the Platonic Ideal-pitch made manifest, so to speak. Notational constructivism could now be translated into a concrete constructivism as compositions would be directly synthesised from component sine-waves, within the strictly formalist permutational aesthetic of integral serialism. As a result a great deal of highly explicable and experientially arid serial electronic music was produced.

Fortunately it did not take a long time for the better composers to realise that to construct just one single interesting sound purely from sine-tones was a painful and arduous task and that such a purist approach was rather pointless in that, once constructed, the new sound-complex was, generally speaking, experienced as a gestalt and in relation to other gestalts as such, and not in relation to its and their internal (Fourier-analysable) structure.

The scientific rationale for the approach had lain in the fact that all sounds may be expressed (in principle) in terms of a sum (possibly infinite and possibly over a continuum of values) of sine-waves. Therefore sounds may be constructed out of sine tones, and relationships established between such sounds and/or between their components. As in the case of pitch combination the same problem arises as to whether the relationships established are experientially valid. However, whereas notational constructivism was backed-up by an (ultimately circular) appeal to the score, the new concrete constructivism was supported by scientistic reductionism. Although in specific cases the constructed relationship between the sine-wave components of two (or more) sound-gestalts may account for the fact that we perceive them to be significantly related, this is neither a necessary nor a sufficient condition. To state that the sounds *must* be musically related because the relationship exists as a physical fact in the structure of the sound waves in the air, or as a physiological fact in the sound-responsive mechanism of the ear is merely an *a priori* assertion. It states merely what we *ought* to perceive, or which relationships we ought to consider important, according to the ideology of this particular school. It appears plausible only because the physical and physiological reduction of mental/symbolic processes has become an intellectually respectable pastime, not to say a major component of technocratic ideology.

Only with notations, abstractions from experiential reality, is our attention focussed upon *relationships between* 'pure' elements, these relationships becoming the substance of analysis . . . the pure elements, the notes themselves, remaining pure figments, beyond actual sense experience. When translated into *sound* and listened to *as sound*, the experiential reality of the sounds themselves loom as large as their notatable interrelationships. Similarly it is only by an act of self-conscious renunciation, an internal visual distancing, that we can confine our attention to the constructed relationships between constituent sine-waves of a sequence of electronic sounds (except, of course, where relationships have been chosen in some way which has *independently* proved to be experientially valid). This mode of listening requires an ideological commitment to visual rationality, in the form of a reductionist theory of perception, and it is this commitment which completes the circularity of the system. To the listener without these preconceptions however, the sine-wave cannot have this special status of a 'pure' element. It is yet another concrete experience impinging on his 'state'. Hence the focussing of attention on the relationships between sine-tone constituents becomes an arbitrary and pointless exercise. Either the relationships between these elements will affect his experience, or they will not. The electronic constructivist merely equates the syntax of his own musical action with some theoretical syntax of

149

response, demanded of the listener.

In contrast, in the sphere of rock music, the new but considered aurality made possible by direct sound-recording, has been a major factor from the start. For example, the successful singer will exploit the unique expressive qualities of his particular voice-tone, directly capturable by the recording apparatus, rather than attempting, like the trained 'straight' singer, to approximate to an ideal 'pure' type. Similarly, as in jazz, the group achieves a democratic solidarity in the immediate dialectic of their performance experience, which may, however, be further refined in the recording studio by repeated attempts to musically 'act' the new track in immediate response to the tracks already laid down. The tape-recorder and gramophone have further enabled this new, direct experientially-based musical tradition to extend to millions of young music-lovers, far beyond the realms of any scribal domination and certification of 'musical competence'.

The real potentiality of direct recording techniques for 'straight' tape-composition is to re-establish a direct, but repeatable, experiential dialectic with the sounds we use and hence make considered composition identical in substance with the experiential dialectic of aural-tradition performance art.

In striving for new possibilities of musical expression and communication, we must adopt the empirical, as opposed to the rationalist-constructivist method, just as the musically 'uneducated' group musician does when he is putting together an album in the studio. As our basic material is no longer dictated by instrument technology and notational restrictions we can begin with any generation procedure, from search and find missions with portable tape-recorders to open-ended improvisation sessions with any desired sources of sound (any type of object, including musical instruments, and electronic synthesis) and so on. We may generate gestalts which are not premeditated by notational rationality. We may also perform tape and electronic operations on such material to produce further material.

From this field of unique sound-events, which could not have been pre-conceived in their total complexity, we may select sound-events and relationships amongst them, which we wish to use. But all the time, the usefulness of any material and the validity of any relationships which we may wish to establish between such sounds must be checked *experientially* by our direct response to these relationships. In particular, we cannot automatically assume that the relationship between sounds which are inter-derivable by some electronic process of transformation is therefore *necessarily* experientially valid. This can only be checked by listening, otherwise we fall back into the rational-constructivist trap and the technical operation of transformation becomes its own rationale. This empirical procedure does not rule out the use of notation as part of the process whereby sound-events are generated but choice of materials and relationships to be used is ultimately governed by experiential validity, and not by the rationale of the notation or construction itself.

In this way we may produce utterly inexplicable, but successful musical communications which should as a result also re-establish some contact between avant-garde 'straight' musicians and a wider, non-filtering, musical public[11].

NOTES

1.　This is not strictly true. Notational procedures have led some people to the view that music is essentially abstract. This view will be discussed below.

2.　An interesting example of this is to be found in the neumic notation of Tibetan chant (cf. Kaufmann, 1967, where a single curvilinear neume might indicate changes in pitch, duration and timbre).

3.　This is not *strictly* the case. Different letters do not *necessarily* correspond directly to different sounds, but this does not alter the fundamental basis of our argument here.

4.　Bach's *Art of Fugue*, arguably one of the finest achievements of the traditional Art-music of Europe, illustrates our thesis in an interesting way. Bach confines himself to the notation of pitch and (summative) rhythm, leaving unspecified dynamics *and even timbre (instrumentation)*, both of which are usually notated (or at least indicated in the score).

Although this approach may appear to approximate very closely to the 'abstract' view of music, we would argue that the work is, however, *not* an illustration of 'rational formalism' as discussed below, as the score notates sets of relations between sound-qualities which are experientially valid (see text) even if the range of possibilities is necessarily restricted by the nature of the notation system itself.

5.　In fact there arises a distinction in musical consciousness between precisely-notatables (pitch and summative-rhythm, the 'basic' elements of music) and less precisely-, or non-notatables (dynamics, timbre, inflexion, phrasing etc.), a kind of 'colouring-in' of the basic material, akin to that between Descartes' 'primary' and 'secondary' qualities. This parallel is not fortuitous, as both splits may be related in some sense to the cultural effects of the medium of writing (printing).

6.　Generally speaking, any 'note' produced by an instrument consists of a fundamental frequency (which usually determines the perceived pitch) and certain of its harmonics, all with specific relative loudnesses and specific inter-relations of phase. The details of these relationships may vary a great deal over the whole range of the instrument (both its frequency-range and its loudness-range). Furthermore the beginning ('attack') and end ('decay') of the sound may have very different and very specific qualities. The task of accurately analysing, and thence synthesising, instrumental sounds has only recently been achieved, using computer technology.

7.　The whole (footnoted and referenced) style of this book panders to the reification of *written down* opinions. Take care!

8.　I am indebted to Jan Steele for the following line of argument re Bergsonian time and the problem of musical retrogrades.

9.　See note 4 above, particularly the remarks in the second paragraph.

10.   Schoenberg, the originator of the serial method, was clearly not unaware of this notational-Ideal/Experiential dichotomy we have discussed. In actual practice the 'harmonic style' of his later serial works is not greatly dissimilar to that of his pre-serial 'expressionist' works, where the harmonic tensions characteristic of tonal music can still be felt even though traditional tonal progressions have disappeared. Having abandoned tonality as a basis it would seem that Schoenberg still felt the need to rely on an intuitive 'feel' for harmonic relationships, and this approach is characteristic of his musical language with or without serialism. This fact is underlined by the rejection of Schoenberg's 'backward-looking' approach by proponents of the post-Webern school of serial (and integral serial) composition.

The fundamental conflict between the two views of music is in fact most clearly expressed in the symbology of the serial opera *Moses and Aaron*. The conflict between Moses' view of God as the all-pervasive, yet ultimately intangible, Idea, and Aaron's desire to relate God to tangible experience, is represented at a surface level by a *verbal/musical* dichotomy [Moses' part is confined to heightened speech (*sprechstimme*), while Aaron sings expressive melodic lines] and at a deeper level by a *notational/experiential* dichotomy (the tone-row is all-pervasive in the score as the structural material out of which the opera is built, but is not *generally* audible).

The second act (the end of the opera as it exists) ends with a dramatic duologue in which Moses (the speaker) holding the tablets of the *written law*, confronts Aaron (the singer) and finally breaks the tablets declaring 'O Wort, du Wort, das mir fehlt' (O Word, you have failed me). In the archetypal ideology of Schoenberg's biographer, Stuckenschmidt (1959), 'Moses . . . clings to eternity, metaphysics and *real* values . . . Aaron is a materialist of everyday life *who is impressed by the glitter of gold and the successes of the moment*'[my italics]. However, the fact that Schoenberg felt unable to write the third act of the opera, in which Moses' view triumphs has, in the light of the present discussion, far-reaching significance for an understanding of contemporary avant-garde music.

11.   This entire chapter is an expansion of a shorter paper with the same title, forming part of a D.Phil portfolio, University of York (1973).

PART TWO

Chapter Five

Some Observations on the Social Stratification of Twentieth-Century Music

PHIL VIRDEN and TREVOR WISHART

Sociology identifies the rules by which meaningful behaviour is generated and interpreted. But beyond recognising that our behaviour is ordered and made predictable and social by reference to 'normative structures', an explanatory sociology remembers that the institutional arrangements of our lives are maintained or changed by interested people. There is a political-economy, specific material and ideal interests, behind the ordering of life. If sociology serves any purpose, it is to locate the centres of rule systems and to draw forth the implications for the various parties to the interactions that maintain them. Any particular sphere of activity must be situated in its general historical context, the wide matrix of social relations of the time, if the import of that activity is ever to be grasped[1].

In Chapter Three above John Shepherd has argued that medieval music articulated an idealisation of its society, and that the evolution of the tonal system of music out of organum could be interpreted as the encoding of a new hierarchical musical ideology out of a more mutual form. This explicit development of the possibilities implicit in the earlier form not only depended upon the development of new techniques — the notation of music, the tempered keyboard — and the patronage of certain social interests — in particular the emergent bourgeoisie — but, moreover, expressed musically the nationalised and centralised hierarchy that was actually emerging throughout economic, political and cultural life. The transformational generative rules for tonality were thus established as a musical accompaniment to the emergence of a new

155

general sense and organisation of the human world.

John Shepherd's detailed analysis provides a broad picture that is consistent with Marx's dictum that the ruling ideology is the ideology of the ruling class. We will not quarrel with that. But, in this chapter we will discuss certain polar trends in the musics of the 'European' industrialised world of this century. Whereas there is comparatively limited evidence of the variety and constitution of medieval music, with notation and especially electrical recording, we are faced with an embarrassingly rich field of evidence for twentieth century musics. Nevertheless we wish to show a certain connection between some developments in recent and contemporary musics and the ideological functions these developments might entail. Specifically, we will emphasise that within the continuing hegemony of tonality there is evidence for a relatively separate tradition of genuine folk musics[2], which do not operate completely or even mainly according to the assumptions or rules of tonality. And, correlatively, the way the elite tradition in music has tried to come to terms with the century-old crisis in tonality has involved little change in ideology and hence no true transcendence of tonal consciousness. Musics are largely stratified in our culture and this is the musical expression of the general social-political, economic and cultural-class system of industrial societies. If medieval pentatonicism stresses a quite different organisation of musical/social experience from the tonality that emerged from within it, so we can discern different, class-based, musical systems serving different functions and singing of different ideals within contemporary life.

The different musical forms that live within industrial 'Western' cultures are *not* to be understood as nothing more than more or less sophisticated or barbaric approximations to tonality. Church music and the manufacturing of commercially popular songs have mediated between the music of the elite and that of the folk. But throughout the reign of tonality there seem to have existed subterranean folk musical traditions organised on principles different from tonality, and often modal: Celtic songs and blues are obvious examples. But even if the basis for the music of the folk has been tonal the important thing about its production has been that its complexity has not existed in extended and notated harmonic development but in what Chester (1970) has termed an intensional elaboration. Even working from relatively simple (which does not mean ineffectual) chord progressions the Afro-American folk artist, for example, weaves an elaborate extemporisation of melody and an expressive nuance of rhythm, timing and tone, within the given structure. We will argue that the reason this should happen is that the musics of elites and of the dispossessed serve different purposes.

The modern age has witnessed a wide separation of elite and mass, a difference that extends deeply into the very ways of experiencing and uttering reality. Culture has become divided and the divisions are both symptoms and reproductions of class systems of rigidly divided labour. Social theorists have long been aware that participation in the ownership and control of material or intellectual property creates a different relation to the world and a different interest from the non-participation of people who can only sell their labour power. The profit-motivated 'efficient' division of labour has 'rationally' separated functional communities according to the dictates of an industrial technology and market. Schematically, there are those whose habitual practice is theoretical, whose function is ownership and control, and an intellectual, abstract operation upon the world; and there are those dispossessed from their material products and from their own potential of consciousness and decision, who labour according to the dictates of those with authority over them.

Of course, any particular society at any particular time will display a class structure of more varied interest groupings, according to the cross-cutting interests around particular forms of property, of material interests, knowledge and skills. But the dichotomous model expresses the essence of an alienation mandated by a thorough hierarchical organisation of society around the specialisation of functions. The dispossessed are separated not only from the products of their labour but, in the routines of daily drudgery, from certain of their intellectual potentials. We might, for example, view the education process as the separation of children of the working class especially from their full intellectual potential[3]. The experience of the parents in industrial subservience reinforces an attitude against verbal explicitness which we will briefly explore below. Conversely the ruling elements, in possession of power and privilege, tend to be alienated from the possibilities of an immediate life of the unselfconscious body.

There is plenty of evidence from many cultures that a strict, rigid and extensive division of labour produces quite different experiences and differences in symbolic articulation between the classes. In terms of avowed values, the class continuum shows a polarisation of attitudes between the owning, ruling classes and the working classes. Most workers tend to be dissatisfied with their work, and have adapted to an incomprehensible and massively unmoveable physical and human world (including their own 'human nature'). They also tend to be concerned with immediate material interests, to abide by the mandates of external authority, and to seek security in communal strength rather than individual assertion. Their orientation matches a realistic appraisal of their place in the social order. Conversely, the voluntaristic optimism and individualism of better placed groups reflects their actual situation and activity, a tendency to internal compulsion and a competence built on a distanced and abstract mediation [4].

More interesting than this obvious difference in orientations is the way the division of labour entrenches a polarity of communication situations in daily life. Systematically different problems in daily life generate systematically different ways of articulating and dealing with the problems. According to Bernstein, working class role relations favour a communication code emphasising verbally the communal rather than the individual, the concrete rather than the abstract, surfaces rather than processes, immediate behaviour rather than intentions, statuses rather than individual personalities. Different speech codes create different orders of relevance and relations for their speakers, and so determine cognitive, emotive and conative experience. Speech is specific to functions, to the control of environment, and the learning of speech and of roles is thus the same process. Role is ' . . . a constellation of shared, learned meanings through which individuals are able to enter stable, consistent, and publicly recognised forms of interaction with others'. It is ' . . . a complex coding activity controlling both the creation and organisation of specific meanings and their conditions for transmission and reception' (Bernstein, 1973b, p.167). Meaningful, relevant, related behaviour conforms to expectations (although, of course, these change to a greater or lesser extent in the social process). Where, with the 'solid' working class, identifications are closely shared and one person's world is very much like another's, a restricted coding of reality is sufficient. There is no need to elaborate meanings or make speech explicitly or sequentially logical, but a great need to confirm that 'I am like you'. By contrast, where the intent of others cannot be taken for granted, people must elaborate and make explicit and clear their meanings. With working class role systems the child typically enters rigidly defined ready-made statuses, established systems of meaning, and leaves them relatively unchanged. But middle class children typically achieve meaning by verbally manipulating their world. Thus, in such person-orientated role systems (the tendency of the middle-class), roles are potentially flexible and control is psychological, whilst in positional families (which are mostly typical of the working-classes), role and status boundaries are not achieved explicitly through the verbal social process, and emotional sensitivity is not made explicit. People tend to be seen in object terms rather than as unique personalities; control is rigidly authoritarian, and change can only be effected by violent and incoherent rebellion.

The speech of the upper classes will typically be that speech closer approaching the grammarians' ideal, whereas working class people will use a more predictable, less 'complex' (in the grammarians' sense) variety of language. Crucially, a restricted code assumes a shared knowledge of the cosmos and does not make the intent and knowledge of the speaker conscious. It is an exophoric speech style in which the discourse is not reflexive — does not refer back to itself, — but makes *implicit* (i.e., unuttered) reference to the world, reference which the audience is *assumed* to know. Anaphoric speech, on the contrary, is reflexive in that the world is first explicitly named, many more assumptions are carefully explicated, and then speech proceeds by constant reference back to the named subjects of the discourse. The variation between elaborated and restricted codes can be assessed along the following dimensions: restricted speech is simpler synctactically; it is more predictable in construction and lexes; finished utterances are shorter; sentences are 'less perfectly' (in terms of the grammarians' ideal) constructed; there are fewer variations in conjugations, subordination and use of the passive; fewer and less various adjectives and adverbs are used; the impersonal pronoun is seldom used but greater use is made of the nominal head; there is greater use of exophoric than of anaphoric pronouns (pronouns that make reference to objects assumed to be in the *environment* rather than already referred to in the discourse); there is a greater use of sympathetic circularity ('you know?', 'didn't I?', etc.), a greater use of clichés and idiomatic lexes and phrases and, in all, a lower organisation of informational content and less ability to hold a formal subject through a speech sequence.

With a restricted coding meaning depends upon extra-verbal contexts since it is very condensed. The intent of the listener is taken for granted, verbal planning is low and such speech enhances disjunctive thought. Qualification is impersonal rather than individual and the elaboration of the uniqueness of individual feelings is implicit, or gestural. Such speech focuses on the immediate, descriptive and categoric, rather than the mediate, abstract and hypothetical. The social conditions enhancing the development of a restricted code are those of coercive rather than symbolic control, and of a routinised rather than an eventful social process. The status dimensions of coercive hierarchy demand relatively little complex articulation for their comprehension, whereas the more sophisticated utterance and negotiation of liberal bourgeois social life demands a certain curiosity, openness to new experience and exploration. For the extreme restricted code speaker there is only one code, just as there is only one possible role. The code reinforces communality and a premium is on communication, fluency and solidarity, not upon *what* is said [5].

Now artworks in general are best understood as prescriptions for perception, conception and hence, ultimately, the organisation of our moral and political activity. We have suggested above that there is a dialectical relationship between our modes of social organisation around our material needs — the division of labour and power relationships — and mental or symbolic life. This seems very plausible so far as the constructions of speech are concerned. People in different social situations, facing problems of relation similar to those similarly situated, but quite different to those in different milieux, are constrained to develop certain powers of abstract (spoken) articulation but not others. Bernstein's theory of the relation between speech and conceptual modes and social context can perhaps be widened to become a more general theory of the relation between symbolisation and sociality. Since we communicate by channels other than the verbal, it would seem likely that artworks hold different messages and are constructed and interpreted by different rules for different people in widely dissimilar social situations. In general we might expect that, as with the speech of the ruling elements, the functional emphasis is upon explicitness within any of the art modes. And, for the working class the intentions of artworks are best communicated implicitly. The functions, and hence the forms of artworks might be quite different between the classes within a society at one time[6].

Meaning has existence within the relationships between the terms of the social process. Intention is expressed by messages signalled via the various sensory modes. Speech is the abstract way of indicating anything and everything, including events in other symbolic orders and including itself. Music is also intended sound, which indicates symbolically and globally, and moves us globally and concretely as well as intellectually. Speech actually includes more than compounds of the discrete meanings of the words uttered. Meaning is not exclusive to the words which formulate the world in detached abstraction. The gestalt of sounds which constitute an utterance is the 'music' of speech, and the attack, the rhythms, the intonation of the melody are absolutely meaningful. The separation of 'song', or 'music', from 'speech' is an aspect of an alienated sense of the world, a symptom of our denial of the unity of being. So too is our attribution of Truth only to the (written) word and to what we suppose to be the discourses of natural science and our ordering of our sensorial powers or symbolic modes in a hierarchy of importance. Music articulates an essential part of our lives. The relationships of social life — the class structure — and attitudes towards them are articulated as much by musical as by verbal forms.

This analogy between the 'languages' of speech and of music can be highlighted by comparing what Bernstein has to say about a 'restricted coding' of speech with Chester's (1970) formulation of the 'intensional' development of musical form:

> A [restricted coding] contains its own aesthetic, a simplicity and directness of expression, emotionally virile, pithy and powerful and a metaphoric range of considerable force and appropriateness. Some examples [of the writings of working class children] taken from the schools . . . have a beauty which many writers might well envy. This is not to say that speakers of this language interact in a completely uniform manner, for the potential of a [restricted coding] allows a vast range of possibilities (Bernstein, 1973a, p 76)
>
> . . . a restricted code is the basic code. It is the code of intimacy which shapes and changes the very nature of subjective experience, initially in the family and in our close personal relationships. The intensifications and condensations of such communication carry us beyond speech and new forms of awareness often become possible . . . (Bernstein, 1973a, p 78)

Western classical music is the apodigm of the *extensional* form of musical construction. Theme and variations, counter-

PHIL VIRDEN

point (as used in classical composition) are all devices that build diachronically and synchronically outwards from basic musical atoms. The complex is created by the combination of the simple, which remain discrete and unchanged in the complex unity. Thus a basic premise of classical music is rigorous adherence to standard timbres, not only for the various orchestral instruments, but even for the most flexible of all instruments, the human voice. Room for interpretation of the written notation is in fact marginal .... The rock idiom does know forms of extensional development but it cannot compete in this sphere with a music based on this principle of construction.

Rock, however, follows, like many non-European musics, the path of *intensional* development. In this mode of construction the basic musical units (played/sung notes) are not combined through space and time as simple elements into a complex structure. The simple entity is that constituted by the parameters of melody, harmony, and beat, while the complex is built up by modulation of the basic notes, and by inflexion of the basic beat. (The language of this modulation and inflexion derives partly from conventions internal to the music, partly from the conventions of spoken language and gesture, partly from physiological factors.) All existing genres and sub-types of the Afro-American tradition show various forms of the combined intensional and extensional development .... The 12-bar structure of the blues, which for the critic reared on extensional forms seems so confining, is viewed quite differently by the bluesman, for he builds 'inwards' from the 12-bar structure and not 'outwards'. Complexity is multidimensional and by no means strictly quantifiable, and the aesthetic capacity of a musical form cannot be measured by complexity alone, but the example of the country blues shows the complete adequacy of a purely intensional mode of construction to an immensely subtle and varied project of aesthetic expression (Chester, 1970, pp 78-79).

While we would disagree with some of this formulation (for example Chester uses the term 'modulation' in a loose sense), the central intuition is clearly useful. The rural blues, as we argue later, in part two of this chapter, is in fact a simple pentatonic structure but with extremely complex inflexion of pitch, timbre, attack and rhythm which defies notational analysis. The idiosyncratic *sounds* of the different blues artists, rather than the specifiable *notes* they play and sing, are the heart of the artform. Such music, working more immediately from forms which when explicated appear quite simple, develop complex and subtle meanings by the *way* of playing and

162

singing rather than by explicit elaborations upon the central form. The meaning of the music lies not only with *what* is uttered but more importantly with *how* it is uttered in the context of the performance. In a restricted coding of verbal communication a nod's as good as a wink, and so too in contemporary folk musics — in the blues and in strongly Afro-American derived jazz and rock — the nuance of intonation holds much of the meaning.

We are arguing that the symbolic modes of the ruling elements tends to explicitness and those of the dispossessed to implicitness[7]. In music the explicits may be laid bare by the translation of soundflows into visual marks, the score, or vice versa. The emphasis upon the implicit — that which cannot be exactly translated — is favoured by those who live, in a more or less besieged manner, in a close communality which divorces itself from the values of the prevailing culture. We do not deny that tonality remains the dominant musical language within the 'European' tradition[8]. As with any cultural field there will be a tendency for the dominant 'language' to invade others that might try to coexist. So, in music, we should expect that the conventions of the forms favoured by the ruling elements would exert a great deal of influence upon the music of the general population. We should equally expect almost a complete lack of 'pollution' of elite music by any music generated by the peoples. So far as the bourgeoisie is concerned the mass of population has little music, and what can be heard through 'the noise' is a debased, unimaginative copy of tonal music[9]. What we might expect, however, assuming that the great differences in musical preferences and productions between the classes are not differences between good and bad musics, is that there are different rules for generating (both good and bad) music for the ruling and working classes because what the musics have to say is quite different.

We will therefore suggest that any musical production in the twentieth century might be arranged somewhere along a continuum ranging from almost totally extensional or explicit elaboration within the piece to almost totally intensional or implicit elaboration. Very generally, approaches deriving from the traditions of tonal music can be adopted and used more or less intensionally. Thus a great deal of commercially popular music this century, the songs derived from the light operetta, the musical and ballad tradition, especially until the late 1950s, might be seen in this light. Similarly, intensional

163

forms can be elaborated along more extensional lines. It might be argued that jazz, at certain periods in its short history, has shown a tendency towards the explicit developments of harmony and formal procedures (for example, cool jazz and, in particular, third stream music). Likewise certain ('progressive') rockbands, like Emerson, Lake and Palmer and Yes, often containing academically-trained white middle-class musicians, have leaned towards the explicit elaboration of harmony and form.

Within this continuum of musical languages the blues, a major source for many of the significant features of jazz and rock musics, may be viewed as exemplifying one extreme pole, in 'opposition' to the system of tonality. The blues singer-guitarist who could be only two or three generations away from Africa, and living in excommunication or relative isolation from European culture, sang what certainly appears to be a 'restricted' musical coding that develops implicitly by inflexion. It is immediate, non-literate and passed on in an oral-aural tradition. More than this, being pentatonic it organises the terms of its musical system upon the principle of 'mutual communality' rather than within the hierarchy of diatonic harmony. The approach to intended sound and the organisation of the sound is thus quite opposed to the approach and organisation that bourgeois music has decreed in its explicit development of 'pure', well-tempered tones. This tends to confirm our underlying thesis: that different musics encode deeply different relationships between people and between people and their realities.

Furthermore the explosion of Afro-American and Afro-American influenced musics during this century may be seen as strongly related to changes and developments in social relations. The electrification of communication, through recording and broadcasting devices, has brought the whole of the industrial world face-to-face in sound. Sounds competed in the market and, despite the opposition of the dominant culture, the music of those *within* the culture but not *of* it, the blacks, found resonance with the experience of others who felt alienated from the established order. The black basis of today's 'popular' music is the musical expression of a generation in conflict with the values of its elders. For a large part of the young born before the Second World War, 'crooning' and the sweetened jazz way was the ideal expression of the rhythms of life. In the conflict of the generations in advanced industrial countries, the young of the 1950s dug deeper into the American black folk tradition to express a wider difference between the generations' experiences of their times. The heroic voicings of songs began to express not only in the lyrics a more immediate, demystified and tougher individual stance, but the whole musical system turned a darker shade of black[10]. This copying, assimilation and elaboration of black musical conventions and techniques, a strident and unsophisticated assertion of a new mass consciousness, came as a shock to those committed to the established order. Beginning among working class youth, the expression of the dissent of the dispossessed became articulated by ever wider sections of the young. The frontiers of jazz and rock may be seen as expressing not only an alienation from mainstream culture but an alternative attitude to the world. The predominant 'chant-like' nature of the music, often displaying modal features[11], and the focus upon immediate extemporising variation and/or the stress upon idiosyncratic creation of intensional elaboration, makes Afro-American musics expressions of opposition to the bourgeois view of the social order.

In order to throw into sharp relief the very real differences that exist between the extremes of the continuum mentioned above, it is useful to stress the ideological implications of musical systems developed by the *ruling* groups in the twentieth century. Though there is not space here to argue a detailed case[12], it may be pointed out that serialism, the most coherent formulation of a 'new' system of musical organisation, can be viewed as growing out of the well-known 'crisis' of traditional harmony generally agreed to have been precipitated by Wagner's *Tristan und Isolde* and, in a certain sense (especially in the tradition of the second Viennese school[13]), implies tonal hierarchy in its very negation. This thesis, with its clear ideological (and musical) implications, is underlined by the rejection of all that seemed to them 'regressive' in this music by the succeeding school of so-called Integral Serialists[14], itself initiating a new stage in the articulation of ruling class ideology through music[15].

* * * * *

Clearly, the field of twentieth-century music is both vast and extremely diverse (compared, for example, with previous epochs). This diversity can itself be seen as relating to the high level of social stratification in our society. In this short chapter we have only been able to give some indication of how the general approach developed in this book might be applied to an understanding of the many musical systems. In order, therefore, to lend support to our *sociological* interpretation of the ideological bases of twentieth-century musics, the second part of this chapter will be devoted to a more detailed *musical* analysis of the blues. We have chosen the blues because it is an ideal-typical example of the music of a dispossessed group and represents one extreme pole of the continuum of musical production we have elucidated above.

The Blues: An Ideal-Typical Example[16]

This part of the chapter is concerned with the *authentic* blues tradition (including varieties of both country blues and city blues), as opposed to 'the blues as used in jazz' (Schuller, 1968, p 44). Many of the people who have written on the blues have been either jazz musicians or musicians trained in the 'classical' tradition.[17]. Consequently, they have tended to talk about the blues scale from the perspective of jazz musicians. Thus, for example, Winthrop Sargeant (quoted, Schuller, 1968, p 44) suggests that 'the blues scale as used in jazz really divides into two identical tetrachords', and gives the following musical example:

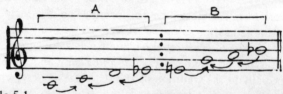

Example 5.1

However, it is clear that these tetrachords (and in particular the notes A and D) are not characteristic of authentic blues itself, no matter how frequently they are used in jazz. Further, there is a tendency for these writers to talk about an accommodation between pentatonicism and tonality (see below). It will be argued here, however, that authentic blues is *fundamentally* pentatonic.

We will begin by considering the alternative theories. Hodeir (1956, p 42) and Borneman (quoted, Middleton, 1972, p 37) suggest that the blue notes arise as a result of the difficulty experienced by blacks in accomodating an assumed indigenous pentatonic scale of the form:

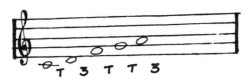

Example 5.2

to Western diatonic practice. Hodeir, for example, states confidently: 'as we know, these blue notes resulted from the difficulty experienced by the negro when the hymns taught him by the missionaries made him sing the third and seventh degrees of the scale used in European music, since these degrees do not occur in the primitive five-note scale.'

There can be three objections to this view. Firstly, the theory ascribes the most characteristic expressive feature of the blues, the inflexion of pitch, merely to a cross-cultural mishap. Secondly, the third and seventh degrees of the scale are not in practice the only bent notes. In particular, the fifth degree is quite often inflected downwards, and to some extent all of the notes may be bent (whether the inflexion is up or down). Thirdly, and most important of all, this theory takes for granted the importance of all the other five notes of the Western diatonic scale (i.e., all the notes except the third and the seventh), *including* the second and sixth degrees (D and A). This assumption is not borne out in practice (see below), and illustrates the culture-specific nature of this approach, since it automatically assumes that blues uses a seven note scale.

The second alternative theory to be considered is that of Schuller (1968, p 44):

> We have also pointed out that while African melody tends to emphasise pentatonism [sic], the use of the subdominant and the leading tone is by no means uncommon. Including these two [see below Example 5.3, Schuller's Example 14] marked x [in Example 5.3], we have, of course, the scale known in European music as the diatonic scale.

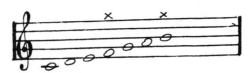

Example 5.3

It should first of all be noted that the pentatonic formation Schuller starts from is different from that assumed by Hodeir (i.e., of the form TT3T3, rather than T3TT3). This merely serves to underline

Example 5.4

the hypothetical nature of these theories of origin. The main point, however, is whether the African music referred to by Schuller is pentatonic or diatonic in its 'deep structure'. As John Shepherd has pointed out in Chapter Three in relation to plainchant:

> It is not necessary, in order to demonstrate the existence of a particular musical structure, that only the notes of that structure be present in the music itself. What is necessary is to indicate that the structure, as articulated by and through the music, determines both the relative importance and function of the notes as used, as well as the more general characteristics of the archetypal melodic (and harmonic) formulae. (p 86).

The mere existence of seven notes does not, therefore, guarantee the existence of the European diatonic scale.

Using the evidence of parallel singing in fourths and fifths often found in pentatonic traditions[18], Schuller manages to derive a 'blues scale' as shown in Example 5.5:

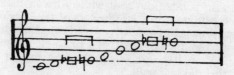

Example 5.5

There are two objections to this line of thought. Firstly, the scale indicated in Example 5.5 — which now has nine notes as opposed to the seven suggested in the previous theory — gives rise to the same objections, in that the second and sixth degrees of the scale are not de-emphasised[19]. More important, perhaps, this combinatorial approach, using Western non-inflected and diatonically derived pitches, in fact gives no insight into the origins of pitch inflexion in blues practice.

It is now possible to put forward a case for the underlying pentatonic nature of the authentic blues. In line with the ideas of Al Wilson (quoted, Roberts, 1973 p.190) the blues scale has the following form:

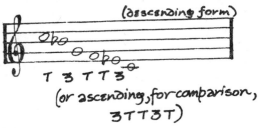

Example 5.6

This conception is supported by Lee (1972 p.26) who quotes the following scale:

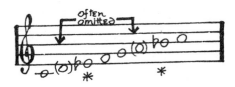

Example 5.7

With reference to the above examples it should be noted that the second and sixth degrees of the scale (D and A) do occur infrequently, but almost always as insubstantial passing notes. Striking parallels for this procedure are to be found in the passing note or *quilisma* theories of Chailley and Yasser with regard to plainchant [20], and in the *pien* tones of much Chinese music.

Many of the notes of this scale are inflected (bent). This inflexion should be understood as part of a fundamentally different conception of correct intonation, rather than the result of an inability on the part of the blacks to accommodate Western diatonic skills. In this connection we might note the following statement by a practising blues musician:

Courlander was once told by an Alabama blues singer that he

'played with notes' just as he 'played with the beats', which suggests not vagueness about pitch, which some authors have attributed to black singers, but a high degree of tonal sophistication (Roberts, 1973, pp 188-189).

Furthermore, whereas in the debate about the possible African origin of the blues, many authors suggest that the 'blue notes' arise from the conflict between African and European traditions, Oliver (1970, p 95) states categorically 'the "blue notes" themselves are found in Africa'. Pitch inflexion is also characteristic of Indian classical music, and Schuller (quoted, Oliver, 1970, p 14) considers it 'worth mentioning that Indo-Pakistani music is divided into six principal modes, three of which — afternoon modes — are nothing but the blues scales. To establish a possible historical link between these modes and the American Negro's blues scale might be an interesting project for a future student of jazz'. Pitch inflexion is also to be found in the practice of Western folk and 'popular' musics. For example, Lloyd 'points out in his book *Folk Song in England* that the vagueness about thirds is a prominent feature of English folk song' (Roberts, 1973, p189). For these reasons, an application of tonal concepts of major and minor to the blues 'bent' third in an attempt to elucidate its expressive function (that is, in an attempt to demonstrate the blacks' supposed ambivalence to white society[21]) is ethnocentric. It is, however, more than possible that whites reacted in this ethnocentric fashion to the blues, and this reaction may possibly have affected the subsequent development of blues-derived music.

Generally speaking, three identical chord shapes are used in the instrumental accompaniment of the voice in authentic blues. This shape is made up of a major third with a minor third above it, and often another minor third above that, i.e., on C:

Example 5.8

It is incorrect to describe this chord shape as a dominant seventh as, for example, has Lee (1972, p 27), when he says that 'the "wrong" notes of the melody could become part of the dominant seventh chord'. The dominant seventh, of course, must be defined not only in terms of its shape, but *in terms of its function* [22]. None of the three chords function in the manner of the various sevenths of tonality, where in the vast majority of cases, the seventh degree 'resolves' to the note below it. This fact, together with the further fact that the seventh degree may or may not be omitted as the musician wishes, is indicative of our proposed argument that the whole aggregate is more akin to a timbral colouration of the melodic note. This consistently used shape may be understood as the externalisation of harmonics inherent in the fundamental melodic note. Thus, on C, the harmonic series generates the notes C,E,G,B flat as the third, fourth, fifth and sixth harmonics respectively. The incompatibility of diatonic functional harmony and colouristic harmony deriving *directly* from the harmonic series is strikingly illustrated through an anecdote related by Big Bill Broonzy, the blues musician: [23]

> To really sing the *old* blues that I learned in Mississippi I have to go back to my sound and not the right chords as the musicians have told me to make. They just don't work with the real blues . . . the blues didn't come out of no book and them real chords did . . . [24] (quoted, Middleton, 1972, p 37)

The argument being put forward is further substantiated by the practice of 'bottleneck' guitar playing. By this technique, an entire chordal shape may be slid up or down the guitar neck. Just as we have argued for the bending of notes as an essential characteristic of blues music, so bottleneck technique allows for an extension of this bending to entire chord shapes built on the notes themselves. Thus, bottleneck inflexion of chord shapes can be understood as an integral aspect of blues style rather than as a further anomalous feature which needs to be explained away. Certainly, there is no parallel to the bending of entire chord shapes in functional harmony, a fact which further backs up our theory. Finally, it may be pointed out that it is possible to find examples of blues where the accompaniment is almost entirely melodic, employing the same pentatonic scale to set off the vocal melody.

In most descriptions of the blues, the chord shapes used are described in terms of the tonal progression dominant (V), subdominant (IV), tonic (I). This description clearly derives from the functional harmony of tonality. However, some authors are quick to point out that blues musicians do not necessarily view their use of chord shapes in this fashion. In discussing riff patterns of the swing era, Schuller (1968, p 48) states:

> Example 18A shows a riff placed over the three root chords (I, IV, & V) found in the blues . . . I hasten to reiterate that the African and the American Negro (at least initially) did not think of it in those diatonic terms. On the contrary, the Negro was simply perpetuating his unawareness of key centres in the European sense.

Since it is admitted here that the blues musicians themselves probably did not understand their music in these terms, then, from the critical stance adopted in this book, we would argue that analysis in terms of tonality is invalid.

But even if we were to view authentic blues within the context of functional harmony, the progression V, IV, I is weak compared with the archetypal progression IV, V, I (or II, V, I), and occurs much more rarely than the latter in such harmony. Most Western popular music (of the Tin Pan Alley/BBC Radio 1 tradition) uses the typical V-I cadence. Therefore the adoption of a V, IV, I progression within a tonal context is extremely surprising. However, it is not necessary to resort to the tonal system to explain the relationship of the three notes on which the chord shapes are built. These three notes form the most basic kernel of the pentatonic scale (see Fig. 1 p 83). It is, of course, unnecessary to refer to the major scale of tonality to derive these notes, since they can most easily be derived from the harmonic series [25]. The instrumental accompaniment can thus be understood as a colouristic extension of the central notes of the underlying pentatonic structure of the melody.

Now although there is insufficient space in this book to pursue the parallel in any depth, there are clearly many features in common between the notion of an 'intensional' or 'restricted' coding of the world 'typical' of working class people and the notion of an implicit world sense that John Shepherd drew from his discussion of pre-literate consciousness [26]. More particularly, there is a striking analogy between the pentatonic coding of the largely implicit ideal feudal structure, and the pentatonic coding of the highly 'intensional' and 'restricted' articulation of black American slaves. Further, in view of this analogy, and in view of John Shepherd's discussion concerning the development of explicit harmony in tonality, it is interesting to speculate that many blues elements 'as used in jazz' cease to be truly implicit, and become increasingly explicit. For example, it seems likely that as one tends towards the 'white' end of the jazz spectrum, the implicit harmony described in the previous paragraphs becomes increasingly explicit, until pieces of genuine tonal syntax can be heard.

Given that some jazzmen tend to view harmonic sequences as the given framework inside which melodic improvisation takes place, it might be argued that these harmonic sequences have become separated or distanced from their original role as colouristic extensions. In view of the discussion in Chapter One, such distancing could be assigned clear ideological significance, and would further explain why most jazz-based commentators on the blues discuss it in terms of the accommodation between pentatonic melody and tonal harmony.

Having made out a case for the underlying pentatonic structure of authentic blues, we will now mention a feature of this music about which there is more general agreement. This feature is the rigid cyclical framework — usually referred to as twelve-bar blues — in which the blues is cast. Mellers (1964, p 267) has drawn certain conclusions of a sociological nature about this framework:

> The rigidity of form was a part of the Negro's act of acceptance: a part, therefore, of the reality from which, without sentimental evasion or even religious hope, he started. That is why, though the blues are intensely personal in so far as each man sings, alone, of his sorrow, they are also — even more than most folk-art — impersonal in so far as each man's sorrow is a common lot.

The absence of conscious individualism, together with its concomitant social mutuality, is, of course, highly symptomatic of an implicit world sense [27]. But, in this case, the rigidity of the framework reflects the rigidity of an *imposed* social situation [28], rather than the fluid adaptation towards the relatively unpredictable and uncontrollable environment of pre-literate man. However, as argued previously, there is within this framework a rich and sophisticated articulation of the life and experience of the musicians.

At the end of the first part of this chapter, it was suggested that, in view of the different modes of consciousness and symbolic behaviour taken to be archetypal of the ruled and the ruling classes, one might expect to find considerable differences in the musical articulations of those classes. Specifically, it was argued that an 'uncontaminated' working class community would be very likely to give rise to an intensional form of musical creativity. Substantial grounds for this assertion may now be said to exist. These grounds, with their elucidation of white society's ethnocentric musical analysis, throw into sharp relief Blacking's (1973, p 73) insight that:

> since musical patterns are always acquired through and in the context of social relationships and their associated emotions, the decisive style-forming factor in any attempt to express feelings in music must be its social content. If we want to find the basic organising principles that affect the shapes or patterns of music, we must look beyond the cultural conventions of any century or society to the social situation in which they applied and to which they refer.

NOTES

1.   A succinct sociology of the contradictions within Social Scientific activity is contained in Jurdant's (1974, 1975) accounts of the oppositions of science, its popularisation, Social Science and folk myth.

2.   By 'folk music' is meant that music transmitted orally-aurally amongst the people. Folk music may be viewed essentially as the authentic expression of communal consciousness, and the property of no particular individual. In these respects it differs to some extent from music which is calculatedly manufactured for *immediacy* of popularity in a market situation.

3.   This has been one of the main concerns of the sociology of education. For an early account of the typical communication processes within the classroom see, for example, Henry (1966). For a summary of the research charting working-class 'failure', see Banks (1969), and for a summary of the different theoretical interpretations of such 'failure', see Flude (1974).

4.   See Inkeles (1960) and Kohn (1969).

5.   Bernstein's work has been criticised, often quite rightly, by a number of people. Perhaps the most influential criticisms have been those of Labov (1973) and Rosen (1974). Both are concerned with the ideological use which has been made of Bernstein's theory, with the way his theory has been taken to support the view that working class people are linguistically less competent than others. Bernstein has since made it quite clear that he is talking of the constraints of social context upon performance, not competence (Bernstein, 1973a). The term 'competence' has unfortunate Chomskian connotations in this context, and we would rather differentiate potential, practice and a competence that emerges through the practical development of potentiality. (A full discussion of the definition of 'competence' is beyond the scope of this book). The separation of intellectual from motor activity that is decreed by our hierarchical organisation of daily life as experienced through home, community, work and school is a systematic alienation from our *full* potentiality, which takes different forms between the classes.

Bernstein can certainly be faulted for the rhetorical devices he has used, and for the lack of phenomenologically grounded research — for his abstracted theorising in default of a close study of the actual processes of communication that transpire in the various contexts that people move through as they grow up in our society. But the central insights of his theory retain their plausibility. For example Wooton's (1974) field study shows that, at age four, working class children's use of speech is in respects quite different from that of middle class children and is evoked in different contexts, yet no less competent. This points to the role of the school system as an ideological reproduction of the general class system, as the creator of the notorious rates of, in academic terms, working class intellectual incompetence.

G   175

6.   These ideas are dealt with at greater length, and in relation to the production and 'consumption' of works in all the artistic media, in Virden (1972).

7.   The terms 'implicit' and 'explicit' are here used in relation to Bernstein's arguments. There are obvious parallels between our use of the words and the way they are used by John Shepherd in Chapters Two and Three, above. There are also further parallels between this *general* implicit/explicit dichotomy and the distinction drawn by Chester (1970) between 'intensional' and 'extensional' musical development. Elaboration of these parallels is not deemed appropriate within the scope of this book.

8.   See Mueller (1951) for evidence of the prevailing 'classical' preferences of American concertgoers until at least the 1950s.

9.   Even those sympathetic to folk forms of music tend to ethnocentrically 'understand' them in terms of the concepts of their 'classical' European training. See, for example, our arguments with those who approach the rural blues, via jazz, from a tonal perspective, in the second part of the chapter. See also Graham Vulliamy's arguments in Chapter Six.

10.   This happened sometime between the recording of 'Sh-Boom' by The Chords in 1954, the worldwide hit of Bill Haley's 'Rock Around the Clock' in 1955 and the establishment of more permanent popular artistry with, for example, The Beatles in the 1960s. Gillett (1971) gives one of the best histories of rock 'n' roll.

11.   The bending of notes, and the riff-patterns of jazz and rock 'n' roll may be seen as deriving, ultimately, from blues practice. Many examples of basic rock 'n' roll and soul music may be shown to display strongly pentatonic features. Furthermore, in the late fifties there was a movement within modern jazz which its practitioners viewed as a move towards the restoration of modality: '. . . it seems like we are into this thing where we want to solo on a modal perspective more or less, and therefore we end up playing a lot of vamps within a tune . . .' (John Coltrane, quoted on the sleeve notes to *Ole*, Atlantic A 1373).

12.   We intend to discuss the nature of the serial system in detail in a future publication.

13.   The school of composers originating with Schoenberg and his two famous pupils, Berg and Webern. The remarks in the text apply most particularly to the serial works of Schoenberg and Berg, and those of later composers who adopted their style of serial composition. The work of Webern, usually regarded as the point of divergence for post-1950s developments in 'avant-garde' composition, is clearly more problematic in this respect.

14.   See, for example, Boulez (1952).

15.   The ideology implicit in Integral Serialist and related musics is briefly discussed, from a different perspective, in Chapter Four.

16.   Trevor Wishart would like to acknowledge the help of John Shepherd and Graham Vulliamy in writing this part of the chapter.

17. Of the sources we quote below this applies particularly to Schuller, Hodeir and Middleton.

18. In this respect see John Shepherd's discussion in Chapter Three of the probable relationship between parallel organum and the underlying pentatonic structure of plainchant.

19. John Shepherd has in fact argued in Chapter Three that parallel motion between pentatonic scales with passing notes is likely to make those passing notes as structurally important as the other notes.

20. See above, Chapter Three.

21. See, for example, Middleton (1972, pp 38-39).

22. The full musical and ideological *function* of the dominant seventh was set out in Chapter Three.

23. A different approach to this same procedure may be found in Impressionist music, particularly that of Delius (cf. Shepherd 1973). We intend to deal with the parallels between some of the procedures in blues, jazz and rock and some of those in Impressionist music in a future publication.

24. It is a striking comment on the prevailing ideology that Broonzy sees the chords of white musicians, coming out of a book, as 'right' and 'real'. The indigenous oral-aural musical tradition does not attain such a high standing in his own eyes, despite the fact that it was the tradition in which he was brought up.

25. See the discussion in Chapter Three.

26. See note 7, above.

27. See above, Chapter One, *'The Oral-Visual Split'*.

28. That is, a framework and situation imposed by white society.

Chapter Six

Music and the Mass Culture Debate[1]

GRAHAM VULLIAMY

Introduction — The Mass Culture Debate

Much of the debate in contemporary educational theory between those concerned with maintaining high cultural standards and those advocating the use of the pupils' culture in teaching takes as a reference point the sociological debate concerning the origins and consequences of 'mass culture'. The arguments in Bantock's (1968) influential book, for example, are explicitly based on the terminology of the mass culture critique, where three types of culture are identified: high culture, folk culture and mass culture (often referred to as popular culture). The purpose of this chapter is to re-examine the assumptions underpinning the critique of mass culture by looking in particular at the case of music and in the process I hope to make some contribution to the wider educational controversy referred to above.

The debate over mass culture, entwined as it is with the sociological debate over the origins and consequences of a mass society, has a history which predates the rise of the modern mass media[2]. As Gans (1967) has pointed out, the charges against mass or popular culture have been repeated so often that it is possible to view them as part of an established critique. The main themes of this critique in its contemporary form may be identified from a number of articles in Rosenberg and White (1959) and in Jacobs (1961).

I will begin by defining the key terms as they are used by the mass culture theorists. Wilensky (1964) identifies high culture by referring to two characteristics of the product: first it is created by, or under

179

the supervision of a cultural elite operating within some aesthetic, literary or scientific tradition, and secondly, critical standards independent of the consumer of the product are systematically applied to it. He then continues to identify mass culture as cultural products manufactured solely for the mass market, while folk culture is seen as the traditional culture of the people predominant in rural society. Set up in these terms the problem of mass culture, as the critics see it, is that with increasing industrialisation and urbanisation there is a tendency for the culture purveyed by by the mass media to destroy both traditional high culture and folk culture.

The starting-point of the critics of popular culture is that such products are made solely for commercial reasons and consequently they must be standardised in the interests of mass production. This mode of production results in a 'separation of the manufacturers of culture from the consumers' (Haag, 1961, p 58) and the consumers then become no more than passive objects who are unscrupulously manipulated and commercially exploited by the producers of mass culture:

> Mass culture is imposed from above. It is fabricated by technicians hired by businessmen; its audiences are passive consumers, their participation limited to the choice between buying and not buying (MacDonald, 1959, p 60).

It follows from this that the creators of mass culture are denied the expression of true creativity and individuality, which is normally associated with the production of high culture:

> Popular culture does not grow within a group. It is manufactured by one group — in Hollywood or in New York — for sale to an anonymous mass market. The product must meet an average of tastes, and it loses in spontaneity and individuality what it gains in accessibility and cheapness (Haag, 1959, p 519).

Critics of popular culture see it as leading to a deterioration of both traditional high culture and folk culture, since not only are potential artists lured away by the lucrative rewards of involvement in popular culture, but also the products of past and present high culture are actually exploited in the production of popular culture. All the features hitherto attributed to mass culture are perhaps best summarised by Coser:

> It [mass culture] is distinguished from folk culture and from high culture by its standardised mass production, marketability

and parasitic dependence on other forms of art and culture. It embodies a sharp cleavage between the consumer [the audience] and the producer. The latter exploits and manipulates the former. These characteristics radically distinguish mass culture from other cultural forms (1960, p 81).

There are differences of emphasis and opinion amongst the mass culture critics, particularly in the social and political orientation of the critique: both conservatives and radicals agree in many respects in their criticism of popular culture, but disagree in their explanations of the causes of the problem. The conservatives (for example, Haag) tend to be hostile to political democracy or to political, social and economic equality. They explain the existence of popular culture by the inadequacy of its audiences. On the other hand, the radicals (for example MacDonald) argue that it is not the audiences who are at fault but rather the use of the market mechanism, with all its possibilities of commercial exploitation, to provide culture in a society characterised by a 'mass' audience. Gans summarises the differences between the conservatives and the radicals in the following way:

> The conservatives attack popular culture because they resent the rising political, economic and cultural power of the so-called masses; the socialists, because they are disappointed that these masses, once liberated from proletarianism, did not accept high culture or support socialist advocacy of it (1967, p 575).

The Afro-American Tradition in Twentieth Century Music

A historical perspective on music in the twentieth century suggests the importance of an increasing split between so-called 'serious' music and so-called 'popular' music, together with a corresponding dwindling audience for the compositions of those working in the 'serious' music idiom. The increasing failure of contemporary 'serious' composers to communicate with a wide audience is explicitly recognised by the music establishment and has led to considerable debates concerning the problems of communicating the new forms of music, such as the twelve-tone developments of Schoenberg, which mark such a considerable break from earlier forms of tonal music[3]. At the same time the ever-increasing popularity of different styles of 'popular' music throughout this century has been obvious.

This gap between 'serious' and 'popular' music has been interpreted by the music establishment and by many sociologists via the assumptions of the mass culture critique, so that clear differences have been postulated between 'serious' music on the one hand, which it is assumed results from the unique creative potential of the artist unpolluted by commercial pressures, and 'popular' music on the other, whose purpose is seen as chiefly commercial and aimed at a mass market. Thus Routh (1972), for example, in surveying contemporary British music since the last war, begins by defining a musical art-work as the following:

> The term music is taken to include as many aspects of the composer's work as fall under the heading of art-work. An art-work is one which makes some claim on our serious attention. This implies a creative, unique purpose on the part of the composer and an active response on the part of the listener; it implies that the composer possesses and uses both vision and technique, and that the listener in return is expected to bring to bear his full intelligence. This excludes non-art music, such as pop music, whose purpose is chiefly if not entirely commercial. Pop groups are big business; they are socially significant; there is no question that they form a remarkable contemporary phenomenon — but this does not make the result into an art-work, and to consider it as if it were is an illogical affectation (p.x.)

That this is the dominant ideology of the music establishment, by which I mean the institutions (such as music conservatoires), music journals and the composers, performers and critics dedicated to the European 'serious' tradition in music[4], hardly needs documenting[5].

A major tendency of the critics of popular culture in setting up the terms of the debate is to consider 'popular culture' as a homogeneous category whilst high culture is subdivided into many different categories with strict boundaries. Thus, for example, in the sphere of music, 'popular' music is always treated unquestionably as a holistic category whilst 'high culture' music is subdivided into music of the Classical era, the Romantic era, Baroque, the Avant-Garde and so on. An 'intellectual field' exists to differentiate the good high culture music from the poorer variety, whilst 'popular' music, because it is 'popular' music, is *automatically* assumed to be of inferior quality as music[6]. Following the stimulating work of the 'classical' music critic, Henry Pleasants, I have argued at length elsewhere (Vulliamy and Lee, 1976) that such an interpretation is fundamentally misguided, since it fails to recognise the impact of an important musical revolution in this century. The music establishment failed to observe this revolution because it took place in an area of music (jazz and 'popular') which, because of the European culture-specific definitions of music, was not recognised as music at all. The new musical developments came from the Afro-American tradition, springing from the Negro blues and now covering such diverse fields as jazz, rock music, soul and Tamla Motown music, and so on. This tradition has ushered in a new musical language with both musical and aesthetic criteria which markedly differentiate it from music in the European 'serious' tradition. The differences spring from the partial retention of various elements from African musical cultures, such as the use of antiphonal response, varying vocal timbres, the use of improvisation, the emphasis on dynamic polyrhythms, the functional use of music for communal participation and the oral-aural (as opposed to notated) transmission of music[7]. In addition such Africanisms were moulded by contact with a European musical heritage to produce specifically Afro-American musical characteristics such as rhythmic swing[8].

What I propose to argue is that in applying the assumptions of the mass culture critique, critics of 'popular' music during the twentieth century have consistently failed to differentiate between varieties of 'popular' music and in particular have failed to recognise the alternative musical criteria of the Afro-American tradition. The reactions of the music establishment to the growth of jazz have been well documented[9] and illustrate how jazz was dismissed because it did not conform to either the musical or cultural criteria of the European 'serious' tradition. This tendency of the music establishment to judge the worth or seriousness of music in terms of 'classical' music standards has led to highly misleading assumptions being made about the nature both of various so-called primitive musics and of Afro-American musical styles. In the latter case, alternative musical criteria derived from an African tradition of music are not recognised, but other standards of judgment, appropriate to composed music concerned primarily with harmonic exploitation, are imposed on an improvised music, which incorporates complex melodic and rhythmic inflections. A case in point is Meyer's well-known attempt to discover what it is that 'makes music great' (Meyer 1959), where he tries to isolate those factors in music which will enable us to compare the greatness of different pieces of music of all types. In fact his reification of 'classical' music criteria involves a basic misunderstanding of styles of music which are not located in the European 'serious' tradition [10].

It is not only the music establishment which reacted to jazz in this way; so also did a number of sociological critics of mass culture, particularly those like Adorno, himself an accomplished musician, who were associated with the Frankfurt Institute of Social Research. Thus Adorno (1941) analysed jazz and 'popular' music in terms of their submission to the phenomenon of 'standardisation' as a result of a highly monopolistic control of the music and entertainment industry concerned to continually 'plug' records in the interests of the profit motive. Unfortunately his concern to highlight the importance of the means of production and to locate his critique of 'popular' music within the Marxist critique of commodity-fetishism blinded him to the fact that his concept of 'standardisation' was a reification of musical criteria derived from the 'serious' music tradition, where the main stress is on the harmonic structure and form of music. Viewed from this perspective, the simple standard harmonic structure of most 'popular' songs at that time was indeed limited, but such an analysis like that of Meyer's already referred to, in judging styles of music from 'foreign' musical and cultural criteria, inevitably distorts the essence of such music. To the jazz performer in particular, and to a lesser extent to certain 'popular' music performers, the structure of the song is simply the limits within which the piece of music is actively recreated by the performer via the incorporation of complex rhythmic and melodic inflections and other musical nuances derived from an Afro-American performance tradition in music.

Since the time of Adorno's writing there has been a belated recognition of the jazz musicians' art. The increasing legitimation of jazz, a point to which I shall return later in this chapter, means that only very rarely is jazz today lumped together with all other varieties of so-called 'popular' music in sweeping condemnations of mass culture. The ideology of the mass culture critique continues, however, in such a way that, whereas thirty years ago the assumptions underlying the mass culture critique made it incapable of differentiating between jazz and other varieties of 'popular' music, today similar assumptions make it incapable of differentiating between various types of so-called 'pop' music. Thus Parker (1975) has recently drawn explicitly on the terminology of the mass culture critique in his analysis of contemporary rock music. Like

Adorno, his main stress is on the means of production — as he sees it, a commercial machine, providing rock music of the lowest common denominator in taste which detracts from the folk culture of the people (in this case identified as the folk music and Radio Ballads of Ewan McColl and others). I want to argue, however, that such a structural analysis, stressing as it does simply the role of the production system in music, rides roughshod over a more phenomenologically inclined analysis, which takes more seriously the definitions of the situation of the actors concerned — in this case of various participants in the 'pop' music process. This point will now be illustrated by reference to the state of rock music in the early 1970s.

The Case of Rock Music
Just as Becker (1951) found in his sociological analysis of dance band musicians in the early 1950s that such musicians made important distinctions between jazz and commercial dance band music, so an examination of recent 'pop' music suggests similar internal differences within 'pop'. In particular the rise of rock music has led to a situation where 'pop' musicians identify two main types of 'pop' music and differing assumptions are made about the production of these different types of music. In the same way that in Becker's analysis the jazz musician wished to differentiate himself from the commercial dance musician (seeing himself as far more creative), contemporary rock musicians wish to differentiate themselves from 'pop' musicians. These differences may be illustrated by looking at the way in which those involved in rock music — writers and critics, the musicians and the audience — themselves identify differences within so-called 'pop' music[11].

The most important way in which musicians themselves categorise different types of 'popular' music is the degree to which the 'vocabulary of motives' (Mills, 1940) for the production of the music is seen as a commercial one. Writers on rock music invariably make this distinction:

> There are serious 'minority' rock groups, who are trying to expand the music beyond its present limits, and there are commercial rock groups (radio groups as Frank Zappa calls them) who exist merely to churn out sub-three minute hits for A.M. radio. There are serious, creative rock artists and there are

185

teenybopper bubblegum idols who are after a fast buck and nothing else (McGregor, 1971, p.33).

In the late 1960s after the breakthrough of the Beatles' 'Sergeant Pepper' L.P., 'serious' rock music came to be increasingly identified with L.P's (albums), whilst singles were designated 'commercial'. The distinction between a singles and an album band is now a very important one both for the musicians and the audience. The 'serious' rock musicians see the single record as being a severe curtailment of their artistic freedom:

> What we're doing now is simply concentrating on L.P's and if by accident a single should come out of an L.P. session, then we'll put it on the market. Whereas before you'd have two sessions; you'd consciously go to an L.P. session and you'd consciously go to a single session. And single sessions were terrible. I can't make them at all. They're just like — you go in there and the whole big problem is whether it's commercial. That is the problem. No matter what the music is like, it's got to be commercial, it's got to have a hook line; you've got to have this and that, and you just fall into a very dark hole. I can't take it at all. (1967 interview with Eric Clapton, lead guitarist of 'Cream', quoted in Rolling Stone Editors, 1971, p.16).

For the audience the seriousness of the musician's intentions and the quality of the music are often deduced from whether the musician is concerned with producing singles. Letters to music magazines frequently dismiss groups because of their commercial intentions:

> T. Rex have turned commercial! . . . He [Marc Bolan] seems content with a few number one hits in the 'Beeb' charts only fit for teenyboppers. (Letter to *Melody Maker* — a British popular music weekly, August 28, 1971).

Such remarks, however, don't pass entirely without criticism:

> Just because the band [T. Rex] get a few hit singles and some screen-time on Top of the Pops, everyone dismisses them as just another 'pop' group. . . .Their critics are people who feel themselves too superior to be enjoying a band with a load of teenyboppers (Letter to *Melody Maker*, February 19, 1972).

Important distinctions are also made by musicians with respect to the actual nature of the music. Prior to the 'rock revolution' (see Shaw, 1971) there was usually a rigid division of labour between the composer and the performer — a singer would sing lyrics which had been written and orchestrated by someone else. In rock music, however, the originators of the material tend to account for the total product — not only do groups now write, orchestrate and play their own material, but in many cases they also produce their own records thus reducing the possibility of outside control over the finished product. This, rock musicians feel, has considerable consequences for the nature of the music:

> If you want to come up with a singular, most important trend in this new music, I think it has to be something like this: it is original, composed by the people who perform, it, created by them — even if they have to fight the record companies to do it — so that it is really a creative action and not a commercial pile of shit thrown together by business people who think they know what John Doe and Mr Jones really want. (Interview with Frank Zappa of 'The Mothers of Invention' quoted in Hopkins, 1970, p.210).

The fact that rock music can be produced by the artist instead of being mainly influenced by managers, agents or recording companies means that rock musicians regard their music as 'real':

> It's *real*, that's what this new music is — and that's what makes it different from anything which has ever happened in pop music before. (Interview with Marty Balin of 'The Jefferson Airplane' quoted in Hopkins, 1970, p.210).

Rock music is seen as the exact antithesis of 'pop' music:

> The heartbeat of rock soon became protest — protest against the static forms, verbal cliches, tired harmonies, instrumental limitations and the vapid romanticism of Tin Pan Alley song . . . . What counted was sincerity, involvement, saying where it was at, doing one's one thing, blowing the mind. (Shaw, 1971, p.208).

Whereas the musical criteria of traditional 'pop' are mainly 'watered-down' elements of musical techniques of the European 'serious' tradition, the musical criteria of rock music are derived mainly from Afro-American music — the emphasis on improvisation in the latter giving the rock musician scope for creativity and musical development which is essentially denied to the 'pop' musician:

> Progressive music[12] is no longer functional[13] — its audience goes to listen attentively, not to dance. Most important, unlike all previous popular music, it concerns itself with musical development, and not with the statement and repetition of a theme (Lee, 1970, p.xii).

Not only is musical development within a piece of music possible but groups are also expected to develop musically over the course of their careers:

> One of the many things the Beatles would give rock was the concept that groups should evolve and grow — developing musically — rather than stand in place and merely continue to issue dozens of records that sounded like those that preceded them. (Hopkins, 1970, p.72).

In such a situation the audience for rock music will 'put down' a group by referring to them as a 'pop' group, because they are playing musical cliches, in the very same way that at the time of Becker's study the best way to 'put down' a jazz musician was to refer to him as a dance band musician. A reader's letter to *Melody Maker* illustrates this point:

> W. Reeves asks why Deep Purple are labelled 'formula rock'. The reason seems quite obvious to me, they *are* formula rock .... Pop music is by definition 'formula'.... However rock as a medium is not stereotyped and cliched. You only have to hear some of the great bands on the British scene at the moment to realise this. I'm talking about people like Van Der Graaf Generator, Pink Floyd, the Who, E.L.P. etc. (Letter to *Melody Maker*, July 17, 1971).

This last quote also illustrates the tendency for the 'rock community' to differentiate many different types of rock music and the tendency to make value judgements with respect to the differing types. Just as critics of mass culture will treat 'popular' music as a homogeneous category whilst making numerous internal distinctions and value judgements within European 'serious' music (classical, baroque, romantic, contemporary and so on), so rock musicians whilst treating 'pop' as a homogeneous category make numerous internal distinctions within rock music (folk rock, heavy rock, progressive rock, acid rock, country rock, jazz rock and so on). This has had consequences for the nature of the audience for rock music. At one time generalisations about the nature of the audience for 'popular' music could be made simply in terms of the fact that rock music was produced by young people for young people:

> For the first time there is now an intrinsically young people's music. The composers are the performers and they're all young and the audience is mostly young. This has a lot to do with youth becoming so dominant both socially and economically (Mellers, 1970, p.64).

Or again, Herman puts it even more dramatically: 'The distinction between rock and pop music corresponds to the crude physical distinction between younger and older generations' (1971, p.13).

However, discussion of the different musical and artistic merits of different rock bands has been associated with an increasing fragmentation of the audience for rock music itself. This point is clearly made by Landau, reviewer for the rock magazine *Rolling Stone:*

> 3 or 4 years ago, rock reviewing was less problematic than it is today. For one thing you knew what to write about. The Byrds, the Animals, the Dead etc. were fit subjects for comment: Gerry and the Pacemakers, Dave Clark etc. were not. The Beatles, the Stones and Dylan were the first inductees to rock's (as opposed to rock and roll's) pantheon; after that, everyone bowed in the direction of San Francisco and underground British groups until the appearance of Led Zeppelin. Zeppelin forced a revival of the distinction between popularity and quality. As long as the bands most admired aesthetically were also the bands most successful commercially (Cream, for instance) the distinction was irrelevant. But Zeppelin's enormous commercial success, in spite of critical opposition, revealed the deep division in what was once thought to be a homogeneous audience. That division has now evolved into a clearly defined mass taste and a clearly defined elitist taste (1971, p.44).

It is also one of the central points in Marcus' long appraisal of the state of rock music in the early 1970s:

> The kind of all-rock around which the community gathered, that it seized, is not accessible to us today, since as a musical community we have fragmented into little groups of age, taste, politics, geography and self-conscious sophistication (1971, p.39).

One of the most important aspects of this fragmentation of the audience has been its shifting social class composition, and the perceptions of the latter by both performers and their audiences; whilst rock'n'roll, the forerunner of rock, was generally identified with the working-class (and with particular groups like the 'teddy boys' and the 'rockers'), rock music has become identified with the middle-class (particularly with college students)[14]:

> And with them came rock, the music of the 1960s. Rock is the product of a more self-aware and self-conscious group of

189

musicians. It is far more a middle-class music than the lower-class its predecessor certainly was (Landau, 1970).

George Melly makes a similar point in his survey of British 'pop' music:

> The average young pop fan today is drawn in the main from a middle-class or suburban background and is educationally usually in one of the higher streams. . . . An interesting side-effect of the intellectualising of pop and its middle-class take-over is the resentment it has provoked among the working-class young. At the open-air concerts gangs of C stream 15 year-old drop-outs stalked aggressively around the fringe of the enormous hairy crowds. They were surgically clean, wore their hair cropped, brown boots and jeans at half-mast with braces. They were looking for 'bother' and seemed to sense that pop, once a music cutting across the class barriers, was now the property of an intelligentsia (however embryonic), a potential 'them' (1972, p.122)[15].

A recurring theme in the literature of rock music is the almost total neglect of the latter in the mass media; as Bill Graham, the Director of the Fillmore rock concert hall in New York, has said: 'The mass media knows as much about rock'n'roll as the underground press knows about La Scala' (Quoted in *Melody Maker*, May 27, 1972).

This reference to the underground press also illustrates the tendency for the values of rock music to be associated with the values of youth, conceived as being anti-establishment, if not overtly politically radical. Explanations of the lack of rock music on radio and television are usually interpreted in this context by the audience for rock music:

> One has to remember that the establishment must be set on self-survival, naturally enough, and anti-society thinking must be suppressed consciously or not. The BBC is the establishment — check. Whatever happens the BBC is unlikely to encourage on any large scale the music we love (Letter to *Melody Maker*, October 9, 1971).

BBC Radio 1, which is supposed to be the 'popular' music programme, is a constant source for ridicule amongst rock musicians and young people generally, in that it is geared almost entirely to commercial 'pop' singles, despite the fact that since 1968 L.P's have outsold singles in absolute terms (Jasper, 1972, p.27), whilst the two categories of music — namely 'progressive rock' and 'reggae and soul' — which a recent Schools Council survey (Murdock and Phelps, 1973) found to be among the most popular amongst secondary schoolchildren are conspicuous for their absence. As George Melly has noted 'Radio 1 caters to a nation of kiddies and their mums' (1972, p.187).

The prevailing attitude of the BBC is perhaps best illustrated by a comment from Tony Blackburn, one of the most popular (with 'the kiddies and their mums') Radio 1 disc-jockeys (and the one most frequently used as a butt for the 'rock community's' ridicule):

> Pop is not to be taken seriously. That's why I go on and talk complete rubbish which it is. If people want seriousness, they'll tune into Radio 4 [*sic*]; if they want to be a little more easy going they'll tune into Radio 2; if they want background noise and a lot of nonsense, they'll tune into Radio 1. There's terrific variety there (Quoted in Hadingham, 1970, p.68).

Patterns of Legitimation in Twentieth-Century Music
The previous section illustrated how, in contemporary 'pop' music, rock musicians seek to separate themselves from 'pop' musicians by making certain assumptions, which might be summarised as follows:

a) Rock music is not commercial, whilst pop music is.

b) The rock performer is a sincere, creative artist who has control over his product.

c) The separation of composer, performer and producer, in 'pop' music denies the possibility of creativity to the 'pop' performer.

d) 'Pop' music is homogeneous whilst rock music is sub-divided into many different types which tend to appeal to differing sections of the audience for rock music.

e) Rock music is neglected in the mass media; the latter concentrates on standardised ('singles') 'pop' music.

f) Rock music is complex and musically developed (with respect to Afro-American musical criteria) whereas 'pop' music is standardised and musically cliched.

In doing so it could be argued that rock musicians are using categories in their defence of rock music similar to those used by defenders of high culture in their critique of mass culture. Thus a list of assumptions drawn from the introductory section to this chapter, whereby high culture is differentiated from mass culture would look very similar:

a) High culture ('serious' music) is not subject to commercial pressures; commercial gain must inevitably lead to inartistic works.

b) High culture ('serious' music) results from the unique creative potential of the artist.

c) Mass culture ('popular' music) is produced solely for a mass market. Its commercial nature therefore leads to standardisation of the product. This in turn denies the possibility of creativity to the artist.

d) Mass culture ('popular' music) is a homogeneous category whilst high culture ('serious' music) is subdivided into many different types with strict boundaries.

e) Mass culture ('popular' music) inhibits the growth of high culture ('serious' music) mainly due to the former's sheer quantity in the mass media.

f) Mass culture ('popular' music) is imposed from above and the audience (teenagers) are therefore exploited.

For an interpretation of these similarities the work of the Marxist-influenced French sociologist Pierre Bourdieu, is particularly suggestive. Rock music might be seen as being 'in the process of legitimation' in the context of his paper (1966) on the 'Intellectual Field'. Bourdieu sees the legitimacy of cultural forms being influenced by the ways in which certain dominant groups in a society are in a position to impose their social constructions or meanings (concerning cultural values, the production of art-works and so on) on others in a form of what he calls 'violence symbolique'. However, one of the limitations of the paper is that, in concentrating on the processes of interaction within an 'intellectual field', he only gives a static picture which neglects some important questions raised by his own analysis. We might ask how and why the 'spheres of legitimacy' change over time? Bourdieu suggests that jazz is 'in the process of legitimation' but this begs the interesting question of how the meaning of jazz has changed so dramatically from being 'uncivilised' music to music fit for scholarly treatises. Similarly, rock'n'roll, once dismissed as being anti-music, is now interpreted by rock critics as being of considerable musical and historical interest as a forerunner of contemporary rock music. One interpretation of the increasing tendency to use high culture 'legitimating criteria' both with jazz and, more recently, in rock music might lie in the shifting social class composition of the audience for the music and the meaning that this shift has for both musicians and their audience. As Bourdieu has said: 'It may be the upper classes who, by their social standing, sanction the rank of the works they consume in the hierarchy of legitimate works' (1966, p.174); it would seem that when both jazz and rock'n'roll were musics appealing almost exclusively to lower status groups in society (in America: jazz to negroes; in Britain: rock'n'roll to working-class teenagers) there was no tendency towards their legitimation. That only occurred when the audiences for the music extended to higher status groups; thus jazz began to be legitimated when certain French intellectuals (for example, Hugues Panassié) began writing about New Orleans jazz in the 1930s. The increasing legitimation of jazz in Britain might, I suggest, be viewed in terms of the attraction jazz had for certain intellectuals and members of upper status groups (for example, Humphrey Lyttleton or George Melly) who later found their way into the mass media. Similarly, the increasing legitimation of rock music might be seen as accompanying the shift in the social class composition of the audience and the performer. Such legitimation using traditional legitimating criteria ('serious', 'creative', 'non-commercial' and so on) then occurs because members of the upper status groups must justify their likes in terms of the criteria of excellence used by other members of their status group; hence the drive to separate their particular musical taste from ordinary commercial pop music. Thus, for example, Richard Mabey, in commenting on his reasons for starting to write about pop music states: 'I began writing about the sociology of pop in the early 1960s, I suspect in an attempt to justify my liking for the stuff, which was then still regarded as inappropriate and slightly indecent for a middle-class undergrad' (Quoted in Cash, 1970, p.7).

If such an interpretation is used then those types of pop music which appeal to the more educated and high status groups (for example, progressive rock) will have the highest legitimation, whilst those which appeal to the lowest status groups (for example, reggae) will have the lowest. This is certainly the case in that reggae, until recently, was not only neglected in the mass media, but was also the subject for scorn in nearly all the critical books and magazines devoted to rock music. Such neglect is illustrated by the following reader's letter to the British magazine, *Time Out*:

> Your latest issue confirms something that I've suspected all along — you're blatantly prejudiced against anything you can't label as 'artistic' or 'progressive'. You seem to think that rhythm-and-blues, soul and reggae in particular are not worth any kind of serious consideration . . . .You can hardly describe yourselves as 'the living guide to all events in London' when you deliberately choose to ignore what is now the true underground

— the R & B, soul and reggae circuit which flourishes despite the BBC, *Time Out* and almost every other medium apart from one or two magazines' (August 27, 1971).

However, in terms of my analysis of the differing legitimation of different types of music, the question still remains as to why members of upper status groups begin to appreciate particular types of music, thus contributing to their legitimation. Bourdieu's analysis would seem to be unable to answer the question of why, for example, it was the Beatles, rather than any other pop group, who became the candidates for legitimation amongst pop intellectuals. One possible answer to this is that the Beatles' music, more than that of other 'pop' groups, was susceptible to an analysis using traditional legitimating criteria. This is made clear by Wilfrid Mellers' book on the Beatles where he provides a very thorough analysis of their music using the 'accepted musical terminology' which, as he puts it, 'has been evolved by professional musicians over some centuries' (1973, p.15). Now as I have argued earlier (and in his chapters John Shepherd provides an extended background for this argument) this musical terminology is derived from the European compositional tradition. Such an orientation leads inevitably therefore to an over-emphasis on the harmonic structure of the Beatles' songs and on those musical elements which are derived from 'classical' music at the expense of those derived from an Afro-American tradition. One consequence of this sympathetic critical appraisal of a 'pop' group's work by an academically trained musician is that, whilst it plays the valuable role of communicating to the music establishment that even by their criteria the Beatles were fine musicians, it does in the process tend to neglect many facets of the Beatles' music which the rock music lover, untutored in academic music, finds the most musically satisfying[16].

Such considerations point to the need for studies which relate analysis of the changes in legitimation to close consideration of the changing content of the 'art-works' themselves. Thus in an analysis of the increasing legitimation of the Beatles' work we should simultaneously consider the changing content of their music (see earlier comments, p.188, by critics on the 'musical development' in the Beatles' work). One might suggest that, in some cases, the content of the art-work itself is altered as a result of the kinds of drives towards legitimation that have been described. Thus, for example, Third Stream Music (the direct fusion of certain aspects of modern jazz and 'classical' music associated particularly with the work of Gunther Schuller and the Modern Jazz Quartet in the 1950s and 1960s) may have arisen partly as a result of the desire by certain jazz musicians to illustrate their own technical and artistic competence *on the classical musicians' own ground* since classical musicians would not recognise alternative (Afro-American) criteria of musical technique[17]. It is such hybrids which, owing to their dilution of Afro-American ('illegitimate') elements and adoption of certain European ('legitimate') elements, then gain something of the legitimation which the musicians desire, with all its consequences in terms of better financial and working conditions for the artist. That Afro-American music has to be diluted with the European tradition of music before it can achieve such legitimation illustrates the rationale behind musicians' cries of 'cultural repression'. Cecil Taylor, the black jazz pianist, has expressed this view forcefully:

> I've known Negro musicians who've gotten grants, but it's very interesting that no Negro jazz musician has ever gotten a grant. If you're a black pianist who wants to learn to play Beethoven, you have a pretty good chance of getting a grant. That's that fucked-up liberal idea of uplifting the black man by destroying his culture (Spellman, 1970, p.48).

Conclusion

I have argued that our society is pervaded by a pernicious distinction between 'serious' music and 'popular' music, which is part of a more general interpretation of cultural forms in terms of alleged differences between high, folk and mass culture. This viewpoint confuses questions of quality in music with questions of genre, where the Afro-American qualities of various styles of music are not recognised but rather such styles tend to be interpreted through the spectacles of the traditional 'classical' music culture merely as poor quality. This ideological view of music in contemporary society is perpetuated by any number of subtle or more explicit means — notably by various types of media policy, differential subsidisation and by the educational system (the latter to be considered at length in Chapter Seven).

Concerning the media, the British Broadcasting Corporation explicitly organises its radio channels in such a way as to perpetuate the misleading assumptions underpinning the dichotomy between 'serious' music and 'popular' music. Whilst Radio 3 is reserved almost exclusively for 'serious' music in the European tradition, both Radios 1 and 2 are dedicated to the lowest common denominator of 'easy listening' and 'popular' music taste, where internal differences within the supposedly homogeneous category of 'pop' music go largely unrecognised. The most obvious casualty of this situation has always been jazz, which has never satisfied the BBC's spurious categories of 'art' and 'culture' on the one hand or of mass popularity on the other. Less obvious is the fact that within 'pop' music there are numerous sub-types — rock music, reggae, soul and so on — which also suffer by being pigeonholed alongside the purely commercial mass 'pop'. In this respect Parker's (1975) critique of the media's policy towards 'pop' music is a well-founded one. His mistake, as discussed earlier, is both to condemn the whole of 'pop' culture on the basis of viewing only a part of it and also to see too deterministic a relationship between the means of production of music and the content and motives of the music and the musicians. For the mass culture critics' assumption that pop music can be treated as a homogeneous category masks the fact that within so-called 'pop' music there are groups of musicians who see themselves as just as serious creative artists as musicians in the European 'serious' tradition and who also make similar assumptions about 'pop' music as do 'classical' musicians.

The ideological nature of the high culture/mass culture distinction is also maintained through the establishment's attitude to the financing of the arts. Whilst the establishment castigates all 'popular' music for being commercial, its heavy subsidisation of European 'serious' music ensures that much of the latter need not even be concerned with commercial considerations. Thus much classical music (especially opera) which might not otherwise prove profitable is helped by government grants and subsidies, whilst both jazz and rock music, to survive at all, have to be commercially viable, which leads to less commercial and more experimental works in these genres being discouraged[18].

Not only does the mass culture critique contain highly questionable assumptions concerning the nature of 'popular' music, it also makes implicit assumptions about the nature of 'serious' music. Many of these assumptions are those central to Western aesthetics generally and in the sphere of music are often taken as absolutes from which other types of music (particularly 'primitive' music) are criticised[19].

The pervasion of the high/folk/mass culture terminology is illustrated by some rock critics themselves using such terminology to describe rock music:

> By pushing towards higher levels of imaginative excellence, rock has begun to realise one of the most cherished dreams of mass culture: to cultivate from the vigorous but crude growth of the popular arts a new serious art that would combine the strength of native roots with the beauty flowering from the highest art (Goldman, 1968, p.138).

And Durgnat notes that rock music 'has made nonsense of so many old barriers between commercial and folk forms and achieved an expressiveness comparable to high culture' (1971, p.47).

Such legitimations of rock music which incorporate 'high culture' terminology, by using the musical and artistic criteria of the establishment, serve merely to reinforce the acceptance of assumptions which have been shown to be highly questionable. As Morse notes in his discussion of Tamla Motown music: 'For the guardians of culture it means that the name of the game is still the same. Not one of their assumptions about what is valuable or significant in music need be seriously questioned' (1971, p.47). Once these assumptions are questioned one must conclude with Morse that:

> Just as many black speakers have said that there is no 'Negro' problem, only a 'white' problem, so it could be argued, there is no popular culture problem, only an elite culture problem; the former is viewed through the distorting spectacles of the latter (1971, p.51).

NOTES

1.   An expanded version of parts of this chapter appeared in Vulliamy (1975).

2.   For origins of the mass society debate, see Bramson (1961) and Kornhauser (1959); for origins of the 'popular culture' debate, see Lowenthal (1950).

3.   Routh (1968), for example, addresses his book explicitly to the problem that so few people either understand or appreciate contemporary 'serious' music.

4.   The term 'European serious tradition' is used by Pleasants (1969). Many other terms are sometimes used to cover the range of music from the Baroque, through the Romantics to twentieth-century 'serious' music — for example, this range is sometimes called 'western art music'. For simplicity, I will often refer to this range as 'classical' music; the word 'classical' in inverted commas is similarly used by writers on music and music education to describe loosely this range of music [see, for example, Schuller (1968): 'Classical music is used to define the European non-jazz tradition, as exemplified by composers like Bach, Beethoven, Brahms, Debussy, Schoenberg etc.,' (p 7, n. 6)]. The use of classical without the inverted commas will then refer quite specifically to the classical period of music generally identified as the 'serious' music emanating from Austria/Bohemia in the period approximately 1750-1830.

5.   For evidence on this point see Pleasants (1969) and my chapters in Vulliamy and Lee (1976).

6.   See Bourdieu (1966) for some insights into the processes involved.

7.   For a useful, short summary of Afro-American musical characteristics, see Williams-Jones (1975).

8.   See Schuller (1968), Chapter I.

9.   See Berger (1947) and Leonard (1962).

10.   For further elucidation of this point see John Shepherd's chapters in this book. In addition Keil (1966) argues this point with specific reference to jazz by focussing upon the concept of rhythmic swing in jazz. See also the discussion in Chapter Five of the misunderstanding of the blues scale.

11.   The section that follows forms part of a chapter of a dissertation submitted for the M.Sc. in the Sociology of Education at the University of London Institute of Education (see Vulliamy, G., *Music Education in Secondary Schools: Some Sociological Observations,* unpublished dissertation, 1972). Whilst full details and limitations of the methodology used will be found in the 'Appendix on Methodology' of the dissertation, certain relevant points need stressing here.

I do not wish to suggest that there is universal agreement amongst rock writers, musicians and the audience. There are, however, certain shared assumptions concerning the nature of the 'rock ethic' (see Morse, 1971, p 48) — assumptions which form the background to debates over particular issues. The categories by which rock musicians identify different types of 'pop' music would perhaps best be illustrated by a participant observation study, as in Becker's work. Here, however, I illustrate these categories from the literature on rock music. On reading either critical books on rock music or interviews with musicians in rock magazines or letters to these magazines from members of the audience for rock music, I noted any statement that illustrated how rock musicians, critics or the audience for rock music perceived the differences within 'popular' music. I then drew out the categories that occurred most frequently, and these are then used as illustrative material in the text. Two important limitations of this method should perhaps be noted here:

a)   I have necessarily had to be highly selective in my use of quotations. Whilst an attempt has been made to include views which occur frequently in the literature on rock music (and in this sense one might suggest that each quotation used represents a widely held view), my selection must also have been influenced by my own commonsense understanding of rock musicians and their audience derived from practical experience drumming in a number of semi-professional rock bands.

b)   The relation of audience views as expressed in the letter columns to a weekly 'pop' magazine (like *Melody Maker*) to those audience views not expressed in such a manner remains unexplored. So also is the relation between views expressed by well-known rock musicians when they are interviewed and the views of rock musicians generally.

12.   At the time of writing, 'progressive pop' was roughly synonymous with rock music.

13.   'Functional' in this context means that the music is not simply listened to but is also used to accompany other activities such as dancing.

14.   This applies not only to the audience but also to the background of the musicians. As Melly notes:

It was typical of what was changing in pop that, apart from their drummer, all the Who were ex-grammar school and that their leading spirit, Peter Townshend, had been an art student.... By the middle 60s pop had become very conscious of its aims, and was attracting those who would almost certainly have been drawn toward jazz, probably modern jazz (1970, p 103).

Nuttall (1970, pp 11-37) also stresses the importance of the British art schools as a breeding ground for rock groups in the mid 1960s.

15.   By 'pop' in the first sentence Melly is referring to 'rock', as is made evident by his reference to pop festivals ('open-air concerts') which feature rock music. Whilst American writers usually use the term 'rock' to describe such music, many British writers still use the traditional term 'pop'. The latter part of the above quote refers to 'skinheads', a particular working-class 'cult' at the time of Melly's writing.

16.   This point is developed further in Vulliamy and Lee (1976) and lies at the heart of Chester's (1970) argument that rock music must be judged

from 'intensional' rather than 'extensional' criteria, since its dominant musical values are from an Afro-American musical tradition rather than the European compositional one. Thus, whilst parts of the Beatles' work can be analysed in extensional terms since they owe a considerable debt to the 'classical' tradition, any analysis of, for example, Jimi Hendrix's music would need to be exclusively in intensional terms, because his inspiration is derived almost totally from the Afro-American tradition.

17.   'His [John Lewis' — leader of the M.J.Q.] motives were that he wished to insist on the artistic value of jazz, and to this end he projected the group by such means as the still-debated wearing of evening dress, and by formal concert-hall announcements' (Lee, 1972, p 116) and 'In the course of assimilating more and more elements of classical music — and thereby, incidentally, gaining social status — jazz generally turns to early classical forms, especially a free kind of counterpoint' (Stearns, 1956, p 229).

18.   The 1975/76 Arts Council of Great Britain expenditure on grants and subsidies for music breaks down as follows (see 31st Annual Report and Accounts of the Arts Council, pp A10-A11):
Royal Opera House: £3,410,000
English National Opera Ltd: £1,848,000
Other Grants: £3,082,222
of which the only grants to Afro-American musical styles were £18,000 to the Jazz Centre Society Ltd, about £8,000 to other jazz groups or organisations and a few small bursaries to individual jazz musicians. Thus less than 1/3rd of 1% of the total music budget was spent on jazz, whilst rock music received no subsidisation at all.

The ideology of 'pop' music as 'commercial' and 'imposed from above, thus exploiting the musical tastes and emotions of young people' is criticised at length in Vulliamy and Lee (1976).

19.   In this context see Merriam's (1967, Chapter One) discussion of a comparison between Western aesthetics and the aesthetic of the Flathead Indian with respect to music (see also Merriam, 1964, Chapter Thirteen). African and Western aesthetics with respect to music are compared in Walton (1972). The whole debate over music aesthetics would benefit enormously from further comparative studies of the aesthetics of 'primitive' music. Just as Horton's (1967) comparative analysis of African traditional thought and Western science allows us to view Western assumptions concerning scientific rationality in a different light, so do studies of 'primitive' aesthetics raise interesting questions concerning the nature of Western aesthetics. John Shepherd expands on these points in his chapters in this book.

Chapter Seven

Music as a Case Study in the 'New Sociology of Education'

GRAHAM VULLIAMY

Introduction

The Sociology of Education has undergone a far-reaching change of emphasis in recent years. The prime concerns of the 1950s and 1960s, input-output studies focussing on the interrelationships between the educational system and the stratification system, have given way to a more explicit recognition of the social and political nature of education. The change was first heralded by the publication of *Knowledge and Control* (1971) edited by Michael F.D. Young and, whilst the contributions to that book come from widely diverse perspectives, two in particular serve to mark a considerable break with most previous studies of education. The first is the application of the sociology of knowledge to education where in particular the curriculum, rather than being viewed as a relatively unproblematic feature of the educational process, is viewed as a social construct — created, supported and perpetuated by social groups in ways which might be examined by sociologists. The second is the influence of phenomenology where studies in other substantive areas of sociology, notable deviance theory, have radically called into question many traditional empirical research techniques and many of the assumptions of positivist sociological theory. The phenomenological critique of the traditional Sociology of Education suggests that social structural statistical correlations, such as those of working-class background and educational achievement, at the macro level take for granted certain processes at the micro interaction level about which we know very little owing to the paucity of descriptive observation research in schools and school classrooms. One consequence of this has been that explanations of school failure tend to have been located in the home backgrounds of pupils, in theories of cultural and linguistic deprivation, rather than in the social nature of what pupils fail at. The latter would point to a critical consideration of both the school curriculum and the social assumptions underpinning teachers' definitions of knowledge and ability in the context of interaction in the classroom.

Recent studies have therefore viewed the curriculum not as an objective reality independent of teachers and learners ('curriculum as fact') but rather as the product of teachers' and pupils' everyday practices in the classroom, inextricably linked with more general assumptions about teaching and learning, methods of assessment, problems of discipline and so on ('curriculum as practice')[1]. However, an important limitation of phenomenological studies of classroom interaction with such an orientation is that there is a tendency for them to exist in an ahistorical void, and consequently too great an emphasis can be put on the power of the participants (in this case, teachers and pupils) to actively construct their reality, at the expense of the view that actors are powerfully constrained by historical and structural factors.

Since a major section of this chapter is the report of a participant observation study of a music department in a comprehensive school[2] where, like Keddie's (1971) study, a sociology of knowledge perspective is taken to examine what counts as knowledge and ability for the teachers, it is important that such an empirical study can be located in an historical context; by doing so we can perhaps better understand the historical emergence and persistence of particular conceptions of knowledge. Esland's (1971) analysis of the subject and pedagogical perspectives of teachers provides a useful framework in this context since it emphasises that teachers, rather than working in a vacuum, incorporate the institutional culture of schooling, which embodies certain historical assumptions concerning what is valued knowledge, what the purposes of schooling are and so on. He notes that 'the knowledge which a teacher thinks "fills up" his subject is held in common with members of a supporting community who collectively approve its paradigms and utility criteria, as they are legitimated in training courses and "official" statements' (1971, p.99). A brief consideration of the history of music teaching in schools, together with statements from contemporary music educators, might therefore give us some insights into certain key features of the subject perspective of music teaching.

Historical Background to School Music Teaching in England

At the beginning of the present century the teaching of music in all schools (other than the public schools), whether at elementary or secondary level, was confined to class singing. This was a reflection of the fact that in the nineteenth century all the great music educators were concerned primarily with vocal music in schools. Rainbow (1967) suggests that this emphasis on vocal music resulted from music educators of the period seeing the main benefits to be derived from school music teaching as being religious and moral[3]. Singing had been introduced into schools as an attempt to improve the quality of church music, where the singing of the 'yokel choirs' had caused a musical scandal (Rainbow, 1968). In addition, John Turner and most of his fellow pioneers in school music teaching stressed the beneficial moral influence of singing, not so much because of the music itself but because of the 'partially subconscious effect of these frequently repeated maxims and moral ditties which formed the texts of the songs concerned' (Rainbow, 1967, p.157).

Although singing has remained an integral part of the music teaching in most schools to this day, the scope of 'class' music has increased enormously since the turn of the century. A major influence has been the development of the 'music appreciation' movement; this was associated particularly with the writings of Stewart MacPherson and Percy Scholes in the 1920s and 1930s[4]. They emphasised the importance of guided listening to music in addition to the performance of music. The appreciation of music was to be improved by analytic study of the form of the music, by increasing pupils' knowledge of the instruments of the orchestra and by giving historical information concerning the composer and the composition. The importance of this movement in the development of school music teaching is that it enabled music to be established more firmly as a 'class' subject; if music could be shown to have its own grammar, literature, analysis and history then it could be taught like any other subject and deserved a place in the grammar school curriculum[5]. This led to a situation where 'By 1939 it was fairly generally assumed that music should have its place in the secondary curriculum, and that it should have syllabuses and examinations' (Brace, 1970, p.16).

The reorganisation of secondary schools with the Education Act of 1944 resulted in an increase in the specialist teaching of music in schools and an acceptance of the principle of general music classes for all. Courses in music instruction in schools were proposed incorporating 'sightsinging, theory, the playing of recorders, musical appreciation and history' (Brace, 1970, p.16). These still make up the staple diet of class music in most schools, although there has recently been a considerable interest in the possibilities of 'creative' music-making in the classroom, a point to which I shall return shortly.

Running parallel to the growth of music as a class subject has been the increasing importance of extra-curricular musical activities in maintained secondary schools. In this respect the influence of the musical traditions built up in many leading public schools has been dominant. Even in the last century many public schools had strong musical traditions based not only on vocal music but also on orchestral playing. A strong emphasis on individual instrumental tuition led to the possibilities of school chamber music groups and orchestras and house music competitions. However, it was not until the late 1940s, when local authorities began to accept responsibility for providing instrumental tuition in state secondary schools, that there could be a real expansion of extra-curricular instrumental music teaching in these schools. The enormous increase over the last twenty years in the number of schoolchildren receiving instrumental tuition in schools has led to a rapid growth of extra-curricular orchestral music. These extra-curricular activities have placed today's school music teacher in a very difficult position because, as Brace has noted, 'he finds himself in the extraordinary position of having more expected of him *outside* his working day than in it' (1970, p.11).

Music educators give many reasons why music should have an important place in schools:

> Some would stress its purely aesthetic importance, as a mode of experience distinct from any other; some strongly advocate it as a creative medium through which the personality can be developed and enriched; others would emphasise its social function in the community; others again find in music a focus for the interrelation of subject interests, and thus for breaking down barriers between disciplines. (Schools Council, 1971, p.8).

I propose to argue, however, that whatever the stated aim of the music teacher, the content of the music lesson, whether it be a lesson in appreciation, the history of music, in singing or in practical music-making, is restricted to one particular type of music — namely, music in the European 'serious' tradition[6]. This perspective is evident in an examination of the literature on music education; one of the most persistent themes in the latter is an assumed dichotomy between 'serious' and 'popular' music. This is particularly apparent in the way in which music educators see the aim of musical appreciation, where the concept of 'good' music conforms to the types of music in which the writer on this subject has been trained as a musician. Thus Brocklehurst, defining the main aim of musical appreciation in schools suggests:

> The primary purpose of musical appreciation is to inculcate a love and understanding of good music. It is surely the duty of teachers to do all they can to prevent young people falling ready prey to the purveyors of commercialised 'popular' music, for these slick, high-pressure salesmen have developed the exploitation of teenagers into a fine art (1962, p.65).

Similar sentiments were expressed at a symposium on the subject of music education: 'As I see it our job is to get them from this level [referring to pop music] to another level, and quite frankly the schools are not doing it.' (Williams quoted in Grant, 1963, p.14).

Music educators have attempted to promote their aims of a 'love and understanding of good music' in many ways. The emphasis at the beginning of this century was on singing and this also involved the teaching of traditional music notation to aid the process of sight-singing[7]. The 'music appreciation' movement emphasised the importance of listening to good music; this emphasis is usefully viewed in the context of the growing importance of the mass media at that time (the 1920s and 1930s) and the consequent need, it was then felt, for the listener to be able to discriminate between the good and the bad he hears. As the mass media have grown in importance, so has the music teacher become more concerned in this respect:

> They [the mass media] have also however brought daily contact with a stream of commercial rubbish. He [the teacher] is now faced with the necessity of developing the power of musical discrimination in his pupils (Rainbow, 1968, p.32).

Thus until recently the main emphases of class music teaching in secondary schools were on music appreciation, incorporating listening to and discussing the history of 'classical' music, and singing, together with the teaching of 'classical' notation and theory. This I will call the traditional paradigm of music teaching. An examination of the recent literature on music education suggests that within the music teaching establishment there has been a small section of musicians and educators who have challenged the traditional paradigm. They have suggested that far more emphasis should be placed on children actually playing and creating music in the classroom, and that this could be achieved by focussing on the techniques the contemporary avant-garde composers use rather than by teaching the traditional notation of 'classical' music. Thus George Self, one of the pioneers of this approach, which I shall call the avant-garde paradigm of music teaching, has said:

> In school child composers (average children, for we all have some creative ability) are bogged down by a notation which demands considerable technical skill to use and which serious composers have either done away with or modified to suit their needs. . . .With respect to pitch for nearly 60 years composers have been satisfied that any combination of sounds may be effective (in context) both in vertical and horizontal array; yet in schools we are chained to the diatonic scale, and chords derived from it. (Self, 1965, pp.126 and 127).

The shift in such an approach is away from teaching pupils to play instruments the 'right' way and towards the actual composition of music and the creative manipulation of sounds:

> Simple methods — which are often complex in terms of their overall result — are given by which the individual pupil can create his own music. Creativity is encouraged to the utmost degree — a creativity whose roots lie in our own environment and in the work of present-day composers (Dennis, 1970, p.3).

Such an approach to music education requires a radical redefinition of what counts as music; music can be created not only by using traditional instruments but also by using tape-recorders and other electronic means, by using 'everyday' sounds and so on. The criteria of successful teaching will necessarily change:

> If the children's activities are truly creative there will be no one 'right' answer. The only judgement worth making will be those we want the children to make for themselves in the process of composition: does this piece hang together? Does it 'read as a whole'? Does it say what I want it to say? Is there anything in it which should be rejected because it destroys the wholeness of the music? (Paynter and Aston, 1970, p.13).

In my last chapter I showed how the music establishment's conceptions of 'serious' music excluded any really serious consideration of Afro-American styles of music. This provides one way of understanding why recent 'reform' of music education has involved a move from what I have called the traditional paradigm to the avant-garde one, such a change taking place despite the fact that avant-garde 'serious' music has a very small audience, whilst Afro-American musical styles are overwhelmingly popular with young people. Thus the rejection of Afro-American music and the interest in avant-garde approaches in music education is best understood by considering the historical reactions of the music establishment to jazz and rock music and by noting that the 'atonal' revolution associated with avant-garde 'serious' music was a revolution that occurred *within* the music establishment. The avant-garde's leading exponents, whilst violating traditional 'classical' musical criteria, nevertheless preserved the latter's cultural criteria associated with the presentation of musical 'art-works' in the concert hall.

Thus the subject perspective of music teaching contains within it historical assumptions concerning the rigid separation of 'serious' music from 'popular' music. In terms of Young's (1971) sociological analysis of the school curriculum, 'serious' music is defined as high status knowledge and 'pop' music as low status knowledge and, in Keddie's (1971) terms, 'serious' music is the subject-based knowledge of the school and 'pop' music the everyday knowledge of most of the school pupils. It is part of Young's and Keddie's argument that, in order to preserve the rigid stratification of knowledge in schools and the consequent rigid hierarchy between teacher and taught, the culture of the pupils has to be seen as a deprived one, so that cultural deprivation becomes a plausible explanation for educational failure. Such models of cultural deprivation often involve highly misleading assumptions concerning the culture of the pupils where that culture is viewed through the spectacles of a mainstream culture which is treated as unproblematic. Such is the case with music where analyses and views of 'pop' music are filtered through the musical and cultural criteria of 'serious' music, a point developed at length in the previous chapter.

Recent approaches to the sociology of education stress that explanation of school failure should be seen as lying as much in the social nature of the teachers' everyday practices as in the characteristics of the pupils, and a plea has been made for more ethnographic studies of classroom interaction which might suggest how teachers' conceptions of knowledge and ability influence the success and failure of pupils[8]. Such research, carried out from a phenomenological perspective in sociology, treats as problematic those categories (such as intelligence, subject knowledge, criteria of educational success and failure, and so on) which educators and many sociologists usually take for granted. The following case study, exploratory in nature, is of this type and is based on observation of the music department in a large (about 2,000) mixed comprehensive school. The school was chosen because it was known to be highly unusual in terms of the range and quality of its musical activities; the fact that it had not only a school orchestra but also a school dance band meant that the school's musical activities were not confined to 'classical' music as in most other schools. This seemed an excellent opportunity to observe how the music staff interpreted and maintained a situation where 'what counts as music[9]' was far more varied than in most schools.

A Case Study[10]

The school is situated in an area which is very heterogeneous in terms of the social class composition of its residents but this heterogeneity is not reflected in the school's intake; this is due to the close proximity of other public and grammar schools which not only take a large majority of the middle-class residents in the area but also cream off the 'high ability' pupils. Consequently, at the time of my case study, a large proportion of the pupils in the school were from working-class homes (many from a neighbouring housing estate); in addition about 15 per cent of each year's intake were coloured 'immigrants'.

The departments in the school were grouped according to traditional subjects and my own observations of classroom behaviour were confined entirely to the music department, although I did have the opportunity of talking to members of staff in other departments in the general staff common room.

The music department consisted of the Head of Music and two other full-time music teachers (whom I shall call henceforth teacher B — The Deputy Head of Music — and teacher C). The primary responsibility of these three teachers was the teaching of class music and the organisation and participation in all the extra-curricular musical activities in the school. In addition there were also about ten visiting instrumental teachers (for example, teachers of brass instruments, woodwind, piano, percussion and so on).

Class music was taught in the school for two periods (40 minutes each) a week to all groups up to (usually) the 4th year. The Head of Music's intention was that in one of these periods the pupils should learn to play the recorder and at the same time the basis of musical theory and notation; the other period was to be used either for singing or for 'appreciation'. The latter was taken by the music staff to include listening to music, the history of music, the provision of information about music, which might include details of the instruments of the orchestra or of the lives of the famous composers and so on. Class music in the 3rd and 4th years was also used for the teaching of both 'O' level music and C.S.E. music[11]. Each year group in the school was fairly rigidly streamed. There were usually twelve streams in a year but the main divisions were between a couple of 'top ability' groups, a couple of 'low ability' groups (usually referred to as 'remedial') and the remaining 'middle ability' groups. These groups remained the same for the teaching of all subjects, including class music.

Extra-curricular music consisted of a large number of pupils (about 150) receiving individual instrumental tuition from the visiting instrumental teachers. These lessons took place mainly during time allotted to other timetabled school periods; however, a complicated rota system had been instituted to enable pupils to miss a different lesson each week on going for their instrumental tuition. The school has only had two Heads of Music (including the present one) and it was the policy of both these that provision should be made for as many pupils as possible to play musical instruments. The school had, therefore, built up a large supply of musical instruments which could be loaned to pupils for their instrumental tuition. Those pupils who progressed well on their instruments were then encouraged to buy their own, if this was possible, so that their 'school' instrument could be released again to be used for another beginner. This strong emphasis on instrumental music teaching in the school, together with the large number of pupils who were therefore learning instruments, enabled a very wide range of extra-curricular music groups to form. Thus the school had a large orchestra, a senior and junior military band (all these mainly under the direction of the

Head of Music), a dance band (under the direction of teacher B) in addition to numerous recorder groups, guitar groups, woodwind groups and so on, some of which were directed by the instrumental teachers of the particular class of instruments involved. There was also a large choir under the direction mainly of teacher C.

I have arranged my data under the headings of 'teachers' perspectives[12] on music and music teaching' and 'teachers' perspectives on pupils and the school organisation'.

a) Teachers' Perspectives on Music and Music Teaching.

The Head of Music was quite explicit concerning the major aims of the school music as he saw them. One of these aims was to produce 'good all-round musicians', which resulted in a much wider view of 'what counts as music' than is customary in secondary schools. He was critical of those schools who see their aim as one of producing only good symphony orchestra musicians, because there are very few available places for new musicians in orchestras, owing to the limited number of full-time orchestras in Britain. The Head of Music pointed out that most full-time musicians have to earn their living playing a wide variety of music from the 'classics', through the light classics to dance music and session work on 'pop' records. Only a very small minority of members of the Musicians' Union were in fact full-time members of symphony orchestras. A similar point was made to me by one of the instrumental teachers who was critical of the Colleges and Academies of Music for turning out students who, whilst being very good technically on their instruments, could not play anything which wasn't in the 'classical' tradition. He suggested that one of the main advantages of music in the school was that the pupils were required to play an enormous variety of music ranging from orchestral 'classical' through orchestral march band music to dance band music and jazz. Such a variety meant that the pupils had to develop extremely good powers of sight-reading so that they could play adequately in the different contexts. It also meant that pupils interested in becoming jazz musicians, as opposed to 'classical' musicians, had the opportunity for socialisation into a different tradition of music as a result of playing in the dance band[13].

Teacher B, who as a class music teacher was unusual in that he had been a professional musician all his life[14] before taking up full-time teaching, had started the dance band when he was appointed as a full-time teacher in the school. However, it had also been the Head of Music's wish to have such a dance band in order to give the school music greater variety and to get more pupils interested in the school music; teacher B felt that one of the main reasons for his appointment was that he had had wide experience as a professional musician playing in dance bands and orchestras.

The strong emphasis on instrumental music in the school led to a corresponding stress on learning the 'discipline' of music — that is, the 'correct' way of playing instruments which involved learning musical notation and the ability to sight-read well. The equation of 'playing the instrument well' and sight-reading meant that there was a corresponding emphasis on notated rather than on predominantly improvised music. Teacher B did, however, teach some of the instrumentalists in the dance band the principles of improvisation so that they could solo effectively in a jazz style whilst being backed by the rest of the band. But in the context of the school's music, improvisation necessarily had to come after the teaching of conventional notation; this meant that pupils who might have learned their instruments in an 'oral-aural' fashion (for example, from records) would be unable to play in the context of the school music unless they also learned conventional notation. The possible clash between 'reading the dots' and learning to play aurally was in fact apparent to teacher B. In the course of a conversation with me on his experience running the dance band he commented on a coloured saxophone player in the front row of the band:

> It's funny he's not very good at sight-reading but he can *really* play. I found that when I asked him to sight-read a line, he paused and said, 'Can you play it first, please Sir?' Then immediately I'd played it , out it would come . . . ba, doo, ba [imitates sounds of saxophone]. In other words he was learning aurally — he could copy me perfectly with a *real jazz feel,* but found sight-reading difficult [his emphases].

This comment suggests that teacher B (as one would expect from his own professional experience) understood the importance of differing technical criteria in judging the phrasing of a saxophone section. A section reading the 'dots' perfectly may very well not play with a 'real jazz feel' (a jazz musician would say 'It doesn't swing') whilst someone who cannot read the 'dots' at all might very well play with a perfect 'jazz feel'. In fact many jazz musicians would say that

if a 'real jazz feel' is to be achieved then learning aurally must come
prior to learning the 'dots', if indeed the latter have to be learned at
all. In rehearsing the dance band teacher B said he taught the
sections (saxophone, brass and so on) orally by singing the parts
himself out loud and getting the sections to play them as he sang
them, and not as they were written down. He did this because this
was 'the best way to teach them to play in a real jazz style'.

If we return to the school's emphasis on learning the 'discipline' of
music and learning to play musical instruments 'correctly', it is clear
that this aim clashes with some of the suggested aims of the
'avant-garde' music educators — 'plink-a-plonk' approaches[15] were
frequently the subject of ridicule in the music staffroom. The Head
of Music explained to me his reasons for objecting to the 'plink-a-
plonk' approaches. His main point was that if music is to be taught
at all, then this must involve the teaching of conventional music
notation and this the 'avant-garde' educators rejected:

> I believe the reason they're doing that sort of thing is that they
> can't do the conventional stuff. They are not good musicians
> and find it too difficult to teach the conventional stuff. It's just
> the in-thing at the moment. People will do anything to be ultra
> with it.

However, his condemnation was not a blanket one covering all
attempts at music making in the classroom; whilst rejecting the
methods associated with, for example, George Self[16], where a new
system of simpler notation is involved, he did feel that the pioneering
ideas of Carl Orff[17] could be used, because here the music-making
takes place within the confines of the conventional music notation
and can be used to help teach this notation.

He also had aesthetic objections to the 'avant-garde' approaches:
'As I keep saying to Mr. X (visiting school music inspector): "What
great music has been composed in that idiom?" Nothing'. A similar
point was made by the percussion teacher whose views concerning
the 'avant-garde' approaches I explicitly enquired about because I
knew that he had previously been teaching at a school with such an
approach. This teacher's main objection was that so much money in
his old school was spent on buying cheap, simple percussion
instruments to be used by all the pupils in the classroom ('just toys
— they don't even have the full chromatic scale'), whilst 'proper'
instruments were not made available to him for his instrumental
tuition ('I had only one snare drum for 27 pupils'). He continued to

say that the pupils were not taught to play the instruments properly but just told to 'bang away' as they liked: 'None of the kids have the faintest idea what they're doing. The music is dissonant, toneless and artless; pupils just banging away on a brand new expensive timpani with no idea at all.'

The Head of Music's final objection against 'plink-a-plonk' was that the pupils themselves wouldn't like it. Whilst observing a dance band rehearsal at lunchtime which a large number of school pupils (say about 100) were attentively watching, I commented on the interest that the dance band seemed to arouse in the school. The Head of Music agreed and continued: 'How many people do you think would come to listen if we put 'plink-a-plonk' on for them? What these kids like is music with rhythm and melody.' He also felt that it was important that at school concerts, which parents and others attended, the pupils should get well applauded for their performances: 'Nothing succeeds like success. But if we had a "plink-a-plonk" concert the audience wouldn't even know whether a particular item had ended or not.' The dance band, however, he said always went down extremely well with the audience and he felt that it was important that such audience enthusiasm should be communicated to pupils.

My comments up to this point have mainly concerned the extra-curricular music activities; I will now consider certain aspects of the school's class music teaching. As would be expected, attitudes similar to those I have already described prevailed in this sphere of teaching as well. The Head of Music felt that he should play a wide variety of music in the classroom and not just impose a narrow type of 'classical' music on the pupils which is what he took to be the practice of many music teachers. 'Mr. X would be shocked at some of the stuff I play — even Gilbert and Sullivan is not quite acceptable to him. But I believe you should play them as wide a variety as possible.' One would expect 'a wide variety' to mean very different things depending on the standpoint ('relevance criteria') of the actor in question. In this case my observation of classroom lessons given by the Head of Music suggested that a wide variety of music was played ranging from 'serious classical' music through the 'light classics', orchestral dance music and 'pop'[18] music. What is common to this range are the accepted standards of musical technique and form characteristic of the European 'serious' tradition. Music in the Afro-American tradition which has different musical values was not played except in the context of 'letting the pupils play their own "pop" records'. The Head of Music, however, did have a knowledge of the history of jazz as his C.S.E. groups did one paper on 'Jazz', but at the time of my observation this part of the course was taught by a student teacher whose empathy for jazz was unusual (as he admitted) for someone trained in the 'classical' tradition, since he had at one time himself played in a traditional jazz band. Whilst all three teachers were well aware of the existence of jazz, only teacher C, who was young and in her first full-time teaching job, had some knowledge of the internal differences within 'pop' music. She often let her pupils play their 'pop' records at the end of the lesson and she commented to me about the different tastes of the pupils — her 5th year form bringing 'progressive rock' records, whilst the earlier years preferred reggae or 'top 20 pop'.

One interpretation of the use made of 'pop' records in the classroom is that they were used as a control mechanism; that is, the promise was made to play 'their' records at the end of the lesson as long as their behaviour was satisfactory. During my observation there was only one exception to this practice of using 'their' records in this context and that was when teacher B decided to devote a whole lesson to listening to them. The teacher wanted to make the pupils really listen to their records (rather than, for example, treat them as 'background noise') and, therefore, after playing them he asked the pupils questions about them such as 'What instrument is that playing?' or 'What is unusual about the rhythm of this record?' An attempt was made to treat the records in the same way as if they had been the 'classical' records on the turntable which were to be analysed: 'We're not going to use them as a background because if they're worth bringing along they're worth listening to; so let's listen to them.'

But the discussion of 'their' records within the category structure (musical) of the teacher was clearly alien to the pupils: it produced a situation where the natural aesthetic response of the pupil clashed with the technical musical criteria of the teacher. For example, after playing a reggae record teacher B commented: 'The organ was out of tune when it came in', to which the pupil who owned the record replied: 'But it's supposed to be. It sounds good.' Teacher B went on: 'You can do things for effect but you needn't play out of tune for that'. The pupil then mumbled something and after a brief pause the teacher concluded: 'It's either in tune or out of tune.'

Keddie's (1971) discussion of 'classroom knowledge' provides a framework within which such remarks might be usefully analysed. She suggests that it is in the relation between the school ('subject'-centred) knowledge of the teacher and the commonsense or non-school knowledge of the pupils that one might usefully interpret the academic success of certain pupils. However, one of the limitations of her particular analysis is that, in viewing 'everyday knowledge' as an 'alternative system of thought' (p.150) to school knowledge, she fails adequately to specify the criteria by which one can identify 'everyday knowledge'; such criteria are necessary for any discussion of the possible status of such knowledge *vis-à-vis* school knowledge. Although I have insufficient data of classroom interaction (particularly because tape-recorders were not used) the example quoted above is suggestive in that the pupils' natural ('everyday') aesthetic response might reflect musical criteria which are different from those of teacher B, rooted as they might be in the appreciation of Afro-American styles of music rather than 'classical' music. A further example from my data might again be suggestive in this respect. The Head of Music was explaining to 3XY (a third year 'remedial' class) that the correct way to play the piano was not to play it too loudly. He remarked that 'the piano never sounds nice played loud' (this remark was followed by a demonstration, playing a couple of chords on the piano). One of the coloured pupils in the class then turned round to his friend and said 'What about that jazzman; he bangs it!' to which his friend said 'Yea!' Now to this observer it was unclear in what 'spirit' the pupil had made this comment — he may have said this just as a 'put-on'[19] — but in giving his response he is using alternative musical criteria which to a jazz musician would be quite valid. The piano in jazz is often used in a very much more percussive way than in traditional 'classical' music, and such percussive effects often necessitate 'banging it'.

Clearly I have selected these two examples to suggest a certain point; in order to be anything more than highly tentative a close analysis of classroom interaction must be made to see whether it can be shown that pupils, in giving and justifying their 'natural' aesthetic responses, are drawing on musical criteria which could be rooted more in the Afro-American tradition of music than the European 'serious' tradition, or whether in fact their responses are unrelated to either tradition of music. In this respect the results of teacher B's use of 'pop' music in the classroom also raises questions concerning differential methods of aesthetic response to musical styles by social groups. Bearing in mind my earlier reference to comparative aesthetics in the last chapter it might be suggested that, in refusing to analyse his 'pop' records, the pupil's attitude to music is similar to that shown by an African or Red Indian community in their responses to 'primitive' music[20]. This then raises the question of whether it is possible to treat 'their' records in the classroom in the same way as the pupils themselves treat them, and suggests that we might, therefore, investigate the assumptions implicit in the strategy of both listening to and analysing any type of music in the classroom[21].

We have already seen that during the first three years of class music the music periods were divided into one where the recorder was learned, with the emphasis on 'learning to play the instrument well' and on learning musical notation to enable other instruments to be easily learned; the other period being designed for singing and appreciation. The aim of the appreciation side was not only to listen to music but also to provide factual information about music and the history of music.

The implications of the stated aims of music in the school can be usefully viewed in the light of a consideration of teachers' perspectives on pupils and on the organisation of the school.

b) Teachers' Perspectives on Pupils and on the School Organization

The music teachers received groups of pupils which had already been streamed, for their class music lessons and, as one would expect[22], this influenced the teachers' perceptions of the pupils. The prevailing definition of 'what counts as music' in the school with its emphasis on musical literacy, the provision of information about music, and the teaching of musical theory (all of which were strongly emphasised at 'A' and 'O' level music, and, to a lesser extent, in C.S.E) made the 'discipline' of music not unlike other academic disciplines with their emphasis on literacy, abstract theory and so on[23]. It was not surprising to find, therefore, that the music teachers should assume that those pupils (in the upper streams) who were good at other academic subjects might be good at the 'discipline of music', whilst those pupils who had failed in other academic subjects (that is, those in the lower streams) would also fail at music. This assumption clearly had implications for the ways in which the different streams were taught. The top streams, some of whom were taking 'O' level and C.S.E., were taught the relevant parts of the syllabus which involved an elementary knowledge of musical notation (more elaborate for 'O' level), knowledge of aspects of the history of music, information about famous composers and detailed analysis of given set works.

The lower streams, however, presented particular problems to the teacher in terms of discipline (problems perceived by the teachers), and in this context attempts to teach notation or extensive information about the history of 'classical' music were relaxed in favour of playing *their* records or discussing aspects of music (and other topics) which the teachers felt the pupils might find interesting. The lower the stream the sooner was playing the recorder relaxed, as it seemed that in the lower streams there was a considerable hostility towards playing the recorder, especially in the third year. There was a general feeling amongst the music staff that there was little one could do with the lower streams in terms of teaching them music. The Head of Music had particularly strong feelings about 3XY, a third year 'remedial' group who had the reputation amongst all the staff of being the most 'difficult' class. The Head of Music felt that they were uneducable and shouldn't have music at all. With such a group he usually let them play their records (most of which were reggae records) and the coloured pupils would dance to them at the same time. On one occasion the Head of Music commented to me on the pupils in the group dancing to their records:

> See, they're as happy as anything doing that. It's good to let them release energy here, then they'll be less likely to cause a disturbance somewhere else. . . . See, that music is their culture; it's no good trying to give them Beethoven — they're just as happy with that stuff. Of course the musical content of it is nil.

I then asked him whether the white pupils liked reggae as well as the coloured ones. He replied: 'No, not so much. But of course it's a question of ability — generally the lower the ability, the more they like it.'

This linking of certain patterns of perceived ability and tastes in music was an assumption that influenced the type of music made available for pupils in the classroom for listening purposes. Generally speaking, in the higher streams 'serious' 'classical' music was played whilst the lower streams were given a wide variety of 'light classics' and orchestral dance music. The Head of Music felt that the top streams 'have the capacity to concentrate much longer on good music'[24]. The main aim of music appreciation, as he saw it, was the enjoyment of 'good music' and success was partly measured in these terms; as he remarked to me talking about the 'good' classes:

> 4T is a good class too. You know they were terrible in the third year but now some of them are quite interested. I was talking to one of them and I asked him whether he had liked any of the records I had played, and he said 'Yes, all of them'. It's gratifying when that happens. They are much more prepared to listen to good music now.

This suggests that for pupils to succeed in class music they must be prepared to take over the teacher categories of 'good' music, which might be compared with Keddie's discussion of a similar point. Thus in the 'O' level group, discussion of music was couched in terms of the dichotomy between 'great' music and 'popular' music, so that the Head of Music could say in an 'O' level class that I observed:

> A lot of music around today will be totally forgotten in 50 years' time — take pop music for example. Pop music is alright for those who like that sort of thing. But it's just put out for commercial profit — they try to please as many people as possible — the music is deliberately made simple for the listener. But it will soon be forgotten because there's nothing to it. The really great music takes time to appreciate; the first time you hear Bach you may not like it, but if you persevere with it, you will grow to like it more and more.

The Head of Music was conscious of the fact that the main emphasis of the school music was on instrumental music outside the classroom, together with a limited amount of examination teaching in the upper streams in class music. As he remarked to me: 'We concentrate on the instrumental side; we could do more for the lower streams, but it is impossible here due to shortage of staff and space'. By this he meant space to store glockenspiels and other instruments which he felt could be used to good effect with the lower streams. However, he felt that such instruments could not just be left out in the classrooms otherwise the pupils would break them, and there was not the space to store them in the small music staff room. Another constraint on the music teachers, and one which provided a continual source of comment from the three class music teachers, was that of the time and energy needed to run musical activities in a school. This constraint was particularly apparent at the school I observed because so many musical activities went on outside the classroom[25]. All three class teachers rarely got a full lunch break and rarely left the school until an hour after the end of the timetabled day — this was because one of the music groups was rehearsing at these times every day. It is in this context that we might view the Head of Music's comments concerning the difficulty of adequately teaching the bottom streams:

> They [4F — an 'O' level group] do some very good work. I put a lot of work into this class, but it is rewarding — they are very keen. With groups like 3XY one is battling against a brick wall — I would exhaust myself just in one lesson if I tried to get anything out of them. If I exhausted myself in classes like that, I wouldn't have the energy to give my best to the really keen pupils.

Or again: 'I'll only spend time on those pupils who deserve it. If they don't want to learn, what's the point of teaching them? I don't think you can teach pupils who don't want to learn.' (Some implications of making problematic *what* the pupils should learn with respect to music will be developed later in this chapter.)

A final major constraint on the teaching of class music to the lower streams was the whole problem of 'discipline'. The latter was regarded by the staff as a major problem throughout the school. It was generally felt by them (and this was certainly the view of the Head of Music as expressed to me) that problems of discipline, truancy and violence had been increasing in the school, particularly in the lower streams and amongst the coloured pupils. Consequently teachers (and especially student teachers of music in the department commented on this to me) found that the lower streams were very difficult to control in the classroom.

In the school there was only a limited number of school instruments for loan to pupils to enable them to be given instrumental tuition[26]. It was clearly a tribute to the success of music teaching in the school that there was a far greater demand for instruments than the supply (this seemed to apply particularly to certain instruments, for example, percussion and brass)[27]. There was a general feeling amongst the music staff that one of the main reasons for so many pupils wanting to learn instruments was that they wanted to play in the dance band. The Head of Music viewed this very much in terms of incentives; for example, in commenting on a young pupil who was making very fast progress on the trumpet, he remarked: 'That kid's just itching to get into the dance band — see the importance of incentives'. The corollary of this was that those instruments which were not played in the dance band were nothing like as popular, thus presenting occasional problems for the school orchestra; the Head of Music remarked to me on the fact that it was difficult to get pupils to play the cello: 'It's not a very glamorous instrument — it's not in the dance band'.

The greater demand by pupils for instrumental tuition than could be met presented a problem to the music department in terms of who should be given the chance to learn an instrument. The Head of Music emphasised that the main attribute required of a pupil learning an instrument was that he should work hard; all the instrumental teachers were reputed to be 'slave-drivers' expecting their pupils to practise regularly every day. If a pupil showed signs of 'slacking', then it would be suggested to him that he give up the instrument in favour of another pupil who would be prepared to put more work into it; pupils, however, who worked hard but nevertheless made slow progress were encouraged to continue. Thus once pupils had started learning instruments, selection to continue was based on their perceived efforts. The problem of initially selecting those who should be given a chance on instruments still remained. I asked the Head of Music on what basis selection was made. He pointed out that teaching the recorder for one hour a week enabled the class teachers to spot those who showed a particular facility for the instrument — this then became a useful guide to those who might be proficient on a woodwind instrument, because of the similarity of the techniques employed. Pupils who were interested in learning other types of instrument would either consult their class teacher or go straight to the Head of Music. Whether they were selected or not depended largely on what form (stream) they were in, because the Head of Music felt that a pupil in a lower stream would not have either the ability or perseverance to play an instrument well and take full benefit from the instrumental tuition provided. As he explained to me: 'First I ask what form they are in. If they are in a low form it is useless because it will be far too difficult for them'. The brass teacher made a similar point to me when I asked him how the instrumentalists were selected: 'We obviously have to go for the top streams. It takes a lot of intelligence to play a musical instrument'.

The general appearance of the pupil was also important — as the Head of Music remarked to me: 'Pupils who can't look after their clothes won't look after my instruments'. The Head of Music's view was that success on an instrument was a function of both the pupil's ability (for academic subjects) and his family background; as he explained to me: 'we do sometimes get some low ability pupils, but they will always be from a good home. We never get people who are both low ability and from poor homes'[28]. Whilst these selection categories of perceived ability and perceived family background were part of the Head of Music's 'stock of knowledge at hand' (Schutz, 1967), it is not clear where such a perspective originated. There is nothing in my data to suggest whether this might have come from his previous experience in the school having 'given everyone a chance' and having found that it is only the top stream pupils who do well, or from previous teaching experience before coming to this school, or from more vague political or social assumptions.

His perspective was not without criticism by other members of the music staff. Teacher B, who also had a small part in the selection, in that he selected those who wished to learn the saxophone, felt that just because a pupil was not 'academically bright' did not mean that he did not have musical ability, and consequently 'everyone should at least be given a chance'. A part-time teacher also commented: 'There are some good neglected musicians in the remedial streams', but pointed out later in our conversation that 'perhaps the inequalities have to exist for the music to be as good as it is now; I suppose if you gave everyone a chance there would be far more breakages'.

Some Observations on 'What Counts as Music'

Before moving on to some further interpretations of the case study data, it must be explained that my account can only be one interpretation of certain aspects of the social world; in the context of Schutz's (1967) discussion of 'multiple realities' my own account is one such reality accomplished from a very particular 'here and now'. Moreover a central tenet of the phenomenological approach is that in formulating a sociological interpretation the researcher must himself draw on commonsense reasoning as a resource in his own explanation. This makes it essential that the researcher should be able to reveal his own system of relevancies which influenced his particular selection and interpretation of data. In suspending the 'natural attitude' the researcher suspends his belief in the reality of the everyday world, so that he might better be able to uncover the 'taken-for-granted' assumptions which are made by members in the construction of their world (Schutz, 1967). My own system of relevancies directed my attention, during my period of observation, to particular types of assumptions made by the music staff in the school. I was particularly interested in the typifications made concerning the musical ability of different groups of pupils and also in the assumptions made by the music staff in their evaluation of good and bad music teaching. I was also interested in the assumptions made concerning the nature of both jazz and 'pop' music. Thus any direct quotations in the text have been selected according to these pre-conceived categories of relevance.

In the development of an interpretation of the data the most significant 'background relevancy' was my own background in music as a drummer in both jazz and rock groups, and the nature of the commonsense assumptions that I have developed as a result of this. In particular I have known many jazz and rock musicians who, whilst regarded as highly talented musicians by their peers, were nevertheless defined as 'unmusical' at school. In this respect I regard the content of my previous chapter as an important resource for understanding how my particular interpretation of the field work data evolved. To take an illustration: my suggestion that 'for pupils to succeed in class music they must be prepared to take over the teacher categories of "good" music' (see p.218) is influenced by the fact that I do not share the assumptions made about the worth of 'pop' music by the Head of Music (and music teachers generally). The validity of his suggestion that 'the really great music takes time to appreciate' (see p.218) can apply as much, in my view, to Afro-American music as to European 'serious' music. I cite this to illustrate how in this case my own commonsense assumptions have influenced my interpretation of the data, and to show that there could be many other interpretations of the data I gathered, depending on the commonsense reasoning and background relevancies of the particular researcher.

Data from the case study suggest both the possibilities for and the constraints on changing traditional definitions of music teaching. The school music department was highly innovative in widening the scope of extra-curricular musical activities to areas of music, including big band jazz (played very proficiently), beyond the more traditional emphases on orchestras and choirs. But whilst the school was hardly traditional in terms of the variety of music played by the pupils, its approach to instrumental tuition and its criteria of success were conventional ones. In fact, the attraction of the dance band for the pupils might be one interpretation of the remarkable success of the school music, in terms of the very high quality of the extra-curricular musical acitivites, the large numbers of pupils actively involved and the generally very positive attitude towards music among most of the school pupils. Widening the sphere of school music could therefore, in this case, be seen as an effective means for gaining the ends of traditional music education.

We do find, however, that there seems to be an association between, on the one hand, 'what counts as music' — in this case, an emphasis on instrumental tuition, musical literacy and the provision of information about music and music history — and, on the other hand, the particular criteria of success and teachers' perceptions relating to intelligence, family background and musical ability. This supports a suggestion from the literature on music education that music educators with the traditional paradigm make the assumption that only a limited number of people are musical and that, as Long puts it:

> The paramount aim in grammar school music is to discover the talented and to provide the conditions in which they can develop their talents as fully as the school pressures will allow (1963, p.148).

The music education literature in the avant-garde paradigm, however, suggests the possibility of very different assumptions — criteria of success shift from playing instruments 'correctly' to developing pupils' musical creativity and in this respect all pupils are seen as potentially musical, or as Carl Orff has put it:

> I do not think of an education for specially gifted children . . . . My experience had taught me that completely unmusical children are very rare and that nearly every child is at some point accessible and educable (quoted in Horton, 1969, p.25).

Where definitions of what counts as music are much more open-ended, and where stress is not placed on musical *literacy* but rather upon *sounds*,[29] music as a discipline ceases to resemble traditional academic subjects, with their corresponding emphasis on literacy. In such a context it is likely that very different assumptions will be made by teachers concerning the interrelationships between pupils' academic intelligence, their family background and their musical abilities, so that, for example, in another comprehensive school music department I observed, where there was a strong emphasis on the avant-garde paradigm of music teaching, I found that large numbers of pupils from the lowest streams were actively involved in music projects at school concerts.

As was suggested earlier, however, both the traditional and the avant-garde paradigms share one important feature in common, namely they are both rooted in the culture of European 'serious' music and, as such, are far removed from the musical experience of most pupils, centred as this is on varieties of 'pop' music. This suggests the possibility of yet another radically different conception of 'what counts as music' in schools, and this can be elaborated upon by reference to Nicholls' (1976) account of the highly unusual music department of Countesthorpe College, Leicestershire, a community comprehensive school for about 600 fourteen to eighteen year old pupils. The school itself is well known for its innovatory teaching methods which stress the importance of pupils' self-directed work on an individualised 'pupil-centred' curriculum. In the music department such an orientation means that there is no attempt to sell any particular type of music, but rather as Nicholls puts it: 'In group music making the style of the music is not so important providing it results in a sound that is good — so that everyone feels he has contributed something and feels the overall sound is really music' (1976, p.130). As a result, a very wide variety of music is represented in the musical activities of the department and its underlying pedagogical philosophy is to start with the musical interests of the pupils and develop these in whatever directions the pupils, as opposed to the teacher, want. Such a philosophy has crucial implications for the teaching/learning process which markedly differentiates this, what I will call, open paradigm of music teaching from either the traditional or avant-garde ones, even where the traditional paradigm is considerably modified by incorporating a much wider variety of music than 'classical', as in my case study.

Criteria of success are such that stress is placed on performing well in any particular idiom rather than on playing instruments 'correctly' (i.e. according to 'classical' technical criteria). As a result many of the department's best musicians cannot read a note of music, having learned to play aurally by listening to records or by following the example of friends — this applied particularly to guitarists, drummers and singers. In addition many of these talented musicians, working in the field of 'pop' and rock music, are the non-academic pupils, who in a more traditional streamed school would be in the lowest streams [30]. Nicholls notes that in such traditional schools these pupils would not only be regarded by music teachers as unmusical, but would *see themselves* as unmusical, whereas at Countesthorpe taking seriously the musical interests of the pupils (even if this is initially just to reproduce television advertisement jingles on the piano or guitar) results in pupils, who have not previously recognised any musical competence in themselves, taking the school's mode III C.S.E. course.

Another significant feature of the Countesthorpe school music department is that barriers between teacher and taught, and teachers' and pupils' prejudices concerning different areas of music, tend to be broken down. Both because there is only one music teacher for the whole school, and because this teacher is trained in the 'classical' tradition and therefore does not have a very wide knowledge of pop and rock music techniques, much emphasis is placed on the pupils' helping and teaching themselves. Nicholls notes in particular the important influence that both sixth formers and some old boys (who seem to come back to the department on weekends, evenings and in the holidays) can have on younger pupils, since the latter 'always seem readily to respect technical ability, especially when it is part of their own culture' (p.139). Thus the teacher, instead of being an expert, becomes more a guide and an organiser and the process of teaching becomes a two-way one between teacher and taught. In these circumstances the teacher finds he is constantly having to reappraise the assumptions he is tempted to make concerning the musical culture of young people. But just as the teacher is more open to the 'pop' music culture of the pupils than is usually the case, so the reverse is also true. Pupils who might normally be put off the 'classical' music interests of the music teacher find themselves following them up in an environment where prejudices concerning different types of music have been broken down, so that, as Nicholls shows, Bach, Stockhausen and King Crimson can freely intermix in the music department.

A further point where the ethos of the Countesthorpe music department clashes with the emphasis of the traditional paradigm of music teaching concerns examination teaching. Nicholls notes that certain pupils tend to shy away from the music department — in particular passive individuals who do not do well in such a self-directing situation and also exam-orientated pupils, who have the ability to take exam courses, but who see no other value in education. The unusually large number of pupils actively participating in the music department puts great strain on the time and energy of the one music teacher, and inevitably, with a high premium being placed on mixed-group teaching, the highly talented and exam-orientated pupils progress more slowly than they would in the usual circumstances of 'the better you are, the more teacher-time you get'. The problem is particularly acute in relation to music 'A' level teaching where, more than in other subjects, the disparity between the 'A' level syllabus and the requirements of the majority of even musically active pupils is so great as to be irreconcilable. At Countesthorpe such a conflict had to be resolved by two pupils travelling to another school for their music 'A' level lessons — an arrangement about which the Head of Music was very unhappy, but one which was felt to be inevitable given the constraints of time.

Conclusion

I have attempted to show that different ways in which 'what counts as music' is defined are likely to be associated with different criteria of success, different relations between teacher and taught, and different assumptions concerning the musical ability of pupils. Different conceptions of 'what counts as music' involve different cultural choices and Young (1971) has suggested that changing the cultural choices 'would involve a massive redistribution of the labels educational "success" and "failure" ' (p.38). In relation to music teaching, it might be suggested that the widely publicised problems that school music teachers have with teenage pupils[31] might be better explained in terms of the teachers' definitions of music rather than of the supposed deficiencies of pupils. Thus, assumptions concerning the limited number of people who can either play musical instruments well or who are motivated to appreciate good music could depend more on the way in which both 'musical instruments' and 'good music' are defined than on the innate musical potential of the people themselves. A similar point is made by John Blacking, the ethnomusicologist:

If, for example, all members of an African society are able to perform and listen intelligently to their own indigenous music, and if this unwritten music, when analysed in its social and cultural context can be shown to have a similar range of effects on people and to be based on intellectual and musical processes that are found in the so-called 'art' music of Europe, we must ask why apparently general musical abilities should be restricted to a chosen few in societies supposed to be culturally more advanced. Does cultural development represent a real advance in human sensitivity and technical ability or is it chiefly a diversion for elites and a weapon of class exploitation? Must the majority be made 'unmusical' so that a few may become more 'musical'? (1973, p.4).

Sociologists working within the theoretical perspective of the New Sociology of Education have sometimes been criticised for over-emphasising the possibilities for change in teachers redefining their situation with alternative definitions of knowledge, ability and so on[32]. Consequently in both the case study and the discussion of the Countesthorpe music department considerable emphasis has been placed on the power of external forces (limitations of resources, shortage of time, poor teacher-pupil ratios leading to possible discipline problems, and so on) to constrain the activities of teachers. On the other hand, music can be seen as a particularly apt example of the potential of viewing school subjects from the perspective of the New Sociology of Education, because unlike the study of, for example, science subjects it does not involve the epistemological problems associated with tendencies to extreme forms of relativity, which are often seen by its critics[33] as the major weakness of the New Sociology of Education. Whilst relativising the status of scientific enquiries is a controversial exercise, as is shown by the debate generated by the publication of Kuhn's *Structure of Scientific Revolutions* (1962), it would seem that the relativity of aesthetic judgements is a far more acceptable proposition, in that different types of music require different criteria for aesthetic judgement and any attempt to pronounce on the 'absolute' value of music is doomed to failure (a point argued in many of the contributions to this book).

The greatest obstacle to change could be seen as the weight of a historical tradition in the subject perspective of music teaching, which perpetuates misleading ideological views on the dichotomy between 'serious' and 'popular' music and, by implication, on the relative worth of various types of music. For teachers to subvert this by adopting an open approach to music teaching means that not only are they resisting the dominant ideology of the music establishment but, in addition, they are going against the dominant ideology of the educational establishment, by taking seriously the culture of the pupils even when this is in opposition to the mainstream culture. Thus the viability of the open approach at Countesthorpe might be seen not so much as an example of better resources (whilst their music wing is certainly well equipped, there is still only one music teacher for the whole school), but rather as an illustration that such an approach in music teaching can only work when it is backed by an educational philosophy, held throughout the school and supported by the headmaster, that it is pupils who should as far as possible initiate things themselves.

NOTES

1.   The distinction between 'curriculum as fact' and 'curriculum as practice', derived from the phenomenological educational philosophy of Maxine Greene, is developed in Young (1975).

2.   Since this chapter is concerned with the teaching of music in English schools, it may be helpful here to give some brief explanatory notes on terminology for the benefit of readers who are not conversant with the background of the English school system. Prior to the Education Act of 1944, the system consisted in the main of a small section of fee-paying *public* schools (mainly boarding), a larger number of fee-paying *grammar* schools, which also gave scholarships on the basis of educational performance, and an even greater number of *elementary* schools providing free education available to all — the first two taking pupils up to the age of 18, the last only to 14. The financial consequences of access to each type resulted in a social class-based stratification of the educational system. The 1944 Act made a clear separation of primary and secondary stages of education in State schools, covering the 5 to 11 and 11+ age ranges (since 1944 the minimum leaving age in State education has progressively moved from 14 to 16). The Act abolished fee-paying for the secondary stage of education in State schools (including the *grammar* schools, but excluding the *public* schools, since these are private institutions) and introduced a tripartite system of state secondary education consisting of *grammar* schools, *secondary modern* schools and *technical* schools. Since the *technical* schools were small in number, the mainstays of the State system of education up until the 1960s were the *grammar* schools and the *secondary modern* schools. Selection for one or other of these schools was based on a test at the age of eleven. About 20% of pupils went through to the *grammar* schools and received a strongly academic education, whilst about 80% went to the *secondary modern* schools, where the stress was on a more practical and less academic education and entry to nationally recognised examinations at 16 or 18 was not expected. Criticisms of this system and, in particular, of the inequalities resulting from the 11+ exam led in the late 1960s to Labour government moves to replace the *grammar/secondary modern* schools with *comprehensive* schools, to which all State educated pupils would go, whatever their ability. The English school system has therefore moved closer to the American system in recent years — *comprehensive* schools bearing many similarities to the American *high* school and English *public* schools to American *private* schools.

3.   'Music must be an integral part of our education; both for its own sake, and for the sake of the public services of the church' — Joseph Mainzer, 1849 (quoted in Rainbow, 1967, p 133).
John Turner noted (1833) that a more general diffusion of vocal music would 'contribute largely to the rooting out of dissolute and debasing habits' and the chosen texts were to be 'simple in character, but conveying sentiments of pure and exalted morality' (quoted in Rainbow, 1967, p 157).

4.   See, for example, MacPherson (1936) and Scholes (1935).

5.   The process of the increasing legitimation of music as a class subject would make an interesting topic for study. Brace (1970) is suggestive in this context. He attempts to show that the unquestioning acceptance of the neat analogy between music and other subjects — a report of 1923 suggested that 'all arguments for the inclusion of Language and Literature . . . may be used with equal force for music' (Brace, 1970, p 16) — has been one of the biggest obstacles to the healthy development of musical activities in schools.

   For some implications of this process of legitimation, see Bourdieu: 'Whenever literature becomes a school subject — as among the Sophists or in the Middle Ages — we find emerging the desire to classify, usually by genre and by author, and also to establish hierarchies to pick out from the mass of works the classics worthy of being preserved through the medium of the school' (1967, p 196).

6.   See Chapter Six, *n.* 4.

7.   The best way to teach such notation was the major subject for debate amongst music educators in the nineteenth century — see Rainbow (1967).

8.   Such a plea is made, for example, at the end of Robinson's (1974) review of ethnographic classroom research.

9.   I shall frequently be using this expression. I intend it to signify the range and techniques of music that the teachers in the educational institution feel should be dealt with in the context of teaching.

10.   The data from this participant observation study were first reported in a chapter of a dissertation submitted for the M.Sc. degree in the Sociology of Education at the University of London Institute of Education (see Vulliamy, G., *Music Education in Secondary Schools: Some Sociological Observations,* unpublished dissertation, 1972). Details and limitations of the methodology used for the study will be found in the 'Appendix on Methodology' of the dissertation. Proper names and the nomenclature for classes in the school have been disguised in the interest of anonymity. I would particularly like to thank the teachers and pupils in the school for their generous hospitality towards me during the period of research.

11.   During the period of my observation about 8 pupils were studying for 'O' level and 20 for C.S.E. There was, in addition, one sixth form 'A' level candidate who was taught personally by the Head of Music. For those not conversant with the English examination system, the following points may be helpful. There are three nationally recognised terminal examinations, for which English school pupils can be entered:
   Advanced Level ('A' level), normally taken at 17 or 18 years old, after two years of sixth form education;
   Ordinary Level ('O' level), normally taken at 15 or 16 years old, after five years of secondary education;
   Certificate of Secondary Education (C.S.E.), normally taken at 15 or 16 years-old, after five years of secondary education.
'O' and 'A' levels are subject-based examinations and are set and assessed by

Regional Examining Boards. 'A' level grades are used as major criteria for entry into higher education. All three examinations can be taken in individual subjects or groups of subjects.

There are a number of differences between 'O' level and C.S.E., which include:

1. It was originally expected that about the top 20% of pupils in the ability range could reach satisfactory 'O' level performance, and that about the next 20% would achieve satisfactory C.S.E. performance. In practice, these figures vary substantially from school to school, and area to area, and performances have improved over time, so that now only 40% of pupils leave school with no 'O' levels.
2. 'O' levels are set and assessed by the same examining boards as 'A' levels. But C.S.E. has a different set of much smaller Regional Examining Boards with proportionately greater teacher involvement.
3. Both 'O' levels and C.S.E.'s are graded and a Grade 1 in C.S.E. is equivalent to an 'O' level pass.
4. Most 'A' level candidates have taken 'O' levels previously, rather than C.S.E.

12.   For my use of 'perspective', see Becker *et al.* (1969, especially pp 5, 29 and 36).

13.   The dance band played a wide variety of music, but was perhaps closest in conception to a large jazz/swing band, playing head arrangements of both jazz and pop standards. Whilst the arrangements for the different sections were notated in 'big-band' style, performances also featured improvising soloists.

14.   Instrumental music teachers are usually professional musicians, although there has recently been an increase in the number of instrumental teachers who make a full-time career from teaching. The background of class music teachers is likely to be different in that, after either a university degree in music or a conservatoire diploma, they obtain a teacher's qualification and make teaching a full-time career. 'Music teachers' cannot therefore be treated as a homogeneous category; one might expect differences in attitudes relating to the differing backgrounds of the music teacher in question. More specifically, the background of the professional musician is such that he is likely to have encountered a far wider variety of music in his career than has the class music teacher.

15.   This term was used by the Head of Music to denote such approaches; the term itself would seem to be derived from a description of the sounds evolving from 'creative' percussion work in the classroom.

16.   See, for example, Self (1967).

17.   See Horton (1969).

18.   I use the term 'pop' here in the narrow sense of being the type of 'pop' music which excludes strong blues or rock influences. For further elaboration of this point, see my previous chapter.

19.   Just as the pupil's question in note 35 of Keddie's (1971) article, in which he asks how a foetus can go to the toilet, might have been a 'put on'.

20.   See Chapter Six, *n*. 19.

21.   Compare this example of teacher B's use of 'pop' music in the classroom with a later one I give where the Head of Music plays 'their' records to 3XY whilst letting them dance to them.

22.   See, for example, Hargreaves (1968) and Keddie (1971). Whilst we know that streaming influences teachers' perceptions of pupils, what these influences are in different situations remains problematic.

23.   See Young (1971) for a discussion of the 'organising principles underlying academic curricula'.

24.   It was not clear to this observer whether by 'capacity' he meant ability or willingness.

25.   The quality of these activities was extraordinarily high for the performance of school pupils. Whilst this judgement is necessarily a subjective one on behalf of this observer, it is a judgement that was shared by all those I spoke to who had witnessed the school groups performing; this applied particularly to the performance of the dance band.

26.   By 'limited' I mean with respect to the total number of pupils in the school. I should imagine that with respect to the number of instruments available in other schools the number was very large. The Head of Music was certainly very adept at persuading 'the authorities' to make further instruments available if they were needed.

27.   By 'tribute' I mean:
 1.Large numbers of instruments were made available to pupils
  and
 2.A very large number of pupils were motivated to begin learning these instruments.

28.   By 'low ability' in the first sentence he was referring to pupils in the 'middle ability' streams; whilst a few pupils from these 'middle ability' groups were in the dance band and orchestra, there were no pupils from the 'remedial' groups.

29.   This important distinction is more fully explored by Trevor Wishart in Chapter Four of this book.

30.   An interesting analysis of the musical development of one such 'non-academic' pupil is given by Spencer (1976 pp 113-121).

31.   The Schools Council 'Enquiry I: Young School Leavers' (HMSO 1968) found that, out of fourteen subject areas, music was perceived by pupils as the most boring and least useful.

32.   See, for example, Whitty (1974) and Sharp and Green (1975).

33.   See, for example, Pring (1972).

Chapter Eight

On Radical Culture[1]

TREVOR WISHART

In this essay I would like to attempt a redefinition and take a fresh look at what is best described as 'radical culture'. I shall attempt to define this in opposition to two very prominent views held within the European Left . . . those of G. Lukacs as put forward in 'Old Culture and New Culture' (1970), and those of T. Adorno as expressed in the essay entitled 'Cultural Criticism and Society' (1967). I shall attempt to put forward an alternative viewpoint which I feel is closer to radical materialist thought and not beset by the vagaries of Hegelianism.

I do *not* intend to discuss here the validity or necessity of radicalising culture or all cultural activities.

In the essay 'Old Culture and New Culture', Lukacs points out that bourgeois fears of revolutionary change are often voiced in terms of a fear for the safety of culture. But he claims, on the contrary, that it is precisely capitalism which has caused the disintegration of the old culture, and that revolutionary change is vitally necessary in order that a new culture can take shape. Commodity fetishism is the underlying cause of the disintegration of the old culture. The separation of the created object from the creative act (its projection onto the market as a commodity) is merely a special case of the alienation of labour . . . furthermore art cannot be viewed as an end in itself where the capitalist organisation of production forces the rationale of sale upon all human activities. Art can neither be regarded as a form of communication, except in a castrated sense, where it enters into relationships with other human beings as a *commodity*. In such a situation fashion takes over from

233

culture. 'Thus every organic development vanishes and in its place steps a directionless hither and thither and an empty but loud dilettantism.' (1970, p.24).

However, it is at this point that we must begin to take issue with Lukacs' analysis. For Lukacs is drawing a comparison between this and a past cultural epoch (he mentions the Greek) in which such an organic development is assumed to have taken place, and in particular an integration is supposed to have existed between artistic manifestations and the total ethos (or life-style) of the culture. What Lukacs fails to point out is the very partiality of such cultures. The culture as lived and the cultural traditions as shared in this 'universal' manner were the prerogative of a class group . . . and inasmuch as they were so, they were an expression of the cultural solidarity of that group, set *against* the other groups in society. The universality of such traditions was always a nonsense, and it was precisely their pretensions to universality which became a weapon of cultural superiority, the lower classes being regarded of inferior status as they were (mentally) unable to appreciate the (elite) culture, rather than merely timewise unable, or unwilling. This use of culture as a weapon of class-domination has been attacked by many radical writers, who have themselves (almost) always been participants in such a culture, and have hence tended to place a value on at least a part of it *per se*.

Adorno (1967) attacks the particular bourgeois version of this universalist view, when he demolishes the ideas of Valery and others who posit:

> . . . a notion of culture which, during the era of late capitalism, aims at a form of property which is stable and independent of stock-market fluctuations. This idea of culture asserts its distance from the system in order, as it were, to offer universal security in the middle of a universal dynamic. (1967, p.22).

This idea of culture, a culture entirely divorced from life as lived, is itself a fetish and evaluating works against this backcloth, i.e. assuming 'cultural values', is a form of marketing technique.

However, Adorno and Lukacs fall into a similar trap because they need to defend their own intellectual property (those things that they value in their own culture). Therefore, in an attempt to demolish the class-basis of bourgeois aesthetics, they raise up a new aesthetics in its place. For, in the statement . . .

> . . . no authentic work of art and no true philosophy, according to their very meaning, has ever exhausted itself in itself alone,

in its being-in-itself. They have always stood in relation to the actual life-process of society from which they distinguished themselves. (1967, p.23).

the use of the words 'authentic' and 'true' simply imply an evaluative position for Adorno as critic which transcends the social situation, a position which Adorno himself is in the process of demolishing in his essay! And this will be the essence of our criticism, for we will suggest that *no* work of art, or philosophy, *or criticism*, has ever exhausted itself in itself alone, in its being-in-itself. They have always stood in relation to the actual life-process of society from which they distinguish themselves. And hence all appeals to culturally transcendent values, truth or authenticity are spurious.

Culture in general is a manifest addition to, an extension of, man's reality by man . . . (in contrast to physical science, which is an investigation of reality) . . . and as such its general social form is made possible by the underlying economic relations in a society (in which case a society has nothing to fear from its culture, if it has its economic relations well sorted out!!). This does not imply that it is a direct causal result of those economic relations, *nor* a reflection or analogy thereof (nor that it should be). One might expect the type of consciousness unveiled in (semiotic) cultural artefacts to be changed on changing the economic infrastructure of a society, but one cannot change consciousness by changing culture. Once culture is legislated from above, it ceases to express any type of consciousness, it ceases to be culture at all, but merely a mirror for an elite to admire themselves in . . . it becomes *propaganda*. When this is done indirectly, through criticism, then the same is equally true. (We might add here that all cultural artefacts are not necessarily semiotic, but this extends the scope of discussion beyond the issues at present in hand).

For what we must now see is the relation of Lukacs and Adorno, as criticis with a deep knowledge, awareness of and intellectual investment in the cultural traditions of the Western European ruling classes, to the actual life-process of society from which they attempt to distinguish themselves . . . as in their writings they have assumed themselves beyond, 'transcendent of', the social infrastructure which they would criticise so ferociously. And in this 'transcendental' stance they reveal both their failure to grasp their *own* dialectical relationship with society, and the seeds of autocracy.

We must not only attack traditional aesthetics, which judges art apart from the totality of human social experience according to intra-artistic criteria (assumed universal), but the very act of Cultural criticism itself, as it is anti-cultural, for it attempts to isolate the Cultural sphere from the totality of human experience, from human culture . . . it fails to locate Culture within the total (world) social framework, in fact reaffirming the disparity between Culture (and hence Cultural criticism) and culture which does exist in all advanced literate societies.

It is economic specialisation and the class-nature of society which has led to the emergence of Culture, but such an entity, by its very nature removed from the everyday cultural experience of most men, is a partial precedental reality, as opposed to a universal objective reality. For a Culture has extended man's reality in a particular non-unique direction, along precedents established among limited social groups within different societies.

What we are hence declaring is that the root of the problem lies in the confusion between culture and Culture, which Lukacs does nothing to disentangle. Economic affluence provides the time (and inclination) to study the detailed ramifications of an existent Cultural tradition, but the declaration of its 'necessity', 'truth' or 'universality' is merely an ideological defence. In many primitive societies the distinction between culture and Culture does not exist, but for economically advanced societies, with much differentiation and specialisation of roles, the development of art by specialists, creating a particular history of precedents, requires that an individual have sufficient leisure, and therefore adequate economic support, to enter into what is generally regarded as an artistic act (or an act of Cultural criticism), this being viewed as only being possible against a background of knowledge of that history . . . and this is the nature of Culture and Cultural background. However, for most members of society, culture is far removed from this. In most societies it has been an acquaintance with various forms of labour and economic struggle, together with some shared traditions, especially of song (most often relating to work-life, birth, love and death etc.) which have been rapidly destroyed by technological societies (as the very nature of labour, and family life, have changed or will change, and, e.g., the electronic media are rapidly undermining the spontaneous communal participatory traditions).

It is obviously absurd to declare any aspect of the partial Cultures to be 'true' in some historical, class-based sense. It is clear that the more 'cultured' Marxist theoreticians feel their heritage threatened by the more militant advocates of a universal folk-dance, folk-song Culture, but both are suffering from the same delusion, the belief that a Culture will have to be decided upon from above in a post-revolutionary society, that culture and Culture will remain distinguishable even when class distinctions have passed away.

Adorno and Lukacs are both absorbed in the Cultural background of the Western European ruling classes, due to their particular economic statuses. However, there is no reason why those who are not familiar with this should ever desire to acquaint themselves with it, (or conversely, why they should not) especially those for whom it has absolutely no significance (e.g. the European working-classes generally speaking, or even more so, the Indian or Indonesian peasantry!). The belief in the 'truth' or 'universality' of particular Cultural manifestations can be traced to the ideological needs of an economically isolated intelligentsia, and the careful preservation of its traditions to a desire to reaffirm a tradition of cultural and political ascendancy. The very process of aesthetic evaluation, or Cultural criticism, may be seen as the prerogative of this elite, especially in modern Europe. The social grouping for which the activity, and the premises and Cultural knowledge on which it is based, have meaning is very small, and its pretence to objectivity hence all the more dangerous. All such forms of advanced aesthetic and Cultural criticism have become a (conscious or unconscious) tool for reinforcing the solidarity of the group. This applies equally well to Adorno and Lukacs, as to Valery and Eliot, for their appeal to a transcendent objectivity of Cultural assessment implies an attempt to justify their own status *within* the Cultural (and therefore economic) elite of Western Europe. One cannot transcend the dialectical process of material-cultural development, and their attempt to do so in theory reveals the essentially Idealist nature of their viewpoints. (Not surprising that Adorno praises a withdrawal from a social situation from which he can see no practical means of escape, while Lukacs' vision is of a return to the golden age of cultural harmony, which takes no account of the nature of the underlying development of the forces of production). Even Trotsky (1923) declares that the proletariat *should* become as fully acquainted as possible with Cultural history, thus at the same time giving some spurious 'validity' to the particular Cultural tradition of the European elites.

On the other hand, the relative poverty of many folk-cultures, especially the remnants or travesties (Russian choral arrangements of originally good folk-songs) which are artificially perpetuated in advanced technological societies, has been the result of an economic oppression and manipulation which has made the folk-culture very limited in scope and vision, if not in intensity of expression, and which any revolution is dedicated to change. To artificially preserve folk-cultures in a post-revolutionary society is to commit the same idiocy as the Valerys and their reification of past culture.

Hence we have seen how the division between Culture and culture (between the radical intelligentsia and the working classes) in society results in a pseudo-radical aestheticism, which is based upon a divorce between what a work 'really' is, and what people take it to be. In attempting to divorce the value or meaning or truth etc. of a work of art from its value, meaning, truth etc. to real people at a particular place and time, the cultural critic attempts to escape from, to 'transcend' his own class-role, to avoid admitting that he is discussing what a work means *to him* as an intellectual (i.e. *not* as a member of the working-classes), hence avoiding the admission of the (bourgeois) class basis of his position *vis-a-vis* the culture.

Adorno (1967) reveals his true position in his essay on Schoenberg. For example, he declares (p.149):

If one does not understand something it is customary to behave with the sublime understanding of Mahler's jackass, and project one's own inadequacy on the object, declaring it to be incomprehensible.

For here it is implied that the public has an obligation to try to understand the artist, i.e. that art accords with some socially-external laws of meaningfulness, truth etc. while it is our responsibility to judge it against these laws . . . rather than that the artist or critic has an obligation to convey his meaning to the public, i.e. that a work is *only meaningful* via its social existence.

Adorno, in fact, pays lip-service to the latter notion, but when he finally assesses a work in relation to its social context, he fails to include the fact that the social context *as he sees it*, including a view of *a* Culture (if not *the* Culture!!) and a history of that Culture, is *not* the social context against which most men will judge it . . . and therefore he implies some transcendent objectivity to his own viewpoint.

On the contrary, if '. . . it is precisely because of its seriousness, richness and integrity that his [Schoenberg's] music arouses resentment' (1967, p.149), then are we to blame individuals for their resentment, social conditions for their conditioning of aesthetic response, or in fact the composer himself for not attempting, or even being concerned, to assess the social context in which his work would be propagated and which would so profoundly affects its appreciation? Adorno is, of course, content to blame the public, because in so doing he can defend his own ivory-tower elitism. This fact is emphasised by the quotation about, for as most people do not resent Schoenberg but merely have no interest in his music or have never even heard of him, it is clearly directed at an audience of other bourgeois critics . . . in fact its very *existence,* and Adorno's continuing involvement in such cultural criticism, presupposes the existence of bourgeois culture by collaborating in it, for Adorno's intellectual satisfaction is derived from knocking down this image of 'bourgeois' (used in an intellectually perjorative sense) artistic appreciation which he has erected (in order to define himself as outside it) while never in fact departing from the fold of bourgeois culture (in the true class sense), theoretically or *in practice.* Lukacs and Adorno both carry forward an old intellectual tradition, and their forebears were the theological guardians of the 'true' culture . . . this is an academically insulated position which managed to survive the rise of the bourgeoisie and is hoping to be restored to prominence over the heads of the rising working-classes.

The Idealist nature of such a position may be revealed still further by asking why Adorno makes no attempt to uncover the social bases of aesthetic response styles (except in the vaguest of vague Hegelian senses). The reason is that this would involve venturing beyond the secure sphere of intellectual speculation towards an investigation of reality, towards *praxis* . . . and hence the necessity of deserting the secure world of bourgeois academic cultural criticism against which he rails. The Marxist dialectic sees human praxis as an essential constituent of the dialectic of historical progress and is therefore not a deterministic philosophy in the naive sense, whereas Hegelian dialectics absolves one of the necessity of gaining knowledge of the world through praxis, the cornerstone of Marxist epistemology, hence praxis may conveniently be ruled out of account *before* one acts.

In this essay we wish to lay the ghost of a 'true' or 'necessary' or 'universal' aesthetics, which has never existed, and is in fact a mental construct of economically superior classes in *any* society. For this reason we must declare that destruction of the 'Old Culture' is a virtue of capitalism, and with it goes *forever* the notion of a 'true' tradition. Capitalism has precipitated the era of permanent cultural revolution, which will be the only cultural situation compatible with a revolutionary society, the general nature of culture being made possible by the economic infrastructure of society. Lukacs' prediction of a return to the golden age of 'harmony and organic development' is not compatible with a permanently evolving world of new possibilities and new experience which the rational human control of the economic-technological sphere should bring about.

Our ultimate radical critique must be that Idealist aesthetics are incompatible with revolutionary society. The meaning of a work is the meaning which it takes on at a particular time and place in the prevailing social conditions, and any attempt to declare that one's individual view at a particular time and place has any greater validity is absurd, and ultimately dangerous. It is significant that most revolutionary theorists have 'emancipated' themselves from bourgeois views of history and society via a bourgeois education system, which seems to have inspired in them a love of bourgeois (and pre-bourgeois) *C*ulture (generally speaking, not shared by the working-class and especially not in the same way) which they feel obliged to justify in their revolutionary theories, by an appeal to 'truth' in certain cultural artefacts, which, by a false analogy with physical-scientific investigation, re-elects the guardians of the 'true culture' in the future society, and disenfranchises the community at large.

This is not to say that no judgement can be made of what a work may mean to most people under different social conditions, but such statements can only ultimately be verified by observation. Otherwise, they take on a normative (and therefore spurious) validity, which implies a cultural elitism.

But *most fundamentally* the views we have been discussing are all based on the hidden assumption of the intrinsic value of *received* culture (either as socially integrative, or as aesthetically or morally edifying). And this very assumption derives from the separation between *C*ulture and *c*ulture, i.e. from the existence of an economic-political-cultural elite.

On the contrary, in the permanently revolutionary society generated by man's conscious control of the economic-technological-(ecological) sphere, culture can only be integrative through *universal participation*, as cultural production accelerates and diversifies in line with the diversification and expansion of human possibilities of experience and action, and hence it follows that a principal indication that social change has been successfully far-reaching will be the disappearance of the distinction between Culture and culture, the precipitation of a totally participatory culture at the level of previous Cultures (which says nothing about the particular course of development it might take, which can hardly be predicted!)

Lukacs' view of a Culture which is somehow ideologically 'in tune' with the new society perhaps derives from his concentration upon *literary* criticism (i.e. upon Cultural products with a clearly discernible and *intrinsic* ideological viewpoint . . . semiotic — especially linguistic — culture) but is a result of a false perception of the relationship between Culture (and culture) in general and the economic infrastructure, and is ultimately reactionary. For, as we have said before, the general form of cultural manifestations is made possible by the nature of the economic-political infrastructure, but any particular cultural artefact does not therefore necessarily *reflect* that infrastructure. In particular the answer to cultural poverty is change in the economic infrastructure, permitting greater experience of, and possibility of participation in the social world, *not* cultural legislation, direct or indirect.

In a post-revolutionary society *all* cultural artefacts should function as *affirmations of man's universal, and evidently universal culture*, regardless of their individual nature, content and so forth, rather than re-affirming the solidarity of a particular group in a spurious 'universalism' while alienating others. Furthermore, if this were not so, the social order would rightly be regarded as inadequate.

But this critique of aesthetics applies not only to future societies, but to present cultural action. It is precisely because of the persistence of the aesthetic viewpoint that works which describe or reflect the contradictions within any particular society (or merely extend a long-existent tradition beyond the comprehension of the average bourgeois audience) may be assessed as the epitome of revolutionary culture. There is clearly a fundamental error here, for revolution is a matter of *praxis* . . . Social Realists may describe the world; the point however is to change it!

TREVOR WISHART

If a cultural critic or artist dons a radical cloak (and therefore purports to be interested primarily in revolutionary historical change — in the Marxist sense), then the only valid criterion upon which he can assess the value of his work is its *political effectiveness!!* If we wished to develop a politically revolutionary stance towards current cultural manifestations, we would have to adopt a viewpoint oriented towards ideological-political praxis. This, then, will form the basis of the second part of this essay. (Note that the issue of whether cultural action ought to be viewed in this light is *not* being discussed here). It will be written with a view towards clarifying issues of cultural praxis for those artists primarily concerned with Marxist political viewpoints. We have no interest in assessing the value of any work *per se*, but merely as an aid to the understanding of practical problems and hence to the application of insights and methods to the *praxis* of radical cultural action. If the reader is inspired to adopt such methods of assessment in order merely to develop a new, more 'authentic', branch of 'cultural criticism', then this essay may be judged a failure!

In order to apply our previous critique to cultural action in the present, we must first of all make a fundamental distinction between the anticipated nature of culture in a future (post-revolutionary) society, and the nature of cultural action required to bring about this social situation. The belief that one can bring into being a particular social situation by merely acting in accordance with the supposed nature of that situation, is, on the one hand, idealistic, i.e. essentially impractical (and un-Marxist) showing a lack of understanding of the nature of society and social interaction (or a desire to escape from the practical consequences of a radical approach), and may be, on the other hand, self-defeating . . . for the role of cultural action within contemporary society must be, by definition, different from that we have suggested for a post-revolutionary society. As our particular action will function within *this* present society, it must be planned with this in mind.

As revolution is a matter of praxis, the fundamental test of any cultural actor who declares himself to be radical is, what is the practical effect of his work? Does it forward the possibility of social change? We will not adopt the totally negative stance which might be (I think wrongly) deduced from Mao Tse Tung's 'Revolution is not writing a poem . . . it is nothing so refined as that'. The antithesis here is not between poetry and revolution, but between

242

refinement (or aesthetically-defined action) and revolution (or practically-based action). However, we must not delude ourselves into believing that various kinds of innovatory cultural action are, therefore, *Q.E.D.*, revolutionary.

Bearing these factors in mind, we may see that, e.g., a socialist realist novel (e.g. *Cancer Ward,* as viewed by Lukacs) may help some people to understand a social situation better, which may help them to act in a more informed and rational direction, but it may, for many other reasons, have a negative practical effect (e.g., it's boring, too difficult, it may exacerbate anti-revolutionary myths outside the borders in which it was produced and so on depending on the particular social situation of the reader). The creator is not, therefore, to be blamed for this, for the difficulties are enormous, but he should be expected to take this into account, i.e., it is not enough to judge one's actions against aesthetic criteria, even those of socialist realism, but they must be judged by their results (which truly are often difficult or almost impossible to define). The myth that an artist can rise above the practical situation, be declared a success, and receive continued critical acclaim, runs contrary to the whole radical materialist viewpoint. For not only must the cultural actor learn by his mistakes, but in practice if he creates a durable or reproducible artefact, its meaning will change as the social situation changes. No man can foresee all the consequences of his actions.

How, then, can a cultural act be declared radical, at any particular time? The naive answer would be to say, 'If it leads to radical social change'. In this sense, Verdian Opera (partly because of its coincidence with political circumstances) was significantly more radical than Beethoven's *Ninth!* (Viva Verdi!) But this is in fact to ask *too much* of cultural action. For, despite some views to the contrary, we do not always find ourselves at a place and time of imminent social crisis. We cannot all be a Mao Tse-Tung. Given this situation, what cultural action can seek to do is to affect people's consciousness, to bring things and ideas to their attention, to orient them towards social change, to reinforce their hopes and their solidarity, and even to precipitate action, which may be a result or a cause of the former.

In particular, this is to imply that the relationship between cultural innovation and radical social change is a mere analogy. For as Marcuse and others have pointed out, the present system has an enormous capacity to absorb the new, to present it as a fashionable commodity. This is not to say, as many do, that all cultural action (or even all action) is doomed to failure, but merely that newness (fashionable *or* innovatory) is not in itself sufficient.

This is, for many, a disillusioning thesis. It implies a taking into account of the profound limitations placed upon the meaningfulness of cultural action in contemporary society, and hence perhaps a crushing limitation on their own personal creative development. In fact, it might even be declared that such an attitude could completely destroy the creative faculty, and hence part of the personal motivation for social change.

But here we must draw a fundamental distinction between an individual's personal creative action, and the making public of that action, for no-one can have objection to a personal, non-public involvement in cultural action. Such private creation may in fact be fundamentally necessary to reaffirm to the individual concerned the possibility of the new culture (implied in his own ability to transcend the *immediate* limitations of the existent socio-cultural framework). But the making public of such acts may not only be ineffectual as radical action. It may even undermine his credibility (this cannot be judged *a priori* but must be deeply considered). This important distinction is discussed by Godard in comments on his most recent films. Drawing a distinction between making a political film, and making a film politically, he points out that the former involves accepting wholeheartedly the criteria laid down by the distribution-controllers and hence, in a sense, distributing one's film before one makes it, while the latter involves calculating one's film as a radical political agent beforehand and realising that getting it shown on, in this case *(British Sounds)*, BBC Television, is a political act in itself. (In this, I feel, Godard goes too far in ideological purity, for failure to get such a film shown on the BBC, due to its political non-acceptability, must constitute a total failure, . . . from which, however, we can learn much.) This dichotomy is fundamental. On the one hand, if we are to declare that a cultural act must be politically uncompromising, knowing that the means of distribution for most cultural activities are not in our own hands, then we are declaring the impossibility of success in our own terms. And, on the other hand, if any acceptance by the distribution-controllers implies a built-in failure of the cultural act (as implied by some Marcusian views), then of course, *all* such cultural action is futile. However, an acquaintance with praxis forces on us the realisation that things are not so neatly black and white as this analysis suggests, though they may indeed be very tight.

At this point it might be worthwhile to discuss a particular 'case-history', in order to throw some of these issues into relief. I would like to consider Shelley's *Queen Mab* from the radical point of view.

Shelley was particularly concerned with the *effect* of his work. In his later life, this was perhaps confined to a pious hope that in the long term men would be swayed by the nobility of his radical sentiments, but in his youth he was more practically concerned with the effective distribution of what he clearly regarded as radical art. His early attempts in Ireland consisted among other things, in the scattering of pamphlets from a balcony . . . and seem more a gesture of frustration at the difficulty of disseminating radical opinion than a conscientious attempt to overcome such practical difficulties. With later works Shelley contented himself with distributing them anonymously to a number of selected individuals with radical or liberal sentiments, and *Queen Mab* was never intended for public distribution by Shelley himself. This approach related strongly to the aristocratic element of Shelley's radical ideology. However, within the world of bourgeois aesthetics as it stood, Shelley's isolation and practical ineffectiveness in this sphere contributed to the myth of his total romanticism. For Shelley's peculiar failure to meet, head-on, the practical problem he had set himself, and the aristocratic aesthetic ideology which contributed to this, must be judged within the context of the social reality in which he found himself. Nineteenth-century bourgeois aesthetic criticism, by its very failure to relate cultural action to the real social situation, generated the myth of the totally romantic poet (contributed to by Shelley's wife . . . see Preface to first collected edition of 1839). The artist, in his actions and attitudes, hence became an object of worship, rather than a human being trying to act in a particular way in a particular social situation. And hence aestheticism, in this particular romantic form, contributed to the final emasculation of Shelley's radicalism in bourgeois cultural consciousness.

However, there is another side to this story. For, against Shelley's expressed intentions, *Queen Mab* was pirated by the radical press and distributed widely to the audience of newly-literate radical opinion. Here it proved to be effective in the sense that Shelley would originally have wished, i.e., it swayed men's opinions (see

particularly references to it by Robert Owen and his followers . . .
and at a lecture given by George Bernard Shaw on a Shelley
centenary, a man stood up and said it had been one of the most
important influences on his joining the Trade Union movement!!).
And furthermore it became radically effective in a less direct way,
for Carlile and Hetherington used Shelley's work as an instrument
in fighting for the freedom of the press. Here, Shelley's ambivalence
was of use, for Hetherington could turn the censorship laws against
themselves by declaring that a complete edition of Shelley's (largely
'acceptable') poetry should be prosecuted as it contained the poem
Queen Mab.

Thus, although Shelley significantly failed to grasp the ways in
which his work might make a radical contribution, the pre-existing
media of distribution were to determine this, despite his own wishes.

In the same way, Shelley's ambivalent view of the possible or
acceptable role of radical art can be seen in his personal difficulties
over the role of poetry . . . for Shelley was not prepared to entirely
sacrifice the lofty generality (or 'vision' in Shelley's own terms) of
poetry for the clarity of prose, though he did feel that a problem
existed. Some of his reasons were undoubtedly in the tradition of the
aristocratic-aesthetic life-style, but as his work was in fact aimed at
the liberal bourgeoisie, clarity of prose would have seemed a more
acceptable radical solution at the time, as we have already
considered the 'aestheticisation' of Shelley by the bourgeoisie.
However, his decision to use poetry and poetic vision, accompanied
by copious prose notes, in *Queen Mab,* turned out to be effective
for entirely different reasons.

For the new radicals were unwilling to accept clear formulations
of what they ought to do, as passed down from above, due particularly
to a glut of such tracts and counter-tracts, which were often
extremely patronising. In confining himself to the general and the
Ideal, to poetry and philosophic Idealism, rather than prose
prescription, Shelley's work could become an ideological *tool* for the
radicals, something which they could accept for their own reasons,
and on their own terms. And this was important, for it is generally
true to say that the radical readers did not share much of the
aesthetic aspects of Shelley's viewpoint. In particular, for example,
they did not share the aesthetic-philosophical traditions (particularly
the Classical tradition) underlying these viewpoints. Therefore, for
example, in the radical editions of *Queen Mab,* Shelley's foreign

246

quotations were translated, and the references to the golden age of antiquity (as compared with the contemporary scene) must have been lost on his radical audience. (Fortunately, they are not so prominent in this work as in, e.g., *Prometheus Unbound*).

But this aestheticism had its advantages, for *Oedipus Tyrranus,* a mock classical play and satire on the politics of the day (published anonymously in 1820) was suppressed under threat of prosecution for being too forthrightly radical and, had it been published, *The Mask of Anarchy,* (about Peterloo) would undoubtedly have been prosecuted. As such works could not therefore get into the liberal press, Shelley's only attempted means of distribution, they (presumably) never reached the hands of the radical press.

In contrast, let us consider a totally different and less explicit approach to conveying a socially-critical viewpoint, through the criticism of social-domination as it manifests itself within the arts themselves, and implied in the adoption of an alternative approach to the arts as exemplified in the work of John Cage. We shall attempt to form a critique of this approach in its own terms.

In a recent discussion-session at the University of York (1972), Cage related how he had walked out of a recent Stockhausen concert in the USA because, as he put it, Stockhausen was sitting in the middle and controlling the other performers (most probably a direct electronic manipulation of the sounds they were producing). Cage made it clear that this type of composer/performer relationship was merely a particular example of the more general idea of control of one individual by another which he found unpalatable. Cage's anarchism does not stop at the boundaries of music. In sharp contrast he described his own conception of an ideal composer/ performer (and dancers) relationship in terms of his gradually evolved relationship with the Merce Cunningham troupe. This developed to the stage where each individual composer and/or performer worked out his own music without any consultation with the others, or the dancers, and each learnt to accept each others' work as part of the final, simultaneous, performance. (This particular anarchist conception of the relationship between individual action and interaction is clearly an extreme outgrowth of the American conception of liberal 'freedom'.)

Furthermore, this mode of working entails a particular type of perception of sounds. Cage likened this to our perception of a landscape (more of this later) which is destroyed in its wholeness by someone calling our attention to particular aspects of it, though we may enjoy discussing particulars afterwards. For this very reason Cage declared his dislike of people wanting to participate in his events, as he felt that this usually involved some *active desire to make sounds* which contradicted the state of acceptance in which the music was composed and performed.

However, this stricture on participation, and its justification, raises one important objection. There is a fundamental distinction between any landscape and any performance, in that a landscape merely *is*, whereas a performance, no matter to what extent the individual ego is suppressed during the performance, remains an intentional act insofar as it is planned and mounted at a particular place and time and (usually) before an audience (i.e., people who intended to be there). Bearing this in mind, even the silent piano piece does not constitute a landscape, but an intentional relationship between John Cage and/or a performer, and an audience.

In this sense at least, then, Cage's attitude to his audience involves some one-way trafficking. Cage's intentional performance before his audience *is* and is OK, whereas Joe Soap's intention to participate must be suppressed. Are we not returning via a circuitous route to the position of our arch-villain Stockhausen again?

It is important to make a distinction here between the Stockhausen/performers relationship, and a state of forced politico-economic subservience. However, the voluntariness (and temporariness) of the subservience involved in the Stockhausen performance is clearly no defence in Cage's mind. What must be important then is that this relationship exemplifies a social ideology where domination of one by another is acceptable currency. But if voluntariness is no defence, then the voluntariness of the audience's attendance at the Cage concert is no defence of using the artist/audience situation, which is always an act, as we have seen, of temporary voluntary subservience . . . Joe Soap must not participate during the performance but may do so afterwards. Why then does Cage *use* this artist/audience situation knowing that it is of a different order to his relationship with his co-creators? Despite his constant reference to his feeling that he could easily abandon composition altogether now, and that he finds the ambient sounds of the planet more satisfying than any music (including his own), why did he not cease to compose and perform long ago?

Here we come to the crux of the matter. Cage's answer is,

'because the social situation is so bad now', (and a letter from Norman O. Brown reinforces his point). And what is so bad? The only specific issue which Cage raised while in York was America's renewed bombing in Vietnam (this example is in fact crucial, see later). Thus Cage exemplifies the dilemma of the quietist. Though he may improve himself, and near acquaintances by example, the larger world continues to rapidly deteriorate. Therefore he feels compelled to act! This is the crucial problem facing all those who feel that political interference with others is the root of all problems. Where can he draw the line between positive action and domination? Many people do not see this problem in relation to Cage's work. 'How to improve the world, one only makes things worse' becomes merely a call to opt-out, for them. However, it is clear that Cage regards his public appearances as the active aspect of this dilemma.

On the other hand, it is clear that the roots of this dilemma lie much deeper, in fact in Cage's American-liberal heritage. For Cage society is still a result of mere conscious consensus and hence can be changed by withdrawing from the consensus, reaching a perfect rational conception of society, and then returning to the structure to convince others to change their ideas. Thus 'What we're doing in Vietnam' conglommerates the entire American people as personally responsible; it has no conception of structural determinants, and reflects the American illusion of a society guided by rational (or irrational) conscious consensus. In a similar fashion, the concert situation seems viewed as a forum, where a clear presentation of the case might lead to a sensible conclusion. However, it is clear that we cannot step outside our social order as our participation is both material and ideological. The relation of Cage's conception of anarchy to American ideas of 'freedom' has been hinted at and exemplifies the latter. Much more important however is the relationship between any such ideologies and the economic conditions which make them possible. (We are *not* proposing here an economic determinism, but merely suggesting that the extent and form of the solution of the economic problem for man limits the nature of possible viable ideologies or life-styles for man). Cage appears to underplay this completely.

The fact that the concert situation *presupposes* the existence of a particular kind of socio-economic framework, which is itself *mutually dependent* upon an ideology of domination seems quite foreign to the liberalist basis of Cage's thought. Hence the problem of Joe Soap is seen as an unfortunate peripheral problem, rather than the crux of the matter; for the existence of art as we know it is only conceivable in a social structure which precludes by its very nature anything approaching the type of anarchy that Cage desires among men . . . hence it is not surprising to find that Cage's work has often been assimilated as yet another fashionable artistic commodity, while chance operations become just another technique on the old-style artist's list.

Although Cage retorted to the recent BBC question 'Is it Art?' by saying that it doesn't matter, the point is that within the given socio-economic context *it is Art!!!* And that is its essential problematic.

Thus it is vitally important to have a clear practical understanding of the real factors which will affect the reception of our cultural actions, if we are truly concerned about their practical consequences. The problem is, evidently, exceedingly complicated, and not open to lofty historical generalisations. In what follows I would like to briefly outline some of the vital factors in the reception of cultural acts, *not* in order to declare a new universal aesthetic, but merely to attempt to understand some aspects of the social framework, against which our actions take on meaning, as it exists at this time. No such analysis could be final, as the framework changes all the time; neither is this description more than an outline. Every individual must assess for himself what he feels would be the best forms of radical cultural action in his own context . . . and that context must be continually reassessed.

In discussing the nature of music, Hans Keller (1970) has developed an elementary theory of how music works. To paraphrase, the composer raises expectations about what he's going to do which are contradicted by what he does do. The former is referred to as the 'background' of the work, and the latter as the 'foreground':

> The background depends, of course, on the terms of reference which the composer and his recipients have in common before the composition starts: on the knowledge of a musical language and its forms, though this knowledge certainly need not be more than instinctive (1970, p.796).

(This theory derives ultimately from the work of Heinrich Schenker). In fact, Keller's own view of the 'background' of a cultural artefact stops very short of the real situation. For Keller takes for granted the 'objectivity' of his own viewpoint as a middle-class intellectual.

The extreme result of our approach must be that, for most people, the background of which Keller speaks *does not exist,* but another background does (to such an extent that no moral or aesthetic distinctions can be drawn between, e.g., certain pop songs and certain Schubert Lieder; in their present context they are to some extent mutual translations of each other against the differing backgrounds of their respective audiences. More important still, we must not confuse a critique of the general tendencies of capitalist culture with an adulation of German Culture as against all manifestations of pop-culture!!).

Keller's theory is intended to be more generally applicable than the original Schenker theory (which extended only across tonal music). But it is clearly not general enough. Because this is in fact how all art works, though the background of some forms, e.g., the novel, poetry, need not be so clearly formalised, or detached from the entire social continuum as that of musics. But it is worthwhile making the comment that art need *not,* therefore, depend on a special language in the sense in which Keller uses it above, for the contemporary existent real world, its situations, forms, sounds, images, is a background (an extremely rich background) shared by a vast number of people at a particular place and time, largely independently (though not entirely) of the special art-languages which they comprehend. (The basic *syntax* underlying musical languages is also undoubtedly physiologically based, and hence to some extent trans-cultural.) Furthermore, the special art-languages themselves carry with them a meaning against the background of the total social world in which they exist, as we have already made clear, and a work which presupposes that its audience comprehends such a language, carries with it a meaning *before* it begins to be unfolded. (Basil Bernstein, 1971, has developed a useful theory of the differing use and function of language among different social strata in contemporary Britain, which may throw some light upon the background to other semiotic or articulatory systems within a given culture.)

From such considerations as these, it becomes possible for the cultural actor to judge the type of audience he will get for his work, and the limitations upon their response. Furthermore it becomes possible for him to consider what 'background' it would be appropriate to assume for the types of audience he wishes to contact, or in particular, how it might be possible for him to universalise his language to reach various groups in different ways. (We must *not* confuse *language-consensus* with *content*-fashionability!) This is not to suggest that the problem is solved, but merely that it exists, and hence may be considered. To ignore it is not a solution, but merely the entry of arbitrariness into cultural action.

Secondly, we will briefly consider the effect of the particular forms in which cultural action is made public, the effect of media and institutions (the social forms of art). This may be roughly analysed in terms of the degree of choice (and commitment) necessary for the recipient to come into contact with the cultural action. If a high degree of conscious effort is required this will clearly imply a great deal of commitment to certain cultural assumptions which the cultural action hence presupposes. We may also broadly differentiate cultural experiences into the social and the private. Books, gramophone records etc., where the cultural artefact is mass-produced, widely distributed, and bought by individuals to read, play or view in their own homes at their own leisure will be a more or less private and probably repeated experience, hence involving a high degree of choice. The simple fact that the recipient has to choose his artefact, usually before his first experience, means that he must either have some sympathy with the artefact, or some reason for believing that he might have (apart from the effects of fashion, advertising and all the paraphernalia of the capitalist commodity market). Any artefact of this sort which aims to change someone's consciousness must therefore begin by appealing to his present consciousness, or he will never in fact choose to give it a viewing (playing etc.). However, due to the easy repeatability of this type of private experience, the medium has the potential for gradually revealing the intentions of a work, for a degree of complexity and subtlety (this applies more to the musical experience than to the novel, which is not often read frequently, due to its length . . .). We may, however, also note that such factors may alienate or merely discount a larger part of any potential audience. Artefacts in these media may hence tend to polarise viewpoints, the half-persuaded may have their conceptions sharpened, whereas the antagonistic will view the work in purely 'aesthetic' terms, a pleasant or profound experience, a welcome addition to the record collection or bookshelf.

A different type of private experience is provided by the media of radio and television. Here there is little choice (the view that everyone is perfectly free to turn off or on whenever they want, is hopelessly idealised . . . most people just enjoy watching television, especially as a passive relaxing experience after a day's work in a factory or office, regardless of specific content). Nor is there room (or very rarely) for repetition, or for the recipient to choose the pace of the experience (as with written forms). The potential audience is very large, and relatively independent of the cultural presuppositions involved in the above-mentioned forms. Theoretically, in these media, cultural action may be more manifestly radical, but, as in the previous case, though for different reasons, may tend to polarise existing opinion. Furthermore, the very efficacy of such media means that they are at present almost entirely in the hands of existing power-groups within any society, and hence the cultural radical will find almost insurmountable difficulty in gaining access to them, unless he is prepared to compromise his explicitness to a debilitating degree. (Furthermore, as these media in their present form are the *least* participatory, they are unlikely to convey a radical cultural message!!)

The case of public cultural experience is complex. Not only does a visit to the theatre, concert-hall or discotheque presuppose the acceptance of certain cultural criteria (and hence a high degree of choice); it also involves participating in a social event. The discotheque and concert-hall provide the extreme opposite examples of the influence of social event factors on the reception of a cultural artefact or event. For, whereas the concert-hall experience is social *yet* essentially intellectually private, immediately individual (at least until the interval), the discotheque experience is immediately communal and socially participatory. (There is no intellectual distancing from the experience and from the communality of the experience itself.) The concert-hall experience is essentially a private confirmation of bourgeois aesthetic values, to be reinforced, obliquely, in different media (dress, manners, conversation) before and after the event. In all these cases, the social experience may completely outweigh the experience of the artefact or cultural act.

A radical assault on such media seems the most problematic (and even futile). Attempts to set up alternative locations for theatre, music etc. (Arts-Labs and so on) usually merely pre-select a different social type of audience member, and usually a type with a more aestheticist approach anyway. (However, the true community

253

arts-lab cum youth-club, e.g., Great George's in Liverpool, seems a truly radical step forward). Attempts to surmount these obstacles via such methods as participatory theatre and/or music within pre-established institutions may either merely pre-select their audiences, or have to be one-off events relying entirely on the element of surprise. This might, of course, be effective occasionally, but does not seem a viable general method.

Next, we must consider cultural actions which do not confine themselves to pre-specified buildings and institutions, or rely upon the aesthetic response-style of the recipient to pre-select them. Such media are the media of the street, of the real environment. Here the audience is to some extent arbitrary, but greater audience selectivity may be ensured by careful choice of venue. Here the radical actor can choose his audience more directly, and can meet them at a more intimate level, and in situations which presuppose little except the everyday reality of the street. On the other hand, his audience is necessarily small, and definitely not captive.

Street posters have the directness, but not the vast audience, of television. Street theatre has the further advantage of immediate public feedback, especially as the suspension of reality involved in the theatrical spectacle can *itself* be suspended.

Finally, we must consider totally participatory forms of cultural action, i.e., actions which presuppose participation, rather than imposing it upon an unsuspecting *audience*. Clearly, this type of cultural activity requires the highest degree of previous commitment of all the forms discussed, while on the other hand, its success in enlarging radical consciousness is almost guaranteed.

The most important negative factor in the latter two categories is, of course, the economic. Money is always available in vast quantities to reaffirm society's Cultural illusions; a rejection of those illusions may mean an acceptance of impotence, or at least a willingness to be content with small successes. Or it may mean an economic compromise with existing institutions (which always carries with it the danger of circumlocuitous self-deception . . . the radical millionaire, etc.) especially when the real effectiveness of many cultural actions is extremely difficult to determine.

Having briefly raised all these problems let me sum up with the following quotation from Tony Garnett, who produced the films *Kes* and *Family Life* :

Q. Do you accept the Marcusian thesis that no innovation

designed to subvert the structure of post-Capitalist society can, in fact, escape the ability of that society to absorb every cultural threat?

A.   On the one hand, that is saying that so long as there are two classes in society and so long as the capitalist ruling class owns everything, they own all culture. It is their task to assimilate. The task of changing all that is not only the artist's. The historical task is that of the working-class and a lot of middle-class artists, as people who work in the arts, what is laughingly called 'communications', whether they are middle-class by birth, or by adoption, like me, tend to think that they are in the van of all this, and that the responsibility is theirs. But only in a peripheral way is the responsibility theirs, and it cannot be achieved by them. However, and Marcuse did not mean this, some people easily get into a politics of despair over this problem and end up with a very nihilist position. So it's an interesting observation, but not a very important one.

Q.   I would like to ask about Reagan's remark in *The Big Flame* to the effect that the working class have always been sold out by the middle-class Marxists . . .

A.   Of course that's true. I would say to anyone in the Labour Movement, 'Don't trust me'. I mean that very seriously. If in the end I have proved to be trustworthy, then that's great for all of us . . . you won't be disappointed that way. This has always been true of left-wing intellectuals who are needed, but who are dangerous because the opportunities for self-deceit, for class-collaboration, for personal corruption, are almost infinite. If you left school at 15 and are working on the line at Dagenham, in a very real sense you can't be corrupted because you can't beat the line. And all they own is your labour power for so many hours a week. But in another way, if you are an intellectual, society owns you in a deeper sense. If you are a lawyer or a doctor or a film-producer, your soul as well as your body is involved and you are owned in a deeper, more horrifying way, particularly left-wing academics. (Quoted in Field and Sainsbury, 1970).

TREVOR WISHART

NOTES

1.   This entire chapter is a somewhat extended version of a paper submitted as part of a D.Phil. (music composition) portfolio, University of York, 1973. The paper was originally written to help clarify certain problems of practical creative activity. The intention was not to take up an intellectual position and thenceforward defend it, but to continue developing such ideas where practical experience suggested this was essential. The paper should thus be regarded as no more than a frozen 'snapshot' of a past moment of this continuing process.

Epilogue

The major aim of this book has been to provide a re-evaluation of deep-seated assumptions underlying attitudes to music. These assumptions permeate the work of leading musicologists and aestheticians, the policies of arts and broadcasting administrators, and the curricula of schools and universities. But as Trevor Wishart's final chapter suggests, even where musical attitudes have been criticised from an avowedly radical standpoint, such basic *assumptions* have rarely been effectively challenged. Such a challenge, which must avoid perpetuating old established ideas in other guises, should seek to be more than just an isolated academic exercise and concern itself with its practical implications. Hence the book lays the foundations for new approaches towards the understanding, practice and dissemination of music.

Some practical consequences of this new approach might include a re-assessment by broadcasting institutions, particularly the BBC, of their programming policies; a more equitable distribution of Arts Council funds towards different kinds of musics; a more open attitude by school teachers towards the musical cultures of their pupils; and a *serious* reconsideration by university music departments of the value of all kinds of music (*including* present-day 'popular' forms), instead of their acting merely as a forum for so-called 'art' musics.

However, the purpose of this book has been to understand, rather than to prescribe; we have confined ourselves to the general theoretical considerations which must inevitably inform alternative practices. In the main it has therefore been left to individual readers to assess the situation as it affects *them*. The authors of this book do not consider it to be a final statement, but more a prelude to further research and activity.

BIBLIOGRAPHY

Adorno, T.W., 'On Popular Music', *Studies in Philosophy and Social Science*, IX, 1, 1941.

Adorno, T.W., *Prisms*, Neville Spearman, 1967.

Adorno, T.W., *Philosophy of Modern Music*, Bloomster, W.V., and Mitchell, D.G., (trans), Sheed and Ward, 1973.

Banks, O., *The Sociology of Education*, Batsford, 1968.

Bantock, G.H., *Culture, Industrialisation and Education*, Routledge and Kegan Paul, 1968.

Barzun, J., *Classic, Romantic and Modern*, Doubleday, 1943.

Bateson, G., *Steps to an Ecology of Mind*, Granada, 1973.

Becker, C.L., 'Progress', in *The Idea of Progress since the Renaissance*, Wagner, W.W., (ed), John Wiley and Sons, 1969.

Becker, H.S., 'The Culture of a Deviant Group: The Dance Musician', 1951. Reprinted in Becker, H.S., 1963.

Becker, H.S., *The Outsiders: Studies in the Sociology of Deviance*, The Free Press, 1963.

Becker, H.S., *et al. Making the Grade*, John Wiley and Sons, 1969.

Berger, M., 'Jazz: Resistance to the Diffusion of a Culture Pattern, *Journal of Negro History*, 32, 1947.

Berger, P.L., and Luckmann, T., *The Social Construction of Reality*, Penguin, 1967.

Bernstein, B., *Class, Codes and Control*, Vol. I, Routledge and Kegan Paul, 1971.

Bernstein, B., 'A Brief Account of the Theory of Codes', in Open University: *Social Relationships and Language*, E262, Block 3, 1973a.

Bernstein, B., 'A Sociolinguistic Approach to Socialisation', 1973b, in *Class, Codes and Control*, Vol. II, Routledge and Kegan Paul, 1973.

Blacking, J., *How Musical is Man?* University of Washington Press, 1973.

Bloch, M., *Feudal Society*, Routledge and Kegan Paul, 1961.

Boulez, P., 'Schoenberg is Dead', *The Score*, 6, 1952.

Bourdieu, P., 'Intellectual Field and Creative Project', 1966. Reprinted in Young, M.F.D., (ed), 1971.

Bourdieu, P., 'Systems of Education and Systems of Thought', 1967. Reprinted in Young, M.F.D., (ed), 1971.

Brace, G., 'Music and the Secondary School Timetable', University of Exeter Institute of Education, 1970.

Bramson, L., *The Political Context of Sociology*, Princeton University Press, 1961.

BIBLIOGRAPHY

Brocklehurst, J.B., *Music in Schools*, Routledge and Kegan Paul, 1962.

Capek, M., *Philosophical Impact of Contemporary Physics*, Van Nostrand, 1961.

Carey, J.W., 'Harold Adams Innis and Marshall McLuhan', *The Antioch Review*, XXVII, 1967.

Carothers, J.C., 'Culture, Psychiatry and the Written Word', *Psychiatry*, XXII, 1959.

Carpenter, E., and McLuhan, M., 'Acoustic Space' in Carpenter, E., and McLuhan, M., (eds), *Explorations in Communication*, Jonathan Cape, 1970.

Cash, T., (ed), *Anatomy of Pop*, British Broadcasting Corporation, 1970.

Chailley, J., 'Essai analytique sur la formation de l'octoechos latin', in Westrup, J., (ed), *Essays presented to Egon Wellesz*, Clarendon Press, 1966.

Chailley, J., 'Une nouvelle méthode d'approche pour l'analyse modale du chant grégorien', in *Speculum Musicae Artis — Festgable fur Heinrich Husmann*, (eds), Becker, H., and Gerlach, R., Wilhem Fink, 1970.

Chaytor, H.J., 'Reading and Writing' in Carpenter, E., and McLuhan, M., (eds), *Explorations in Communication*, Jonathan Cape, 1970.

Chester, A., 'Second Thoughts on a Rock Aesthetic: The Band', *New Left Review*, 62, 1970.

Cicourel, A.V., *Cognitive Sociology*, Penguin Books, 1973.

Cooke, D., *The Language of Music*, Oxford University Press, 1959.

Coser, L., 'Comments on Bauer and Bauer', *Journal of Social Issues*, 26, 1960.

Crocker, R.L., 'Hermann's Major Sixth', *Journal of the American Musicological Society*, XXV, 1972.

Crossley-Holland, P., 'Non-Western Music', in *The Pelican History of Music*, Vol. I, Penguin Books, 1960.

Dennis, B., *Experimental Music in Schools*, Oxford University Press, 1970.

Douglas, M., *Purity and Danger*, Penguin Books, 1970.

Duncan, H.D., *Symbols in Society*, Oxford University Press, 1968.

Durgnat, R., 'Rock, Rhythm and Dance', *British Journal of Aesthetics*, II, 1971.

Esland, G., 'Teaching and Learning as the Organisation of Knowledge', in Young, M.F.D., (ed), 1971.

Fanon, F., *Black Skins, White Masks*, Markmann, C.L., (trans), Granada, 1970.

Field, S., and Sainsbury, P., (eds), 'An Interview with Tony Garnett', *Afterimage*, No. 1, April 1970.

Fisher, H.A.L., *A History of Europe*, Edward Arnold, 1936.

Flude, M., 'Sociological Accounts of Differential Educational Attainment' in Flude, M., and Ahier, J., (eds), *Educability, Schools and Ideology*, Croom Helm, 1974.

260

Gans, H.J., 'Popular Culture in America: Social Problem in a Mass Society or Social Asset in a Pluralist Society?' in Becker, H.S., (ed), *Social Problems: A Modern Approach*, John Wiley, 1967.

Giedion, S., 'Space Conception in Prehistoric Art', in Carpenter, E., and McLuhan, M.,(eds), *Explorations in Communication*, Jonathan Cape, 1970.

Gillett, C., *The Sound of the City*, Sphere, 1971.

Goldman, A., 'The Emergence of Rock', *New American Review*, No. 3, New American Library, 1968.

Goldschmidt, E.P., *Medieval Texts and Their First Appearance in Print*, Oxford University Press, 1943.

Goody, J., and Watt, I., 'The Consequences of Literacy', *Comparative Studies in Society and History*, V, 1963.

Grant, W.,(ed), *Music in Education*, Butterworths, 1963.

Haag, E. van den, 'Of Happiness and Despair We Have No Measure' in Rosenberg, B., and White, D.,(eds), *Mass Culture*, The Free Press, 1959.

Haag, E. van den, 'A Dissent from the Consensual Society', in Jacobs, N. (ed), *Culture for the Millions*, Princeton, 1961.

Hadingham, E., (ed), *Youth Now*, Kingston Grammar School, 1970.

Hallowell, A.I., 'Temporal Orientations in Western Civilisation and in a Pre-literate Society', *American Anthropologist*, Vol. 39, 1937.

Hanson, N.R., *Patterns of Discovery*, Cambridge University Press, 1965.

Hargreaves, D., *Social Relations in a Secondary School*, Routledge and Kegan Paul, 1968.

Henry, J., *Culture Against Man*, Tavistock, 1966.

Herman, G., *The Who*, November Books, 1971.

Hodeir, A., *Jazz: Its Evolution and Essence*, Secker & Warburg, 1956.

Hopkins, J., *The Rock Story*, Signet Books, 1970.

Horton, J., 'Carl Orff', *Music Teacher*, April, 1969.

Horton, R., 'African Traditional Thought and Western Science', 1967. Reprinted in Young, M.F.D., (ed), 1971.

Hughes, A., 'The Birth of Polyphony' in *The New Oxford History of Music*, Vol. II, Oxford University Press, 1955.

Inkeles, A., 'Industrial Man: The Relations of Status to Experience, Perception and Value', *American Journal of Sociology*, 66, 1960.

Jacobs, N.,(ed), *Culture for the Millions*, Princeton, 1961.

Jasper, T., *Understanding Pop*, SCM Press, 1972.

Jurdant, B., 'Freud and Science', *Nouselit*, 1, 1974.

Jurdant, B., 'La science un drole de je-trimethylamine', *Impascience*, 3, 1975.

Kaufmann, W., *Musical Notations of the Orient*, Indiana University Press, 1967.

a

Keil, C., 'Motion and Feeling Through Music', *Journal of Aesthetics and Art Criticism*, 24, 1966.

Keddie, N., 'Classroom Knowledge', in Young, M.F.D., 1971.

Keller, H., 'Towards a Theory of Music', *The Listener*, June 1970.

Kenyon, F.C., *Books and Readers in Ancient Greece and Rome*, Clarendon Press, 1937.

Kitto, H.D.F., *The Greeks*, Penguin Books, 1951.

Kohn, M., and Schooler, C., 'Class, Occupation and Orientation', *American Sociological Review*, 34, 1969.

Kornhauser, W., *The Politics of Mass Society*, The Free Press, 1959.

Krebs, S.D., *Soviet Composers and The Development of Soviet Music*, W.W. Norton, 1970.

Kuhn, T.S., *The Structure of Scientific Revolutions*, Chicago University Press, 1970.

Labov, W., 'The Logic of Non-Standard English', in Keddie, N., *Tinker, Tailor*, Penguin Books, 1973.

Laing, R.D., *Self and Others*, Penguin Books, 1971.

Landau, J., 'Rock 1970', *Rolling Stone*, 2 December, 1970.

Landau, J., 'Rock and Roll Music', *Rolling Stone*, 1 April, 1971.

Langer, S. K., *Philosophy in a New Key*, Harvard University Press, 1960.

Langer, S.K., *Feeling and Form*, Routledge and Kegan Paul, 1953.

Leach, E.R., 'Primitive Time-Reckoning', in Singer, C., Holmyard, E.J., and Hall, A.R., (eds), *A History of Technology*, Vol. I, 1954.

Lee, D., 'Lineal and Nonlineal Codifications of Reality', in Carpenter, E., and McLuhan, M., (eds), *Explorations in Communication*, Jonathan Cape, 1970.

Lee, E., *Music of the People: A Study of Popular Music in Great Britain*, Barrie and Jenkins, 1970.

Lee, E., *Jazz: An Introduction*, Stanmore Press, 1972.

Leonard, N., *Jazz and the White Americans*, University of Chicago Press, 1962.

Lévi-Strauss, C., *Structural Anthropology*, Jacobson, C., and Schoepf, B.G., (trans), Penguin Books, 1968.

Long, N., 'Some Problems of Grammar School Music', in Grant, W., (ed), *Music in Education*, Butterworths, 1963.

Lord, A.B., *The Singer of Tales*, Harvard University Press, 1964.

Lowenthal, L., 'Historical Perspectives of Popular Culture', *American Journal of Sociology*, 55, 1950.

Lukacs, G., 'The Old Culture and the New Culture', *Telos*, Spring 1970.

Lyle, R., 'Delius and the Philosophy of Romanticism', *Music and Letters*, 29, 1948.

McDonald, D., 'A Theory of Mass Culture', in Rosenberg, B., and White, D., (eds), *Mass Culture*, The Free Press, 1959.

McGregor, C., 'A Magical Connection', in Somma, R., (ed), *No One Waved Goodbye*, A Fusion Book, 1971.

McLuhan, M., *The Gutenberg Galaxy*, Toronto University Press, 1962.

McLuhan, M., *Understanding Media*, The New American Library of Canada, 1964.

McLuhan, M., 'The Effect of the Printed Book on Language in the Sixteenth Century', in Carpenter, E., and McLuhan, M., (eds), *Explorations in Communication*, Jonathan Cape, 1970.

McPherson, S., *The Appreciation, or Listening Class*, Joseph Williams, 1936.

Marcus, G., 'Rock-a-hula Clarified', *Creem*, June 1971.

Mellers, W., *Music and Society*, Denis Dobson, 1946.

Mellers, W., *Music in a New Found Land*, Barrie and Rockcliff, 1964.

Mellers, W., *Caliban Reborn*, Victor Gollancz, 1968.

Mellers, W., 'A New Tribal Music', in Hadingham, E., (ed), *Youth Now*, Kingston Grammar School, 1970.

Mellers, W., *Twilight of the Gods: The Beatles in Retrospect*, Faber and Faber, 1973.

Melly, G., *Revolt into Style: The Pop Arts in Britain*, Penguin Books, 1972.

Merriam, A.P., *The Anthropology of Music*, Evanston, 1964.

Merriam, A.P., *The Ethnomusicology of the Flathead Indian*, Aldine, 1967.

Meyer, L.B., *Emotion and Meaning in Music*, University of Chicago Press, 1956.

Meyer, L.B., 'Some Remarks on Value and Greatness in Music', *Journal of Aesthetics and Art Criticism*, 1, 1959.

Meyer, L.B., *Music, the Arts and Ideas*, University of Chicago Press, 1967.

Meyer, L.B., *Explaining Music*, University of California Press, 1973.

Middleton, R., *Pop Music and the Blues*, Victor Gollancz, 1972.

Mills, C.W., 'Situated Actions and Vocabularies of Motive', 1940. Reprinted in Cosin, B.R., *et al.* (eds), *School and Society: A Sociological Reader*, Routledge and Kegan Paul, 1971.

Morse, D., *Motown*, November Books, 1971.

Mueller, J.H., *The American Symphony Orchestra: A Social History of Musical Taste*, Indiana University Press, 1951.

Murdock, G., and Phelps, G., *Mass Media and the Secondary School*, Macmillan, 1973.

Nef, J.V., *Cultural Foundations of Industrial Civilization*, Cambridge University Press, 1958.

Nestyev, I.V., *Prokoviev*, Jonas, F., (trans), Oxford University Press, 1961.

Nettl, B., *Music in Primitive Culture*, Harvard University Press, 1956.

Nicholls, M., 'Running an Open Music Department' in Vulliamy, G., and Lee, E., (eds), 1976.

Nuttall, J., *Bomb Culture*, Paladin Books, 1970.

Oliver, P., *Savannah Syncopators: African Retentions in the Blues*, November Books, 1970.

Ong, W.J., *The Presence of the Word*, Yale University Press, 1967.

Ong, W.J., 'World as View and World as Event', *American Anthropologist*, LXXI, 1969.

Parker, C., 'Pop Song, the Manipulated Ritual', in Abbs, P., (ed), *The Black Rainbow*, Heinemann Educational Books, 1975.

Paynter, J., and Aston, P., *Sound and Silence*, Cambridge University Press, 1970.

Pleasants, H., *Serious Music and All That Jazz*, Victor Gollancz, 1969.

Poulet, G., *Studies in Human Time*, Coleman, E., (trans), Johns Hopkins University Press, 1959.

Pring, R., 'Knowledge Out of Control', *Education for Teaching*, Autumn, 1972.

Rainbow, B., *The Land Without Music*, Novello and Co., 1967.

Rainbow, B., 'The Historical and Philosophical Background of School Music Teaching', in Rainbow, B., (ed), *Handbook for Music Teachers*, University of London Institute of Education, 1968.

Rayburn, J., *Gregorian Chant: A History of the Controversy Concerning its Rhythm*, 1964.

Reese, G., *Music in the Middle Ages*, W.W. Norton, 1940.

Reti, R., *Tonality, Atonality, Pantonality*, Rockcliff, 1958.

Riesman, D., 'The Oral and Written Traditions', in Carpenter, E., and McLuhan, M.,(eds),*Explorations in Communication*, Jonathan Cape, 1970.

Roberts, J.S., *Black Music of Two Worlds*, Allen Lane, 1973.

Robinson, P., 'An Ethnography of Classrooms', in Eggleston, J., (ed), *Contemporary Research in the Sociology of Education*, Methuen, 1974.

Rolling Stone Editors, *The Rolling Stone Interviews*, Straight Arrow, 1971.

Rosen, H., 'Language and Class: A Critical Look at the Theories of Basil Bernstein', in Holly, D. (ed), *Education or Domination?*, Arrow Books, 1974.

Rosenberg, B., and White, D., (eds), *Mass Culture*, The Free Press, 1959.

Routh, F., *Contemporary Music: An Introduction*, The English Universities Press, 1968.

Routh, F., *Contemporary British Music*, MacDonald, 1972.

Scholes, P.A., *Music, the Child and the Masterpiece*, Oxford University Press 1935.

Schools Council, *Music and the Young School-Leaver*, Schools Council Publications, 1971.

Schuller, G., *Early Jazz*, Oxford University Press, 1968.

Schutz, A., Collected Papers: Vol. I — *The Problem of Social Reality*, Martinus Nijhoff, 1967.

Schwarz, B., *Music and Musical Life in Soviet Russia 1917-1970*, Barrie and Jenkins, 1972.

Self, G., 'Revolution', *Music in Education*, May 1965.

Self, G., *New Sounds in Class*, Universal Editions, 1967.

Sharp, R., and Green, A., *Education and Social Control*, Routledge and Kegan Paul, 1975.

Shaw, A., *The Rock Revolution*, Paperback Library, 1971.

Shepherd, J.C., 'The Social and Theoretical Background to the Music of Delius', unpublished, University of York, 1973.

Shepherd, J.C., 'Adorno's "Philosophy of Modern Music" ', *Contact*, Spring 1975 (a).

Shepherd, J.C., 'The Implicit-Explicit Paradigm', unpublished, University of York, 1975(b).

Shepherd, J.C., 'Meyer's "Explaining Music" ', *Contact*, Spring 1976.

Spellman, A.B., *Black Music : Four Lives*, Scholsen, 1970.

Spencer, P., 'The Creative Possibilities of Pop', in Vulliamy, G., and Lee, E., (eds), 1976.

Spiess, L.B., 'Introduction to the Pre-History of Polyphony', in *Essays on Music in Honour of Archibald Thompson Davison*, Harvard University Press, 1957.

Stearns, M.W., *The Story of Jazz*, Oxford University Press, 1956.

Stevens, D., 'Ars Antiqua', in *The Pelican History of Music*, Vol. I, Penguin Books, 1960.

Stuckenschmidt, H.H., *Arnold Schoenberg*, John Calder, 1959.

Titiev, M., 'Social Singing among the Mapuche', *Anthropological Papers*, No. 2, University of Michigan at Ann Arbor, 1949.

Trotsky, L., *Literature and Revolution*, Moscow, 1923.

Virden P., 'The Social Determinants of Aesthetic Styles', *British Journal of Aesthetics*, III, 1972.

Vulliamy, G., 'A Reassessment of the "Mass Culture" Controversy: The Case of Rock Music', *Popular Music and Society*, IV, No. 3, 1975.

Vulliamy, G., and Lee, E., (eds), *Pop Music in School*, Cambridge University Press, 1976.

Walton, O.M., 'A Comparative Analysis of the African and the Western

Aesthetic' in Gayle, A., (ed), *The Black Aesthetic*, Doubleday Anchor, 1972.

Werner, E., 'The Origins of the Eight Modes of Music', *Hebrew College Annual*, Vol. 21, 1948.

Werth, A., *Musical Uproar in Moscow*, Turnstile Press, 1949.

Westrup, J., 'Medieval Song', in *The New Oxford History of Music*, Vol. II, Oxford University Press, 1955.

Whitty, G., 'Sociology and the Problem of Radical Educational Change: Notes towards a Reconceptualisation of the "New Sociology of Education" ', in Flude, M., and Ahier, J., (eds), *Educability, Schools and Ideology*, Croom Helm, 1974.

Whorf, B.L., *Language, Thought and Reality*, MIT Press, 1971.

Wilensky, H., 'Mass Society and Mass Culture: Interdependence or Independence?' *American Sociological Review*, April 1964.

Williams, R., *Culture and Society 1780-1950*, Penguin, 1961.

Williams-Jones, P., 'Afro-American Gospel Music: A Crystallisation of the Black Aesthetic', *Ethnomusicology*, September 1975.

Wooton, A., 'Talk in the Homes of Young Children', *Sociology*, Vol. 8, 1974.

Worsley, P., *The Trumpet Shall Sound*, Granada, 1970.

Yasser, J., *A Theory of Evolving Tonality*, American Library of Musicology, 1932.

Yasser, J., 'Medieval Quartal Harmony', *Musical Quarterly*, Vol. XXIII, 1937.

Young, M.F.D., (ed), *Knowledge and Control: New Directions for the Sociology of Education*, Collier Macmillan, 1971.

Young, M.F.D., 'Curriculum Change: Limits and Possibilities', *Educational Studies*, I, No. 2, 1975.

Zuckerkandl, V., *Sound and Symbol: Music and the External World*, Trask, W.R., (trans), Routledge and Kegan Paul, 1956.

Explanation of Musical Terminology
JOHN SHEPHERD
and
TREVOR WISHART

This Appendix attempts to give the non-musician some insight into the nature of physical sound processes, different musical languages, and musical vocabulary in general. For the sake of clear understanding, we have therefore sought to make the descriptions and explanations adequate rather than definitive. Although a few of our descriptions may consequently lack all the finer details that might have been included for the specialist musical reader, we trust that this possible deficiency will be fully compensated by the greater ease with which the general reader may approach the musical sections of the book.

PITCH

Frequency and Pitch

Physically speaking, the sensation of sound is produced by vibrations transmitted through the air, themselves causing the eardrums to vibrate. The number of times per second that the air molecules vibrate is called the frequency, and is measured in cycles per second (usually known as herz. We will, however, refer to cycles per second in this Appendix as this label serves to remind us of the physical process involved). Below about 16 c/s the individual vibrations are heard as distinct pulses. Above about 20,000 c/s (20 KHz) the human ear no longer responds to the vibrations, i.e., nothing is heard. (Certain other animals e.g., dogs, bats can hear sounds in and above this range). Between 16 and 20,000 c/s the vibrations produce the sensation of a continuous sound. As the frequency of the vibrations increases, the perceived quality of the sound changes (gets 'higher'). This perceived quality of the 'height' or 'depth' of a particular sound is referred to as its *pitch*.

Scale: Pitch Notation

Usually in musical practice a certain limited set of *discrete* pitches is used. (It would be more strictly true to refer to a limited set of discrete pitch-relationships. See below). These may then be arranged in ascending (or descending) order to form scales of pitches. Most scales have between five and twelve pitches. Such scales of pitches *may* be notated (as in the West) by using a system of height lines on which the discrete pitches are marked as dots. The dots may occur either on the lines (see diagram 1a) or between the lines (see 1b), but nowhere else. A typical scale might look like this (1c):

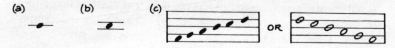

Diagram 1

The number of height lines in general use in the West, (i.e., five), is a matter of convention. The group of lines is known as a *stave*. Pitches written down in this way are usually referred to as *notes*. To notate pitches lower (or higher) than those on the stave shown above, we may use another stave covering a lower range of pitches. To differentiate between these different stave-ranges a sign called a *clef* is used. For example the two in most general use in the West (though these are by no means exclusive) are the treble and bass clefs (often in combination as in piano music, see below):

Diagram 2

Pitch Relationships

The pitches used in any particular scale will obviously give rise to a finite set of possible relationships between themselves. Any *one* of these relationships (expressed as the ratio between the frequencies of any two specific pitches) is called an *interval* (see below). Ultimately it is the pattern of relationships set up between the pitches of a particular scale which distinguishes it from other, different, scales.

MELODY

Motif

A (usually) very short sequence of notes used as a basic structural unit of a melody or of larger forms.

Phrase

A constituent part of a melody or theme (cf. the relationship of a phrase to a sentence in language).

Passing-note

Any note in a melody which fills in the gap between two structurally more important notes. This distinction between important and passing notes in any particular piece depends on the syntax of the relevant musical language.

Monody: Monophonic

A monody is an unaccompanied melody. Such a melody may be said to be *monophonic*.

RHYTHM

In the context of this book rhythm may be most easily understood in terms of the following three categories:

Pulse

Pulse is the continual recurrence of the fundamental temporal unit in any piece. Pulse is sometimes described as 'beat'. Good examples of pulses which exist outside music are provided by the heartbeat, regular walking, a pile-driver, a clock, etc. The rate of recurrence of a pulse is known as *tempo*.

269

Rhythm

Rhythm (in its strictest sense) refers to the actual pattern of individual durations (lengths of discrete sounds and silences) used in a piece. The succession of these durations does not necessarily coincide at any time with the imagined articulation of either pulse or metre (see below) although the pulse or metre (if any) will always be felt *through* the rhythm. In music outside the tradition of tonality, the duration of these individual units need not bear any simple relationship (such as *summativity,* see below) to the duration of the units of pulse.

Metre: Bar-line

Metre (which applies most particularly to the music of tonality) occurs when regular and recurring stress patterns are imposed on pulse. Metre can be basically duple:

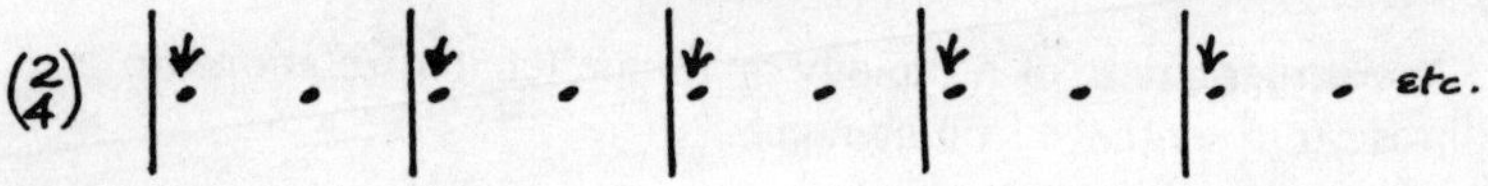

Diagram 3

or triple, thus:

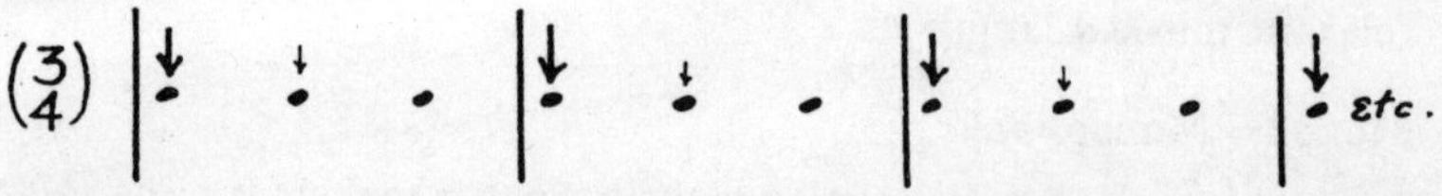

Diagram 4

Quadruple metre is a complex form of duple in which the third 'pulse' or beat contains the second strongest stress, the second beat the third, and the fourth the weakest, thus:

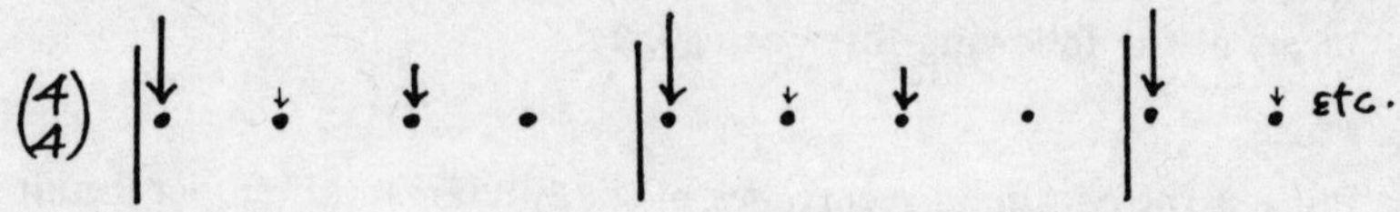

Diagram 5

These metres are known as simple metres. (In this respect metre is sometimes loosely referred to as 'rhythm', as in 'simple duple

270

rhythm'). There are also 'compound metres'. A good example is when simple duple metre is subdivided into triple metre, thus:

Diagram 6

The strongest beat of the metre always occurs after the *bar line*, indicated in the above examples and in conventional notation by a vertical line.

Rhythm Notation: Summative Rhythm

Rhythm notation in Europe since approximately the twelfth century may most easily be understood by reference to a bar of 4/4 metre (see above, Diagram 5). The duration of a sound persisting throughout such a bar is indicated by the notation:

Diagram 7

(the pitch used is of course irrelevant for the purposes of this explanation). We may now derive smaller units of duration by dividing this unit into a number of *exactly equal* parts. The conventional notations for these units are given below. Thus (dividing by a factor of two):

Diagram 8

Thus any note may be expressed as a *sum* of smaller units, e.g:

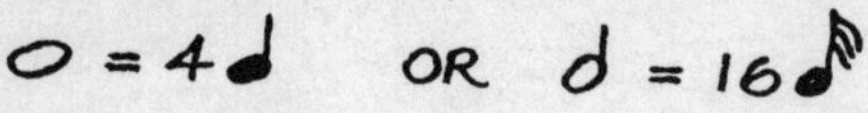

Diagram 9

These various units may be combined to form rhythm-patterns in which this relationship of simple *summation* of units is always retained, e.g:

Diagram 10

As indicated above, metres may also be devised by dividing the basic unit into three (or, much more rarely, five, seven, etc.). This requires various refinements to the above system. However the basic principle of summation is retained. Exceptionally, notes of short and unspecified length may be introduced into this framework and are indicated by the schematic (imprecise) notation ♪.

DYNAMICS

This refers to the relative loudness of sounds. Gradations of relative loudness are notated in the tradition of tonality as follows:

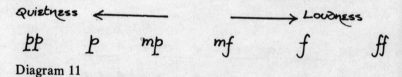

Diagram 11

Gradually increasing loudness is indicated thus:

Diagram 12

and its opposite by:

OR "*decrescendo*"

Diagram 13

SCORE

The complete notation of a piece of music is known as the *score*.

HARMONIC SERIES

Frequency Spectrum: Timbre

In order to generate the vibrations in the air which produce the sensation of sound, we must use some form of mechanical apparatus, e.g., musical instruments, the larynx, a loudspeaker cone. In practice, in attempting to vibrate some medium at a specific frequency, it will usually vibrate simultaneously at a number of other subsidiary frequencies (an exception to this is the sine-tone generator, see below). The complete set of frequencies at which the medium is vibrating, and which will be characteristic of the medium and the mode of vibration, is called the frequency-spectrum. The difference between the typical frequency-spectra of one instrument and those of another is heard as the difference in tone colour or *timbre* of the two instruments.

Fundamental: Harmonics: Harmonic Series

For most instruments which produce clearly defined pitches, the subsidiary frequencies will be closely related to the principal frequency. The latter is known as the *fundamental,* and the former as the *harmonics* of the fundamental. The frequencies of the harmonics are simple whole number multiples of the frequency of the fundamental. Thus, for example, if the fundamental frequency is 100 c/s the harmonics will occur at such frequencies as 200, 300, 400, 500 etc. The entire set of such frequencies is known as the *harmonic series* of the fundamental.

It is important to understand that it is the ratio between two frequencies, and *not* the absolute numerical difference, which determines the size of the interval between them, (q.v.). Thus the interval between 200 c/s and 300 c/s (absolute numerical difference 100, ratio 2:3) is not the same as that between 300 c/s and 400 c/s (absolute numerical difference 100, ratio 3:4). Hence the set of *intervals* generated by the *harmonic series* will be the same whichever fundamental is chosen i.e:

Fundamental	120 ⎫		
1st harmonic	240 ⎬ ⎫	1:2 interval X	
2nd harmonic	360 ⎫ ⎬	2:3 interval Y	
3rd harmonic	480 ⎭	3:4 interval Z	
	etc	etc	

Fn 37 ⎫		1:2 interval X	
1H 74 ⎬ ⎫		2:3 interval Y	
2H 111 ⎫ ⎬		3:4 interval Z	
3H 148 ⎭		etc	
etc			

These intervals generated by the harmonic series, and expressible in terms of exact whole number ratios, may be called the *natural* intervals.

TONALITY

Tonality

Tonality is the musical system prevalent in European art culture between approximately 1600 and 1900. It is the musical language with which most readers of this book will be generally familiar. All the terms explained in this section are drawn principally from the analysis of tonality, although *some* are used in descriptions of other musical systems.

Tempered Scales: Letter Names: Pitch Classes

The tempered scales are the scales of tonality. The intervals which determine these scales are close approximations to the simpler natural intervals (i.e., 1:2, 2:3, 3:4, 4:5, etc.). The interval around which the tempered scale pivots is the *octave*. It is the only interval in the tempered scale to coincide *exactly* with its counterpart in the harmonic series. *Both* intervals have precisely the same frequency ratio of 2:1. This interval is so basic in the tonal system, that all pitches having that relationship to one another are given the same name and from the point of view of the system's operation are regarded as essentially the same note.

To clarify this we will begin to describe the way letters of the alphabet are used to refer to the notes of the scale. Imagine these notes to be written in ascending order, the first note being labelled 'A' and the others 'B', 'C', 'D', and so on. On reaching the note an octave above the first 'A', the name 'A' is again attached to this second, 'higher' note. We can thus begin to refer to the notes of succeeding octaves in the following fashion:

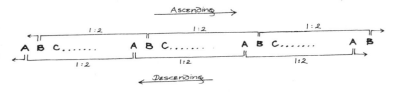

Diagram 14

The tempered scales have basically seven notes which are represented by the first seven letters of the alphabet, i.e., A — G. Recent terminology refers to all those frequencies which share the same letter name as a *pitch class*. The octave series indicated above may now be completed:

←*etc.* A B C D E F G A B C D E F G A B C D E F G A B *etc.*→

Diagram 15

The letters as used here correspond to the lines and spaces of staves in the following simple manner:

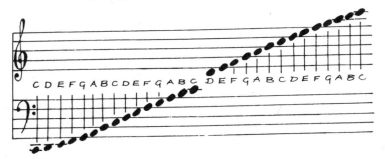

Diagram 16

Intervals: Tones: Semitones

The intervals between notes are named in the following manner:

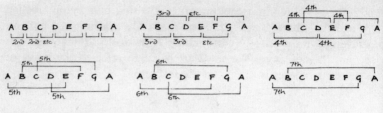

Diagram 17

This may also be demonstrated on a stave:

Diagram 18

However, not all the intervals between adjacent notes on the stave are of equal size. For example, in the scale beginning on C the two intervals indicated below are half the size of the rest:

Diagram 19

Intervals of this size are called *semitones*. The remaining intervals between adjacent notes in this scale are called *tones*. As the result of this inequality there are two types of second, third, sixth and seventh. These types are referred to as 'major' and 'minor'. There is also one special interval which occurs between the fifth and the fourth and is called an augmented fourth, a diminished fifth or less commonly a tritone. In the case of this special interval the name used depends on the function it performs in any specific tonal context:

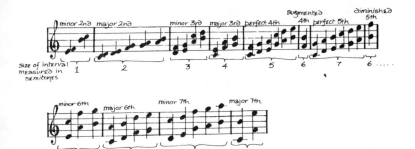

Diagram 20

Inversion of Intervals

If we take any interval and 'subtract' it from the octave, the remaining interval is called its *inversion*. Thus, e.g:

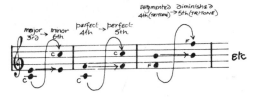

Diagram 21

Hence the inversion of a minor second is a major seventh, of a major second a minor seventh and so on. The only interval which is its own inversion is the tritone.

Chromatic scale: Sharps: Flats: Naturals

Although the basic tempered scales have only seven notes, the fact that the semitone is exactly half the size of the tone enables us to construct a scale consisting entirely of semitones. Thus (using 'T' for tone and 'S' for semitone) a seven note scale T T ST T T S will generate a scale of twelve semitones, thus: SSSSSSSSSSSS. This twelve note scale is known as the *chromatic scale*.

At this point the letter-name scheme indicated earlier becomes problematic because there are now more notes than letters. This difficulty is obviated by using special signs called *sharps* (♯) and *flats* (♭) to indicate notes in between those we can write directly on

277

the stave. A sharp sign before a note indicates a new note one semitone higher, and a flat sign a note one semitone lower. Thus a complete chromatic scale might be written as follows:

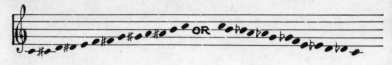

Diagram 22

The use of sharps and flats can be best illustrated by reference to the piano keyboard:

Diagram 23

Here, the white notes are referred to simply by letter names. The semitones in between, the black notes, are indicated by the use of sharps or flats as described above. Note in particular that C sharp and D flat (for example) are the same note. Also note that in most musical practice, a sharp (or flat) sign occuring before a specific note in any bar (see above) is meant to sharpen (or flatten) every occurrence of that specific note *throughout* that bar *and no further*. If the specific note is to be used again within that same bar *but unsharpened* (unflattened) it must be accompanied by a 'natural' sign (♮).

Micro-intervals: Sliding inflection

It is convenient at this point to explain these concepts, though they occur extremely rarely in tonal music. A micro-interval is simply some interval less than a semitone. Some micro-intervals are given special names, e.g., a quarter tone is half a semitone. A sliding inflection is a continuous movement in pitch away from or towards (or both) a specifiable pitch. Although this cannot be definitively notated, some idea of the device may be given by the following (crude) signs:

Diagram 24

In blues and jazz such inflections are in common use. The procedure is sometimes referred to as 'bending' the note.

Major and Minor Scales: Key

The sequence of tones and semitones (and, in the case of the harmonic minor scales, q.v., the minor third) in a seven note scale (in the tempered system) determines its characteristic shape. There are two basic shapes in the tonal system. These are referred to as *major scales* and *minor scales* (of which there are two variants). Using 'T' for tone, 'S' for semitone and '3' for minor thirds, the major scale shape is as follows:

TTSTTTS or on the stave, starting (e.g.) on C

Diagram 25

The harmonic-minor shape is:

TSTTS3S or on the stave, starting (e.g.) on C

Diagram 26

The melodic minor *ascending* shape is:

TSTTTTS or on the stave, starting (e.g.) on C

Diagram 27

279

and *descending*:

TTSTTST *or on the stave, starting (e.g.) on C*

Diagram 28

Note that it is these interval relationships which determine the characteristic shape of the scale and *not* the note on which it begins. It is in fact possible to begin any of the above shapes on any note of the chromatic scale, e.g., the harmonic minor:

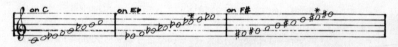

* *Note, by reference to Diagram 12, that Cb = B(♮), and that E# = F(♮).*

Diagram 29

The note on which the scale begins and ends is called the *Key-note*. Furthermore, the music using that scale is said to be 'in the key of' the note on which that scale begins.

Transposition

Just as major or minor scales can begin on any note of the chromatic scale, so can any melody, because it too is characterised by its shape. The process of moving the melodic shape from one key to another is known as *transposition*.

Cycle of Fifths

At the beginning of this section on tonality it was noted that all intervals in the tempered scale, apart from the octave, are *only approximations* to similar natural intervals. The reason for this may now be made clear.

Starting on any note of the chromatic scale and proceeding by steps of equal intervals we will eventually return to the note we began on, as the system is finite, e.g:

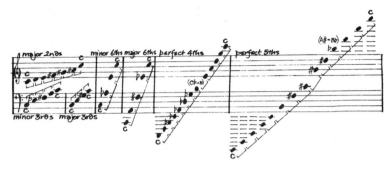

Diagram 30

Only the intervals of a fifth, and its inversion, a fourth (and a semitone) however, will take us through all twelve notes in this process. This cycle is known as the *cycle of fifths*.

In contrast, if this process is attempted with fifths taken from the harmonic series (i.e. intervals of the exact frequency ration 3:2) we will not in fact return to the original note *exactly*. This may be demonstrated mathematically by noting that:

$$\text{Interval of 5th} = \frac{3}{2}$$
$$\text{Interval of 5th + 5th } (= 9th) = \frac{3}{2} \times \frac{3}{2} = \left(\frac{3}{2}\right)^2$$

$$\text{Interval of Octave} = \frac{2}{1}(= 2)$$
$$\text{Interval of 2 Octaves} = \frac{2}{1} \times \frac{2}{1} = 2^2$$

$$\text{But } \left(\frac{3}{2}\right)^{12} \neq 2^7 \text{ & in fact } \frac{\left(\frac{3}{2}\right)^{12}}{2^7} = 1.014 \ (i.e. \neq 1.000...)$$

Diagram 31

(Note that twelve tempered fifths span seven octaves. Hence the powers in the equation above).

We note, however, that the 12th natural fifth approximates quite closely to the 7th octave. The tempered scale attempts to rationalise the natural intervals by adjusting the size of the fifth to make this correspondence exact. As a consequence, the sizes of all the other intervals in the tempered scale have been adjusted by varying degrees away from the natural intervals, and all the semitones in the chromatic scale are equal in size, as indicated previously. This system has the advantage of being totally symmetric and permits us to move freely from scales based on one keynote to those based on others. It is this which makes tonality possible, and separates tonal and related musics from all other musical systems.

Tonal Relationships: Harmonic Relationships: Tonal Harmony

In tonal music, when two or more notes sound simultaneously, the result is known as a chord. Combinations of different intervals produce different chords. The different types of chords may be classified according to these internal relationships between the notes. The rules derived from compositional practice, governing the succession of chords in a piece (e.g., so-called 'discords' usually 'resolve' onto so-called 'concords') are known as the rules of tonal harmony. In practice we must also take into account that the notes of a chord are derived from the scale of a particular key-note and consequently perform a specific function in relation to the key of that scale. The most important chords in this respect are the *triads* based on the notes of the scale of the particular key-note. Thus, for example, in C major:

Diagram 32

This results in three major and three minor triads. Major triads have a major third below a minor third (making up a fifth) and minor triads have a minor third below a major third (also making up a fifth). The 7th triad is known as a diminished triad (because it is composed of two minor thirds, making up a diminished fifth):

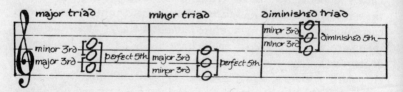

Diagram 33

The three major chords, known respectively as the *tonic* (on the key-note), *subdominant* (at the fourth), and *dominant* (at the fifth) triads are essential to establishing the key of a particular piece. A similar, but slightly more complex, process occurs in minor keys.

Note also that a particular chord may in fact be derived from three different scales, e.g:

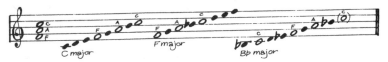

Diagram 34

This potential 'ambiguity' of function allows us to move from one key to another. Note that such a unified and highly inter-related system would be impossible without a small finite set of pitches.

Modulation: Tonic Key

This is the process of moving from one key to another during the course of a particular composition, In a similar manner to that in which different chords establish a key, so movement through different keys in a composition establishes an overall feeling for the basic key of that composition, which is called the *tonic key*.

Pentatonic scale

A pentatonic scale is comprised of five notes. The purest form of such a scale may be derived from either the cycle or fifths of the cycle of fourths, q.v. Thus, for example, starting on C, the cycle of fifths generates the notes C G D A E, giving rise to the pentatonic scale C D E G A. Similarly, starting on C, the cycle of fourths generates the notes C F Bb Eb Ab which give the pentatonic scale Ab Bb C Eb F. Both of these end products are the same basic shape. Clearly it is possible to start the scale on any one of the five notes, thereby generating different forms. No matter which letter names of the tempered scale are used to denote this scale, *only* five forms can be derived. Using 'T' for tone and '3' for minor third, the following five shapes emerge:

```
T 3 T T 3
  3 T T 3 T
    T T 3 T 3
      T 3 T 3 T
        3 T 3 T T
```

MEDIEVAL SACRED MUSIC

Medieval music operated in a very different way from tonality. Although it is *convenient* to use tonal notation in discussing medieval music, it is very wrong to assume, *a priori*, that medieval music has anything at all in common with tonality. The reader should thus approach this subject with a completely clear mind and only refer to earlier sections of this Appendix when the use of 'general musical terms' requires him to.

Plainchant

Plainchant refers to the tradition of sacred monody codified by Pope Gregory around the turn of the seventh century.

Organum: Free Organum

Organum refers to the early forms of parallel polyphony (q.v.) which evolved from Plainchant and which date approximately from the ninth century. Occasionally there were brief deviations from strictly parallel motion, and this is known as *free organum*.

Modes

In classic medieval *theory* there are eight modes. A mode is a medieval scale, and the term 'mode' is used because there are substantial differences between modes and the scales of tonality. Modes are classified in four sets of two. In each set one mode is known as the 'authentic' and the other as the 'plagal'. Their names are as follows:

AUTHENTIC	PLAGAL
DORIAN	HYPODORIAN
PHRYGIAN	HYPOPHRYGIAN
LYDIAN	HYPOLYDIAN
MIXOLYDIAN	HYPOMIXOLYDIAN

There are two important notes in each mode. One is the tenor, which is the reciting note (that is the note on which the chant centres before descending to the final). The other is the final, which is simply the note on which the chant ends (and frequently begins).

The crucial difference between all eight modes lies in their shape, *and in their shape only*. There can be absolutely no question of the modes bearing any definite relationship to one another, with the possible exception of the plagal to its authentic partner, and *vice versa.* There is no modulation between modes, and the final or tenor of a mode — in terms of our *tempered* scale with its *fixed* pitches (e.g. A = 440 c/s) — can be any 'note' a singer chooses.

The shapes of the modes are as follows:

DORIAN:	TSTTTST
HYPODORIAN:	TSTTSTT
PHRYGIAN:	STTTSTT
HYPOPHRYGIAN:	STTSTTT
LYDIAN:	TTTSTTS
HYPOLYDIAN:	TTSTTTS
MIXOLYDIAN:	TTSTTST
HYPOMIXOLYDIAN:	TSTTTST

[n.b., it is very important to realise that the 'tones' and 'semitones' referred to here are not necessarily the same size as those in the tempered scale (see below, modal intervals).] All these shapes are clearly different, except for the dorian and hypomixolydian modes. However, these modes have different tenors, so the difference of shape is very noticeable in actual performance.

All the shapes *may be viewed* as 'slices' out of the *natural gamut*, though this must not be regarded as an explanation of their historical origin. The natural gamut is the *recurring* shape . . . TSTTTSTTSTTTSTTSTTTS . . . Thus:

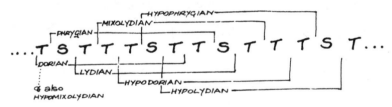

Diagram 35

The most likely reason for this correspondence is that the natural gamut contains only one augmented fourth or diminished fifth, an interval that is complete anathema to medieval music. Any other sequence involving 'tones' and 'semitones' would result in more than one *diabolus in musica* (i.e., augmented fourth/diminished fifth). Reasons for the development of these modal shapes and the natural gamut are put forward in Chapter Three.

The reader might notice that by beginning on a particular interval of the natural gamut we *appear* to be able to generate the major scale of tonality. But this would be to assign a spurious importance to just one of the 'notes' (the first of such a sequence) and is not justified *in view of the different shapes of the modes*. However, one may usefully employ the tempered scale of tonality to gain some appreciation of the different modal shapes. Using the white notes of the piano, the modes have *approximately* (see modal intervals below) the following shapes:

DORIAN:	. . . D e f *g a* b c d . . .
HYPODORIAN:	. . . A b c d e *f* g a . . .
PHRYGIAN:	. . . E f g a b c d e . . . .
HYPOPHRYGIAN:	. . . B c d e f *g a* b . . . .
LYDIAN:	. . . F g a b c d e f . . .
HYPOLYDIAN:	. . . C d e f *g a* b c . . . .
MIXOLYDIAN:	. . . G a b c *d* e f g . . . .
HYPOMIXOLYDIAN:	. . . D e f g a b c d . . . .

(in the above examples the final is indicated by a capital letter and the tenor is italicised).

The *ambitus* or range of any particular chant will *not* necessarily coincide with the octave. It can be greater or less. Also, once above the tenor, the notes assume a less important stature. There is no question of a 'reaching up' to the key-note as their frequently is in tonality. The *ambitus* commonly extends to one note below the final.

The Modal System is not Unified

It is essential to understand that the most important 'instrument' in medieval music is the voice. All other instruments were initially regarded as imitators of the voice. In many ways the voice thus held a position similar to the piano (or tempered keyboard) in tonality. And precisely because there was no tempered keyboard in medieval music, the voice was the 'instrument' in terms of which all theory was thought out from a performance (as opposed to a scholarly or theological) point of view. This is partly the reason why the modes are not inter-related (i.e., the modal system is not unified). That is, since plainchant was fundamentally of an oral rather than a notated tradition, there was no easily available *visual* device in terms of which the different *oral-aural* shapes could be related to each other.

It is also the reason why the octave is a relatively unimportant interval in medieval music. For the untrained voice, the octave is a particularly large interval to take as a frame of reference. The fifth and the fourth are much more comfortable and manageable. 'Practical' theory was thus thought out largely in terms of these intervals. Because the octave is essential to any inter-related musical system (see *Tonal System* above), the limited range of the 'classically untutored' voice is another factor militating against a 'unified' modal system.

Modal Intervals

Because medieval music was originally an oral-aural tradition with a limited range of vocal reference, it seems highly likely that the more important intervals (fifths and fourths) would correspond exactly with those generated by the harmonic series. This is yet another factor militating against the formulation of one unified tonal shape (cf. above) since such a shape requires adjustment of the intervals (as in the tempered scale). Further, since these intervals are the strongest in the series (apart from the octave) and the easiest to define vocally, it is more than possible that other smaller intervals were derived by filling in the larger intervals. Because the difference between a fourth and a fifth is a 'tone', this interval became the basic unit of stepwise motion. All other intervals can be derived from these three. Firstly, minor thirds, then semitones as a result of passing notes within the minor third. The major third would result from two consecutive tones. It is again essential to underline that they would not correspond exactly with those of the tempered scale. The semitone in particular might well have been a very fluid interval (both from the point of view of size and stability).

Ambiguity of Mode

The section entitled *Modes* above dealt with classical *theory*, which probably had as much to do with theological preoccupations (numeric symbolism) as with musical practice. The ensuing sections dealt with *probable* practice. It is quite possibly because of this difference that there are a minority of chants which are modally ambiguous, and some which cannot be placed in any mode. The theory put forward in Chapter Three seeks to account for these 'anomalous' chants.

Tetrachord: Pentachord: Hexachord

Units of four, five and six (respectively) consecutive notes which served as the basis of theoretical speculation about modal structure.

287

SERIAL MUSIC

Twelve Tone Technique: Serial Technique

During the nineteenth and early twentieth centuries the possibilities and implications of various types of discords, of modulations to more and more distant keys, rapid movement through many keys and other possible facets of the tonal system were explored by composers. By the turn of the century it was not surprising to find (e.g., in the works of Wolf, Schoenberg, etc.) a tendency towards frequent use of all twelve notes of the chromatic scale, and a breaking down of the conventions governing the progression from one chord to another in the functional framework of tonality. With these developments, the clear hierarchy among the pitch-classes within a piece of music, which had been the basis of tonal organisation, was becoming extremely tenuous.

During the years of the First World War, Arnold Schoenberg invented the twelve-tone, or *serial,* system based on an acceptance of the equal importance of all the twelve pitch-classes of the chromatic scale. All the material, both horizontal (i.e., reading along the stave, and hitherto thought of as 'melodic') and vertical (i.e. reading down the stave, and hitherto thought of as 'harmonic'), of a particular composition is to be derived from a *tone-row* or *series*. The series for any particular composition will generally be different from that for any other, but *not* necessarily so.

Series: Tone-Row: Basic Set

The series, tone-row or basic set of a piece consists of a specific ordering of the twelve pitch-classes of the chromatic scale, e.g:

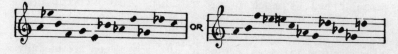

Diagram 36

Although a series seems like a (chromatic) melody (and may sometimes be used thus) it does in fact differ in that, as it is an arrangement of pitch-*classes,* any note may occur in any register. Thus the *same* series may appear in any one of several forms, e.g:

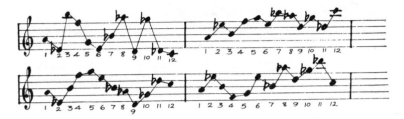

Diagram 37

Thus, unlike a melody, the pitch-contour, or shape, of a series is not usually of primary significance. If, however, we consider any *specific* form of the basic set we note that, just as with the major and minor scales discussed above, it is the *intervals between* the pitches of the series which determine its basic character, rather than the actual pitches themselves. The series, or basic set, can in fact begin on any one of the twelve notes of the chromatic scale (the twelve transpositions of the basic set), e.g:

Diagram 38

289

Prime: Retrograde: Inversion: Retrograde-Inversion

Apart from the basic set and its transpositions, certain other transformations of the series are used. Thus the pitch-classes may be used in the reverse order, and this is known as the *retrograde* form, the basic set in its original form now being referred to as the *prime* form, e.g:

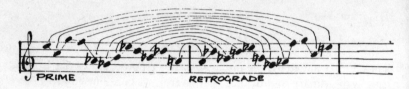

Diagram 39

Considering again a *specific form* of the prime, we may take its intervals in the opposite direction. Thus if it begins by moving down a major third and then up a fifth, we could begin by moving *up* a major third and *down* a fifth (see diagram 40a below). Continuing in this fashion we generate a new twelve-note set, known as the *inversion* of the prime (see diagram 40b).

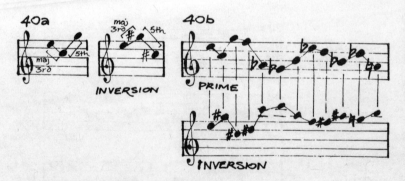

Diagrams 40a and 40b

Finally we may take the notes of the inversion in the reverse order, forming the *retrograde inversion* of the prime, e.g:

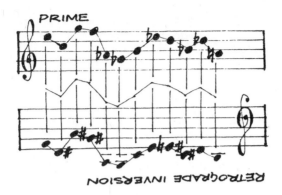

Diagram 41

The retrograde, inversion, and retrograde-inversion will, of course, each have twelve transpositions, giving a total of 48 forms deriving from one basic set.

Integral Serialism: Parameters

After World War II a movement developed among the so-called 'avant-garde' to extend the serial procedure to all elements of a piece. Not only the pitch-class, but also the duration, dynamics and even timbre of a note were to be determined by reference to a series. This was known as *integral serialism*, and the different factors to be serialised (pitch-class, duration, dynamics etc.) were referred to as the *parameters*.

Duration Series

The extension of the serial procedure to the organisation of note durations is not entirely satisfactory, as there is not an agreed finite set of 'duration-classes' to correspond to the twelve pitch-classes of the pitch-class series. However, we may select twelve note-lengths e.g., (as in Boulez' *Structures 1,* deriving from Messiaen's *Modes de valeurs et d'intensites*):

Diagram 42

and arrange these in some order to form the prime of a *duration*

291

series. If we take the sequence of durations in diagram 42 as our basic set, then the *retrograde of the duration series* will be as follows:

Diagram 43

The reader may now puzzle over the problems of inversion and transposition of such a series (there is no *satisfactory* solution). A more interesting approach to relating pitch organisation to that of durations is to be found in Stockhausen's *Gruppen.*

ELECTRONIC MUSIC

Sine-tone

We have previously noted that sound is composed of vibrations of the air. The simplest vibration we can describe is that of the so-called simple harmonic oscillator. This motion can be summarised by the graph:

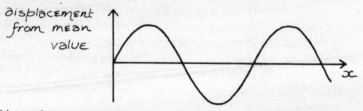

This graph may represent:-
1. the variation of pressure, with time (x), at any fixed point along the path of a sine sound-wave.
2. the variation of pressure, with distance (x), along the path of the sine sound-wave, at any given time.
3. the variation in position of the prong of an *idealised* tuning-fork, with time (x).

Diagram 44

The curve represented here is known as a sine curve. This curve might, for example, represent the movement of the prong of an (idealised) tuning-fork vibrating at a fixed frequency. Thus, as the curve moves back and forth across the horizontal (time) axis, the prong moves back and forth across its mean position. The tuning-fork would set up a corresponding pressure wave in the air around it, and this pressure wave can also be represented by a sine-curve. The resulting sound is a *sine-tone*. The closest instrumental approximation to this sound is given by notes in the higher register of the flute. Sine-tones can be generated by means of an electronic device known as a sine-tone generator, or sine-tone oscillator.

Fourier Analysis

It can be demonstrated mathematically that any vibration, no matter how complex, can be described by a sum (possibly infinite and possibly over a continuum of values) of sine-wave oscillations. The mathematical breakdown of a vibration into its sine-wave components is known as Fourier analysis. Conversely this implies that any vibration (and consequently any sound) can *in principle* be synthesised by superimposing sine-waves.

Sound-Gestalt

Any real sound we may hear will have its own special characteristics. Not only will it have its own Fourier-analysable internal structure, but this structure may vary from moment to moment. In particular the way in which the sound begins (the *attack*) and ends (the *decay*) will be especially important in determining its perceived character. Under normal circumstances the internal processes of (e.g.) an individual sounded instrumental note will take place so rapidly that we will apprehend it only as a *single form*, or sound-gestalt.

Envelope

The overall form of a sound as it varies through time (the nature of its attack, its internal fluctuations and its decay) may be indicated by a graph. Thus, considering only the loudness of the sound, we may describe a single piano note by the following graph:

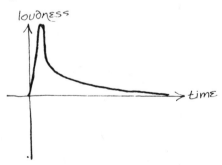

Diagram 45

Such a graph represents the (dynamic) *envelope* of the sound. In a similar way we may describe the variation of the timbre of the sound through time as its *timbral envelope*.

Electronic Sound-generation: Sound-recording

Just as it is possible to set up oscillations in a mechanical medium, it is possible to generate and control oscillations of electric current (voltage, power) in an electrical circuit. If these vibrations are then used to control the vibrations of a mechanical object (e.g. a loudspeaker cone) we can produce *corresponding* oscillations in the air (i.e. corresponding sounds). Hence we may generate, or synthesize, sounds from an electronic apparatus (a *'synthesizer'*).

Conversely, using a microphone, we may convert oscillations in the air into electrical oscillations and ultimately, on a tape-recorder, into variations in the magnetisation of a band of tape, hence 'recording' the sound.

Electronic Process of Transformation: Filtering

Such electrically 'captured' oscillations may themselves be altered in some predetermined way while passing through our electronic circuitry. When we now convert the electrical oscillations back into corresponding sounds, we will hear a different sound to that originally recorded. The sound has undergone an electronic process of transformation.

A simple example of this is the process of filtering a sound. For example, if we have recorded a sound-gestalt consisting of some high-frequency vibrations and some low frequency vibrations, using a suitable electronic circuit (a low-pass filter) we may remove the high-frequency components, and hence in the resulting sound we will hear only the low frequencies which were present in the original sound-gestalt.

OTHER TERMS

The Greater Perfect System

A theoretical system invented by the Greeks which is a *two* octave rationalisation of their system of tones. Whether this system bore any meaningful relationship to the practice of music in ancient Greece is questionable.

Raga

In Indian music a very large number of different scale shapes are used. A raga is defined not only by the particular scale shape chosen, but also by a series of characteristic melodic formulae. Each raga is thought to define a different mood, feeling, or state of being; different ragas are felt to be most appropriately played at specific times of the day or of the year.

Heterophony

The simultaneous sounding of two different melodic lines which are not necessarily related to each other harmonically or metrically.

Polyphony

The simultaneous sounding of two or more melodic lines in such a way as to produce specific metrical and/or harmonic relationships.

Parallelism

Polyphony in which the two (or more) melodies follow exactly the same contour and are hence always the same interval apart.

Imitation

Originally imitation occurred when one group of people reproduced a melodic line that had just been sung by another group of people or an individual. When the imitators 'rushed' the original statement, thereby causing an overlap, this is one way in which harmony may have originated. This practice was later systematised so as to produce precise harmonic and metrical relationships, and became the basis of various composed forms (e.g. where this overlapping imitation was exact, but not necessarily starting on the same pitch, it was called *canon*).

Fugue

A particular and complex form of musical organisation based on various imitative devices, and a single theme known as the subject. (On the minority of occasions where there is more than one theme the form is known as Double, Triple, etc., Fugue).

Fugato

A piece or a musical texture which relates loosely to fugal procedures.

Augmentation

A device whereby all the note-values (i.e. durations of notes) of a theme or motif are increased in length by a constant factor (e.g., doubled, tripled, etc.).

Diminution

Exactly the reverse of Augmentation.

Sonata Form: Exposition: Development: Recapitulation

A musical form originating in the eighteenth century. The form has been developed and expanded in many different ways but its basic formulation is as follows: two important (and usually contrasting) themes are presented in different keys. This section is known as the *exposition*. It is followed by a transitional section in which the music usually modulates through distantly-related keys and in which the themes may be developed or transformed in a variety of ways. This section is known as the *development section*. The music (usually) returns to the tonic key, and both themes are then presented 'reconciled' in the same (tonic) key. This latter section is known as the *recapitulation*.

Arch-Form

As its name implies, a musical structure the succession of whose constituent parts is in the form of an arch e.g. ABCBA or ABCDCBA.

Name Index

297

NAME INDEX

Kaufmann, W., 152, 261
Keil, C., 198, 262
Keddie, N., 202, 207, 215, 218, 231, 232, 262
Keller, H., 250, 251, 262
Kenyon, F. C., 47, 262
King Crimson, 225
Kitto, H. D. F., 49, 262
Kohn, M., 175, 262
Kornhauser, W., 198, 262
Krebs, S. D., 57-59, 262
Kuhn, T. S., 227, 262

Labov, W., 175, 262
Laing, R. D., 124, 262
Landau, J., 189, 190, 262
Langer, S. K., 2, 8, 21, 24-26, 33, 42, 46, 50, 60-62, 115, 130, 262
Lao-Tse, 127
Laplace, 29-31, 68
Leach, E. R., 16, 46, 262
Led Zeppelin, 189
Lee, D., 16, 23, 50, 262
Lee, E., 169, 171, 182, 187, 198-200, 262, 264, 265
Lenin, V. I., 57-59
Leonard, N., 198, 262
Levi-Strauss, C., 55, 262
Lewis, John, 200
Lloyd, A. L., 170
Long, N., 223, 262
Lord, A. B., 26, 116, 262
Lowenthal, L., 198, 262
Luckmann, T., 46, 117, 259
Lukacs, G., 1, 5, 233-237, 239-241, 243, 262
Lunacharsky, 57
Lyle, R., 64, 262
Lyttleton, Humphrey, 193

Mabey, R., 193
McColl, Ewan, 185
McDonald, D., 180, 181, 263
McGregor, C., 186, 263
McLuhan, M., 2, 13, 27, 28, 30-33, 37, 38, 40, 47, 49, 50, 124, 260-264
McPherson, S., 203, 230, 263
Machabey, 81
Mahler, Gustav, 238
Mainzer, J., 229
Mao Tse Tung, 242, 243
Mapuche, The, 75, 265
Marcus, G., 189, 263
Marcuse, H., 243, 244, 254, 255

Markmann, C. L., 260
Marx, Karl, 50, 57-59, 65, 128, 156, 184, 237, 239, 242, 255
Mellers, W., 63, 78, 79, 91, 93, 117, 173, 188, 194, 263
Melly, G., 190, 191, 193, 199, 263
Melody Maker, 186, 188, 190, 199
Merriam, A. P., 72-76, 115, 116, 200, 263
Messiaen, Olivier, 137, 291
Meyer, L. B., 2, 7, 8, 21, 24-26, 33, 34, 42-44, 46, 50, 61, 115, 139, 183, 184, 263
Middleton, R., 166, 171, 177, 263
Mills, C. W., 185, 263
Mitchell, D. G., 259
Modern Jazz Quartet, The, 195,200
Morse, D., 197, 199, 263
Mothers of Invention, The, 187
Mueller, J. H., 176, 263
Murdock, G., 190, 263
Musicians' Union, The, 210

Nef, J. V., 28, 263
Nestyev, I. V., 66, 264
Nettl, B., 76, 77, 111, 120, 264
Newton, I., 29-31, 48, 68, 141
Nicholls, M., 224, 225, 264
Nuttall, J., 199, 264

Oliver, P., 170, 264
Ong, W. J., 10, 13, 14, 22, 38, 41, 42, 46-49, 75, 79, 264
Orff, Carl, 212, 223, 261
Owen, Robert, 246

Palestrina, Giovanni, 129
Panassié, H., 193
Parker, C., 184, 196, 264
Paynter, J., 206, 264
Phelps, G., 191, 263
Pink Floyd, 188
Plato, 41, 42, 126-128, 130, 143, 148
Pleasants, H., 182, 198, 264
Poulet, G., 23, 49, 92, 120, 264
Pring, R., 232, 264
Prokofiev, S., 59, 66
Pythagoras, 79, 144

Rainbow, B., 203, 205, 229, 230, 264
Rayburn, J., 120, 264
Reese, G., 81, 84, 86, 88, 89, 98, 104, 105, 118, 264
Reti, R., 90, 119, 123, 264

299

NAME INDEX